Echoes of Terror

Contributing authors:

Jodi Lee
Matt Hults
Dave Field
John Everson
Nancy Jackson
Garrett Peck
Keith Gouveia
Meghan Jurado
Stephen C. Hallin
Ken Goldman
Katherine Smith
J. Edward Tremlett
Giovanna Lagana
Nicholas Grabowsky
Andrea Dean Van Scoyoc

Lachesis Publishing

www.lachesispublishing.com

Published Internationally by Lachesis Publishing
1787 Cartier Court, RR 1,
Kingston, Nova Scotia, B0P 1R0

The 2007 copyrights © for each story in this anthology are hold by the authors of the individual stories.
All rights reserved.
Exclusive cover © 2007 Jinger Heaston
Inside artwork © 2007 Carole Spencer

The use of any part of this publication reproduced, transmitted in any form or by any means, electronic, mechanical, photocopying, recording, or otherwise, without the prior written consent of the publisher, Lachesis Publishing, is an infringement of the copyright law.

National Library of Canada Cataloguing in Publication Data

A catalogue record for this book is available from the
National Library of Canada.
ISBN 1-897370-06-7
Also available in multiple eBook formats from
www.lachesispublishing.com
ISBN 1-897370-07-5
Credits:
Editors: Katherine Smith, Garrett Peck and Giovanna Lagana

This is a work of fiction. Names, characters, places and incidents are either the product of the author's imagination or are used fictitiously, and any resemblance to any person or persons, living or dead, events, or locales is entirely coincidental. The author and publisher recognize and respect any trademarks mentioned in this book by introducing such registered titles either in italics or with a capital letter.

here's LOOKING at you, kid :)

of you, kid!"

Looking

here's

Katherine Smith, Giovanna Lagana and Garrett Peck would like to thank the wonderful Carole Spencer for supporting them in this project.

They would also like to thank all the authors who participated in this anthology. Your stories gave them chills and many memorable nightmares.

CONTENTS:

"Looks Like A Rat To Me" by Nicholas Grabowsky:

By the time I'd reached the den, my foremost destination of concern, five of these vile and monstrous things had already begun their bloodthirsty assault on my wife ...

"With Love, Veronica" by Ken Goldman:

Ambrose Woodhouse is not a good-looking man, and he knows it. No woman will look at him without revulsion, and Ambrose has come to expect and accept this reaction. And then, seemingly from nowhere, comes Veronica. Mysterious, sensual, every man's vision of the ideal woman, Veronica causes Ambrose to become completely obsessed with her. Just who is this woman and what does she want from a man, who is, as he sees it, "long past the point of fooling myself into believing I might hope for a normal life living among those who are not themselves social lepers"?

"Eating Crow" by Garrett Peck:

Carol Mitchell and her husband David are on their way to their weekly bridge party with their friends the Brightmans when Carol is inexplicably attacked by a black crow. She considers it a fluke, but the evil bird is waiting for her when they leave and attacks again, this time sending her to the emergency room for stitches. When the crow assaults her at home the next day, she realizes this is no coincidence. For some unknown reason, this crow has a personal vendetta against her and its agenda is nothing less than her death.

"Fowl Play" by Keith Gouveia:

When Gary Lund is fired from the Peabody Hotel, he enlists the help of his best friend to get back at his manager, but the friends soon discover the hotel's secret, and nothing will be the same again.

"Bug Powder" by Meghan Jurado:

So where do the drugs come from, anyway? Just who are these suppliers, what *are* these chemicals? Dealing in narcotics is never safe or easy, and when a strange new supplier hits town, everything goes to hell. A local small-time dealer gets in deep with the new heavy, receiving more free product than he ever dreamt possible. He gives samples to his favorite customer, hoping to make a sale. But when the customer starts having a less than pleasant reaction to the new drug, the dealer has a choice of ending the madness or continuing to sell – and he's not about to make his new boss angry.

"When Black Fades To Grey" by Andrea Dean Van Scoyoc:

Can time change a person so much that he is no longer himself?
    Andrew and Guy had always been friends … until things with Guy turned darker, much darker.

After high school, Guy tracks his best friend down and asks to meet him and reluctantly, Andrew agrees.

Guy's further changes make Andrew's blood run cold as he tells Andrew a terrifying tale of his journey, a journey that no one should make ...

There is a catch to hearing Guy's horrifying tale. Will Andrew make it out of the meeting alive after hearing it?

"November Girls" by Katherine Smith:

In a disturbing encounter with a ghostly visitor, a young woman begins to wonder if she were to disappear, would anyone care, or would she just be another of the November girls ...

"The Tree" by Katherine Smith:

A bitter old man finally faces the Nemesis of his past in the form of an ancient tree that has evil powers ... or does it?

"Clown School" by J. Edward Tremlett:

Did you ever get the feeling that modern life, as we know it, is just one colossal joke? Bill's been certain of that for some time. Viciously divorced, saddled with sole custody of an ungrateful child, and left to twist in the winds of the job market, he's been watching his life go by and wondering when he'll hear the punch line. A chance encounter with a fun yet unsettling clown school in the middle of Nowhere, Wisconsin may end the gag once and for all. But what is left in the stark silence when the laughter stops...?

"Crushing Giles" by Stephen C. Hallin:

During the Salem witch trials, nobody was above suspicion. Anybody accused was sentenced to hang and suffer eternal damnation. The necks of many good people snapped at the gallows and many more good people learned to fear their friends. But when the trials ended, everything changed – people learned that the real evil in Salem was paranoia. So, what happened? How did the tide shift? The executions stopped thanks to several heroes and one of them was Giles Corey. This story, *Crushing Giles*, is an extension of what occurred during those dark days.

"Door Bitch" by Dave Field:

People rescued from strife oscillate through a range of exhausting emotions – relief, fear, anger and concern. 'Door Bitch' portrays that situation – gone awry.

"Tempest" by Matt Hults:

Logan and his friends know they can't outrun the coming thunderstorm, but when the rain begins burning through their clothes like acid, they take shelter in the first cabin they can find. Only they aren't alone. Something else has sought refuge from the rain, something that will kill to remain unfound. Now the group is left with two equally grim choices: face the unknown horror lurking in the cabin, or flee outside and try to survive the Tempest.

"A Baker's Dozen" by Nancy Jackson:

The cost of redemption has gone up to thirteen. An unlucky baker learns a harsh lesson in betrayal after being visited by a stranger seeking revenge.

"Interludes" by Jodi Lee:

Risking his career and his life, Kaine rescues a tortured and terrified 13-year-old boy from the belly of the ancient asylum where he is a Psychiatry resident. Later, unable to deal with the strange child, Kaine leaves him behind ... until the day he meets Claire Davis and she leads him back into the nightmare.

"One Hell of A Deal" by Giovanna Lagana:

Award-winning author Jack Truman should never have answered his phone this morning. Because on the other end of the phone line is a demon who is out for more than just selling him a simple subscription to a book club. No, this demon is out for much, much more and he definitely won't take no for an answer.

"Ice Cold Shakes" by John Everson:

When four co-eds head to the Appalachians for a final summer fling, they have no idea how final it might be ... but when Lisha invites them to her backwoods hometown for a seductive strawberry shake, they'll learn that not every sweet is as sweet as it seems ...

Echoes of Terror

1

I used to raise rats around the time I entered high school, had several different cages in the shack in my backyard, and my parents let me raise them and train them. But in recent years, I bought a very used, run-down Jacuzzi for my patio and there was actually what my fiancée called a 'vole' that lived in it for awhile. Without that particular little vermin, this story would never be.

LOOKS LIKE A RAT TO ME
By Nicholas Grabowsky

I never liked rats much. They scare the bejesus out of me. It's a fact ... some folks are frightened by even the smallest, seemingly least imposing creatures on this planet. Mosquitoes, bugs, bees, spiders.

Themselves.

Sometimes, it's so senseless it must be hereditary, or perhaps the syndrome hails from some otherwise inconsiderable traumatic episode straight from childhood. Me, I can't figure it out.

All I know is I hate rats.

But I love dogs.

I love *my* dog.

At least, I *did* ...

My name is Jeremy Sytes. I used to be a middle-aged, run-of-the-mill average Joe Family Guy, so to speak. During the day, I was an assistant sales manager for the retail giant Kempco, and every night I returned to the suburban home life I shared with my wife Helen, toddler Terrance, and infant Jody. I had recently self-published a collection of my own anecdotes for weary travelers, *Sytes for Sore Eyes*. Might as well mention it whenever I can, and it's doing well at online bookstores.

Now, onto Viceroy ...

Viceroy was our Border terrier. He was a scruffy, spunky little canine with a face like Benji and a bluish, wiry double coat that thinned down to tan-colored 'socks' at his thighs and feet.

Viceroy hated rats, too.

We all did.

I'd stretched myself out over the blue fescue of the backyard lawn, around 11:30 pm, gazing up at the stars and wispy rogue clouds and the quintuplet of spotlights from the Lakefest Auto Mall's Midnight Madness sale dancing like a major Hollywood movie's premiere in the southern sky.

A half-empty bottle of Bud stood on a bald spot of the lawn and within comfortable reach of me. My kids were in their beds; Helen reading a paperback in the den; Viceroy likely lounging at her bunny-slippered feet with his snout buried into his paws.

I was alone.

I was loving every minute of it.

I was surrounded by a peaceful quiet but for the sickly hum of the weathered Jacuzzi at the corner of the patio. I was used to that hum, didn't mind it a bit. The Jacuzzi had cost me only a couple hundred bucks. It was previously owned by a succession of heavy partiers and building contractor acquaintances of mine, who'd convinced me the tub's appearance was only a result of moving it from points A to B, C, D, and E. But they were right, it operated with rarely a tick. Yeah, it wasn't supposed to hum the way it did, but Helen and I'd enjoyed a good few months of otherwise unaffordable recreational relaxation in spite of that. It was a four-person tub held upright by a weary wooden frame encased by cobwebs and redwood-stained plywood along its four sides. The patio had no shelter, and the sauna's thick foam/cloth cover was green with algae from the rain and riddled with splotches of brown stains from my using it as a tabletop when I barbecue. And I 'que quite often.

It didn't matter to us that it was such an eyesore. What mattered to us was that it worked.

We were nearly into the first week of enjoying the tub when the yellow jacket wasp population in our yard grew to nightmarish proportions and I discovered they'd made a sizeable nest of the Jacuzzi's wooden innards. I took care of that, but it was a pain in the ass.

The other week, I spotted a small rodent scurry across the patio's cement floor and squeeze itself into a hole in the wood of the hot tub's casing.

My God, it was attracting pests.

"That must've been a vole," Helen had told me. "An above-ground mole. I hear we have 'em up here."

"Looks like a rat to me," I'd told her. "So ... you're fine with it living inside our Jacuzzi?"

"We can phone the exterminators."

"We have exterminators? We can sick Viceroy on it ... "

"Don't let our dog near that thing, it might have rabies," was Helen's final word, and the matter hadn't been brought up since, for we hadn't seen the damn rat in the stretch of time afterwards.

But lying there on the grass that night below the stars, I saw it again, the little prick.

I turned my gaze to one side, reaching for my beer bottle in my visual foreground and at my fingertips. The rat darted across the landscape no more than a few feet beyond. I could've sworn I heard children's laughter coming from the other side of the fence, the neighbor's kids, but I paid no mind to their business. I had my own.

"*Godammit!*"

I rolled onto my belly, alert with adrenaline. Damn vermin could've been right there with me the entire hour or so that *I'd* been, foraging in the grass inches away from my head, and me blissfully unaware. I watched it as it went up to the patio, sniffed the air, made a leisurely promenade across the cement until it crept into the same crack of plywood it had the last time I'd seen it, into the recesses of the Jacuzzi structure's dank interior.

The rat had been utterly oblivious to my presence, or downright just didn't care, and this discernment upset me further.

I thought to get up, get Viceroy after its ass, and I did just that. I crept carefully across the patio, slid open the glass door, called inside, with a voice soft but firm, my dog's name.

Viceroy came running. He leapt over the sofa, into the air, and in graceful avoidance of the living room's glass coffee table, ran out to me in the patio and humped my leg.

"Good dog," I told him, pulling him from me, patting him on the head and moving us both away from the door. "Now. *Go get the rat!*"

Viceroy spun around a few times in a chasing-his-tail kind of fashion, stood on his hind legs with paws in the air like a gallant steed, and bolted for the Jacuzzi. He knew *exactly* what I meant.

He went to sniffing around the parameter of red-stained plywood; thrust his black nose into the abysmal hole of the rodent's lair.

"That's it, Viceroy, go get it," I cheered, and while the dog was preoccupied, I crossed the yard to retrieve my beer.

I stopped cold for the brief distraction of rustling in the bushes at the fence to my left. Something the size of my dog disappeared into that fat bulk of foliage the second I'd laid eyes on it, and I looked over my shoulder at Viceroy. He was exactly where I'd left him, now barking into the rat's hole. I would have instantly hushed him for fear he'd awaken the kids or alert Helen to our antics, but what I'd seen steal away into the bush concerned me a bit more.

As I began to doubt I'd seen anything at all, my interests fell momentarily beer-ward. I looked, but I could not for the life of me locate my bottle of Bud.

It had been right there, on the bald spot in the middle of the grass ...

But no; another quick look behind me and there was my beer bottle, resting safely atop the Jacuzzi's foam covering. Like I'd put it there myself.

A bit disoriented from the apparent brain fart of not remembering placing it there, I went to it, downed the remainder of it in jealous abandon, craving another immediately. I withdrew inside and into the kitchen, then emerged onto the patio with fresh beer in hand to find no sign of Viceroy.

But I saw the rat scurry away from its Jacuzzi refuge, then out again onto the grass; this time, a family of more than a handful of the buggars in various sizes followed suit from out of the hole in one mass exodus. I was dumbfounded. Acting upon absolute frustration and in a bit of a panic, I threw my beer bottle at the last rodent to reach the grass. The bottle missed, the bursting of broken glass echoing into the late night, the foot-long tail of the last rat declining into the thickness of grass blades like a wiggle-worm toy pulled along by a string.

And that was my last beer.

I whistled, called out for my dog.

"Viceroy, come here, boy!"

I sojourned into the dark of the yard, suddenly finding myself overcome by a hell of a dizzy spell, which brought me to my knees despite the fear of my knowledge of rats wandering through the grass.

There I met my Viceroy, his body limp and motionless and utterly pulverized. It took me several minutes to realize his true condition ... I could see him clearly before me, sprawled out across the grass, and the bulbous black trail, which extended from his belly and down over the lawn into the bushes, I found to my horrified observation, was likely an intestine.

As well, it took me a while to become aware of the movement all about me.

Something stirred from within the bushes before me.

I looked up at them, then drew my gaze higher.

Black shadows of at least a half dozen, dog-sized rodent beasts shot across the electric power cables and phone lines above me, past the tree branches of the rear neighbor's yard that extended over my property. I couldn't believe what I saw. One, two, three, four, five, six, and they each disappeared down a utilities pole, down into the dark brush of the corner of my yard.

I bolted to my feet, found myself out of breath as though I'd jogged all the way to the Lakefest Auto Mall and back, and I hadn't exerted myself but to stand.

Another rustling of the bushes before me doubled me back in surprise towards the house in several steps, and I could not take my eyes off my beloved Viceroy as I went. Then there came a moment within the bushes of furious commotion, until a black rodent, with a head the size and shape of a two-gallon funnel, poked itself out from the bush, seized my Viceroy between incisors long enough to resemble two scythes, and dragged his body into the obscurity of branches and heavy leaves.

Backing towards the patio had at this point been a series of reflexes in my favor, but my feet could only propel me as fast as my disbelief could give way to the certain urgency it would've taken for me to escape.

I finally turned, and already one of these creatures was making its way inside the house, through the inviting entrance of open sliding glass doors I'd neglected to shut. The sight of this gave me the urgent strength I needed to pick up speed and run for those doors.

I entered the house, saw the vermin avoid the coffee table and scale over the sofa to the hallway like Viceroy had done in backwards fashion coming out to my summons not long before.

I kept running. In my inept clumsiness, I couldn't avoid the glass coffee table. I fell upon it, its foundation crumpled under my weight, and the glass shattered like a hundred beer bottles had been thrown with great force around and beneath me. I caught sight of my own blood escaping from a multitude of areas on my person and saturating my clothing as I pushed myself up, determined to continue pursuit rather than inspect my wounds.

By the time I'd reached the den, my foremost destination of concern, five of these vile and monstrous things had already begun their bloodthirsty assault on my wife ...

... tearing her to shreds against her struggles and screams right there on her recliner chair deathbed and to the point where she already resembled a grisly pile of blood-soaked beef having gone through a tremendous delicatessen cold cut shaver before I could even *hope* to save her ...

The window behind her was slid open, and another two or three dog-sized rats made their way through the gaping screen and into the room, unconcerned with my standing there baring mute witness to this unspeakable calamity.

One rat was fiendishly chewing on something red and glistening and an obvious appendage of Helen's, all by itself in the opposite corner of the room like a squirrel happily laboring over a morsel of nut it scored, turning it about in its hands. I observed from my petrified stance in the doorway that Helen's head had been stolen away too rapidly for me to have seen it happen. The invaders permeated the air with the sounds of feasting, gnawing. It echoed throughout the house.

I believe I'd been standing there unable to move for quite a good deal of time. I was like a ghost to these damnable beasts, a distant spectator, and I regarded this as I became able to think more and more clearly. As I captured my senses, I remembered my children ...

I turned about in mad abandon, furiously animate, leapt up the flight of stairs to the kids' rooms in record time and came upon my three-year-old's room first.

Kicked open the door.

Flicked on the light switch.

There were no rats.

And yet, Terrance was awake and wide-eyed, and he stared straight at me.

"Daddy, *no!*"

"Come on, Terry," I said, racing for his bed, but the closer I got to him the more frightened he became, and his eyes never left me.

My eyes likewise never left him but for a moment when I chanced to look down on my way to his bed and noticed my tennis shoes were absent from my feet, as were my socks. My trousers were suddenly nonexistent and my lower torso had been stripped of all clothing. The exposed vastness of hair on my legs stood on end as if responding to electric static in the air.

I was stricken with a single thought, a rational supposition, a powerfully sane element of enlightenment in all this madness: *This can't be real. Either I'm seriously hallucinating, or I passed out, and am actually physically catching some zzz's out back on the lawn.*

But there was no time to entertain this thought.

Any thoughts ... no, no time for a single goddamn one of them.

I snatched Terry into my arms as he kicked and flailed against me as though *I* was the threat and not the onslaught of rats. Fast as lightning, I carried him from his bedroom, across the upstairs hallway, and into baby Jody's room.

I switched on the light.

I fell to my knees yet again, as I had a couple times already that night, and for the final time.

In the room, there was a chest of drawers, the drawers of clothes having slid fully out and thrown on top of one another over the carpet. The large rats climbed out of the gaping space where the drawers had been, probably having chewed through the wall behind the furniture piece in no more time than it took me to fetch Terrance.

That sight alone wasn't what brought me to my knees.

One of the rats was perched with his hind feet atop the curved metal frame at the foot-end of Jody's crib, its body elongated and flexing over her, front paws limp and against its body, whiskered snout nostrils collapsing then expanding like two respirator bags.

That nose was black.

Its ears were not like the other rats'; they were more folded over their front and drooping. The tar black hair of its body thinned into a noticeable tan color around attenuated legs and feet that receded into dog-like paws the next second. The thing that before was a rat took a swan dive right into my baby's cradle. Jody wailed.

And what emerged from the cradle with my daughter's neck clenched tightly between its jaws was no rat, but Viceroy. It took Jody with it into the doorway to Hell that became of the section of dresser that once harbored drawers, into the wall.

I wanted to follow after him. Then I did not know *what* to do.

Again, I noticed the rats were oblivious to my presence, for they still could've attacked me, as vulnerable as I was, at any time. For a mere mortal, fragile man engaged in a foiled and useless attempt to rescue his wife and children, I knew I was as easy a prey as any of them. It was as if my house was on fire, and the flames overtook everyone else yet did not harm *me*.

I began to hallucinate again, as I can describe it, if that was indeed what I was doing.

I was somehow, suddenly, out of place. I was oddly overwhelmed with hunger. I couldn't see at first, like I'd blacked out and had come to in a heartbeat. I experienced the sensation of biting down on something writhing and struggling in my mouth between my jaws, keeping whatever it was forcefully at bay as it fought to live, tearing away at it as ravenously as I would the barbequed ribs of an all-you-can-eat restaurant parlor after getting stoned out of my mind.

But as I returned to the immediate events surrounding me, my vision focused onto the sight of my poor son Terrance, sprawled out before me with his midsection exploded like he'd swallowed a hand grenade, which detonated from his insides out. Blood and carnage, like an animal carcass freshly slaughtered and split from throat to groin, spilled over and about me, and I realized that I myself had been feeding on him.

Possibly for quite some time ...

I lost consciousness after this, not long after, and I knew this for certain as well as everything else I'd experienced that night, that I succumbed to a deep sleep, and that was it for me.

Except ...

I distinctly remember in the midst of that void of tranquil blackness a young police cadet returning his perplexed gaze down upon me and replying to someone else, as if there were others around him I did not see. And he said to this unseen person: "I dunno. Looks like a rat to me."

Here I am, several weeks or months later, I do not know, describing my account to you in detail, halfway across the country away from what was once my home. You won't believe what I've been through since ... the men in white coats, the men in blue coats, the men in suit coats endlessly questioning me and clicking their ball-point pens, keeping me contained in this twelve-by-twelve metal cell most of the hours of each day until they come to a decision they all can agree upon as to what to do with me.

You won't believe *this*, either:

You remember the incident in California where that average Joe Family Guy went suddenly psycho and ripped his family to shreds with his bare hands?

It was in all the papers. The media lapped it up.

That was *me*.

And I know clear as day there was a cover-up, on the part of the police, the government, the Great Institution responsible for regulating everything we know, a sensational exchange of misinformation to rival even the Roswell alien aftermath, executed somewhere between the time I'd eaten my son and the time of my writing this confession of sorts.

On one hand, *Dateline*'s now-famous television segment brought up strong arguments but shaky evidence regarding their story about the growing myth of a colony of wererats wandering from house to house in West Coast United States suburbia, increasing their number and leaving numerous families dead and dying and devastated in their wake. Their case in point was my own infamous tragedy.

But if you ask me, my personal opinion of this entire ordeal is that the neighbors' kids had spiked my beer.

About the Author

Nicholas Grabowsky's novels, collections, and nonfiction have been traditionally published since the mid 1980s, and more recently published under his own small press Diverse Media, to worldwide fans and the critical acclaim of much of the top brass in the horror field today. Under his own name as well as pseudonyms such as Nicholas Randers and Marsena Shane, his works include *The Everborn*, *Halloween IV*, *Pray Serpent's Prey*, *Diverse Tales* and *The Wicked Haze*.

Currently he writes, directs, produces, drinks cheap rum and is content living vermin-free.

You can visit him at: http://downwarden.com/

I was inspired to write "With Love, Veronica", of all things, by two locations. I have family in New England and visit often. Massachusetts has its many little seaside towns dotting its coastline, and the bluffs along the sea could easily motivate any writer ... or any killer, depending upon one's inclination. Ditto for the hidden little towns deep within Maine's wooded interior. My story's narrator and his Veronica come from those parts, and there's a different kind of scary about those New England locales and their inhabitants. Just ask Stephen King ... or me.

With Love, Veronica
By Ken Goldman

They told me the fish were cold and they felt no pain.
But they were not the fish who told me.
— Anonymous

I am, as you can see, an ugly man ...

... not deformed, but certainly freakish in the Grand Guignol sense of the word, the make-no-mistake-about-it sense, and long past the point of fooling myself into believing I might hope for a normal life living among those who are not themselves social lepers. The schoolyard taunts are behind me now, but I have little doubt there are those who call me hideous behind my back.

Does my candor surprise you? It shouldn't. I don't pretend not to see the disgust on the faces of others and how people nervously avoid me. Impossible not to notice. There are none so blind as those who will not see. Isn't that what they always say, Dr. Antonelli?

I admit this without anger despite the unfairness of my circumstance, and I don't tell you my story to elicit your pity. I accept my ugliness and I want you aware of it before I go on. Knowing this will explain a lot about Veronica. At least, that's my hope.

It will certainly explain why growing up in Portland offered me little refuge from my daily agonies. There are few places in this New England seaport for a child to hide a face like mine, and I spent my boyhood wandering the hilly streets of the harbor district fully understanding how Quasimodo must have felt returning from his bell tower.

I found no sympathy walking these streets, and as a grown man never saw any desire in women's eyes beyond the desire to leave my presence. Their revulsion was similar to someone who has seen a bloated and filthy rat slither from a kitchen after they have eaten a particularly hearty meal.

Of course, I now understand the perfect logic of their reaction. The hatred of ugliness is, after all, the prejudice that never dies. Regardless of the culture or the enlightenment of an age, the truly hideous seem not to belong, as if features like mine are a kind of outrage. I've learned to recognize the double take that confirms something about me is not quite right, then the abrupt turning away. It's the same gag reflex of one who has bitten into what at first appears a perfectly good Winesap apple only to discover that his mouth has gorged on blood.

But as I've told you, I accept these judgments, having no choice in the matter. I admit to remorse and some resentment, but there's no real anger. I experience my own revulsion whenever I catch an accidental glimpse of myself in a mirror.

My mother? Why is it you couch surgeons always link a man's sexual wiring with dear old Mom?

Okay, it was like this ...

Have you ever seen a face so ugly only a mother could love it?

You're looking at one ...

I always suspected my father's leaving had something to do with me. While the man was never handsome by any stretch of the imagination, I'm certain his refusal to marry my mother wasn't an entirely irrational choice. One glance at her explained why. Before I grew old enough to gurgle 'Dada' the man had already packed his bags.

Mother knew his reasons for walking. What the woman lacked in appeal, she made up for in frankness, often explaining: "Ambrose, some were never meant to be beautiful. Those whose beauty lies within learn to expect nothing from this world." She had assumed her words offered comfort or, failing that, consolation. Of course, they offered neither. From others I received the kindness a mackerel might expect from the fisherman about to club it. Just the same, I learned my lesson well. I saw how far Mother's inner beauty had taken *her*.

The poor woman couldn't see that I was no more beautiful on the inside than I was externally. Not talented or artistic, I lacked even rudimentary social skills which might have coaxed others to venture closer.

And do I appall you, Dr. Antonelli?

Maybe you're asking yourself if I appalled the girl in the photo you're holding, this beautiful young woman posing on the rocks?

But we can't really ask her, can we?

Mother's death left me with a meager inheritance. I found a room inside a boarding house in Diamond Vespers, a small town hidden deep within the wooded interior of Maine that, like myself, had secluded itself from the world outside. I worried where I might find employment in such a remote outpost, knowing that any person I met would curse the encounter, swearing never to set foot anywhere near my workplace again.

The task proved less difficult than I'd feared. There's always a dark and remote alcove somewhere for persons like me to cloister themselves, a hidden cache that enables others to get on with their lives feeling no guilt. Coworkers stepped lightly around my station in the mail sorting room as if Ambrose Woodhouse were some kind of secret, an abhorrent mushroom growing in the dark. They exchanged the minimal requisite niceties and quickly moved on.

"How ya doin', Ambrose? Okay? That's good."

I didn't mind. If I were to be the local bogeyman, better I appear invisible than grotesque. What would a therapist call my reaction? Withdrawal? A defense mechanism to conceal a massive inferiority complex? Yes, that sounds about right.

So the mail sorting room position worked out well for all concerned. It seemed oddly appropriate that my postal consignment at the local branch was inside the place where all undeliverable local mail winds up, called the 'D.O.A. letter' office to those on the inside, a dusty chamber dimly lit by several 75-watt bulbs hanging from filthy strings, where my only companions were the huge mail sacks that had no other destination than myself.

In the sorting station inside the Diamond Vespers postal branch, they have these new rapid fire systems that automatically sort mail going to the adjoining counties, using high-speed optical scanners reading bar codes and machine-printed addresses, bringing and purging on third class envelopes by the hundreds. But with damaged or illegibly printed addresses, those fancy machines can't always scan as they're meant to, and discarded letters that have made it as far as our county eventually find their way to the sacks of undeliverable mail, and to me. My job is to determine what the machines can't. I'm the mail's last hope of deliverability, the last human component before the mail man; that is, I try to figure out where these 'dead-on-arrival' letters are meant to go even if it means I have to open the damned things myself, although I'm not supposed to tell anybody about that.

The woman had written an address on a 9 x 12 manila folder that proved all but unintelligible for man or machine. Only the words "Vespers" and "Maine" were legible, and not very. It appeared she had probably mailed the folder during a rainstorm because the ink had run in thick rivulets to the bottom edges of the envelope.

Don't say you heard it from me, but once a mailer finds itself in our D.O.A. office, all bets are off regarding the privacy of its contents. The logic is, of course, that there might be some indication of its destination, or at least a return address inside. More often than not, it's a kid writing to Santa in July or some fool addressing his memorandum to a town or street that exists nowhere on the map. Undeliverable letters are sometimes good for a laugh during a lunch break, but not usually for much else.

Veronica's letter was different.

It contained the 8 x 10 photograph you're holding, Doctor, clearly not intended for a stranger's eyes. That beautiful and shapely young woman, that's Veronica reclining comfortably upon those ocean-soaked rocks – a jetty or promontory of some sort – as if she were a sea nymph posing for a Renaissance painting. Whether the waves behind her are crashing to shore in Scarborough or the French Riviera, I couldn't tell you. Their inclusion in that photograph always seemed extraneous to me because, as you can see, Veronica is completely nude, basking upon those rocks.

Go ahead, Doctor. Take a long look at her smiling, relaxing while a brisk wind musses hair black as onyx, beads of seawater glistening on perfect breasts burnt gold by the sun. I know you're feeling what I felt when I first saw her.

I never learned who took this snapshot. I didn't want to know. Maybe you're thinking it was the same guy whose name and address dripped down that manila folder, the intended recipient of Veronica's gift package. Yes, that was my first thought, and it might have made perfect sense excepting one small detail.

Paper-clipped to the photograph was a small and delicate sheet of perfume-scented pink stationery, its texture so rose petal-like I wondered how anyone could have written a sentence on material so thin without tearing it to shreds. I had to rub my eyes to convince myself the words really were there. I can still smell that stationery as if it were in my hands right now.

Dear Ambrose,
Just my way of showing that I hope we can
get to know each other much better.
With Love,

Veronica

Dear Ambrose ...
The truth took a moment to fully register.

She had intended that photograph for me all along! *I* was the only person stationed in the small 'D.O.A.' office. Although the smudged handwriting on the envelope – illegible as it appeared – bore no likeness to my name or address, the coincidence factor was too great to consider any other possibility. Ambrose isn't exactly a household name, is it?

I shoved the folder into my jacket; fully aware the action might cost me my job – and maybe a whole lot more – if anyone saw me. The envelope didn't contain my address, and there are federal laws to warn postal employees about that sort of thing. But I'm no fool, either. Women never go out of their way to meet me. Especially beautiful women who aren't vision impaired.

She wrote no home address on the folder, but on her stationery, she had placed a post office box, 111-B located somewhere in Boston. I seriously considered tracking the location down. But then what? Could I stake out Veronica's box in the hopes of catching a glimpse of her? Not likely I'd pull off that trick unnoticed. People remember me whether they care to or not. I didn't feel very much like justifying my mailbox curiosity to strangers.

I considered doing nothing, writing off the entire incident as a probable trick played by some hardhearted jokester. Perhaps Maurice with the greasy hair? Or maybe Jake who works the front counter, always sneering when he thinks I don't see? I tried erasing from my brain the pink stationery and its accompanying photograph. But the image of the woman prone on those rocks wouldn't fade, nor would her words ...

'Dear Ambrose ... '

Suppose she was for real ... just suppose ...

After days spent considering my alternatives, I chose the most direct course. I won't deny my hand trembled the whole time I wrote back to her.

Veronica,

Thank you for the photograph. I'm hoping we can get to know each other much better too.

Ambrose

It took all of my courage to mail that letter.

It took the last of it to endure the pain that followed.

For weeks, there was nothing. Day after day, I emptied the thick sacks arriving at my station, covering the floor with envelopes and folders of every possible size and description, hoping to find the one purposely ink-smeared address that proved a companion to the first.

Nothing ...

I'm no stranger to pranks, Doctor. I imagined the likely scenario. Some contemptible fellow employee, bored with his routine, had gone to great lengths to humiliate me. Maybe he had discovered the woman's alluring photograph somewhere. Perhaps he had gone so far as to persuade a girlfriend to hop on those rocks and remove her string bikini. Together maybe a dozen coworkers had re-christened the woman in the photo 'Veronica', and I pictured them convulsed with laughter at the way I so easily took the bait.

Are you laughing yourself sick, Maurice?

Enjoying this, are you, Jake?

As more agonizing weeks passed, my hopes faded that somehow another communication from Veronica might yet find its way to my station.

It never happened.

I waited for the inevitable smirking question from someone, from everyone.

"So, Ambrose, receive any interesting letters lately?"

"You up for a day at the beach, Ambrose, old pal?"

But that never happened, either.

Clearly, my tormentors preferred anonymity. I expected the punch line would arrive with a late night telephone call. I limited my phone use to weekly communications with farmers' markets for the delivery of groceries and shared a party line with my landlady, an old crone named Sarah Barnes, one of the town's widows whose social security checks needed some stretching. Such was the extent of my Diamond Vespers telephone communications.

Until one midnight after I had given up all hope of ever hearing from her again ...

... a shrill ring jolted me from my sleep.

"Ambrose?"

Her voice was impossibly soft, practically childlike.

"Who ... What time is—"

"Did you really like my photograph, Ambrose?"

I shook myself awake.

"Who is—"

I didn't have to ask.

"You know who I am, Ambrose. So, did you like my photograph?"

Not a joke. Please, not a joke.

"Are you really ... who you say you are?"

"I am exactly who I say I am. But the photograph? You liked it?"

"Yes."

A hesitant schoolgirl giggle ...

"How much did you like it, Ambrose?"

"Very much. I liked it very much."

"Would you say you loved it?"

"Yes. *Yes.* I loved it. But why did you route it with the undeliverable letters? Why didn't you just send it to me here? How did you know I would read your note?"

"You *did* read it, didn't you?"

"Yes."

"And you enjoyed my photograph? Loved it? More because you knew you shouldn't be looking at it?"

"Yes."

"Then you have your answer, Ambrose."

I knew she was toying with me and savoring her enjoyment. For a moment, I heard only the woman's light breathing. Then:

"You would like to see more, wouldn't you?"

I found it suddenly difficult to speak. "This is a joke, right? Goddamn you, if this is a joke ..."

"No joke, Ambrose. No joke. But you didn't answer my question."

"Yes. I would like to see more. I would love to see more."

"Perhaps to do more than see? Perhaps to touch?"

"Yes. Yes ..."

"Let me hear you say my name, Ambrose."

"Veronica ... *Veronica"!*

Another giggle.

"That's good. That's very good. Now, are you listening? Are you listening very closely? Because there is something I want to tell you. Something very, very important ..."

The words spilled from me in a rush as if independent of my will.

"Yes, I'm listening. Yes."

The faintest of whispers, an exhalation, as if Veronica breathed her words, impossible words – unthinkable and absurd – meant for the ears of anyone but me.

"I want you, Ambrose. I want you now ..."

... And I wanted her, too, Doctor. I wanted her more than I ever wanted any woman.

Because in that single moment, I really believed ...

... that Veronica had killed the twisted gargoyle living for so long inside me. The moment she arrived at my door, I believed I could never revert to the deplorable creature I'd been all my life; that my appearance no longer mattered. Not so long as I had her.

I was wrong.

A woman like her, a man like me ...

Don't you see? Beauty may only be skin deep, but ugliness ... Well, you know the old saying.

The grotesque creature with my face remained for the world to see. During our few weeks together, I prayed no one would discover us in the dismal spots we frequented, that I might find some refuge from the meddlesome interference of others if only in my own room.

That proved impossible. In Diamond Vespers, the walls have ears, and they have eyes. People see. People always see ...

... and people talk.

"I'll bet your companion cost you a piece of change, eh, Ambrose?"

"Hey, Ambrose, you finally find a woman who won't puke her dinner into your face?"

Of course, Veronica pretended not to hear the ridicule, not to see the sneers. But they were there, all right. They were there.

None so blind as those who will not see ...

"Make them all invisible, Ambrose," she tried to convince me. "See only me. There are no others while I'm with you."

But I couldn't make them invisible, Doctor. Worse, I saw the flaws in Veronica as clearly as I saw my own – even while pretending not to see them.

Tunnel vision, isn't that what you head examiners call it? One sees only what he chooses even with the truth glaring him in the face? Yes, I saw the prostitute whom I paid to perform her masquerade, reimbursed to say and do anything – no matter how detestable – just to pocket another dollar from her trusting john. It's the oldest cliché in the book: the whore with the heart of gold.

Just a nickel a dance, boys ... a nickel a dance and I'm yours.

I think I need a glass of water, please.

Don't misunderstand. Time spent with Veronica remained precious. I convinced myself that I didn't give a sweet damn about how much I'd paid for her company. And that wasn't all I'd paid for, either. I bought her things – jewelry, clothes – all the while enduring Veronica's other men, strangers who were probably as wretched as myself.

Knowing nothing of them, for months I almost managed to convince myself they didn't exist.

Almost.

I would have gladly lavished my fortune on the woman, had I possessed one. Of course, Veronica saw to it that I exhausted what little I *did* have from my mother's estate. Oh yes, she was good, she was very good.

But she wasn't very smart, Doctor. She wasn't very smart at all.

Near Halibut Point, the air at sunset feels crisp enough in October to sting. The sudden gusts churning off the Atlantic felt brutal last Sunday, and watching the distant whitecaps I knew a storm was approaching off the Massachusetts coast. On a jagged abutment, Veronica held me close, braced against the sharp wind squalls, thick tufts of that raven hair doing a brisk polka beneath her scarf as the waves crashed far below.

"What's wrong, Ambrose? You've hardly said a word."

I felt like a cancer had grown inside me. I couldn't look at her, but somehow I found the strength to speak.

"Was it on rocks like these you took that photograph, the one you sent to me? Whose idea was it to show your tits that day, Veronica? Maybe the guy who took your picture?"

My words struck her harder than the sharp slaps of wind.

"I never lied to you, Ambrose. You know what I am. You've always known."

Inside hot bubbles of anger roiled and I pulled the woman hard against me.

"Do you want to know what happened inside our post office yesterday, Veronica? Would you like to hear about my conversation with my good pals Jake and Maurice? *Would you?"*

"Ambrose, I never meant to hurt you. I thought you understood—"

The rain started that same moment, thick dollops of it pelting our faces. But I didn't budge from our spot on those jutting rocks, and together we stood as if paralyzed – afraid to move – in the soaking torrent.

I reached into my slicker for the two manila folders. I didn't have to explain their contents.

"One addressed to Jake, the other to Maurice. The photos are the same, showing you bare-assed to the wind. Of course, you mailed your pink promotional ad to their home addresses this time. No need to play head games when you're soliciting guys whose deliveries don't have to pass the inspection of some shriveled landlady with her nose in everyone's business. Do I have it right so far?"

"Ambrose, you don't under—"

"Don't I?" I shook her, crushing the two folders in my palms. "Tell me, do you as a rule follow guys like me as your homework assignment, knowing the easy marks we are? Is that how it's done, your little scam?"

I held the folders out for her, but their addresses had become smeared in the rain. They were completely unreadable.

"I swear to you, Ambrose! I never—"

"You know what those guys said, Veronica? Their exact words when they cornered me inside the office? Maurice, he starts off like he's mimicking an insipid love song. *'Ver-on-i-kah ... Ver-on-i-kah ...'* He's chortling at me like he's come up with this brilliant comedy bit. The man just tears a gut until I'm thinking he's going to woof a lung right there on the floor.

Then Jake passes me your photo just as serious as he's able to pull off, and I'm thinking these two are working in tandem and that Jake's handing me this letter telling me I'm fired because of you. And all the time he's looking like any second he might howl like a goddamned wolf.

"But, no, what he hands me is *this* ...

"Recognize the pink paper? Two identical letters addressed to each of them, Veronica, identical to the one you sent me! And Jake, he says to me, 'Ambrose, don't you be gettin' this photo all sticky, now. 'Least not 'til quittin' time. Maurice and me, we gon' to write to this post office box in Boston, and maybe we'll even tell your little cooz pot here that you sent us.'

"Jake is right, isn't he? That's just what you are! A goddamned cooz pot, just like the man says!"

There I was, Doctor, screaming at that woman even while the tears ran down my face.

Right on cue, the thunder started, and the world cracked in half. Thick bolts of lightning spiked the coastline as if the sky were pissed off, too.

I couldn't stop myself. Veronica struggled, but I just couldn't stop myself.

Damn her, Doctor! Damn her!

She begged me to let her explain, said I was hurting her. But I *wanted* to hurt her; I wanted to hurt her the way she'd hurt me. And so I shook her; I shook her so hard on those rocks with the waves crashing below and the thunder so loud inside my head I couldn't hear myself think ...

... so loud I couldn't hear Veronica scream when she slipped from my grasp. The rain made the rocks so slick,

Doctor. And she just lost her footing, just toppled over the edge before I could grab her, then plunged from the bluff to the waves below.

She tumbled in the wind like a kid's discarded rag doll. I watched her thump against the sharp rocks; saw her head smash open like an eggshell. Seconds later, the surf just rolled her over, swallowing what remained.

Then she was gone.

I'm sorry, Veronica ... so sorry ...

But I didn't push her, Dr. Antonelli. She slipped. I swear to God I didn't push her ...

Dr. Morton Antonelli hit the STOP button of his Sony, snapping into silence the desperate recorded pleas of his patient.

"Poor bastard," the therapist muttered. This guy the police had brought in had himself one mother of an identity crisis. When no one was around to drop kick his ego, Ambrose Woodhouse found a pretty effective way to do it himself.

He poured a fresh cup of coffee, gazing at the Atlantic just outside his window, then turned his attention to the photograph Woodhouse had handed him of the nude woman reclining like a siren on the rocks. The woman in that 8 x 10 was indeed beautiful. But she was probably not worth confessing to the police for having killed, as Ambrose had done.

"Poor pathetic bastard," the therapist muttered again, rereading the brief letter Veronica supposedly had scribbled concerning her hopes of getting to know the message's recipient better.

Antonelli jotted down more notes.

Ambrose Woodhouse wants so desperately to feel loved, he insists the letter sent on the pink stationery bears his name. He sees his name there because he wants to see it there, just as he wants to see his relationship with Veronica as real.

Antonelli again searched the contents of the large catalogue envelope with the smeared address, but Ambrose's name appeared nowhere inside. Why should it? No one had sent that letter to Ambrose Woodhouse. The salutation on the pink paper read only 'Dear Sir' and explained how the woman hoped they could get to know each other better, blah, blah, blah. The photograph was a nice touch, of course, although Ambrose chose to disregard the elaborate brochure that came with it. At least until he had filled out the form and sent the cash.

No doubt Ambrose Woodhouse was completely delusional and had imagined seeing his name on that flimsy pink tissue paper, all right. And that wasn't the only thing the pathetic guy had imagined.

But the body washed ashore yesterday at Halibut Point, that was real.

In a manner of speaking, at least.

Christ, was there anyone in Diamond Vespers who didn't know about Ambrose Woodhouse and his woman? The secrets those little towns always kept under the floorboards.

Poor, ugly bastard.

The Doctor examined the frilly pink stationery, so impossibly delicate that Woodhouse had wondered aloud how the woman could have written anything on it. That answer was deceptively simple to anyone not into self-delusion.

No one had written on it. The damned thing was mass-produced.

The old woman named Sarah Barnes who shared Woodhouse's party line had cleared up the tangled mess of the whole lurid affair. Antonelli jotted into his notes how the old lady had heard Ambrose talking on the phone late one night, speaking in some freakish woman's voice as well as his own. Luckily, the guy wasn't very good at playing the two roles, at least not convincingly enough to fool the widow who listened in on her tenant's complete conversation. Old Sarah had retained enough of her faculties to reconstruct the entire exchange. The conversation between Veronica and Ambrose had gone just as Woodhouse had said almost word for word:

"Did you really like my photograph, Ambrose?"

"You would like to see more, wouldn't you?"

"Fucking incredible," the therapist muttered. He studied the colorful and tantalizing brochure marketed through the mail by some anonymous entrepreneur operating out of a private postal box in Boston.

Probably fucking illegal too, the doctor thought. After all, there were federal postal laws.

Which was too bad.

Because the woman in that photograph was every bit as magnificent as Ambrose Woodhouse had claimed. And for a mere $3000 sent to Luv-Mate Inc., c/o P.O. Box 111-B in Boston, Doctor Morton Antonelli might have seriously considered buying the incredibly lifelike love doll named Veronica for himself.

With Love, Veronica originally appeared in *The Edge: Tales of Suspense* #2 (USA: September 1998). It has also appeared in *The Dream Zone* #3 (UK: June 1999), and *Storyteller Magazine Vol. 9, #3* (Canada: winter 2002-2003). This story was a *Futures Magazine* 'Fire to Fly' Short Story Contest Semi-finalist (January 2004).

About the Author

Former teacher Ken Goldman has homes on the Main Line in Pennsylvania and on the South Jersey shore, depending upon the track of the sun. His stories appear in over 435 publications in the U.S. and Canada, the UK, Ireland, and Australia. He has received honorable mentions in Ellen Datlow & Terry Windling's *The Year's Best Fantasy & Horror #7, #9, #16*, and Ellen Datlow, Kelly Link & Gavin J. Grant's *YBF&H #17*. Anthologies due in 2007 are *Potter's Field 2* (Sam's Dot Publishing), *A Time To… The Best of The Lorelei Signal 2006* (Wolfsinger Publications), and *The Macabre Underground* (Splatterpunk Press). A chapbook of Ken's stories, as yet untitled, will be issued by Sam's Dot Publishing in early 2007.

As a 14-year-old I encountered a crow with baleful eyes that looked like it wanted to kill me. Having just seen Damien: Omen II, I imagined it might try.

EATING CROW
By Garrett Peck

Chapter 1

It was finally the Friday night Carol Mitchell waited for. It was the third Friday of the month, when she and her husband David ritually met at the home of their friends, Betty and George Brightman, for several relaxing rounds of bridge. Perhaps it wasn't that exciting, but Carol liked living a quiet life. Excitement usually meant trouble.

At the moment, Carol applied the last vestiges of her makeup. She didn't use as much as she used to, having finally succumbed to David's protests that wearing so much made her look like she was preparing to perform a war dance. As she smeared a sparse amount of blush on her left cheek, Carol heard the bathroom door open behind her. She looked up to see David, with a large brown towel wrapped around his waist, emerging through a thin curtain of steam. They were going to be late getting to the Brightman's, but he insisted on grabbing a quick shower before they left. He was fanatical about cleanliness. "Some people are good looking, and some people are ugly," he once pontificated, "but anyone can be clean."

"Hurry up, dear," Carol ordered as she looked back at the mirror to finish rubbing in the blush. "We're running late."

"I know, honey," David replied while he unceremoniously unwrapped the towel from around himself.

Carol paused in her beautifying to watch her husband's reflection in the mirror. A pleased grin formed on her lips as she admired his lean, athletic legs and firm, muscular buttocks. *How lucky I am,* she thought with satisfaction. *Twelve years of marriage and the sight of my husband's ass still turns me on.* Her grin turned slightly mischievous as she considered suggesting they call off the bridge game and spend the rest of the night in bed. But she knew David wouldn't miss going over to George and Betty's. He enjoyed their regular bridge parties as much as she did. Besides, there would be plenty of time to make love when they got back. They had all night, and all of tomorrow morning for that matter.

As Carol picked up her lipstick, David slid into a tight pair of briefs. He turned to look at his wife worrying over herself in the mirror. He lifted his hand to beat against his smiling lips and gave a whooping Indian war cry. He saw his wife look over her shoulder with a mock frown on her half-painted lips.

"Okay, you kidder," she admonished him. "Let's get a move on. Betty promised me a slow death if we were late again."

"That's one thing about Betty," David commented wryly. "She always keeps her promises."

With Carol egging him on, David finished dressing and grooming. By the time he was ready, they had fifteen minutes before they were due at the Brightman's. The drive took twenty.

"We'll be about five minutes late," Carol predicted after consulting the dashboard clock of their Buick Lucerne. "Do you think Betty will let me slide?"

"I suspect she's busy sharpening her meat fork at this very moment," David replied.

They drove in their accustomed silence, with the radio blaring. Even though he was thirty-six, David still enjoyed heavy metal. That was one of the few things Carol didn't understand about him, but she suspected it was one of the ways he kept his mind as young as his body. She wasn't a great fan of the music, but occasionally caught herself tapping her foot in rhythm to a few of the songs she came to recognize and enjoy.

True to her assessment, they arrived at exactly five past eight. They leapt out of the car with what looked liked a choreographed unison. Carol reached out to hold her husband's hand as they walked up the Brightman's driveway.

There was a moderately cool October breeze ruffling the leaves of the big oak tree planted in the front yard. Carol listened to the soothing music it made. Then she heard another sound from the branches… a shrill, inhuman shriek. She turned around and looked up at the source of the noise. With a maddened flapping of wings, something dark streaked down from its perch and flew toward her face.

Carol instinctively ripped her hand away from David's to ward off the attacker. She didn't know what it was – only that it was black and had wings. *A bat,* she thought with horror. When it struck her hand, however, she felt feathers. Her brain barely had time to register the fact before she felt talons ripping into her flesh. Carol screamed and the bird answered with another eerie screech. She flailed her arms about wildly to fend off the beast. The violence of her actions finally succeeded in driving it away. It flew off into the night sky while Carole continued waving her arms in its direction.

A hand grabbed one of her swinging limbs. Carol collapsed, sobbing, into David's arms.

"There, there," David soothed, running a hand through her hair.

The whole event had taken place in less than five seconds.

There was a squeaking sound and for one terrified instant Carol thought the bird had returned. But a pale light followed the noise and she realized it was only the front door of the Brightman's house opening up. George Brightman stepped out onto the porch, followed a second later by Betty.

"What the hell's going on here?" George demanded.

"A crow," David explained over Carol's muted sobs. "Goddamn crazy thing flew right in her face."

Without replying, George and Betty jogged out to where David was examining his wife's arm. There were three raw claw marks marring her skin. Two of them looked nasty, while the third was barely a scratch. Blood beaded along the tears.

"Good Lord," Betty intoned with concern upon seeing them. "Come inside the house, honey. Let me help you fix those up."

Carol accepted David and Betty's support as they lead her into the house.

Chapter 2

"You probably just frightened it," Betty said above the rush of water splashing over Carol's wounds. She was in the bathroom, doting over her friend's injuries.

"No," Carol protested. "It flew right out of the tree. It purposefully attacked me."

"Nonsense, dear. Why on Earth should it do that?"

"I don't know," Carol admitted. "You don't suppose it was rabid, do you?"

"I doubt it," Betty reassured her. "I don't think I've ever heard of a crow going rabid. I can't remember there ever being any rabid animals found out this way, either."

As Carol reached over to turn off the faucet, Betty took her wet arm and dabbed a dry hand towel over the cuts. The flow of blood had diminished, but not entirely quit.

"Don't," Carol muttered. "You'll stain the towel."

"You let me worry about that. Now hold still."

Betty reached over to grasp a bottle of alcohol sitting on the edge of the sink. She dampened the dry end of the towel with a generous amount of the liquid. Carol braced herself for the sting she knew was coming. She relaxed after Betty began scrubbing out the scrapes. They didn't sting so badly after all. Upon examining them closer, she realized they really weren't all that deep. Her face reddened when it occurred to her how badly she had over-reacted. She made a mental note to apologize to David and George for acting so silly. A fine example of the tough, modern woman she made.

"Won't need any bandages," Betty announced. "Therefore, I predict that you will live through the night."

"Thank you, Betty," Carol replied. "I'm sorry I acted like a child."

"Think nothing of it."

They walked into the parlor together. David sat at the card table and George was busy mixing drinks behind the bar. The bar was a monstrous, old-fashioned mahogany thing. It was George's pride and joy. He always kept it polished to an admirable shine. It was one of those things that just wasn't being made any more and would have cost George an arm and a leg if he hadn't inherited it from his parents.

"Who ordered a Tom Collins?" George asked with a friendly grin as the women approached him. He thrust the drink into Carol's grateful hand.

Carol took a long swallow of the refreshing beverage. Without asking, George had mixed it a little stronger than usual. To help calm her nerves, no doubt. She took another sip, but didn't thank him. She knew he preferred to have the little things he did for people taken for granted. Her mental note of apology forgotten, she walked over to join David at the card table.

"Are you okay, honey?" he asked.

She nodded. "Yes, I'm fine. I just don't understand why that thing attacked me."

"Maybe this is its mating season," George suggested. "It was probably just horny."

"Oh, George ... " Betty began, but she was too late to stop the room from bursting into laughter. It was just what they all needed to dismiss the incident and return to high spirits.

Soon George and Betty, drinks in hand, joined the Mitchells at the table and their first game began. They played long into the night. The decks were kept dealt and the glasses were kept full, though Carol watched David carefully to see he didn't have too many. She respectfully reminded him he had to drive them home. Twenty dollars apiece would be awarded to the winning couple. This was because if it were up to David and George, they'd be playing poker. But as long as there was some money in the kick, they agreed to play bridge.

At well past twelve, they decided to call it quits. Points were unnecessarily added up and Carol and David found themselves twenty dollars richer.

"Well, ready to head home, Mrs. Trump?" David said teasingly.

"Better a trump than a tramp," George added.

Carol yawned in answer. "Yes, handsome hubby. You have one very tipsy lady to take home."

George and Betty saw them to the door, where they idled with parting chatter. There were smiles, embraces, handshakes, and assurances they would be in touch.

While David lingered relaying a last minute message to George, Carol opened the door and stepped out onto the porch.

It was there, waiting for her.

Carol gasped and took a step backwards. She finally got her first decent look at the bird perched on the porch railing. It was large, even for a crow. Large enough to be mistaken for a young raven. Its head and body were black as death. Its fiery yellow eyes transfixed her with their evil intent. Dimly, she heard David rattling on behind her inside the house, but she couldn't speak. Her mouth gaped open; her jaw twitched to no avail. She didn't scream until the bird launched itself at her.

Her paralysis broke. Her first instinct was to duck and throw her uninjured arm over her face. The furious beast fluttered onto the top of her head. It tore at her hair, trying to reach her scalp. She flung her hand up to push it away, but when she did, the monster hooked its pointed beak into the soft flesh of her wrist. She yanked it away, tearing a deep, gaping gash.

Then David was there, driving it away with shouts and swings. It dislodged itself from her hair and flew back to the railing it had assaulted her from. It looked her dead in the eyes and gave one challenging, high-pitched squawk before again flying off into the night sky it had come from.

Carol clutched her new wound to her chest. She was momentarily speechless. With silent coaxing, David was able to pry her hand away to get a better look at it in the porch light. The ragged slash in her wrist was welling over with blood, which beat a macabre rhythm as it splattered on the wooden floorboards.

George broke the silence by saying, "It's going to need stitches. Let's get her to the hospital."

Chapter 3

Carol's wrist received six stitches after a two-hour wait at the hospital. George and Betty had insisted on waiting with them, though they didn't talk much. The late night emergency room seemed to suppress their will to make conversation. Carol was certain they had stayed out of a sense of duty and guilt, as if her being attacked in their front yard somehow made them responsible. She felt an inner warmth course through her from the reliability of her friends. They were good to have in this tough old world.

It was just after four when Carol and David arrived home. They held each other close as they strode up to the house. They slid into the security of their home and barred the door against the night with the turn of the deadbolt. Leaving their coats on a chair in the foyer, they made a beeline for their bedroom. Nothing was said. Each one knew what the other needed.

Carol unfastened her pants and pushed them down to the floor as soon as she entered the room. David followed suit, hooking his thumbs in his briefs and pulling them down with the same fluid motion. Carol pulled off her panties while David continued with the rest of his attire. Carol felt a twinge just below her shoulder where she had received a tetanus shot as she stripped her blouse off. David was there to help her with the bra. He unhooked it and let it drop to the floor. Carol gave herself over to chills of pleasure as she felt her husband run his hands over her shoulders and down to her breasts. He massaged her nipples into hardness using his thumbs and forefingers. At her first moan, he eased her down gently onto the bed. Carol forgot the dull pain in her wrist. It was beautiful ...

Chapter 4

It was so, so beautiful. The sun was shining and she and David were walking through the woods. It was a lazy summer day, the kind just made for a walk through the forest. Cheery sunlight sparkled through gaps in the trees and songbirds filled the air with their light-hearted melodies. David was holding her hand. Not the way he did now, but the way he had when they were courting. She felt frozen in time. Each step she took gladdened her heart. Joy dared her to deny it.

That was when David dropped her hand and walked ahead of her. The woods became silent. Eyes from the branches assailed her. She stopped in her path, knowing something wasn't right. She cried out to David. He was stopped ahead of her with his back turned towards her. The forest screamed back in return. Hundreds of birds – robins, sparrows, cardinals, blue jays and others zoomed out of the trees surrounding her. Wings, beaks, and claws thudded against her and grabbed for purchase. A pigeon flying into her face forced her to the ground. The cloud of feathered creatures fell upon her. Even though she knew she couldn't be helped, she reached up through the flurry of beating wings towards David. He turned around. The crow that had started it all perched on his shoulder. The bird glared at her in malevolent triumph. David also stared at her, but not with *his* eyes. The eyes now staring from his face were yellow and fueled with venomous hatred. The last thing she saw before a gull plunged its beak into her horror-filled eye was her husband tilting his head back and uttering the long, victorious screech of a crow …

Chapter 5

...before she sat up in bed, stifling a gasp. Shaking her head, she sank back down to the pillow. *Great way to start the morning,* she thought with newly awoken sarcasm.

The first fact she noted was that she was alone. Remembering it was Saturday, she rolled over and looked at the clock. It was 12:13. David must have woken up earlier and gone downstairs. She decided not to lie in bed for a while as she usually did on Saturdays. It was no fun without David. Instead she felt like cleaning herself up and getting started with the day.

She was reminded of her stitches when she pushed herself out of the bed. They smarted even worse now that the Novocain had worn off. "Novocain doesn't kill pain," she remembered a comedian saying, "It postpones it." She smiled at the offbeat truism and headed to the bathroom for a thorough sponge bath.

Downstairs she found a pot of warm coffee and a note from David. "*Went to play tennis with George. Be back at two,*" the note informed her. Carol shook her head in secret admiration. It never ceased to amaze her how much energy her husband had after only a little sleep. She'd gotten more sleep than he had and still felt a little woozy. Maybe working forty hours a week managing a food warehouse did something for you. As for her, she would stick with coffee.

Sipping from a lukewarm cup, Carol looked out the window to judge the afternoon. Indian summer, her grandmother always used to call weather like this. The autumn sun heated the days, but the warmth began to fade at sunset. Since it had been dry lately, Carol decided it would be a good idea to water the flowerbeds. She needed something to do until David got back. She might as well do something useful rather than watching TV. She gulped down her coffee and went out to the garage.

It had rained often enough during the last month and the flowers hadn't needed watering, so David had rolled up the hose and stored it in the garage. There was precious little crime in the neighborhood, but David knew it had less of a chance of being stolen or vandalized by kids if they didn't leave it out. It took Carol a moment to locate it. She found it curled up under his workbench and snatched it up with triumph. It still looked brand new. There was not a kink or a rip in it. David took very good care of his property.

Carol hummed an unidentifiable tune as she pushed the button to open the garage door. She always felt compelled to make some sort of noise to cover up the hideous rumbling the door made as it traveled upward. Sunlight sprayed into her eyes when the door opened past her line of sight.

Carol walked, slightly blinded, into the driveway. Standing back from her flowerbed, she saw her decision to water had been a good one. The petals of her pink roses were dried out and the stems were wilting. She went over to the water faucet and bent down to reach her hand behind the bushes to connect the hose to the nozzle. There she froze.

A crow sat under the faucet, blinking its eyes with demonic intent.

Carol didn't need to be told. This wasn't just any crow. It was *the* crow. For some unknown reason this black beast wanted to kill her. She knew it. It had chosen her and it meant to kill her.

Bird and woman both stayed rigid; both waiting for the other to make the first move. They stayed immobile for at least thirty seconds before Carol began drawing slowly away. The bird followed her with its piercing gaze but made no move to attack. When she had gained enough distance, she inched into the garage.

Carol's gaze darted frantically around the room, searching for a weapon. She continually glanced back at the door to make sure the bird wasn't flying in after her. She couldn't see it from where she was and had no idea if it was still where she had last seen it. Eventually, her roving gaze locked onto her husband's golf bag. She crept over to the far wall it leaned against. Yanking a heavy iron from the bag, she turned back toward her adversary and began to advance on it.

No lousy bird is going to ruin my life, she thought with fury. It had taken her too long to build this nest. Damned if anything was going to rip it down now.

Her hands tightened on the club, much to the protest of her injured wrist, as she came into view of the faucet. The crow was still there. It watched her with amused intimidation, as if it were waiting for a reason to tear her face to shreds. It refused to retreat as she came closer. There was a suggestion of a smile on its curved beak. *Make your move,* the smile said.

Carol got within three feet of the bird. She thought she saw it tense up, but it still didn't make any threatening moves. Baring her teeth, Carol raised the club over her head. Then, with all the strength she could muster and a silent prayer for aim, she swung the club down.

The bird was moving even as the heavy metal tip came swishing down toward it. The five-iron thudded into the dry soil ineffectually. It wasn't even a close miss. Carol felt rough talons closing around her bandaged wrist in a sharp, lancing pain. Light and dark became one at that instant and she could feel herself falling off the edge of the driveway and the edge of the world …

Chapter 6

Pulling ... something pulled her awake. Her eyelids fluttered. Bright light shined into her dilated pupils and forced her to squeeze them shut again. There was something rough under her back. It felt like concrete. Still there was that pulling sensation. There was pain. Her disoriented head bowed and she looked down at the ground. She tried opening her eyes and this time, they obeyed her.

She saw red and black. The red was her blood. The black was the crow. It stood over her wrist and she saw its beak dip down into her naked gash. With revulsion, she felt the familiar pulling sensation and saw it rip out the last stitch. Her blood flowed freely again. The bird stood in a pool of it.

Sensing that she was awake, it turned to look at her. Its beak was red with gore and the stitch it had just torn out of her clung to the sticky coating. It squawked loudly and flipped its wings up threateningly, like a vampire's cape. It was not finished with her yet.

Feeling something born of desperation surge through her body, Carol brought up her leg and tried to bring it down on top of the bird. It was too fast for her. Taking flight, it easily dodged the pathetic blow. With the same movement, however, Carol pushed herself to her feet using her unmarred hand. Making use of her momentary advantage, she sprinted for the garage. She left the golf club and the shredded bandage on the driveway and did not look behind her. She nearly ripped the door off its hinges getting into the house.

Once safely behind the door, her hand groped for the lock. She found it and turned it. It did not occur to her that there was no way for the bird to get through a closed door.

She was ready to attribute the beast with all the powers of Satan.

There was a beating against the window. She snapped her head around and saw what she expected to see. The crow was outside, its wings slapping against the smooth glass panel in a vain effort to obtain entry. Carol took an involuntary step backwards, lest the window implode and allow the creature to rush in and finish her off.

Another sound joined the clattering at the window. It was a slow, meticulous dripping. Carol glanced down to see her reopened wound drooling blood onto the counter, where it collected and dripped to the floor. She moved over to the sink and grabbed the cleanest dishtowel in sight. She wrapped it tightly around her wrist to stop the flow of blood.

Her mind raced to surmise the situation. The bird had her trapped in her own home. She could not get outside without being attacked. Her hand definitely needed more stitches, but she didn't have a hope of getting to the hospital herself. She couldn't call the police. There was no way they would believe her story. They would take her for a crank caller or a college student who'd had too many mushrooms or whatever the hell kids took to get high these days. She discovered David's cell phone on the kitchen counter. He hadn't taken it with him. That meant she had to call Betty. She was the only person besides David and George who would believe her.

Trying to ignore the god-awful racket at the window, Carol reached for the kitchen phone. She had trouble making her trembling fingers push in the proper number. She managed to make the connection after taking a moment to steady her hand. Thirteen empty rings echoed in her skull before she gave up hope that Betty would answer.

She turned back to look at the monster outside her window. It noticed her looking at it and that only seemed to enrage it further. It redoubled its efforts to break through the barrier that separated them.

"You bastard!" she screamed at it. "What do you want from me?"

The bird paused in its assault to nail her in place with its stare. She could see the answer in its beady, malefic eyes. It wanted *her*... and it meant to have her.

It flew away from the window, then flew back into it, causing the pane to rattle and Carol to jump. It drew away once again and she waited for it to deliver another blow. It never came. She stood there a full minute before she allowed herself to believe it wasn't going to come smashing into her house to tear at her unmercifully until she was dead.

Her shoulders sagged in relief. Maybe it had hurt itself, hope suggested. Maybe it had fractured its skull and was out there dying this very moment. Her comforting thoughts were quickly followed by a different one – what if it had given up on that window and was trying to find another way inside?

Carol found herself running around from room to room, making sure all the doors and windows were secured. Finding nothing amiss downstairs, she charged up the stairs to repeat the operation on the second floor. There she only found one unlocked window in the bathroom, which she hurriedly remedied.

Trudging down the stairs again, Carol felt a dizzy spell coming on. The loss of blood mixed with exercise had finally caught up with her. The gore soaked towel dropped down the remaining few steps as her injured arm reached out to catch her near fall. After recovering, she trotted weakly down to the ground and bent over to retrieve it. Standing up, she looked through the kitchen. The door to the garage was wide open.

Carol bit her lip in panic. It was in now. She was sure of it. That's when she heard a familiar voice calling from a concealed area of the kitchen.

"Hi, honey, I'm home. Say, why is my five-iron out in the driveway?"

Chapter 7

They asked her a lot of embarrassing questions at the hospital. She couldn't tell her doctor how she had really lost her stitches, so she was forced to make up a story. "I never could stand the idea of having thread laced up in my skin," she told him, "so I took them out this morning. Then it started to bleed again. I'm so sorry. It won't happen again."

Away from the humiliating ordeal with the doctor and sitting safely next to her husband on the drive back, Carol asked David what they were going to do.

"I've already got it arranged," he assured her. "When you were with the doctor, I took the liberty of calling George and Betty. I asked them if they wanted to accompany us up to my parents' place in the mountains. I thought we could all use a change of scenery."

David's parents had a cozy cabin in the Appalachians. They told David and Carol they were free to use it whenever they pleased.

"Up there?" Carol replied. "But honey, what about your job?"

"I had time to call Mr. Ferguson, too. You were back there quite a while. Knowing I had all that vacation time piled up, he said it would be no problem."

"What about George?"

"He's got time saved up as well. I can't see why he couldn't get a few lousy days off. We'll call him when we get home. He'll know for sure by then."

"But, David ... " Carol faltered, not wanting to voice the question she had to have answered, " ... what if it follows me there?"

David glanced at her. "What if what follows you there?"

"You know what I mean. The crow."

"What?" David replied incredulously. "Don't be silly, dear. How could a crow follow us to Union County?"

"I don't know," she admitted, "but it followed me from George and Betty's."

David shook his head. "That's impossible, honey. It couldn't have been the same bird."

"It was, David."

"How could that be? It was just a coincidence."

"It wasn't a coincidence. If that wasn't the same bird, then Hitchcock is laughing in his grave!"

"Well, even if it was," said David, the tone of his voice telling her he still didn't think it was, "there's no way it could follow us up to the mountains. You'll be safe there. You'll see."

Chapter 8

A call to the Brightmans confirmed the trip. They would go over to pick them up at eleven the next morning. Carol would have been happier leaving that night, however. After thinking about it, she figured the seclusion and peaceful beauty of the mountains would give her the feeling of security she needed to regain. David laughed when she asked if they could make the drive that night. "We'd get there after dark," he explained. "We need some light to split wood for the stove. Now come upstairs and help me pack."

David pulled a pair of tremendous suitcases from the top shelf of the closet. He opened them up and laid them flat on the bed. From there he proceeded to pack a generous supply of old clothing into one of the cases. Carol caught sight of him opening his underwear drawer. He chose numerous pairs of socks and arranged them neatly around the shirts and pants he had already packed. When he lifted out his brief collection, she saw what he kept hidden under them.

David bought the .38 snub-nose during their first year of marriage. This had caused a small argument between them. Carol finally gave in after David told her he only wanted it to protect her from thieves, rapists and other bad guys. He put it in his underwear drawer and it had only been out a few times for cleaning since then. Now Carol was glad he had bought it. The gun, she decided, would give her all the security she needed. If that crow showed up again, she would blow it to kingdom come. She didn't think David would approve of her bringing the weapon, however. She would have to get it while he wasn't looking.

"Don't forget your toiletries," she reminded him.

"I won't," he returned. He went to the bathroom to collect them.

Carol waited until she heard the medicine cabinet open, then she hopped over the bed. She reached in and pulled the gun from the drawer. Its weight gave her a feeling of power and independence she didn't quite recognize, but liked. She unsnapped the holster and slid the pistol out. Opening the cylinder the way she had been shown, she found it was fully loaded but for one chamber which David kept empty to 'avoid accidents'. With a smile, she clicked the cylinder shut and walked back to her suitcase. She just had time to hide it under the jeans she added before David came back into the room.

That night David cooked them a steak dinner. He wasn't a very versatile cook, but he could broil a steak that would shame the Devil. After dinner and a few glasses of wine, they made love by the fireplace. They went at it for hours. Carol was consumed by his passion. It seemed to her that he had never been as kind or gentle since their honeymoon.

When it was over, she was exhausted. She dragged herself up to their bedroom and slipped naked beneath the sheets. She tried to wait for David, but sleepiness overcame her willpower.

Though her confidence had recovered and her feelings of foreboding were diminished, it never occurred to her to take the gun out of her suitcase.

Chapter 9

Carol experienced a moment of discomfort on the two-and-a-half hour drive to the cabin. It was when Betty asked her to relay what happened the other day in her own words. She told it in lavish detail, excluding none of the gore. Betty was shocked and consoled her. Carol thanked her, but assured her she was fine now. Running through the whole thing again helped to purge the experience.

The road leading to the cabin was a winding dirt affair that David drove a little faster than she would have liked. The dust storm shooting out from under the tires would have blinded anyone driving behind them, but no one was following. When David brought the car to a halt, Carol heard him yawn.

"What's the matter?" she teased. "Didn't you sleep well last night?"

"I was up all night worrying about you," he explained.

"You should worry in your sleep," George advised. "You'll get more rest that way."

The group hopped from the cozy velour interior of David's Buick and met behind the trunk. David produced the key and unlocked it. Four pairs of arms reached inside to haul out the luggage. George and Betty paused to drink in and comment on the rustic scenery surrounding them, and then trudged up to the weather-beaten wood door David was unlatching. They all walked in together with their suitcases banging against one another and the doorframe. David, carrying both Carol's suitcase and his own, took them to their room.

"Nice place," George complimented David when he returned.

"We aims to please," David drawled in his best mountain dialect.

"Where do we stay?" Betty inquired from above the wood stove she had been marveling over.

"Right next to us," David said as he stooped to pick up her suitcase. He motioned for George to follow him.

David set Betty's case next to the bed in the adjoining room. George laid his flat on the mattress. He flipped the twin catches and lifted the lid.

"I wouldn't unpack that, George," David recommended. "Those bureaus are pretty cruddy. It's better just to live out of the case."

"So who's unpacking?" George cackled. "I was just getting out my little surprise." With a smile of mock anticipation, he produced a large brown bottle from under a pile of clothing.

"What the hell have you got there?"

"Come on over and have a look."

David stepped over and looked at the yellow label on the bottle. It was a brand of Scotch he had never seen before.

"Heard this was a dry county," George remarked.

"Not anymore. Jesus, where did you get this stuff? The label says it's twelve years old."

"That's what it said when I bought it six years ago."

"Damn. Will it still be good?"

"Are you kidding? Good Scotch is like a good woman; it improves with age."

David nodded, but added, "Up to a point."

"Only one way to find out how good it still is," George said. He picked up the bottle and headed back to the ladies with David in tow. "Who wants a drink?" he asked with revelry.

Before either of the women could answer, David cut in. "Hold up a second, George. We better chop some wood for the stove before we start getting soused. That is, if you don't want to freeze your balls off tonight."

"Uh oh," Betty threw in. "You better help him out, George. You might need those some night."

"So might you," George threw back. Betty's mouth dropped open. George had to wait for Carol and David to stop laughing before speaking again. "Come on, Dave. Just one drink. I've been saving it for six years. I can't wait anymore."

David looked up at the ceiling in thought before saying, "Okay. One. Just don't get drunk and chop your hand off."

George clapped his hands in satisfaction. "Great! Now, does this place have anything civilized, like glasses?"

"They're in the cupboard above the sink," Carol told him. She was still absent-mindedly stroking her bandage after David's remark about chopped off hands.

George brought down four glasses and examined them for cleanliness. Uncertain, he rinsed them out. Then he grasped the cap on the bottle and was about to twist it when he caught David's attention. "Take a long look, buddy. This may be the last eighteen-year-old virgin you ever see." With that, he twisted off the cap. He moaned orgasmicly as he brought the bottle up to his nose, then poured a small amount into each glass.

The glasses were passed out and the group met in the middle of the room for a toast.

"I've been saving this bottle for a special occasion," George said with unaccustomed seriousness, "and I can't think of anything more special than spending a little time with the people in this room."

"Here, here," David called as their glasses clinked.

Carol and Betty winced as they took their sips. Even David had some trouble with his. Only George polished his off with relish.

"Ready to hit the old woodpile, pal," George proclaimed after setting his glass down.

"All right," David agreed. "Let's get it done."

"Hey, this is the mountains. Don't you mean 'git-r-done'?"

"Ain't no cable guys out here, I promise you," David rejoined.

As the men went out the front door, Betty turned to Carol. "I have to use the bathroom. Where is it?"

"There is none," Carol informed her. "Just an outhouse out back."

"An outhouse? My God, when David told me we'd be roughing it, I thought he just meant there'd be no television."

Carol smiled and followed Betty out into the sunshine. She saw George and David out by the woodpile. Both held axes raised over their heads. They swung them down almost simultaneously and the two logs became four. Carol watched, proudly grinning, as the muscles on David's forearms rippled. George may have the more sparkling personality, but she knew her husband would beat him in a beauty contest any day. A hand on Carol's shoulder brought her back from her thoughts.

"I'm going to use this so-called outhouse," Betty told her. Carol saw her trot around behind the cabin.

"Honey," David's voice came, "could you run inside and get those old gloves under the kitchen sink for me?"

"I sure can," she replied. "Be back in a moment."

Carol jogged back into the cabin. Before going directly to the sink, she collected the empty glasses. After setting them down, she turned on the water. It was the rushing water that covered the sound of beating wings flying in through the door she had left open. She only sensed the crow a split second before the familiar claws latched onto the back of her neck.

Chapter 10

George heard the scream the exact instant his axe blade hit the log in front of him. He let the axe slip from his grip and sprinted for the cabin. Behind him he heard something heavy strike the ground, punctuated by an expletive. A glance over his shoulder identified the noise as David tripping over the log he had just split and landing on his face. Four more long strides and George was through the doorway.

Carol was on the floor in front of her bedroom. The black crow was still latched onto her neck and she was trying to grab a hold of it. Every time her hands drew near they were bloodied by the creature's flashing beak. She was too panicked to even cry out again.

George was frozen by the insanity of the situation. *Birds do not attack people,* his rationality insisted. *This couldn't be happening.* But the bird was real, and so was the damage it was doing to Carol. He shook off his indecision and went to her aid.

The bird was so busy with Carol it didn't even realize George was behind it until his hand grabbed its wing. Reacting with surprising speed, it let loose of Carol and jerked its body around to face its new enemy. It sank its beak into the hand that trapped its wing and parted them, splitting the flesh wide. The quick counterattack was enough to loosen the hold on its wing. The crow wrenched itself free and fluttered to the top of George's head. George didn't have a mass of thick hair to protect him like Carole did. The monster's talons found easy purchase on his scalp.

Carol rolled over and looked up at the scene. She saw George shielding his eyes with his hands against the violent pecks the bird was raining down on his face. All it needed was one lucky shot and its beak would slip between his fingers and blind him. Its beak was so long she thought it might even be able to push it straight through to his brain. She had to get to the gun fast. It was George's only chance.

She lifted herself to her feet and stumbled into the bedroom. Shatteringly aware of George's agonized shouts, she searched for her suitcase. David had stored it under the bed. She yanked it out, undid the locks and dumped the contents onto the floor. A second's worth of rummaging and she produced the .38. She fumbled with the safety and flicked it off before racing back into the living room. George was on his knees with his attacker still clinging to his scalp. Carol raised the pistol and took careful aim at the murderous beast. She was concentrating so hard she didn't even notice David standing in the doorway with his cheek scraped and dirty from his fall. She centered the crow in her sights. *This is for you, bird,* she thought with venomous glee. She fired just as George stood up.

The bullet struck George full in the throat. It shattered his spinal connection on its passage through. It lodged in the wall after bursting out of the other side of his neck. The bird released its death-grip and George's body slumped to the floor, where it began to shudder.

Carol was struck immobile with shock. The gun hung limply from her hand. She didn't raise it again even when the crow landed on the table and stared at her in defiance. It seemed to know she wouldn't try to shoot it again. It gave her a raucous squawk that promised its return, then flew out the door, forcing David to duck out of its way.

The .38 slipped from Carol's fingers and landed on the oak floorboards with a hollow clunk. She opened her mouth and said, "I ... " then shut it. There was nothing she could say. There was nothing she could do to take back what she'd done. She began to shake in a way not unlike George's corpse at her feet.

"Sweet Jesus," David muttered. "Sweet Jesus."

Betty came running up behind him. He turned to face her, blocking her view of her husband's body.

"What happened?" she asked frantically. "I heard Carol scream, then I heard a shot ... "

"Betty." David choked. "Don't go in there. Please don't. It's ... messy ... "

Betty pushed David aside and walked into the room. She was just in time to see George's last quiver. Her mouth gaped open and she took a few stops closer to him. She didn't get too near, as if death by gunshot might be catching. Then she turned around slowly to look at Carol. She saw the gun at her feet and the vacant look of horror in her eyes.

"What did you do to him?" she whispered.

Carol's mouth opened, but nothing came out.

"It was the bird," David explained. "That goddamn crazy crow. It was here. George heard her scream and ran in to help her. Then the fucking thing attacked him and Carol tried to shoot it. Oh, God ... "

Betty didn't seem to be paying attention. She was staring at the body of her husband. "George?" she said as if she expected him to answer.

"Betty, he's dead," David told her. "We ... we've got to call someone. There's no cell signal out here, but I have the CB in the car ... I'll call the police." He turned to go outside.

"David, don't!" Carol cried out. "It's still out there! It might get you!"

"Honey, we have to! I'll be all right, I promise. But we've got to call."

David went out to the car, leaving the distraught women by themselves. They didn't look at or even speak to one another. There was so much to say and no way to say it.

Chapter 11

The three of them waited by the car. Betty had wanted to cover George's body, but David insisted they leave it alone until the police arrived. They went outside to avoid looking at it. Carol had protested the idea violently, but finally agreed when David assured her the shot must have frightened the bird off for good. After all, Betty couldn't be expected to stay inside and he wanted them all to stay together.

David handed Betty the bottle of Scotch he had picked up before going outside. Betty shook her head. "I can't," she said. "It was George's."

"Drink it anyway," he insisted. "You need it. We all do."

She took his advice and swallowed a sip. Carol mutely accepted it after Betty was through. When the two police cruisers pulled up, they were still passing the bottle between them.

The two troopers exited their vehicles and walked up to the group at a brisk pace. One was heavyset with graying hair; the other was slimmer with short-cropped black hair. The heavier man walked with a strut that displayed his sense of authority. He was the one who spoke first.

"I'm Sergeant Grant Masters. This is Officer Richard Perkins. We understand there has been a shooting."

"Yes, sir," David replied.

"Who is the victim?"

"George Albert Brightman."

"Who had the gun at the time of the shooting?"

"My wife, Carol Mitchell."

"And your name is?"

"David Mitchell, her husband."

"And the other lady?"

"Betty Brightman, the victim's wife."

"Where is the body, Mr. Mitchell?"

"Inside the cabin. Do you want to see it now?"

"Yes, sir."

They all walked back into the cabin with David leading the way and Officer Perkins bringing up the rear. Once inside, Sgt. Masters bent to examine George's corpse. He made sure not to step in the sizable pool of blood that was pooled around it. He shook his head and straightened up. "Right through the throat. Bastard never had a chance," he commented unthinkingly before turning to Carol. "Were you holding the weapon when it discharged, ma'am?"

"Yes," Carol answered softly.

"Then I'm afraid I'm going to have to place you under arrest, Mrs. Mitchell. The charge is currently manslaughter, but we'll reevaluate that after the coroner's report. You have the right to remain silent. Anything you say can and will be used against you in a court of law. You have the right to speak with an attorney prior to and during questioning. If you cannot afford an attorney, one will be appointed to you by the court. Do you understand these rights as I have read them to you?"

Carol swallowed audibly. "Yes." The rather clichéd manner in which the policeman had read her rights might have made her smile if the situation weren't so grave.

"Do you wish to give up the right to remain silent?"

That almost did make her smile. It had been exactly what she expected him to say. "Yes," she repeated.

"Wait a minute, honey," David interjected. "This is very serious. You shot a man. I think you should talk to Jerry first." He was referring to Jerry Klein, their lawyer.

Carol considered it. When she answered the sergeant, her tone was apologetic. "I think that would be a good idea."

"Very well, ma'am," Masters conceded. "Perkins, take Mrs. Mitchell to headquarters and let her call her attorney."

"I'm going with her," David announced.

"I'm sorry, Mr. Mitchell. I'm going to need you to stay here for a while," Masters told him.

Officer Perkins walked over to Carol. "Come with me, Mrs. Mitchell."

Carol took a longing look at David. "It'll be okay," he promised her.

She followed the trooper out to his car. He stopped in front of the back door and removed a pair of handcuffs from his belt. "I'm sorry, Mrs. Mitchell, but I'm going to have to put these on you. Standard procedure."

Carol lifted her arms. "Please be careful. I have stitches under the bandage."

"I'll put them on as loosely as possible."

True to his word, Officer Perkins slipped the cuff over her bandage and pushed the two halves together just barely enough for them to catch. Then he opened the door for her and she stepped into the car with as much grace as she could muster under the circumstances.

The meat wagon was pulling in as they were pulling out.

It was all so surreal to Carol. She had always been a decent, law-abiding citizen any community would be happy to harbor. She had never been in any trouble with the law outside of a parking ticket she received when she was twenty. The idea of her sitting handcuffed in a patrol car was laughable. And George dead? That seemed equally impossible. Someone like George should live forever. But she had put a bullet through his throat. He would never tell another nasty, but good-natured joke again. Tears threatened to start flowing down her face and it took all her effort to keep them inside. She did not want to cry in front of a stranger. That could wait until she was alone with David.

The road was worse heading back down the mountain. It always frightened Carol the way David drove down it, but Officer Perkins handled it expertly. He drove with one hand on the wheel and the other hanging out the window. The excellent suspension on the large Chevy smoothed out the bumps. They were coming around an exceptionally wide turn that overlooked a forty-foot cliff.

That was when the demon bird soared in through Officer Perkins' window and into his face.

Carol screamed as Perkins' foot smashed down on the accelerator in surprise. His hands left the wheel and grappled with the bird at his face. One of its talons hooked into his left eye and his screams joined Carol's as the cruiser smashed through the flimsy guardrails and plunged down the cliff. It struck an outgrowth of rock on the way down and wound up landing on its roof.

Chapter 12

Carol was barely conscious. Her breath came in quick, dusty snatches. She was crushed between the front and back seats. Her left shoulder and right leg felt as if they were clamped between vices and she was certain they were broken. Her face, neck, and arms were cut up by shards of glass from the broken window. She heard no sound from up front. She knew the chances were Officer Perkins was dead.

Carol tried to move herself. There was always the possibility the car might explode. She doubted it, but didn't feel like staying inside to find out. She was unable to budge herself. Her broken shoulder and leg screamed with pain and the handcuffs rendered her arms useless. She was hopelessly trapped. With that realization, she heard the familiar call of the crow.

It walked in through the window nonchalantly and fluttered over to land on her chest. Carol cringed away, but knew there was no escaping from the bird this time. Sensing it had won the battle at last, it was in no hurry. Carol began screaming at it, but it didn't flinch. Its beak came flashing down to jab into her neck and closed around the jugular vein. It yanked up on it as if it were an earthworm. Blood began to jet from the wound in long spurts. Satisfied that its job was finished, it leapt up to the window, gave one last squawk of victory, and flew off to parts unknown.

So this is the way the world ends, Carol thought bitterly as her lifeblood pumped out of her. *Here I am – a murderer trapped handcuffed in the back of a police car that drove off a cliff, slowly bleeding to death from a wound inflicted by an ordinary black crow.* She would never see another sunset or sunrise. She would never drink water or eat bread. Worst of all, she would never kiss her strong, handsome husband ever again. They had never even said goodbye.

As she began sinking into unconsciousness, she wondered which God she had offended in order to die this way. In a shocking revelation, just before she fell into her final rest, she figured out which one.

It was Venus.

Chapter 13

The crow's beady yellow eyes observed the man who fed and trained it through the bars of its cage. It ruffled its feathers and squawked when a knocking came on the front door of the apartment it called home. It watched its master cross to the door and open it. The two humans who entered were quite familiar to it. It saw the male of the couple hand over a stack of narrow green papers to its master. It thought the papers would make fine nesting material.

The bird certainly didn't understand the words being spoken, but this is what it heard the male say: "Thanks to Carol bringing that gun along, our plan worked out even better than we expected. You don't come cheap, but you're certainly a lot less expensive than a divorce."

The crow seemed to nod its head in approval as it watched David Mitchell lean over and kiss Betty Brightman with a deepening passion.

About the Author

Garrett Peck's short horror fiction has appeared in 15 previous anthologies. He has also co-edited three anthologies, including *Personal Demons* (with Brian A. Hopkins), *Tooth and Claw* (with J. F. Gonzalez) and *Small Bites* (with J. F. Gonzalez). He has twice been nominated for the Bram Stoker Award in nonfiction. You can visit his website at: http://www.authorsden.com/garrettpeck

During a company business trip to Memphis, Keith Gouveia fell in love with the city's beauty and history and immediately wanted to write a story set in the region. While walking the streets in and around Beale Street, many tourists talked about visiting the Peabody Hotel to see the ducks march. Since he didn't have time to see them for himself, he made do with researching them on the Internet and "Fowl Play" was born.

FOWL PLAY
By Keith Gouveia

Gary Lund stared down the hallway watching one of the maids in the Peabody Hotel bend over seductively to retrieve the dropped roll of toilet paper from her cart. The low cut, blue dress she wore rode high, exposing the bottom of her butt cheeks.

She knows I'm watching. He grinned as she stood and turned toward him and then winked. *Probably did it on purpose just to tease me.*

"You like that?" she asked with a smile.

"You know I do, Veronica," he said, tilting his mop and leaning against it, turning on the suave macho act.

Behind Veronica, the elevator door chimed, and Gary's demeanor changed. *Damn*, he thought as his boss stepped off the elevator.

"Ms. Veronica, I'm certain there are rooms that need attending to."

"Yes, sir," she said and quickly pushed her cart toward the elevator doors.

What an asshole. She just started her shift and was only stocking up, Gary thought, returning his attention to mopping the floors.

"Don't think I don't know what you and the ladies do in the empty rooms during working hours," Mr. Cevasco said as he approached.

"I don't know what you're talking 'bout," he said, eyes on the floor as he continued to mop.

"Don't play coy with me."

Gary stopped and straightened his back. "Who's playin'?"

The anal retentive bastard released a nasal sigh and the look in his eyes relayed to Gary that he was mentally counting to ten. *What a coward.*

"I'll be bringing the ducks down in a half an hour, and I'm sure guests will be lining up soon. I want this floor mopped and the carpet rolled out by the time we arrive."

How the hell did a simple prank turn into a nearly seventy-five year tradition? "I know how to do my job."

"Consider it a friendly reminder."

Gary didn't like the snide look on the man's face. "If you'd stop talking to me, I could finish sooner." Gary narrowed his eyes, testing his boundaries.

Without another word, Mr. Cevasco turned around and walked away.

That's what I thought, prick. Look at you, sashaying your ass like a little bitch. Fucking faggot, he thought and then quickly averted his gaze as the idea of him looking at another man's ass made him gay.

Gary returned to mopping the floor, and though he knew he'd only be doing it again within a couple of hours, he put his full effort into it. Getting the orange marble floor, with white veins running through, spotless before Mr. Cevasco returned, was top priority.

That faggot is going to recognize my hard work, he thought. *There's a reason pets aren't allowed in fancy hotels. No matter how well trained they are, they're still animals and keen to destructive behavior. All this work to give the false impression that we have the best-trained ducks.*

The more he thought about it, the angrier he got, until finally the floor was sparkling, but he soon discovered it was all for naught. Outside, a slight rain drizzled down. The beaded water that formed on the tourists, who came into the hotel to see the marching ducks gather at the marble fountain, pooled on the floor.

Son of a bitch! I can't catch a break, he thought as he placed yellow 'Slippery Floor' caution signs around the viewing area. *I won't be able to just spot mop later, the whole thing will need to be done again.*

He looked outside to see the rain had stopped. *Too late. Damage done.*

The music began to play and the crowd clapped enthusiastically, waiting for the elevator to open and for the ducks to come marching to the tune.

The children roared in laughter as Mr. Cevasco led the march with his brass duck-head cane. The five North American Mallard ducks waddled to the fountain and jumped into the cool, crystal clear water.

The people gathered around "oohing" and "aahing" at the ducks and their master.

I'll never understand it, Gary thought. *They're just ducks. There's plenty of other things in this town to see.*

With his attention averted, he failed to see the only male duck approach him.

"Look, Mommy, he's poopin'," a young boy said, pointing toward Gary.

I am not, he thought, then realized the boy aimed behind him and not directly at him. He turned to see the duck standing on the ledge of the fountain, ass in the air and dangling over. Taking a quick glance down, Gary's anger boiled over. *Son of a bitch shit on my shoes!*

Without thought, Gary back-handed the mallard, sending it splashing into the water.

"Mommy, he's a bad man," the boy cried. This time there was no denying he was pointing at Gary. Looking around the viewing area, all eyes were upon him.

"Mr. Lund, you're fired!"

"What! You can't do that!" Gary argued, and for the briefest of moments, he would have sworn the portrait of Edward Pembroke sneered at him. *Too much stress, that's all*, he rationalized as the portrait was in his peripheral vision. *A trick of the eye.*

"I can and I did. I want you out of here in five minutes. Get your things and go."

Shaking the icy chill away, Gary returned his attention to his boss. "I've got my stuff on me. Thank you very much, sir. Fuck you, sir!"

Several mothers squealed their displeasure with Gary's choice of words as they quickly covered their children's ears.

"Out!"

Bite me, he thought, exiting the Peabody's lobby. *Fucking bastard! Just because I don't swing that way doesn't mean you can treat me shitty.* Though Gary knew he was merely speculating, it made him feel better thinking that way – believing all the extra work was because Cevasco harbored deep feelings for him. He fished his cell-phone out of his

Dockers. Scrolling through the numbers listed in his phonebook, he chose Ralph Corhin, his roommate and good friend.

"Yo," Gary said when Ralph answered. "Can you get off? I need a drink."

Feeling a bump against his right side, he quickly spun around. "What's your prob—" There was no one there.

"Hey, what's wrong?" Ralph asked.

"Nothing." Gary took one last look behind him, but he was alone. *Weird.*

"I'll be there in twenty."

"All right. See you then." Gary hung up.

"I can't believe you got fired," Ralph said before taking another swig from his imported beer. They were sitting leisurely at their favorite watering hole just around the corner from the famous Beale Street.

"Shut up."

The anger on his friend's face almost caused Ralph to spit out the mouthful of beer in a fit of laughter. "C'mon, Gary, lighten up."

"It's not like I can't find a better job ... it's just the principle, you know?"

"Yeah, but you had it made there," Ralph said, placing the bottle on the table and noticing his friend had polished off two beers before he even arrived, but chosing not to say anything. "That hotel is walking distance from every major attraction Memphis has to offer; it's going to be tough finding something better."

"Tell me about it. Not to mention all the great tail I got. It was ridiculous."

"Don't remind me."

"All those hot, bored cleaning ladies, especially Veronica, she was hot. Damn that bastard! Damn those ducks!"

Several heads turned in the bar.

"You want to keep it down over there?" said the bartender.

"Sorry," Gary replied, then finished his second beer.

"You know, there's other Peabody hotels, what about Florida? I bet the bitches are mighty fine down there."

"No way, man, I love this town. Where else in the world can you have a three-block, outdoor party? Name a finer sports arena than the Pyramid. And don't get me started on the King."

"I love this town's history just as much as you. I'm just saying—"

"Oh, so I take it you'd move to Florida with me?" Gary asked, cutting him off.

"Hell no! You got fired, not me."

"Speaking of which, think you can get me a job at the Aquarium?"

"Yeah, right! Like they'll hire you after punching a duck." He half-laughed.

"I didn't punch it," Gary said indignantly.

"It really doesn't matter."

"The damn thing shit on me. What was I supposed to do?" Gary said, leaning into the table so as not to be too loud. "They don't have to know."

"They'll find out ... trust me. Can't you just say you're sorry and beg for your job back?"

"I'm not apologizing to that pompous windbag. Just because he's got the title of Duck Master doesn't give him the right to be such a prick. I mean, who cleans up all their shit?"

"You do."

"Damn right. I could do his job, easy. I'd really like to teach that faggot a lesson."

"Hey, easy," Ralph said, noticing several heads turn toward them again.

"Look, what do you say we go have a little fun?"

"I don't like that look in your eye."

"Don't be such a pussy," Gary said, reaching into his back pocket. He pulled out his wallet, opened it, and removed a key. "C'mon, it'll be fun."

"Where did you get that?"

"Remember when I got reprimanded for losing my key. Well, I had a spare made of the new one they gave me. Just in case."

"You're not supposed to do that."

"Fuck you; will you fucking grow a set already? Jesus H. Christ!" Gary's voice was a soft whisper, but filled with malice.

"What do you have in mind?" Ralph asked, leaning into the table, trying to be discrete. He could tell there would be no talking Gary out of it. Once he had his mind set, that was that.

"I'd love to see the look of horror on that bastard's face when he goes into work tomorrow and finds those feathered beasts dead and rotting."

"You want to kill all five?"

"Why not? But I'm starting with the drake; he's a mean little fuck. You should have seen his eyes. I swear he did it on purpose."

"You know animals can sense our demeanor. It's probably why he doesn't like you."

"Ah," Gary said, waving his hand. "What do you know?"

"Fine, count me out then."

"I'm sorry. Please. I'm not asking *you* to kill them. I want to do it, but I need your eyes. You can be my look out, that's all."

Shaking his head in disapproval, Ralph knew he couldn't say no.

The two had been friends for seven years and roommates for five. Besides, if it wasn't for Gary, Ralph would probably still be a virgin and he owed him. He was never really good with the ladies, but Gary was a true ladies man. With his curly blonde locks, blue eyes, and broad shoulders, no woman could resist his charms. Especially if they heard the rumors of his well-endowed member, which Ralph knew to be true. He couldn't help but steal a glance one day at Gary in the shower after Phys-Ed class, and even he was impressed.

"All right, let's do it. But I'm out of there at the first sign of trouble."

"Deal."

Since the Peabody Memphis Hotel was only two blocks away from Beale Street, they decided to hike it rather than have their car spotted. They concealed themselves in the shadows of the neighboring buildings and treaded carefully. Once there, they slipped in through the employees' entrance and made their way to the fountain area where they could ride the mallards' personal elevator to their penthouse palace.

"All this for a few ducks?" Ralph asked.

"Sick, isn't it?"

"Who's this guy," Ralph asked as they passed a portrait hanging proudly in the Grand Lobby.

"That's Edward Pembroke. He's the guy who first trained the ducks to march on the red carpet to John Phillip Sousa's *King Cotton March*. Listen to me, I sound like a fuckin' tour guide; that's how trained I am. Anyway, he's the original Duck Master. They say he worked in the circus, training animals before he worked here as a bellman. I'm not sure when they'll be hanging the second Duck Master's portrait; guess I'll never know now."

"He's a creepy looking bastard."

"I know. I had a strange feeling earlier, but don't worry about it. The guy's dead; he can't bother you. C'mon," he said, pushing the call button for the elevator.

As they stood before the brass doors, Ralph couldn't shake the feeling of someone watching them. His head nervously swiveled around, searching for justification of the feeling, but found the place to be oddly deserted.

"This is a little weird, isn't it?"

"What do you mean?" Gary asked, turning to face him.

"Shouldn't there be workers around?" he whispered.

"They're probably on break or something," Gary rationalized.

Before Ralph could continue, the doors chimed and opened to them. They stepped inside and pressed the only button there. The elevator was specifically used by the ducks and the Duck Master twice a day.

Inside the elevator, Ralph began gnawing on his thumbnail – he knew it was a nervous habit, and this only added to his anxiety. His shoulders twitched slightly as he felt a sudden drop in temperature. Just as his breath formed a white cloud in front of his face, he felt a hand touch his shoulder. "What the—" He jumped, startled by the firm grip and turned around to see who it was.

No one was there.

"What's wrong with you?"

"You asshole," Ralph said, punching Gary in the arm, a knee jerk reaction believing Gary to be his tormentor.

"What?"

"You know what. You scared the shit out of me, that's what."

"What are you talking about?"

"You grabbed me."

"I did no such thing." Gary's facial expression relayed to him that he truly had no idea.

Before he could protest, the doors chimed again, and Gary immediately stepped off the elevator as the door opened then he ran off.

Not wanting to spend another second alone, Ralph darted off behind him. "Hey, wait up!"

"Shhh," Gary hissed as his index finger rested against his lower lip.

"Sorry," Ralph said, this time in a barely audible whisper.

"The ducks could be anywhere in here." Gary's hands firmly grasped the brass door handles to the suite. "Are you ready?"

"Yes."

Gary turned the knobs and slowly opened the doors. "We'll split up and round them up—"

"I know what you are planning!"

"Jesus!" Both Gary and Ralph said as their hearts skipped a beat. They stood face to face with an old man.

"Look, buddy, if you know what's good for you, you'll get the fuck out of our way and keep your nose out of this," Gary said, removing his hand from his chest.

"I saw you hit my baby. How dare you show yourself here again?"

Recognizing the man as the one in the portrait in the lobby, Ralph tried to warn Gary. "It's him ... Edward Pembroke."

"Get out," Gary replied, leaning in for a closer look.

"You will not harm the pride of this hotel," said the man, shoving his hands into Gary's chest. Gary hurtled into the air, landing several feet away in the hallway.

"Oh, shit!" Ralph shouted, running to his fallen friend. "We gotta get out of here," he said, helping Gary to his feet. Both Ralph and Gary watched wide-eyed as the old man stepped out of the suite toward them, the air around him rippling as if he didn't belong there.

"Let's go!" Gary shouted and ran to the elevator. He frantically pushed the call button. "What's wrong with this thing? Why won't it open? We just stepped off!"

"Hurry," Ralph said with the old man slowly and methodically approaching.

"What do you think I'm doing?"

The doors chimed and they stepped in. Gary immediately slammed the palm of his hand against the 'Close Door' button. Ralph saw a smile appear on the old man's face as the doors began to close and couldn't help but quake in fear. The old man just stood there, smiling as if knowing there was no escape for them.

"Whew," Gary exhaled, obviously believing the worst to be over as their descent began.

"I thought you said that guy was dead."

"Ever hear of ghosts?" Gary asked snidely.

"But that's not possible. It's just not—"

Before he could finish, the elevator stopped, causing them to stumble forward. The lights went out. They screamed like little girls. Then the lights came on again, but they were no longer alone.

The old man stood in front of the brass doors smiling, exposing blackened gums, yellowed teeth, and a rotting tongue. The pale complexion of his wrinkled skin was broken only by the dark patches under his opaque eyes.

"You will pay for harming my beloveds."

"Look, man, we're sorry. We didn't do anything," Gary pleaded while Ralph stood there, paralyzed by fear.

The old man laughed as his body levitated backward, passing through the doors and vanishing. Silence encompassed the elevator causing the two men to pull close. A trickle of crimson fluid ran down from the lobby button on the elevator panel. Gary extended his index finger and swiped it. Rubbing the visceral fluid between his fingers, he said, "It's blood."

The buttons on the elevator panel exploded from their housing, launched by a jet stream of the crimson fluid. Both Gary and Ralph screamed as the sound scared them. They jumped into each other's arms, holding tightly in a loving embrace as the blood rose to their knees, their sobs masking the dull music playing over the loud speaker.

"We're going to die. We're going to fuckin' die!" Ralph screamed.

"I'm so sorry I talked you into this. I love you, man." Gary wept.

They closed their eyes as the rising blood reached their chins.

"Please, God, don't let us die like this," Ralph said and the doors chimed.

Slowly, both men opened their eyes to see the magnificent fountain where the ducks spent most of the daylight hours. Looking upon each other, they stepped backward, breaking their embrace. There was no trace of the blood.

"Let's get the fuck out of here!" Gary said and Ralph followed him out of the elevator.

Ralph ran straight into Gary, who stopped abruptly. Without asking what was wrong, Ralph turned to the left and saw first hand what caused Gary to stop. Thousands of snakes slithered along the floor, walls, and ceiling, making their way toward them, their hissing echoing in the hallway, causing Gary to cover his ears. Ralph turned the other way to see countless more.

They were surrounded and whether they were poisonous or not, he wasn't willing to find out.

"C'mon!" Ralph shouted, grabbing Gary by the arm and pulling him toward a hotel room door.

Ralph tried the handle, but it was locked. His gaze trailed off, and when he saw the snakes closing in, he rammed his size thirteen boot into the door. "Damn it!"

"What are we going to do? It's hopeless. They're going to kill—"

A slap across the face silenced Gary's incessant whining.

"Pull yourself together, man. I need your help. If we work together, we should be able to break the door in."

"All right," Gary said without a trace of anger from being hit.

"On the count of three."

"There's no time!"

"Okay, then three!"

The force of both their bodies against the door caused it to fly open. Quickly, Ralph got behind the door and slammed it shut.

"Oh, shit!"

"What's wrong?" Ralph asked, spinning around.

"Look," Gary replied, pointing a shaking finger at the bed.

Atop the bed lay a naked, ravaged woman. The skin on her chest and abdomen was peeled back, exposing her ribcage, and her intestines were strung about, dangling from the edge of the bed.

Ralph covered his mouth with his sleeve as he approached the bedside.

"This can't be happening," Gary said, following Ralph. "It's Veronica."

"Are you certain?"

"Of course I'm certain," Gary said, taking a step closer. "What a fuckin' shame, I hadn't gotten the chance to hit that yet."

"I can give you two a minute if you'd like."

"Not funny, man. Not funny."

"I know, I'm sorry," Ralph said. "Hey, check the window, see if we can climb down," Ralph ordered, reversing roles. It had always been Gary to give the orders, he had always been the strong one, but never in their lives would they have dreamed of facing something like this.

"Okay," Gary replied.

As Ralph approached the body out of morbid curiosity, the small intestine shot upward and wrapped around his throat. Veronica's eyes burst open; she had the same opaque eyes as the old man and a devilish grin stretched across her face, cracking the dried blood on her cheeks. He tried to scream, but the hold was too tight.

Fortunately, his gagging alerted Gary to the danger.

"Oh, shit!" He ran to Ralph's side and grabbed hold of the spongy intestine, trying to give Ralph enough slack to breathe, but his efforts were in vain. Gary turned his attention to Veronica. "Let him go, bitch!"

Ralph felt the grip tighten.

"Sorry, Veronica, but bros before hoes," he said and began wildly punching her in the face. She continued to refuse, and Gary continued his assault.

With the darkness swelling in his mind, and with the last of Veronica's features to fold into the bloody mess that was now her face, Ralph clamped his teeth onto the decaying flesh and bit through. She wailed as the intestine retreated. Ralph staggered back, spitting the bitter taste out, and Gary quickly put enough distance between him and the she-bitch.

"Are you all right?" he asked Ralph.

"Hell no. We have to get out of here. How high are we?"

"A couple of stories."

A loud thump against the door caused both of them to jump.

"Either way, we're dead," Ralph said.

"What are you going to do?" Gary asked.

"Jump. But before I do, this is all your fault." With that said, Ralph ran toward the window, leaped into the air, and crashed through the glass.

Gary's screams told Ralph he had followed.

Ralph screamed wildly too as his fall increased in speed. He closed his eyes, not wanting to witness their demise.

"Ahem!"

The screaming stopped.

Who is that? I'm not falling anymore, Ralph thought, slowly opening his eyes. He found himself lying on the cold, marble tile floor looking up at a man in a blue uniform.

"Oh, shit," Gary exclaimed, seeing the officer's demeanor.

"You two are under arrest."

Officer Barnett listened to the two perpetrator's stories through a one-way mirror. When he arrested them, both were stark raving mad, screaming how the Peabody Memphis Hotel was haunted. Though the hour was late, he called in the local psychiatrist to evaluate them before deciding where they should be sent: the county jail or the nuthouse. The two were separated and their individual stories documented; both were identical.

He watched as the good doctor excused himself and exited the room.

"Well, doctor, what's the verdict?" Officer Barnett asked as the visibly tired man entered the room.

"In their minds, they're telling the truth. Whether it's their conscience, the alcohol, or a real ghost plaguing them, I don't know. But I do know that all you have is a case of breaking and entering, and even that is thin considering the hotel is open to the public."

"I didn't ask you how to do my job. I asked if they're dangerous."

"They are of no threat to anyone. Now, if you'll excuse me, I've got an important meeting in the morning and would like to be well rested. Good night."

"Good night," he replied as the doctor left. He took in a deep breath, held it, and released it before exiting the small viewing room and entering the holding tank.

"When do we get to talk to a lawyer?"

"Never mind. You're free to go, but I'm warning you. If I catch either of you near that hotel again, I'm locking your asses away. You understand."

"Don't worry. Neither of us wants to go there again. Right, Gary?" Ralph said, nudging him with his elbow.

"Right."

"Good. Now get out of here."

"Thank you, sir."

"Just get out!"

Without another word, Gary and Ralph left. Quietly they walked through the precinct and exited the station. Once outside, the two thanked God for seeing them through the ordeal. As they took several steps away, an all too familiar sound echoed in the night.

"Quack!"

Both of them stopped dead in their tracks. Slowly, they turned around to see a brown mallard staring at them. Their eyes opened wide, their arms shot upward, and they ran away screaming.

As they fell out of sight, the duck's shape transformed into Mr. Pembroke who grinned devilishly. He watched the two grown men behaving like children

Before vanishing into thin air, he said, "That'll teach ya!"

About the Author

Keith Gouveia is an author for today's reader. He cuts through the fluff and delves into the action teasing with suspense and intrigue. Some of his more memorable projects have been the Halloween chapbook *Devil's Playground*, co-written with AP Fuchs as well as *On Hell's Wings* and the Dark Fantasy *Children of the Dragon*, all available from Coscom Entertainment. He can be found here: http://www.keithgouveia.com

I was watching David Cronenberg's Naked Lunch, and was struck by a comment made by the character Joan Lee after injecting insect poison into her veins: "It's a Kafka high; you feel like a bug." I began to wonder: What would a Kafka high be like? Could you come down?

BUG POWDER
By Meghan Jurado

I got this shit that will blow your mind.

If I told you where I got it, you wouldn't believe me. But I'm gonna tell you anyway. What else have I got to do?

See, normally I'm a small time kinda guy, nickel and dime stuff, keeping people going with little baggies of powder here and there. I'm not much of a user myself, but a little bump now and then is hard to resist, you know, to keep going. But this new stuff, I wouldn't touch with a ten-foot pole.

So here's how it happened: I was walking home from dinner, my leftovers in a shiny silver packet tucked in my coat pocket, when *bam*, this guy hits me over the head with something. He didn't hit me too good, neither, 'cause all he did was make me wobble a bit and make me mad.

The second whack got me, though.

So I went down and got a face full of pavement. When I woke up, it was dark and there's this horrible smell and a rat was gnawing at my coat pocket. I screamed like a little girl and scooted away. I think even the rat was disgusted.

There were all these sounds, these clicking sounds, like drumming your nails on the table. They were all over. It echoed.

Some guy stepped out from the darkness and then I saw him, *really* saw him; it was some *thing*, bunched up under an overcoat that was stretched in the wrong places. The guy looked *pointy* under there.

I screamed again, and the clicking sounds got louder. The guy stepped up and dropped a big bag at my feet – a gallon zipper bag, filled to the brim with white powder. It could have been anything.

"Take," the thing said in a rasping buzz that sounded like an intercom. I didn't make a move.

He reached out with this thing I'm pretty sure was his arm, but it had these big pinchers that made me whimper a little. He opened my coat for me and dropped the baggie inside. "Take," it repeated, and I tucked the baggie down in my coat lining, inches away from the spreading piss in my trousers. It left a conspicuous lump.

He gave me a shove and I fell on my back, but there were these things under me that kept me held up, kinda. It was like lying on a waterbed. I didn't move, but I *began* to move – if that makes sense – to glide across the floor like I was rolling on ball bearings. It didn't take long to figure out after one of the roaches climbed up over my face I was being propelled by bugs. Thousands of 'em.

They dumped me out of wherever I was at down by the subway tracks. I climbed up the platform, real careful but real fast, in case there was a train. Then I ran all the way home, me, a guy who gets winded walking up a flight of stairs.

When I got back to my place my heart was pounding so hard I couldn't hear anything else, and my eyes were pulsing in time. I locked the door behind me and ran into the kitchen, ready to make a date with a stiff drink.

As I was tipping the bottle, I remembered the food in my pocket. I pulled out the bag of white powder first, giving a theatrical little shudder as I tossed it on the table where it landed with a thud. The bag wasn't sealed too good and a little poured out.

Next came the food. It looked all right, but when I peeled back the foil to give it a sniff, a couple of bugs came out. I smushed 'em and dumped the food in the trash.

Now it was down to me and the powder. I sat across from it, staring at the little white pyramid that had spilled from the baggie. Its mystery was as great as the pyramids of Egypt.

Now, I may be a fool, but I'm not a big fool. I wasn't about to just go ahead and snort a big old line of that powder without knowing what it was, especially given where it came from. In fact, I had half a mind to just dump the whole bag in the john and forget I ever saw it.

I was rising from my chair to do just that when my phone rang. It wasn't an odd occurrence; customers were always calling me day and night and I'd have to unplug the damn thing just to get any sleep.

I let the machine get it, as usual. There are certain people I am simply trying to avoid.

The machine spit out its perfunctory message: "Not home. Leave name, number." Then it beeped.

The most God-awful sound came over the line. A loud basso buzzing, so deep and loud that my eardrums seemed ready to rupture from the vibration. I clapped my hands over my ears but the sound was inside, vibrating me to pieces from the inside out.

The sound stopped. I uncovered my ears cautiously and the tape was still rolling, recording a number of weird clicks and clatters. Finally, there was something that resembled speech, an insect humming forced into words.

"We're coming in three days. We're coming for the money. We're coming in three days. We're coming for the money ... " The message repeated over and over again until the tape cut off.

I looked at the baggie on the table, leaned over, and snagged it with a finger to pull it close. A long thin line of powder stretched out across the table as I dragged it toward me, looking ready for the world's most ambitious nose candy freak.

I had to sell it. The bugs would be coming for their money. I did not want to go toe to toe (or *whatever* to toe) with the guy in the stretched out coat; I was a 'show the underbelly' type. I decided to call a friend of mine, Charley-Girl, to come over and test the stuff out. Charley would put anything in her nose at any time. She came in handy for testing new product, and she knew she could count on me to dump her at the emergency room door in case something went wrong. Or in the river if it killed her.

I rose to make the call. My legs were shaking.

Charley-Girl showed up an hour later, as promised. She stood at my front door, sniffing and shivering. I peered through the peephole and she seemed to sense me, and grinned up at the door with her gap-toothed smile.

"I's here, man," she called, and I let her in.

I took her to the kitchen table and we sat and contemplated the bag for a while.

"Where is this from?" she asked, peering at the small cone of powder, which I had yet to remove.

"New guy in town. Seems like a heavy. Wanted to try his stuff out on someone special." I winked at her. She rolled her eyes and began to spread the pile with her pinky nail, sorting it into thick lines for the express train up her nostril.

"Riiight." Having sorted and narrowed the lines to her satisfaction, she whipped out a twenty and rolled it. She lowered her head, filthy money to her nose, and took in the lines with a mighty inhalation.

When it was over, she sat back in contemplation. I bit my tongue so I would not demand "well?" She would tell me when she was ready.

A thin line of blood ran from one nostril. I was not duly concerned, as it had been a lot of whatever it was, and powder makes your nose bleed sometimes. She closed her eyes and rested her head on the back of the chair.

"Charley?" I asked, tentatively, after she had sat that way for a minute or more.

She raised her head and smiled at me. She opened her mouth to say something and that's when the vomiting started.

"Oh, my God. Oh, my God. Oh, my God—" I was driving at breakneck speed, around and around as we argued, her with her head out the window blowing chunks to the wind. Whenever she put her head out the window, I would turn towards the hospital. When she brought it back in, she would scream at me to turn around and take her home, right now, *goddammit*. Blood and thick fluid flew from her mouth as she screamed at me.

"You got to go to the hospital, Charley, some of that coming out of your mouth is your guts, shit, I gotta take you—" She punched me in the side of the head then, and despite the rushes of sickness, Charley-Girl was still stronger than me; when she hit you, it hurt.

"Take ... me home," she hissed, a runner of blood coursing from her mouth all the way down her neck. "I can't go to the hospital again or they'll pick me up; I got warrants out. Come on and just take me home. I'll be fine; I just gotta settle my stomach or something." Then she threw up in my car, covering us both with a thick red liquid lurking with chunks. I screamed and twisted the wheel again. I'd take her to her place, the moon, fucking *anywhere*, just to get her out of the car.

We arrived at her house. I screeched up to the curb and parked at a sideways angle. Traffic behind me swerved; horns blared. I ran around to her side and yanked the door open, and she came out on her hands and knees, falling hard on the pavement but still crawling, struggling to get inside. I grabbed her, hauling her up under her arms, threw my arm around her back and shoulders, and tucked my hand into her hot armpit to help hold her up. Gore was splashed down the front of her ragged t-shirt and jeans, all the way down to her shoes.

"I can make it," she muttered through a mouthful of thick sludge, and as it escaped and ran down her chin, I was horrified to see a couple of her teeth fall to the pavement.

I wrestled her to her door and she managed to get it open after a few stabs with her key. She started to slip inside and I grabbed her arm, thinking to tell her to be careful, to call me if she needed anything – or something else that people say in these situations – when she twisted violently in my grip and wrenched herself the rest of the way in, leaving two fingers behind.

To my horror, I could not let go of them at first. I stood, staring at the blood-smeared digits with their knobs of bright bone, wet, smeared with viscous fluid, before I shrieked and threw them down the hallway, where they tumbled into a dark corner.

I turned tail and clattered down the steps, screeching like an effeminate fire alarm, dove into my disgusting vehicle, and had my foot on the gas before I put the car in gear.

I sped toward home, talking to myself the whole time, trying to rationalize, internalize, and put some order to the thoughts that were tearing through my head like a frenzied pit bull. The car reeked of sour vomit and blood, a thick meaty smell that assaulted the nostrils and pushed away any thoughts that threatened to solidify.

I pulled up in front of my house without any real idea of how I had arrived there. I tried to get out, but was hindered by the seatbelt, which I had fastened at some point in the haze. I fought myself free and ran up to my apartment, leaving behind a set of bloody footprints.

I hid in my apartment for a while. Real hiding – under the bed kind of stuff. The phone rang a couple of times, but my answering machine was still busted from whatever those fucking bugs put it through, so it would call out shrilly and then fall silent.

I peeked out from under the box springs a couple of times, and the only thing in the world that made me move out from under the sagging springs was a roach that skittered over my legs and sent me out squealing and brushing at myself.

After a few false starts, I sat down next to the telephone and finally picked up the receiver. I put it cautiously to my ear and started to dial Charley's number, one button at a time. The call took hold and the phone began to ring, and I imagined all sorts of awful things, a big puddle of Charley on the bathroom tile being one of them.

Something picked up on the other end. I asked, "Hello?" not wanting to get an answer. There was a thick and bubbling sigh – a sound like a child chewing a mouthful of mashed potatoes – and then the receiver was gently dropped back into place. The smooth sound of the dial tone went in one ear and out the other.

I decided, despite my previous satisfaction in my cowardice, to pay Charley a visit and see how she was doing. I got the feeling she wasn't so hot. A glance at the clock let me know that I had two days at most to get rid of the rest of the bug powder and come up with some cash. I needed to know what I was working against. Obviously, I couldn't sell this stuff close to home.

I looked down at myself. I looked like I had thrown a pipe bomb in a butcher shop; gobbets of meat stuck to my shirt and pants, half dried in congealed blood. I peeled off my clothes there in the living room, leaving the bloodied pile by the phone. Then I walked into the best shower of my life.

I called my friend Monkey as soon as I got out. I told him to come get me, that there was some shit in it for him. If only he knew.

He pulled up outside and honked his horn, so I clattered down the steps. I left the bug powder on the table, on hold until I got back.

I climbed into the car and there was Monkey, dirty, dreadlocked Monkey. He tried to pass himself off as a hippie, but I never saw any free love from him, and he did have a job. Maybe I just don't know how hippies work.

He was glad to see me, at any rate, and I bumped him up from a baggie of my regular stuff. I told him we were going to see Charley-Girl, and his face just lit up.

"I dig that chick; she's crazy," he said, pleased.

"I think she's sick. Last time I saw her, she didn't look so good." I didn't look at him while I said it. If she was dead, or about to kick off, it had just occurred to me that I might be a little responsible for it. I felt bad.

"Eh, everyone gets some bad shit now and again. We'll fix her up." He began to whistle as he pulled away from the curb.

The ride to Charley's was uneventful. I listened to Monkey's various philosophies and he would pat me every so often to make sure I was really listening. I was fading in and out, so I mostly got a jumbled mish-mash of Monkey-speak.

"... And then I told her that they were crabs, man, but not like the ocean kind, the kind you get rid of with a comb ..."

We pulled up to Charley's curb, and I hopped out before Monkey even finished – not that he ever would be. He slid out from behind the wheel at a leisurely pace, still talking.

"What's your hurry, man? We got all day," he said, smiling and sliding his hat down low over his eyes. Coke seemed to have the opposite effect on Monkey; it calmed him down.

I turned and punched the buzzer on the door. No one buzzed me in at Charley's, but the third buzzer I pressed was the magic buzzer, and the door swung open.

Charley lived on the second floor. There were still swatches of gore up the hallway, and I could see my footprints intertwined in and out of the central puddle. Monkey came in behind me, and miracle of miracles, fell silent.

I crept down to the stairwell, past the broken elevators, their gaping maws looking to swallow me whole. Monkey followed.

I opened the stairwell door and walked up the stairs, keeping to the sides to avoid the crimson stripe up the middle.

"I thought you said she was sick, man. Looks like she got stabbed or something." Monkey's courage was faltering. I turned to look at him for a minute and the look on my face must have convinced him. He started up the stairs behind me, muttering under his breath about cops and crazy chicks.

We reached Charley's floor. The blood path ended at her door, and I thought of her two fingers lying in a jumble down the hall and shuddered.

I knocked once. Monkey stood behind me, holding his breath.

I thought I heard something move inside, something stealthy, chittering. I knocked again, louder, and heard nothing but smooth silence. Monkey and I leaned toward the door, straining to hear anything.

Monkey reached past me and twisted the gory knob. The door swung open, slowly.

The inside of Charley's apartment looked like a slaughterhouse. It was worse than the hall, worse than the puking in the car, because in here, it was everywhere. It looked as if the house had been repainted red, using entrails for a kicky sort of texture effect. It was even on the ceiling.

"Bad news," said Monkey, somber, quiet, a completely un-Monkey state. I started forward as if to go in and he caught my arm. "You really want to go in there?"

I turned to him; I could feel my mouth pulled down in a grimace that was supposed to be reassuring. "Don't you think we have to?"

He didn't say anything, but he let go of me.

We tiptoed into the apartment, careful and quiet as mice. He kept close behind me, and I inventoried the living room, but didn't see Charley in any shape or form.

"Where is she?" Monkey whispered, making me jump a mile.

"I don't know," I whispered back, and had we had been better friends I might have grabbed his hand.

We made our way towards Charley's bedroom. The snail trails of mucus-like blood lead up to the door. The door itself was open a crack.

Monkey whimpered a little in his throat. I was thinking of leaving, just shutting the door and pretending I had never heard of Charley, but I had done this to her, and that thought made my feet keep moving forward, one step at a time.

Monkey was right behind me as I swung the door open. There was something on the bed. I reached over and flipped the light switch. Lights came on, bright and unforgiving.

Monkey and I screamed in unison, clutching at each other blindly.

On the bed was Charley-Girl, or what had once been Charley. Now it was not anything alive, but a skin bag, with the basic features of Charley but nothing inside. I could see her face, deflated, like a balloon, spread out on the pillow like a discarded Halloween mask. Her arms and legs were still present and accounted for, but her torso had an oddly caved look, and she was split, from sternum to pubic bone. There was a huge tear down her torso and it looked like something had come out, had eaten its way free of Charley.

Monkey reared back and puked, and I scrambled out of the bedroom, slipping and sliding in blood and guts. I made it to the kitchen where I stood by the sink, letting water run but not drinking it, not touching it, just listening to it run. Monkey came out of the bedroom, walking stiff-legged like a zombie. He stopped and looked at me with sad, sunken eyes.

"What happened?" he choked out, and that's when the blood dripped from the ceiling, dripping and dripping between our feet. We looked up, and I opened my mouth to scream, but he beat me to it.

The thing that was on the ceiling dropped down on him.

It was a bug; it was a huge fucking bug, with too many legs and eyes, big black eyes, and it ripped at Monkey, bored into him right under his chin. He made muffled noises and held his hand out to me for help. I reached for him, oh, I tried so hard to reach for him, but he kept moving and the bug was scaring me so bad I couldn't get around it.

"It's Charley!" I said, backing up against the counter top, sliding around the counter until I was clear for the door. "It's Charley!" I said again to the weakly waving hand, and I backed out of the apartment and shut the door firmly. I stood in the hallway for a minute, hearing the tearing sounds from behind the door. Then I realized I had an audience; people were coming out of the apartment to see what all the noise was about and there I was, smeared with blood and looking like a madman.

I took off down the hallway, people staring. "It's Charley!" I shouted, and it made me feel better to say it for some reason.

I made it down the stairs and took off into the night, running, running, not waiting for anything. I made it most of the way home before my legs gave out and I spilled to the pavement, my pounding heart making bright lights bloom before my eyes, my ears roaring with exertion.

"It's Charley," I whispered, and then I passed out.

I came back into myself screaming, but my body was already in motion. I snapped back, sitting at my kitchen table, my hands working themselves in the powder, packing it in tiny little bags. A pile of full baggies sat next to me; my idle hands really had been the Devil's tools. I was packaging this shit to sell. I knew what it did, but I didn't want to know what those bugs would do to me, and my unconscious self had made up my mind. I was going to get rid of this shit quick, and I was going to get the hell out of the city. Man, maybe the hell out of this *world*. I could do it with the gun. It would be quick.

It had been dusk when I started over to Charley-Girl's house with Monkey. By the time I had everything bagged up, it was dawn. I grabbed my backpack, the candy bag, crammed a handful of baggies in my pocket for easy access, bumped up from my own supply, and headed down to Haven Park, where there were a bunch of kids who stayed up all night and shook. A bump of this shit and they would shake, rattle, and roll.

As I clattered down the stairs, tired beyond tired, but still humming with my shit – my nice *ordinary* blow – a flier caught my eye. It had been stapled on the banister at a crazy angle. It seemed to twitch and waver, and I saw there were roaches on it. Fucking roaches. This town was infested in more ways than one.

I brushed at the roaches, retched as they touched my hands, and stomped them as they hit the ground. They stuck to my soles like gum.

Love Fusion, the flyer trumpeted, and it was my lucky day, oh thank my lucky stars, hallelujah. An all weekend rave and I knew the promoters. I could just sail right in there with my candy bag; no one would check me twice.

I went down and hopped on the bus, beating out some scumball crackhead for the last seat. I sat with my bag close in my lap, and muttered to myself about bugs. How much money would they want? They never told me. What *was* this shit? Didn't know that either. It had to be, in my honest opinion, a plot by the roaches to take over the world, to make everyone into bugs. It was a mass plan to exterminate the human race, and I was a part of it! I was even causing it – I was the delivery system! It was just then the girl next to me got up and moved, and I noticed people were talking about me behind cupped hands. I realized I was talking out loud, and about a global bug conspiracy. Jesus Christ.

I jumped off at my stop, leaving behind the whispers and the stares. I walked the four blocks to the warehouse on shaking legs. Hell, everything was shaking; my lips were quivering, my hands twitched, and I could feel my eyelid ticking in time to my heartbeat.

I walked right up to the back door and knocked, and there was Murphy, all-around security guy for this kind of thing. He let me through with a wink and a smile, and I flicked him a baggie of the bug powder. A tiny bag, but hell – it would kill him anyway. I'd become a one-man execution squad.

Inside was bad, oh, so bad, with all the lights and the music and the thumping. There were so many flashing lights, and the kids were everywhere. Most of them knew me, so I was bombarded. I was selling out there on the floor like I wasn't supposed to do, but I wanted to get this done fast; I wanted to be done before anyone opened the baggie and made their nose bleed.

I had worked my way upstairs when it started. There was screaming below, horrible screams, and then it started to smell hot, like a slaughterhouse, the hot smell of guts spilling. The sounds, the horrible gut-wrenching sounds, and still people were buying it; they wanted to get their hit before the place got closed down. The sick kids had nothing to do with them; they were shoving money at me and I was handing out Death. But then the bag was empty and I was done, free; I got rid of it all!

Soon there was the sound of sirens, but I couldn't have left if I wanted to; there were too many bodies on the floor writhing, spurting blood from everywhere. It was a soup of human parts; teeth and fingers and organs floated in the mix. I tried to make it back downstairs, but suddenly there were cops, so many cops, and the cops were screaming and yelling too, and someone was yelling for an ambulance, a battalion of ambulances, and that's when I remembered I still had baggies in my pocket. I wasn't done at all. I sunk down onto the stairs. People rushed by screaming and puking and I just began to cry. I was still crying when the cops grabbed each of my arms and hauled me to my feet. I was crying as they cuffed me and turned out my pockets, taking the bug's money. They took it all and shoved me in the back of the car.

The cop car was quiet; the officers looked at me like I was some kind of freak, and asked me what kind of shit I had been selling.

"C-coke," I sniveled, and I knew it wasn't true, but what could I tell them it was? What the hell was it?

The cop on the right snorted. The cop on the left looked at me in the rearview.

"Asshole," he said.

I had to agree, and wouldn't the paramedics get a big surprise when they carted off the bodies? I could see it in my mind, the bugs wriggling out of empty skin bags, and I wondered: could they fly?

We arrived at the station and I was yanked out of the car. I could tell the cops didn't really want to touch me. The other one grabbed my bag and I swear I saw him slide a couple of white baggies into his pocket.

I could tell him, but I won't.

They think I killed Charley-Girl, and Monkey too, in light of my flight from 'the scene of the crime', and that's fine. I don't want to get out of here. The bugs haven't come for their money, but now I see that isn't what they wanted at all; they just wanted me to spread this shit and spread it fast.

So now I'm in jail, just sitting here spinning my wheels. I can see the rest of the city from my cell; I see smoke rising from the center somewhere, and I can hear more sirens than usual. It could be nothing, but somehow I doubt that. Just think: there are hundreds of dealers right here in this city, and I bet you a million dollars that some of them are selling the bug powder. It could be anywhere. Everyone likes a snort now and then.

Don't you?

About the Author

Meghan Jurado is a horror fanatic. She lives in Colorado with her husband and her three hairless terriers. She has been published in *The Undead*, *The Undead II: Skin and Bones*, *Shadowbox*, *Revenant Magazine*, and *The Travel Guide to the Haunted Mid-Atlantic Region*. Meghan can be spotted lurking on the Internet at http://www.demonnurse.com

Thank you for taking a stroll in the moonlight with me ...

Established fans are used to my graphic and shocking works. After having continually asked me for werewolf stories, I had never obliged ... until now.

So I am pleased to present to you my newest creation. I do hope that you enjoy it ...

Oh, and go ahead and leave the lights on. No one will blame you...

WHEN BLACK FADES TO GREY
By Andrea Dean Van Scoyoc

MEMORIES OF THE BEGINNING

The night wind chilled him as he sat in his car, staring at the closed gates before him. Was it colder here than usual? Of course it wasn't. His mind was being overactive, as it always was. He couldn't help but think though that somehow this night held a sense of foreboding ... a dread that he had never felt before while visiting the cemetery.

He slowly opened the car door and made his way from his transport to the heavy iron cemetery gates. He paused. Andrew Flanagan had no idea why his long lost friend from so many years ago had summoned him here. If he had business he needed to discuss with him, couldn't he have simply come to his house with a twelve pack, like he used to?

Andrew had always loved this cemetery, with its tall and ornate stones that dated well back into the early1800s. It reminded him of a more genteel culture and refined era with its gently sloping hills and well manicured landscaping. The care with which the entire area was tended made it look as if it were privately owned instead of being a public burial ground.

On this night, though, the wind howled like the collective souls of the damned. He could not help but feel apprehension as he looked through the formidable gates at the graves. He felt as if he knew those who rested beneath the bright green sod. Never had he felt ill at ease with the prospect of going inside ... until tonight.

Guy Falton had always been unusual, though. Odd, eccentric, bizarre, he had been called those names and many more in his life and during the duration of their friendship that spanned from middle school to the present.

During school, Guy was always secretive and aloof. It seemed as if Andrew was the only person who he could talk to and who could talk to him. Even the other smart kids wouldn't have anything to do with Guy.

"Jealousy," Guy used to proclaim, and then stick his nose in the air as he walked off. Andrew would simply follow him, mute to his outbursts, but secretly knowing that Guy was right, no matter what anyone else thought.

Andrew's school days and his lonely trips down the halls were punctuated with questions of: "Hey ... Andrew ... man, why do you hang out with that geek? Don't you think he might be dangerous?" "Hey Andrew, what is with your friend? Does he think he's Albert Einstein?" "Hey Andrew, what on Earth could the two of you have in common? Are you two sweet on each other or something?"

Andrew knew that it looked weird, their friendship, him being a rich kid with the best wardrobe that money could buy and more money from a week's allowance of doing nothing, than most kids saw in a month of hard work. Guy, on the other hand, had worn and rumpled clothing, but they were not 'sweet on each other', and when he wasn't going on about one thing or another that went completely over his head, Andrew enjoyed his friend's company. His answer to the irritating and oftentimes really stupid questions was the same each time: "Guy's just really smart, that's all, so why don't you lay off?"

It wasn't very often that Guy allowed anyone a glimpse of his work, but when the teacher told the class about projects, Guy jumped on the opportunity to bring in what he had, or create an all new 'oddity' based on what the teacher wanted. Extra credit was no stranger to him.

People used to laugh and point at Guy's collection of oddities, anything from forgotten manuals on dead languages to nuclear fusion and any and everything in-between. The truth was that Andrew believed every word of what he told people about Guy's smartness. There was no way that with how he acted, how he couldn't communicate with others well, and the grades he made, that he wasn't *extremely* intelligent.

The biggest accolade to Guy's name and the one that sealed his fate as the most hated nerd in school, especially amongst his peers, was when he was asked to intern at the local museum for a summer between their junior and senior year. He was supposed to learn all about Paleontology, some kind of space something or other that he tried to explain but that Andrew could not grasp, and ancient cultures in South America. That was also the summer that Guy changed and not necessarily for the better.

Was it possible for a person to get used to the way another person had been their entire friendship and then not be able to absorb a change in them? That was how Andrew felt about Guy. He simply could not get used to the 'new' Guy.

After that summer at the museum, instead of becoming smarter – if that were possible – Guy seemed to almost dumb down. Maybe that was a poor choice of words, but Andrew honestly had no other explanation. Guy changed, the typical changes that people think of when kids go through stages in their lives, but for Guy it was odder than anything Andrew could have fathomed. First, he started getting in trouble at school. The fact of the trouble he got into would make any experienced troublemaker laugh, that was beside the point. *It was the fact that Guy had gotten into trouble.*

Then as his troublemaking spree continued, his grades began falling. Guy was caught with books on the ancient occult studies of lost tribes and he began drawing occult symbols on walls, carving them on desks, any place he could think of to draw them, *even on himself.*

"They give me power, at least that is how I feel. As long as I feel powerful, I have the confidence to act as if I am powerful. It's all in the mind, Andrew, if you think you are powerful and you can convince others that you are, whether you are or not, you have achieved power."

Guy's books on physics, space, and alternate life forms, among other odd things he had previously studied, were replaced by dusty and fragile tomes on witchcraft, lore and legends of curses and cursed objects ... He even managed to get his hands on a book, bound in skin – Andrew was too afraid to ask what kind – of cursed people, which he studied more than he did his schoolwork! Andrew didn't know why Guy's new studies troubled him, but they were very uncharacteristic for his friend and he was troubled from then on, up until the day of their graduation.

Many times, Andrew thought of ending his friendship with his strange friend, but how would Guy take that? Guy had become scary, *powerful and scary,* and Andrew worried what would happen if this new power that Guy supposedly had accumulated for himself were real.

Could he distance himself from Guy? Could he just laugh and tell Guy if he tried to 'curse' him, that he had been right ... that power was all in the mind and if the mind of the person that one tried to harm didn't believe then he or she couldn't be touched? Andrew liked to think that he was strong enough to laugh at Guy and his power ... but was he? What if the power was real? *What if?*

Andrew did try distancing himself from his friend, and for a while, it worked. He registered for college in another state and went an entire semester without hearing from Guy. He prayed daily that he never would hear from him again. But, as fate would have it, almost as in mockery of his pleas, no sooner did he think that he was rid of his weird friend than he came back into his life.

Andrew studied hard, made good grades, and then his life changed forever. He was called into the Dean's office one afternoon with news that would forever change him and the direction he would go.

He scarcely heard Dean Kizer's words: "I'm sorry, son, but your father has passed away. I have arranged a leave of absence for you for one month. Please let me know if I can do anything for you. Again, I'm terribly sorry."

The Dean's words were kind, but Andrew was numb. He didn't even feel the reassuring squeeze on his shoulder as Dean Kizer walked out of the room, leaving him alone with his thoughts. He knew that everyone outside the office could hear his mournful sobs; he could see their shadows outside the door. *Please don't come in*, he silently prayed. He knew they meant well, but he wished to be alone.

The trip home for his father's viewing and funeral was the hardest that Andrew ever had to make. The only other people in his life who had ever died were his grandparents, but they had been very old. His parents got married later in life and since he was a very late baby, his grandparents had been very old when he was born. He hardly remembered them ... except his Granny Thompkins. Her, he remembered....

His mother met him at the door of their neat little home, her eyes red and swollen. They fell into each other's arms, sobbing hysterically.

For a while, Andrew seemed lost. His father had always been his rock and he was lost without his guidance. He learned what a distinguished family history he had quite by mistake when his mother asked him up to the attic after the funeral. He sat in rapt attention as his mother pulled book after book, old and dried parchment out of the trunk, and faded photos from so long ago that the dates were no longer legible on them. He drank in all of what his mother told him, but he was still in shock and awe and wondered if he could ever live up to what was expected of him. His father's shoes were big ones to fill, but he would do his best.

In the meantime, Andrew and Guy had drifted apart. Andrew took the entire month's leave of absence from college and went back only when he was sure his mother would be all right. He returned to school, got his head back on straight and pursued his studies. Andrew wasn't sure whatever happened to Guy and couldn't rightfully say that he cared.

He would never forget the day that it happened. He had finished with classes for the day and was getting ready to meet some of his classmates for a pizza and beer at the local hangout. His phone rang and only one person had his number. He almost hated to answer it. He loved his mother, but she was such a pain, she always had been. Since his father's death, she became unbearably clingy. He knew that she was lonely, but for God's sake, why didn't she get a hobby? Tentatively, he glanced down at the ringing metal oval in his hand. The screen read 'Out of Area'. He laughed. There was one other person who had his number, but that was more of a coincidence than the fact that he had actually given the number to him. It had to be him, the drunken guy who kept calling him by mistake. The man was always apologetic, swearing that Andrew's number was just one number off from his pal's, yet he continued to call. At least he was funny. He hadn't heard from him in about three weeks, so he was due for another slurred barrage of jokes and giggles. Andrew had no idea who the guy was, but he didn't mind hearing from him occasionally.

"Hello."

"Long time no hear! How have you been, Andrew?"

Andrew gripped the phone so hard he surprised himself that he didn't break it.

"Guy?"

"The one and only, back and better than ever! So, how have you been this past year or so? Lonely without me?"

Andrew swallowed, hard…

That was just the beginning of Andrew's troubles …

Andrew kept the conversation general and upbeat but didn't give his former friend any information about his whereabouts nor did he invite a 'let's get together' type of conversation, either. By the end of the chat, though, he feared his cavalier attitude had been for naught.

"Hey, Guy, how did you get this number?"

"Your mom, dopey! I called your house and she and I had the best time catching up."

Andrew gripped the phone again. Was his mom all right? He knew that while his mother and father hadn't really disliked Guy, neither one had cared much for him. "He's weird, dear," his mother used to say. "Something isn't right about that boy, son," his father used to also say.

Andrew hung right up after 'catching up' with Guy and called his mom. Sure enough she had given him the number, which he asked her *never* to do again ... not for anyone else, and while she admitted she was pleasant to him, she in no way chatted with him, nor did she have a desire to.

"Mom ... did you tell Guy where I was?"

"No son, I didn't."

"Mom ... you're sure?"

"I only gave him your number, son. He can't use it to track you down, so I thought it would be harmless if he had it. Can't you block his number?"

"Yeah, something like that, Mom. I have to go. I'll call you later, okay? I love you."

Andrew didn't even wait for his mother to respond before he hung up the phone.

What was he going to do now? He would just have to play each day by ear and worry about what he would do *if* Guy did show up in his life. His mother was correct, cell phones were untraceable, so Guy really had no way to find him. He was being paranoid and worrying for no reason. He smiled and headed off to the pizza joint.

For a while Andrew didn't sleep well and he worried that Guy would somehow find him. One week turned into two, two into three and soon the semester was over. Summer Break would be good for him, he could go visit his mother and hopefully continue to avoid Guy.

He did indeed enjoy his summer. He and his mother went antique hunting, something that he had always enjoyed doing with both his parents; they went to the beach and enjoyed just being around each other. Andrew knew that his mother was lonely and he was happy that he could bring her some comfort. While at home, he felt more at ease with his new station in his family as the head and patriarch of their proud heritage. His mother told him even more about his roots. Andrew was still mesmerized by just how little he knew of where he came from.

"Mom, why didn't you and Dad ever tell me about this before? What if I said I didn't want this responsibility? What if I said I wasn't interested? What if I just said 'no'?"

"Son ... you know that your father and I had you late in life. Your father was not interested in carrying on the family's duty and, until you came along, was quite happy to just live with me until we both grew even older than we were, and died. Had you said 'no', your father would have been just fine with that. You weren't planned, so he had no issues with the legacy dying out with him."

Andrew's gaze darted up with his mother's kind ones.

"But neither of us *ever* regretted bringing you into this world. When your father looked at you for the first time, with that little blue knitted cap on your head that they gave you at the hospital, your tiny pink face all screwed up in a scowl, he fell so in love with you that the only time I ever got to hold you after we brought you home was when I fed you. That was when your father and I decided that when you graduated from high school, if we were still here, we'd tell you. Had we died before you graduated, the family legacy would have died with us. We were happy with that and I hope that you don't think ill of your father for wanting to wait."

Andrew smiled. "No, Mom, I don't."

Andrew went back to school refreshed and with a new outlook on life. He could understand why his father never told him of the family's secret, and how they came to be as prominent as they were. Some people would be jealous, some wouldn't understand and then there were always those who would think that *they* were more deserving of such honors than the actual recipient. This way, his father had saved the entire family grief. Andrew had even more respect for his father than he thought he ever could.

However, his tranquil peace of mind would not last. School started back in the fall and he had been lax about getting his class schedule. Would there be any good classes left? He looked over the listings of what was left when a shadow fell over him and he shivered. His stomach knotted up and he turned around into Guy's glaring eyes and wide grin.

"Well, well, what do you know? Are you stalking me? I can't get away from you! It's bad enough I had to put up with you in high school, now I have to share a campus with you, too?"

Guy laughed and grabbed Andrew firmly by the shoulder, hurting him. Andrew winced but knew that he had to play along. If Guy were this strong, what would he do if Andrew angered him?

"Hey, you spaz! Are you on steroids? You have gotten strong! You going out for the football team or what?"

Guy laughed and grabbed Andrew around the neck.

"Nah ... I don't want to be manhandled by those gargantuans. I have been traveling to South America. I joined the Peace Corps and had a great time! I saw things that you would not believe, man. I tell you, it was a life-changing experience."

As Guy said the words 'life-changing', his countenance seemed to darken and then go back to normal. Andrew visibly shivered.

"What's wrong with you, weirdo?"

Andrew knew he had to think fast.

"Coming down with something, I think. You know, I went all through high school and was hardly sick a time ever, and yet I get to college and become like that sickly kid, what was his name ... "

"Patterson Himley, that rich little weakling, spoiled twerp ... God if you had ever been like him, I'd have had to kill you, you know that, right?"

Andrew would have known that Guy was joking ... until he looked at his expression again and into those eyes that chilled him to the bone. "Uh ... yeah, him, I couldn't stand that kid. Well anyway, I need to get my schedule done, Guy. Take it easy and watch out for that newfound strength of yours, you brute!"

Andrew laughed and patted Guy on the shoulder as he walked off. He could feel Guy's gaze bore through him. He hoped, he prayed, that the meeting was the first and last time that he would see him again.

Andrew avoided Guy for a while and Guy didn't seem so interested in being around him, then all that changed. One day, just as quickly as Guy had become unbearably stranger than he had ever been, he just stopped. He stopped everything when he got around Andrew. There was no more shows of strength as Andrew considered them, no talk of power like he had done back in high school, no more talk of using people for his own gain, no more spells and occult symbols. It was as if he had changed again, but this time the change was for the better. Andrew's joke about Guy playing football turned out to be rather ironic as the once odd young man started going to football games with him. He even came over to watch them on television or they met at the local wing place to watch it with a group of guys. Andrew was relieved that Guy seemed almost ... normal. He knew that Guy had always been difficult for others to figure out, but he'd never been difficult for him to understand. Now he saw what everyone else had gone though and just how bothersome it was, but what could he do?

THE MEETING

Now here he was, after five long years, and he couldn't help but be worried. What possible motivation could have caused Guy to make such a strange request of his friend? Andrew had often quipped – jokingly at first – over the years that he wished to write about Guy's interesting, albeit strange life, and had done so again just the other night when he called. Guy always said the same thing anytime Andrew brought the subject up: "My life is a whirlwind of adventures, some great, some small, but they are mine and I can't share them ... unless I wanted to kill you afterward." Guy would always guffaw and grab Andrew in bear hugs, jostling him around. Guy was kidding about killing him if he told him of his adventures ... right?

Could this be what the meeting was about? Could this be what Guy had called him to the cemetery for? Had he changed his mind? To some people that might seem odd, but for Andrew, that was actually normal and no one could comprehend just *how* normal such a request was for Guy, to meet in a place that would creep everyone else out.

It was true that Guy had strange journeys to tell about and even stranger items he had collected over the years that Andrew wished to photograph and include in the book if that was what he had called him about. But why the cemetery? Why now? It was cold out in the cemetery at night, it being December and so close to the holidays. And besides, these 'modern cemeteries', as Guy called them, did not hold much interest for him. Unless the inhabitants of a cemetery were at least five hundred years old, he wasn't interested in them, so why had he chosen a place to meet at that held absolutely no interest for him? The oldest grave in this cemetery was two hundred and ten years old. Definitely not anything remotely attention-grabbing to Guy, although Andrew found it fascinating.

Andrew admitted that his upbeat, hip, and ultra modern studio loft didn't set the stage for writing something as unusual as an autobiography for such an eccentric individual, but wasn't meeting in the cemetery going a little overboard? He shook his head as his mind chided him, *yeah right ... did the cold freeze your brain? Look who you're dealing with!*

His mother had always loved cemeteries too, which was where Andrew always swore he took his interest from. She in turn had gotten her love from her mother. Andrew remembered his Granny Thompkins talking for hours about family history and lore and legends that spanned so far back in time that Andrew simply couldn't fathom it. But as she got older, and the dementia took her in its cruel grasp, that changed. Her love went to abject terror. Andrew's mother asked him not to talk about cemeteries in front of her any longer, as she had nothing helpful to contribute. Her "You know, Andrew, I used to go visit cemeteries in search of epitaphs too, would you like some company?" was replaced with thunderous warnings and her dire tales of how she claimed that the dead spoke to her in sibilant, sinister, and tortured whispers. Her frightening stories did nothing to scare him or dissuade him from going. He simply shook his head as his mother gently reminded him: "It's just the ramblings of a sick and tired old woman, honey. You go on and have fun."

Nothing could change how he felt ... he had always loved cemeteries and this one in particular. In his family, spending a day in the cemetery *was* considered fun! Many nights when he couldn't sleep, he would get in his car and drive to the beautiful old burial ground where he would wander amongst the graves, talking to the long dead inhabitants as if they walked with him. He was sure that if anyone could see him, they would think him mad, but he had never concerned himself with what others thought and nothing could change that.

Andrew stopped and cocked his head. Maybe his grandmother had passed some of her gift or madness depending on how one perceived her ramblings, onto him. There were many times that if he thought hard enough and listened attentively enough, he swore that he could hear them too, luring him and tantalizing him with their soft-spoken keening.

The cemetery gates swung noisily open, creaking loudly, as if protesting being roused from their solemn slumber. Andrew was almost afraid to go in. What awaited him, the normal Guy or the weirdo reverted Guy who had come to take his soul? He mentally chastised himself for being so foolish. What was he thinking? What could be awaiting him other than Guy being what he always was, just Guy! For some reason though, some feeling that both chilled him and frightened him, made him wish that he were meeting his friend elsewhere this night.

Like a child who had been summoned to the Principal's office to face discipline, Andrew summoned his courage to face whatever Guy had in store for him. He really did feel silly, him a grown man and being apprehensive of a place that he came to all the time, but he found that he couldn't help himself. With a knot that suddenly made its way from his stomach to his throat, he walked through the gates.

He pulled his coat tightly to him. Why was he shivering? Sure it was cold, but was it really the cold that was bothering him, or was it the fear of the unknown that gnawed at him like a starving dog coveting a bone? Could it be death reaching out to him in retaliation for him coming and disturbing its charge's eternal rest? Maybe it was his grandmother. She told him while on her deathbed that she would never leave him, and she'd meant it. Many times since her death, he had sensed her: things fell off the wall after being securely hung, items came up missing, and sounds that no human or animal could make wafted through his loft on stormy nights. It only stopped when he left for college. It was a relief to him actually. His mother reported some of the same happenings, but she ignored them.

"Honey, your grandmother was very sick, mentally sick when she died, so don't you think that a part of her maybe hadn't been able to cross over to the other side? Just ignore her. If she gets too troublesome, just tell me. I will see what I can do."

Andrew didn't really want to think about what his mother could do to rid him of his grandmother's spirit, and he wasn't sure he wanted to know. He was grateful that he had been accepted to a college far enough away that maybe his grandmother couldn't follow him. His grandmother had always loved storms and in the years that passed her death, with each one that approached, he had dreaded her coming to him. He knew that that was her way of telling him that she was there with him. Andrew too loved storms, the more violent the better, but had only been able to enjoy them after he left home. It took him a while to get used to being gone and the first few times a storm raged, he would jump and look around, but after a while he knew that he was rid of his grandmother.

Guy loved storms too, but that was only so he could summon the Earth's power to him ... or so he said back in high school. Andrew looked up, as if such a simple gesture might call down the Heavens to comfort him, like storms always did. He knew that no such thing would be possible this night and he felt naked and alone. He looked up again, but this time to actually look at the sky. The moon was barely visible, obscured by thick, gray clouds that seemed to shimmer from shades of white, to pure black.

He took a step further into the cemetery, then two, and then found that with each step, his feet moved easier. He hurried deeper into the cemetery, his heart pounding. He didn't realize until he stopped just how fast he had been traveling. He was not much of an athlete and he hated to run, but that was what he had actually been doing. He found it odd that on this night, his place of solace left him feeling uneasy and did not offer him the comfort that it normally did. It was as if the cemetery itself was upset at his presence.

He saw something in the distance, faint at first and then brighter and then fading away, as if a fire were being fanned and then allowed to die away. The sweet smell of Cavendish caught his nostrils and it was as if he were being pulled toward the smell that he had always loved so much. Though not a smoker himself, Andrew had always loved the smell of pipe tobacco. Cavendish was his favorite, although he would not turn his nose up at a nice cherry, either.

He knew that Guy was close by. Guy was never without his pipe. He had smoked pipes laden with Cavendish since high school. When other kids were smoking clove cigarettes or pot, he was smoking a pipe loaded with Cavendish.

Andrew had always found it funny that when he would go outside to the smoking area at school where most of his friends hung out – even though he was not a smoker himself thanks to his asthma – he would find Guy and the History teacher, Mr. Arnon, discussing ancient Roman architecture and language while each smoked their Cavendish-filled pipes. Andrew used to laugh. He couldn't help it. All the kids called Guy 'the teacher's pet' and maybe it was true, but Andrew couldn't help but think, that if the truth be known, Guy knew as much as the teacher did if not more.

Andrew stopped. Guy was only a few feet in front of him. He smiled and then chuckled silently. Guy would think he was such an idiot. Actually, Guy thought that most people were idiots . How the two of them had ever become friends was still a mystery to him. They met in the library where Guy was researching his next 'A+' paper and where Andrew was serving detention for skipping class. They were both putting away books and struck up a conversation, which in itself was unusual as Guy talked to few people. The rest was history. Andrew tried to remember even how they started talking, but he couldn't. Was it he who initiated the conversation? It had to be because Andrew knew Guy was perfectly happy if no one *ever* talked to him.

He strained and strained his mind to think back all those years ago, but it refused to cooperate. One thing was certain, though, Andrew and Guy were as different as daylight and darkness and Andrew *had* to have been bored out of his mind to even consider talking to a nerd like Guy.

"Ahhh, I see that my power has lured you to me, like a fly caught in the spider's web!"

Guy's words, which Andrew would have thought funny coming from anyone else, chilled him even more than he already was.

"You wish, dork. It was the Cavendish and you know it."

"Well ... sounded good anyway, didn't it?"

Andrew laughed. Guy had the strangest sense of humor, but he really could be funny at times. Most people in school hadn't understood his sense of humor and so that was another thing that, instead of making him gain friends, made him an outcast. However, that wasn't saying a lot, as most people just didn't understand Guy.

"So tell me old friend, what is it that is so important that you had to drag me out to the graveyard to talk?"

Andrew spoke the words as if he and Guy were the best of friends and had no secrets between them. But Andrew was nervous and the knot in his stomach kept telling him that he was in danger, at least *some form* of peril.

Guy grinned.

"Yeah, like I *dragged* you out here. You know that you love this place. You come out here all the time. Remember, you told me that you like it here. Creep."

Andrew laughed. If anyone was the creep, it was Guy. *Stay calm, Andrew.*

Guy emptied his pipe and set it down. The pipe was an antique, hand carved with a gargoyle in bas-relief on the ivory bowl and set in dark cherry wood. Andrew knew the pipe had been passed down to Guy's father from his grandfather at his death, and his father had passed it down to Guy. Guy had mused aloud one time as to whether or not he would have started smoking a pipe if it had not been for his heirloom. With Guy, one could never just assume anything.

Andrew looked up. Guy was staring at him curiously. He often did that and it gave Andrew the creeps. It was as if Guy stared through him and attempted to see into his soul. Andrew scolded himself. After so long, he should be used to Guy's odd ways, but that was only if he could be comfortable being around his former friend – and he couldn't be, not now. Something about this meeting, and the air of heavy apprehension that all but strangled his heart this night made him even more sensitive than usual to Guy's bizarre behavior.

"Sit down, Andrew. I have an issue that I need to discuss with you, one that I can't tell anyone else."

Guy moved over on the bench and motioned for Andrew to sit. Andrew had sat on this bench before. The gravestone that it sat in front of was one of Andrew's favorites. It was of a life-sized, weeping seraph, in utter anguish, lying over a small column, surrounded on each side by urns of cascading roses. The woman's name who was buried there was Eva Larrington, and she had died in eighteen hundred at the age of seventeen, in childbirth according to the epitaph. Andrew had always thought that while the stone was gorgeous, the circumstances of it being erected were so sad.

There it was again. As Andrew sat down, the knot that had been plaguing his stomach intensified into a burning ball of fire. Why was he feeling this way? He had always had good instincts, but this signal, while he had only had it one time before, meant that he was in danger! The last time he had felt this way was when he walked home from a friend's house through a neighborhood that was better left alone, and was nearly shot and robbed. He had always been sensitive and psychic, he had second sight, whatever you wanted to call it. It was another gift passed to him by his grandmother, and he hated how he felt. He hoped, like he did every time he got one of his 'feelings', that he was wrong.

Andrew fidgeted. "I guess this has nothing to do with your autobiography?"

Guy shook his head glumly.

"No, I'm afraid it doesn't. What I am about to tell you this night, Andrew, I must beg that you keep to yourself, not only for my safety, but for yours."

Andrew nodded. It was almost as if he nodded out of instinct. It didn't feel as if he nodded his head, but that he was on some sort of string and an invisible puppeteer orchestrated his every move.

"Then by all means, old friend, tell me. You know that what is said between us, stays between us."

Andrew hoped that he sounded convincing. What would Guy do if he thought that Andrew would betray him? The Guy he was sitting with was not the Guy he once knew and he couldn't assume anything about him ... especially not after so long.

Guy nodded. He knew he could trust his friend. Through thick and thin, they had weathered the best and the worst of times, from hating mutual enemies in school, to hating each other even at one time. But their friendship had always prevailed ... until Guy *changed*. Then their friendship became strained and strange and Andrew had hoped to honestly never see Guy again.

Had Guy ever felt the same way?

Guy looked at Andrew. His old friend was graying already. He had been quick to gray, but he was still as handsome as he had always been. In high school, he always had his pick of any girl that he wanted. He still had the body of the football player that he had been in school. Guy couldn't help but be a little jealous. He always had been. He, on the other hand, had never had any luck with women and was still a virgin. It wasn't that he didn't want to have sex, but his studies of ancient languages, ancient civilizations, and obscure customs of people of the world took up all his time. He had been delighted to send his best friend postcards from his travels to every part of the globe and to places that no man should have ever traveled alone. He always sent them to his parents' home in case Andrew happened to switch dorms or move off campus. Guy was always thoughtful like that. He didn't like to assume anything and he certainly never left anything to chance.

What would he have done if he knew that Andrew threw all of them away?

Guy smiled. People in such technologically developed countries always thought they were so smart and had so much going for them. Yet when he traveled to the remote and never-heard-of countries, islands, and mountains of his travels, it was in those places, many which had never seen anyone other than those in their small towns, that he had found the most enlightenment. Guy's dark eyes searched Andrew's green eyes for any sense of how he should start his tale. Andrew simply stared at him, like he always did, his large green eyes curious, but willing to lend a neutral glance or a quick stare of disapproval if the situation merited it. Guy smoothed his black hair and exhaled. He'd never had trouble with his words, and speaking in front of anyone was what he lived for. That was one of the perks of being smarter than everyone else and he knew it. Whether people actually *wanted* to hear him speak or not, he was a legend on the high school debate team, he knew they would listen nonetheless because he was so much smarter than they. He had always been a show-off of his knowledge and oftentimes to the chagrin of his teachers, who could not disagree or discipline him for what he did or said because he was *always* right. He had enjoyed the debate team, running circles around his opponents, giving class presentations that no one could follow or lecturing at the local college at night on ancient customs. Whatever he had to do to show off his vast wisdom, which far outshined anyone else's in school, he did. Now, here he was, alone with his friend, in the middle of a bunch of dead people, and he was speechless. He would open his mouth and see what came out.

"Andrew, you know how I have traveled the world, how I have seen things and been to places that most people, if they lived two or three lifetimes, could never be fortunate enough to see?"

Andrew nodded, but again, it was not a nod of anything but pure instinct. The burning knot in his stomach had increased to an all out searing pain, which threatened to engulf him. Had Guy contracted a deadly disease while in one of those far away places? Had he summoned Andrew to the cemetery to say goodbye? Was he going on a trip that he feared he might not come back from?

Now Andrew kind of felt bad for his thoughts about Guy.

Guy looked at the ground and continued speaking. It was not like him to not keep eye contact with whom it was he addressed. It was intimidating to look Guy in the eyes when he spoke, but Andrew was used to it. Now he found that he looked at Guy, but Guy would not look at him. Andrew's stomach burned badly.

"I never told you much about my trips in the postcards and letters I sent you, only to say that I had seen things and done things that most men could never dream of, but I never elaborated on any of my stories. That was what my biography was supposed to be for if I ever decided to allow you to write it. I know for many years that you have tried to get me to put my travels into words, which would be part of that autobiography. I just can't, Andrew. As much as I'd like to, I can't. But I will tell you *my* story and ask that you keep it to yourself. Right now, I must tell you another story, a story that I have told no one, a story that is probably better kept to myself, but I can't. I can't keep what I know a secret any longer. It is killing me to bear such a burden alone. I wish nothing more from you than to have your understanding and loyalty, which I have always had."

Andrew waited, but Guy did not give him an opportunity to acknowledge him in any way. He paused for only a heartbeat, it seemed, and then continued.

"What I am about to tell you happened two years ago in a small, unpopulated part of South America. I was there attempting to find any shred of ancient artifact that I could to show that the land had pre-historic inhabitants. I had gotten a grant from a museum and they wanted results. I had written and documented evidence that people had been living there for thousands of years before modern civilization; all I needed was physical proof. The tribe that had lived there originally seemed to have simply disappeared in the mid sixteen hundreds, and even though there were still villagers around the area, they were not the original inhabitants. It was they, the original inhabitants, that I was curious about, as local history just suddenly stopped mentioning them. I wanted to know what might have happened to those that lived there for so long and how they lived. I figured that the newer inhabitants were simply creatures of convenience. They found an abandoned village, probably still stocked with foodstuffs, clothing of sorts, and all manner of necessities for life and they simply moved in. I stopped in town and asked for directions. I had at least a day's hike ahead of me and I wanted to make sure that I didn't get lost. In remote places like where I was going, if I got lost, it was conceivable that I might never be seen again."

Guy paused and took out his pouch of tobacco.

"All those stories you hear about people getting lost and not coming back are not myths made to scare tourists away. They are true accounts of what can happen if you don't know where you're going or what you are getting yourself into when you venture off into the unknown."

Guy exhaled and then lit his newly filled pipe.

"The villagers were *uncooperative* to put it lightly, and a few were even hostile, asking me what business I had on the mountain and why I needed to get involved in something that I had no right to. I finally found a small boy whom, when I paid him what amounted to a week's worth of wages for his family, told me the path to take up the mountain. I was set. I was excited and a bit frightened too about my adventure. What could possibly be so important that the villagers were so hateful to me? It is typical in those small places for people to be secretive, to a degree. They have nothing as it is; the last thing they want is for someone to come in and find something that they could use themselves or to find riches that they could sell to survive. But these villagers were unnaturally protective of *something* and I was going to find out just what.

"I got a week's worth of provisions, and even though I didn't plan to stay more than a few days, when traveling like that, it is better to have it and not need it, than need it and not have it. I made my way up the mountain. I climbed so high up that it was difficult to breathe. I had been up high mountains before, but never one that high. I made camp and determined that I would start my search first thing in the morning and work until nightfall.

"I slept well that night under the stars. It was so peaceful, but it was cold, too. I was thankful for a heavy flannel shirt and some long johns that I had with me. I tended to carry the same clothes for the similar or even remotely similar regions, where weather was concerned, that I traveled to. When I was in the desert, I carried flannel and long johns, headgear to protect me from the elements. And I tended to carry the same things, in the same bag, when I went to South America. Of course I kept a hot – as hot as the thin air would allow me to – fire going as I had no idea what type of creatures I might encounter, but the solitude and the sheer beauty of such desolation at night was one in which I knew that I wouldn't soon forget.

"After a hearty breakfast the next morning, I set about climbing even higher to see where the mountains would take me. There were a few paths, but they were not well worn and it looked as if it had been ages since anyone had walked them. All the better for me or so I thought; still clinging to the hope that I would find some undiscovered treasure that I could carry back with me. I was going into what the little boy had called '*La montaña del inexplicado, la montaña de la muerte*' – the mountain of the unexplained, the mountain of death.

"Those people like that are always full of stories, so I ignored him of course when he told me of the dire and awful tales that came off that mountain from those few lucky enough to survive even a night in its clutches. They simply didn't want me poking about and while I could respect and understand that, that didn't mean that I was not going to do so anyway. I had studied all forms of ancient hexes, curses, and other magicks back in high school. Please ... whatever they had, let them throw their best at me. I was certain that I could take it on and defeat it. What could a bunch of illiterate, inbred monkey worshippers do to me? I had studied powers that would make them wish to die where they stood rather than face them!"

Andrew shivered. He knew that what Guy said was true, he had been privy to Guy's studies ... well, he had been privy to the fact that he had done them in high school, and this self-centered, scary Guy was the same one that he had come to loathe and fear.

"I laughed at the kid. There is no such thing as the 'unexplained'. Everything has a rational explanation, and I had proven it time and time again with my studies."

Guy dropped his eyes and his expression. For just a moment, he looked troubled.

"It turned out that all of my knowledge combined could not have prepared me for the lesson I would be learning on that mountain. The townspeople's advice of leaving while I still could and never coming back went unheeded.

"I cleaned up my campsite before I left. No matter what a jerk I was to others, I had and still do have the utmost respect for nature. I buried my fire pit, made sure to cover up any embers and wood, hoisted my backpack on my shoulder and set off for the top of the mountain and riches beyond belief. Or so I thought ...

"I came across an old and obviously rarely to never used cave and went inside. There were so many paths, twists and turns that I was like a child on Christmas Day. I had no idea where I would go first. I simply stood there, drooling all over myself trying to pick which adventure to begin first. I chose the cave tunnel to the left. I figured I would just work my way around and have an adventure a month if I had to! I could always go back into town for supplies and take my time. As long as the museum was seeing results, they would continue to fund me. I had a satellite phone with me with batteries that would last a while and I was set. I would send them updates every day. They'd be like dogs salivating over a plate of hamburger meat.

"I took off down that first tunnel anxious to get started. I had a flashlight and small lantern both with me and would use one when it wasn't convenient to use the other. I am used to hard living and I can go from modern to primitive to back again in mere seconds. The cave tunnel was dark and a bit spooky, I don't mind admitting. My heart was in my throat and my breath was like tiny gasps as I made my way through that precarious path. In places, the tunnel had no walls and was just a ledge or so to walk on. Bats were all over the place. Thank God, I know how to move quietly!

"I traveled for what seemed like all day. I never sat down, took a leak over the ledges when I needed to and walked until I was sure it was nighttime. Eventually, the pathway emptied out into a large room with even more tunnels leading out of it.

"In the middle of the room was an altar and strange markings on the walls. I had never seen such markings and I was fascinated. I really thought I had stumbled onto something huge. I held the lantern up and walked over to get a better look. Even with the lantern, it was so dark that I tripped on something sticking out of the floor and fell. I was okay, but my lantern flew out of my hand and shattered against the wall, spilling oil onto the ground. A fire started, but that was okay, it illuminated the entire room and it was then that I could see where I was. It appeared to be a burial chamber and what I had tripped on was a bone sticking up out of the ground! Broken pottery littered the ground and as my eyes adjusted, I could see more bones.

"I cried out for joy and got out my flashlight. I knew the fire from the lantern was not going to last much longer and so the flashlight would just have to do. I hoped that maybe if I was lucky, I would get some light from somewhere in the morning.

"I decided to lay all of my tools out and go to sleep for the night. I have to admit that I hardly slept.

"When I woke up the next morning, there was faint light trickling in through a crevice in the ceiling. I was elated. It didn't give me much light, but with the flashlight, too, I had enough to start excavating.

"As I dug and scraped, dusted and searched, I lost myself in my greed and in my desire for knowledge. Even if I found but an entire skeleton or *one whole piece of pottery*, anything proving who and what lived there and how long ago, it would be *my* discovery, *mine to brag about* and maybe to make it into the history books with! *I* was the one who climbed that mountain, *I* was the one braving the dangers of a dark cave, me, *I had done it and I wanted all the credit!* Such a find of an, as of that moment, undiscovered culture and people would catapult me to instant respect and success in the communities that had snubbed me just months before!

"I worked into the late afternoon and decided to call it quits right at sundown. No matter how I dug and pleaded with the chamber to give its secret up to me, it wouldn't. I was so close, right there, I had found a burial chamber that had been abandoned for centuries, but obviously at some point someone had cleaned it out. Judging by how unused the path to the cave was, either people had found an easier accessible way in or they cleaned it out centuries ago shortly after the burial. God was I pissed off."

Andrew's eyebrows shot up. He had never heard Guy swear before and though most people wouldn't consider the word 'pissed' a swear word, he knew in Guy's book it would be.

"There went all of my hopes and dreams for showing up those jerks who'd made fun of me, making them eat a healthy dose of dried out crow. I had nothing. All of those other cave tunnels led back out to the same spot where I had entered the cave to begin with. I can only assume that those other tunnels were carved out to confuse any would-be robbers. It didn't work as they obviously had looted the entire cave at some point, but it exhausted me to the bone. I took a bit of time, more than I wished I had, and explored the cave tunnels. Each of them led to that one room, but some were shorter than others. Of course the one I originally took to get to the room was the longest."

Guy stopped and exhaled in apparent abject disgust, shaking his head, slowly.

"I packed up my gear, and I was bawling my eyes out like a little girl, I swear I was. I was angry, I was sad, I was disheartened that I had not found one thing to add to my collection, and knew that I could even have been centuries late. I don't know which would have made me feel better, being a day late or a century late. I felt just as bad with both thoughts that even though it had been a while since anyone had been on the mountain, whoever trod those caves before me had taken every last bit of artifacts. I consoled myself by thinking that whoever had taken all the treasures, trinkets, and articles of interest no longer had them. I'm certain they sold them for a *pittance* of what they were worth and then spent the money, probably on booze or cheap drugs and gone right back to the starving, poverty-stricken level they had been before they robbed the chamber. Serves them right. At least if *I* had taken them, they would be in a museum! I guess when I really thought about it, thinking that way made me feel better because I just could not bring myself to think that anyone had been to the area within the last few years and 'beaten' me to the precious finds.

"It took me a while to get out of the cave and I started down the hill to the trail when a noise that chilled my blood made me whip around. By that time it was pitch black and there was no moon at all so I saw nada. The sky was etched with dark, black clouds, like a storm was moving in, but I could have sworn that I heard a howl.

"I shook the thought from my head and continued on down the trail hoping that I wouldn't slip on some rocks or break my neck getting down it. I had my flashlight, but it was of little use except to scare the crap out of me with every movement I saw. I am not the type to be afraid of much, you know, Andrew. I have seen too much, too many weird things, archaic things, evil things in my travels to get a case of the crawlies from a noise in the darkness, but for some reason, this place was a lot different than any of the other treks I had been on. There was definitely a far older magic than I had ever encountered on that mountain.

"I hadn't planned on stopping but I needed to. I was beat and still fuming about being cheated out of my treasure. I figured that the place I had camped before would be just as good as any place to stop. I still had my fire pit, I just needed to dig it out again and the area was peaceful, as peaceful as could be expected for a jungle.

"When I got back to camp, there was a very old man sitting there. He had a fire going and had food cooking on a spit. I was angry at first that someone would do such a thing. I mean come on; it was *my* spot first! Who did he think he was? He had dug out *my* pit and was using it! I know the ground there was hard, but that's too bad! That was *my* pit, I practically broke my back digging it out and he had no right to use it. He needed to dig his own! But then I thought about how much trouble he'd saved me. Already dug, soft ground or not, at least I didn't have to do it and he had food. My first thought was that he better share it since he was using *my* pit. I wouldn't hesitate to tell him that because he was in my camp that I wanted some of his dinner.

"I wasn't sure what was cooking on the spit and I wasn't about to ask, but it smelled good and that was all that mattered to me. I was famished. I sat and introduced myself. At first the man paid little attention to me. Nice, he hijacks *my* campsite, whether I was there or not, I was there first as it was obvious no one had been there in ages. I guess he just suddenly decided to take a day trip?"

Guy stopped and ran his hand down his face. It was not often that Andrew had heard Guy run his sentences together and ramble. Usually, at least as far as Andrew had always known, Guy was articulate and a bit Histrionic, speaking in phrases and sentences that were over most people's heads.

Guy sighed, appearing to calm himself and continued:

"I introduced myself *again* and thanked him for digging *my* fire pit out again for me. I figured that if I told him that he was using my pit, he might show a little manners. It worked ... at least to a degree. He told me that his name was Paulo and that he lived nearby. I tried to get more information out of him as to where he lived because there was no village 'nearby', but he was as secretive as I was when he asked me what I was doing there. I explained that I was doing research on the local culture and why it died out. He eyed me like he didn't believe a word I said, but nodded. I didn't like the way he looked at me, as if he knew I *was* lying. I hate it when people can read me. I was lying! I wasn't there necessarily for research. If I could find things to make me powerful in the museum's eyes, in the archaeological society I was trying to get into as well, great, but I was more interested in gaining some form of power, more so than that stupid social circles could hold for me. Granted, the thought of some form of archaic power came only after I left the caves empty handed, but hey, it was worth a thought anyway.

"Anyway, the guy glared at me like he was some kind of judge and jury as to why I shouldn't be there. But when he spoke, Paulo was polite and told me that he had been born in the village that occupied the far side of the hill and had lived there his entire life. I was intrigued. Maybe I could get something out of the wasted trip after all. Paulo and I sat up until the wee hours of the morning and talked. I enjoyed speaking to Paulo, but I honestly wanted to know what he was doing in my camp. Did he come to stop me from taking any of the treasures that had been there at one time? Was he some sort of caretaker that was charged with keeping the place safe? I also wondered if he were some backwards policeman. In those bassackwards countries, cops don't always look like cops. I finally got sick of the pleasantries and flat out asked him why he came to my camp.

"I figured he would lie, but I guess he appreciated my honesty with him, so I got it in return. He told me that he had had two reasons for coming to my camp – one, to make sure that I was safe, as the area was dangerous, and two, to tell me a story worth more than any trinkets or treasures I could find. He wished to tell me the history of the area's bloody, macabre and troubling past.

"Well of course, I was all ears! My dig had yielded nothing, as I have lamented to you since I started this story, and a first hand account of the area's past would make the trip worth something and keep the museum interested! How many opportunities would I have to talk about the area's history with such a knowledgeable individual? He was old and I was sure that his knowledge was vast in the area's folklore! Besides, no matter how much I could have found in the dig, I would have still had unanswered questions. Maybe this man could tell me from start to finish everything I needed to know. Hey, I am used to hard work, but that doesn't mean that I wouldn't take the easy way out if it happened to present itself!

"I could ask anyone in the village to tell me the tales of old, and had thought about doing so, but just like with anything else, what assurance did I have that the stories wouldn't be embellished or intentionally and profoundly inaccurate? I would understand why, to lead treasure seekers away from the real riches, which would be the area's people, culture, and heritage, at least in their opinion, but that was not the riches I was looking for and I think Paulo could see that.

"Paulo took the food off the spit, divided it up between us and pulled out a bottle of drink from a well-worn and threadbare satchel. I had tasted the native drink before and it was divine, so I didn't hesitate to agree to share it with him. I knew that this bottle would be no less delicious as Paulo boasted that he had brewed it himself. He passed the bottle to me and I took the first drink then passed it back. He handed me a small portion of the meat and I ate hungrily. The food was good, smoked perfectly and the conversation was of the utmost interest, so I had, what I considered to be, the perfect night before me.

"Paulo drank from the bottle and took a bite of the food. We ate in silence until we were both done. There wasn't a lot to eat, but it was very filling, dense, as if all muscle. I still had no idea, even after consuming every morsel, what it was, but I enjoyed it. I really hoped that my dinner wouldn't be spoiled by a revelation from Paulo as what it really was. As if he read my mind, he looked at me most curiously before he spoke.

" 'Shall I tell you?' he asked, smirking at me.

" 'No,' I politely declined.

" 'Then shall I tell you my story?'

The story on the other hand, I was most eager to hear.

" 'Yes, by all means. I am excited to hear it!'

"So Paulo settled back and looked up at the sky.

" 'It is said that this mountain was made by an ancient evil, an evil that no one could contain. It came to the mountain because it had been banished from the Other Realm, the realm where all the power of the Heavens lies. The Other Realm is where all the good and bad cohabitate, existing in truce and equality. Being as they cannot fight amongst themselves there, the Earth is their battleground. Every disaster that happens, every famine, every baleful damnation that Mankind can endure is because of the wars that cannot be fought there, but must instead be waged here.

" 'The evil hated Mankind, which is why it was banished to Earth. The Supreme Power, the power that ruled over all the good and evil alike made a mockery of its banishment by sending it to the very place it hated. At first it was totally alone and it liked it that way. Then the loneliness that it thought it wanted so desperately consumed it until it decided that it wanted company. The evil made a beautiful forest with flowers, green grass, lots of animals and riches, riches untold and beyond mortal man's comprehension. Then it waited. It knew that it wouldn't be lonely for long and it was right. Soon, people came from all over and settled in the mountain. If evil could be happy, it was. It had people to watch and it had company, whether it could interact with them or not.

" 'The inhabitants discovered the jewels and riches the evil made for them and they were very happy. They were wealthy, even by your standards in the modern world that has left mine behind; they were wealthy. Everything was gold, everything was bejeweled ... everything was decadent. At first the people were grateful and made weekly sacrifices to the evil in the mountain for their good fortune.

" 'However all that changed with each generation that came after the original inhabitants. The sacrifices stopped and the evil became angry and sullen because the people became thankless. After centuries of watching the people it had made rich and prosperous, it decided that it was time that it be paid back in full for their ungrateful hearts. The evil wanted all the pleasures that mortal man had and that it did not and knew it could not have. The evil tortured, maimed, and made miserable the people of this area in its anger until they begged their heathen gods for release. They prayed for years and years until finally, a great god of old was sent from the Other Realm to deliver them from the evil. The god, a god of light and purity, dug a huge hole in the earth and captured the evil by leading a trail of jewels, wine, and other mortal riches into the hole. Once the evil was contained, the god filled in the hole with ash, rock, and foul mud and then planted a great and poisonous plant over the area, that would grow and swallow the mountainside, to keep those of a curious nature away."

" 'I remembered seeing a terrible, sprawling plant so many times on my trek up the mountainside. For as far as I could see, it seemed that there was no beginning or end to this plant, it just simply seemed to be everywhere so at least that part of his story made sense.

" 'Is that that horrible, needled and ghastly-smelling bush I keep seeing?"

Paulo nodded eagerly.

" 'Yes. The god made sure that the evil could not escape, so he made this plant cover the entire area, so that the evil would not want to come out of its banishment because of the foul smell that the plant emanates, but also that it would be poisoned and die if stuck by one of its needles. The god told those natives of this land, those who had been here when the Earth was new, that they would have to lead pure and humble lives in order to keep the evil at bay. The evil could not live if it had nothing to feed off of. If they would live like the angelic beings he was descended from, then they would be free forever from the evil that had plagued them for so long. The elders of all the local tribes agreed and the pact was made, an otherworldly pact that it was felt nothing could break. My ancestors lived for many centuries in peace and relative calm, until one day, all the evils of man resurfaced. Men began sinning in great abundance and the evil escaped its hiding place, fueled by new and even more wicked sins than it had ever witnessed before. However, after so long of being fed nothing to grow on, it had shrunk to the size of a mortal man, only a slight bit taller and misshapen. The evil began hunting and causing mayhem again. However, the evil did not kill those it hunted, it turned them into something else, something hideous, something evil, like itself.' "

" 'Well, what was that?' I asked anxiously, not having any idea that my own life was in danger. Paulo looked up and the clouds moved away from the moon and silvery silky light drifted down to us. Paulo smiled.

" 'Are you sure you wish to know?' he asked.

" 'Of course I wish to know!' I blurted out, still unaware of what was about to happen to me.

" 'So shall you be told the truth of why no one has been to this mountain in so long, so shall you know why this mountain has the reputation it does, so shall you be cursed, like those of us who live here!' "

"Paulo looked up and howled. My blood froze in my veins. It was the same howl I had heard earlier. I was frightened, frightened and stunned, but not so stunned that I didn't know I had to get out of there. I got up to run, but I fell over the log that I had been sitting on. I tried to scramble to my feet again, but Paulo pounced on me and turned me over. I looked up in horror as a great shadow blacked out the moon. Paulo had changed, not the gradual metamorphosis like Hollywood shows you in movies, but it was instantaneous, as if one of those new morphing special effects they do with movies now."

Andrew was a bit surprised by Guy's analogy of morphing scenes and transformation. He knew Guy never went to the movies, as he thought them a waste of time, so Andrew was impressed that he even knew that morphing existed in movies.

Guy continued speaking, as if not even aware that Andrew was impressed.

"One minute Paulo was human and the next, he was a werewolf; at least that was what he looked like to me. I don't know how many people have actually seen werewolves and lived to tell about it, so I am only going by what Hollywood has used as examples. I was petrified. I have seen many things in my life, things that most men could not see and live to tell about, but I had never been at the jaws of what could have been such a brutal death before, and I was nearly hysterical with fear.

"I screamed and begged Paulo to tell me what he was going to do to me. Not that it would have made much of a difference, but I wanted to know what to expect. You probably don't understand that, but anticipation of death is worse than death itself. I could have prepared myself mentally if I just could have gotten him to tell me what he planned on doing. All he did was laugh. Then he stopped laughing, which terrified me even further."

"He stated, 'You wanted knowledge! You wanted to know about the history, heritage, and culture of this area! Now you know! We are werewolves! We are the descendants of those people who had a chance at blessed immortality and instead, threw it away for carnal pleasure and riches! We are damned, pure and simple, we are damned for all eternity, as are our descendants damned, like our ancestors before us damned us. The cycle will never stop. That is the punishment inflicted upon us for the bloodline we carry!'

" 'But I have nothing to do with this! Why would you kill me? We could have sat here and ate and talked and enjoyed each other's company! Why did you feel it necessary to do this charade?' I said.

"He replied, 'Because you were told to stay away from this mountain. You were warned time and time again as you asked about town. I checked and each person I spoke with told me how they tried to warn you away, to no avail. You see, as long as the people of the town below us keep visitors away from this mountain, we leave them in peace. They serve a purpose for us, so why should we kill them? That would do us no good, as then we'd be totally defenseless against people such as you. For many years, people have not ventured up this mountain, as they listen to the old tales at the bars and in the streets, that we make sure are frightening enough to scare away even the most determined of scavengers!

" 'Each child is raised with the knowledge of what they must do when they grow into adulthood, and that is to keep our secret and this mountain safe from trespassers. Can you imagine what would happen if word were to get out about us? We'd be hounded and harangued until the day we die, and yes, we can die. Old age claims us, as it does humans, it merely takes longer. If people knew about our secret, it would be a nonstop investigation of us! We cannot allow that. We are a peaceful people and wish no one any ill will, unless they are not persuaded to leave by the stories we have fabricated, some from real events and others from our imaginations. Now, you will join the few others whom have ventured up here in search of whatever it is that you look for. You have no right to anything that we have. Our greatest treasures, what little we had has been taken from us over the years, and we barely are able to scratch out a living now. You have no right to our knowledge, you have no right to what treasures we do have left; you have no right to *anything* of ours! We have nothing and you can't take anything from nothing. You were warned, you would not listen, and now you will pay!' "

"I tried again to scramble to my feet. I would not be allowed to make amends, Paulo had made that painfully obvious, but if I could just run away, I would never go back and my knowledge-seeking days would be over. I have never believed in any type of god, but I said every prayer I had ever heard as a child, while I experienced the last moments of my life. If there is a god, He didn't listen. I was not spared. I knocked Paulo off of me and jumped to my feet, only to see shadowed shapes at the outskirts of the firelight. I knew that any escape attempt would be futile. I turned around and Paulo jumped on me with all his might, knocking me to the ground. Even though he knocked the wind from my lungs, I was determined that I would not go out without a fight, so I just began swinging blindly at him. He grabbed my wrists, both of them, in one of his huge hands and held them over my head. He bit deeply into my arm and ripped away part of the flesh. I cried out and he let me go."

"He said, 'You see, there was no need for you to fight me. Your punishment didn't have to be bad. You are punished either way. There was no need for me to kill you. I am not hungry now. Remember our dinner? That was the last human that ventured up here.' "

"I turned on my side and puked. I continued to vomit profusely, disgusted at what I had eaten. I have heard tales of cannibalism and seen evidence of it in most of my journeys, but when it happens to one's self, it is a much different feeling. Paulo simply laughed and when I looked at him again, he was Paulo. He looked up and once again, the moon had gone behind the clouds. He shrugged, smiled and walked off, leaving me bleeding and, though I didn't know it at the time, dead, as far as my humanity was concerned."

Guy stopped and wiped his eyes.

"Now you see, Andrew, you see, you know what I truly am. What I had prized above everything else about myself, my thirst for knowledge has proven to be my undoing. I feel better now that I have told you. I know that you won't tell anyone."

Andrew stared, open mouthed, at Guy.

"Of course I won't tell anyone, Guy. You're my friend! Besides, who would I tell that would believe such a story? Your secret is safe with me."

Guy smiled and stood.

"I know but that is not why I know that you won't tell anyone. You won't tell anyone because you won't live past this night to tell anyone. I'm sorry, Andrew. I did need to clear my soul and under different circumstances, I would have been interested in you writing my autobiography, but now I wish to erase you from my life. You are afraid of me. I can sense it and have for years, even before I was endowed with this power. What have you told others about me? What would you tell others about me now? I have watched your expressions as I relayed my tale. You are terrified and horrified of me.

"This was a test, Andrew, a test to prove your loyalty to me as a friend and you failed. I was afraid you would. Now you must pay. I never told you how much your friendship meant to me, but it meant everything to me. I wanted to talk to you, I wish I could have, about what I was doing back in high school and since then, but even back then you were plotting to rid yourself of me. I know it because those that came to me told me. You never saw them, no one did, but they were my real friends ... at least for a while. You were never my friend."

Andrew continued to stare open-mouthed at Guy, scarcely believing what he heard.

"Guy, I am so sorry about what happened to you. Please, please spare me. I haven't said a word about you to anyone, I swear! We have drifted apart, sure, but I never thought ill of you! No one has to know about this meeting but us. I already said that there is no one I could tell, no one that would believe such an incredible story!"

Guy shook his head.

"I'm sorry, old friend. I wish I could believe you, but I can't take that chance. It will end here tonight. I won't mutilate you, don't worry. I care too deeply for you to do something like that to you, even though you don't care for me any longer. One bite to your throat, I will tear it away, lay you on a beautiful, soft piece of ground, and you will be gone. I will spare you my fate. *At one time,* you were a good friend to me and I haven't forgotten that."

Andrew panicked. Having his throat ripped out was not what he would call being rewarded for being a good friend!

"Well, if I had been such a great friend to you, *at any point in your life*, why not spare my life? I told you, I won't tell anyone, we can go on and live like we have for our entire lives and no one has to know!"

Once again Guy shook his head. In the pale moonlight, Andrew could see tears roll down his friend's cheeks. Andrew's stomach burned so badly that he doubled over. He looked up to see Guy bearing down upon him.

"Go ahead, just kill me now if that is what you want!"

Guy's eyes were still wet.

"Just because I have to kill you, Andrew, doesn't mean that I will take any pleasure in it. You know I can't stand to see you in pain. That damned stomach of yours. I wish you had gone to the doctor about it when I asked you to so many years ago. How about you lie down here, the grass is soft and I will make it quick. I promise."

Guy forced Andrew onto his back on the ground and ran his hand over his head.

"I will miss you, Andrew, and I take absolutely no pleasure in this. It's just that you have left me no other choice. You were all I had and you betrayed me. I still care for you. If that offers you comfort, please take it and hold tightly to it."

The clouds moved and silver moonlight nearly blinded Andrew. He put his arm over his eyes and when he removed it, Guy was gone. In his place, was a snarling werewolf, who didn't even seem to recognize the man that he had shown such care to, just moments earlier.

Guy opened his mouth and began to clamp his teeth around his friend's neck. Andrew knew that his life was over and closed his eyes. He nearly gagged at the rancid emanation from his friend's dark orifice. How many people had he killed before he targeted Andrew? Suddenly howls of pain broke the night sky and Guy, or what was once Guy, fell backward off of his friend and onto the ground, writhing in pain.

Andrew reached up and caressed the necklace he wore. Had it saved his life? No, but it had always brought him immense comfort. Since he was a young man, he had worn a sterling silver, large crucifix around his neck. Guy tried to sit up, but Andrew's foot slammed him back down. He looked at the silver dagger in his hand and the large, smoking hole in his friend's chest.

Guy continued howling and thrashing as the silver seemed to torturously burn him. It didn't take long to do what it was supposed to. Contrary to the movies they had sat up and watched many times in their youth, in the hopes of scaring the hell out of each other, Guy didn't get up and come back for more, attacking and snarling like some super creature. In moments, he was dead, and where there had been a large and terrifying wolf creature lying just moments earlier, now lay a naked Guy, the same man who had, at one time, been a good friend to him.

Guy's chest was decimated and Andrew turned his head. The sight of his friend's melted and burned body made him very ill. His lifeless eyes stared up at the full moon that bathed them both. Except this time there would be no transformation, no morphing, nothing. Guy was dead and no amount of moonlight could or would change that.

Andrew sank to his knees and sobbed, gently closing Guy's dead, cold eyes. He sobbed for what he had to do.

"I'm so sorry, Guy. I'm so sorry. I never told you what happened when my father died. I never told anyone. You never knew my lineage ... and neither did I until he died. A burden, a terrible burden was thrust upon my shoulders, but in the essence of family history and respecting my roots, which are firmly entrenched in the 'Old Country', I had no choice but to do what I was born to do, as my father before me did and as *his* father before him did. Werewolf hunters have been in my family for generations! I know you didn't know that, but you grew up around my father ... we used to laugh at his tall tales as we thought they were. He was telling us, Guy, he was warning us and giving me a glimpse into what lay ahead for me. He spoke of the old ways, the old magic, the old powers, and when he died, my mother told me that those powers were a part of my family and a part of me!"

Andrew screamed at Guy's lifeless body in anger and in sadness.

"Why didn't you just come to me? Why did you have to play this game with me? Had I known that this was the hell you had been living with, I would have put you out of your misery a long time ago. No one should have to endure what you did. I'm just sorry that I couldn't help you."

Andrew sobbed harder as he realized that this whole game, this cruel, and unholy thing that Guy had done, was maybe his way of crying out for help. He had to have known that Andrew would help him, but maybe he didn't want help. Maybe he wanted release but was too afraid to ask for it. Maybe he was afraid to be alone. It made Andrew heartsick to have to kill his friend, even though it was the right thing to do. Guy's tortured soul was finally at peace.

It was dirty, it was underhanded, and it was unfair what Guy did to Andrew, but if he had simply asked Andrew for his help, he would have told Guy his story and then killed him mercifully and with great respect. Andrew could not help but wish that his old friend had showed that kind of faith in him, to trust him, to ask him if he could help instead of deceiving him and using the autobiography as an excuse to trick him to the cemetery. Maybe Guy thought it would be easier for Andrew to die in a place he liked? Instead, it was Andrew who ended up fulfilling the first of his heritage's burdens and he hated it.

He had not been prepared, as he honestly had no idea that Guy was a werewolf. He had simply been very lucky that his station in life now dictated that he carry the special knife with him at any and all costs, no matter how he had to travel to avoid detection or the authorities.

Andrew dressed Guy in his tattered clothing and laid him gently on a soft, grassy knoll. He knew that someone would find him. The crew that took care of the cemetery during the daytime hours would be in, in only a few short hours and they would find him.

Andrew took one last look at his friend and wiped his eyes.

"Goodbye, Guy. May you finally rest in peace."

Andrew turned his back to the moon and to his dead friend. He would leave him slumbering peacefully in the soft grass. It was what Guy deserved. After all, he would have done the same for him, wouldn't he?

About the Author

Andrea Dean Van Scoyoc is a best selling, award winning Horror Sinisteria author. The very popular but sadistic brains behind such hit novels as *The Two* and *A Man of Two Worlds* (which won the 2005 Preditors and Editors Horror Novel of The Year) her newest novel *Michael* already has fans up in arms and clamoring to get their hands on it.

'A force of nature' as she has been called, Andrea has in just a short amount of time since her arrival into the world as a first time author in April of 2005 managed to do what many other authors will not be able to do in a lifetime of writing.

Please visit Andrea on her website at:
http://thelosttheforgottenthedamned.com
and look for her at the many conventions she does a year.

Drop by and say 'hello' if you do see her. She doesn't bite …very much.

The idea for this story came on a cold November day, hence the title. I simply love atmosphere, and what is bleaker than the encroaching winter? What if you disappeared and no one missed you? What if you were a nice person, but alone, unremarkable, as most of us are, just a face, a casual friend ...

In this story, you might become one of the November Girls.

NOVEMBER GIRLS
By Katherine Smith

It was a dismal day. Fearful clouds scuttled across a tarnished sky and skidded into the dark horizon. There was rain, cold and thin, tingling on the skin and chilling the bones. The wind whispered past, sounding as mournful as I felt.

Two blocks of walking had cold water running under my collar and dribbling down my neck. My sodden shoes made disgusting noises as I slogged along the drenched sidewalk. What with the usual turmoil at the office, it hadn't been my day all the way around, and I grimaced as a small hole in my umbrella allowed a light mist to dust my face.

Perfect.

The doorway was warm, welcoming. It beckoned with jewels of light behind glass doors. The rich smell of coffee and yeast wafted outward as a man came out of the door, his collar turned upward against the inhospitable evening. My stomach, deprived since an inadequate lunch, answered that blissful odor with unadulterated pangs of pure, lustful hunger.

It wasn't much of a decision to go inside the cafe. The two remaining blocks of squelching along in the cold would be more palatable after some warmth and refreshment. Setting aside my dripping coat and ineffectual umbrella, I slid gratefully into a small booth and shook out my damp hair. *Mocha Java*? I wondered in furtive ecstasy, or espresso? Sugar, cream, the works. Maybe even hot chocolate. To hell with the diet.

"Charlie?"

The place was small, cozy, upscale. The polished tables were set in corners among hanging ferns and glass partitions. This illusion of privacy made me start at the sound of my own name.

A girl moved into my line of vision, standing by the side of my table. I hadn't noticed her when I came in, but I hadn't exactly been looking either. She still wore her coat, long and rain-spotted, so it was possible she had come in right after me. I blinked at her in some surprise, feeling I should know her.

"Charlie." She said again, quite softly, tentatively, as if she was worried she'd made a mistake.

"Yes." I cleared my throat a bit uncomfortably. My given name is Charlotte. People who know me well call me Charlie.

"You don't recognize me, do you?" The question was wistful, spoken carefully into the spice-perfumed air. She stood facing me, her damp coat hanging from slim, dispirited shoulders.

Blessedly, revelation came just as the moment stretched toward total awkwardness. I said quickly, "Of course, I do. Megan. From the office. How are you?"

"Okay, I guess. I don't like the rain much, though. It seems to go right through you, doesn't it?" She smiled slightly, feigning a shiver. "Fancy running into you. I saw you coming down the street and knew you at once. I just thought I would stop and say hello."

"It's great to see you," I replied, just a shade too heartily. Megan Watson had been a passing acquaintance, just another secretary, like myself, at the huge and impersonal insurance company where we worked. She'd quit some months back and apparently moved on to greener pastures.

She stood, in dripping eloquence by the side of my table. Pale, blond, with thin hands and light blue eyes, she was unremarkable, but pleasant enough. I'd liked her, or at least hadn't *disliked* her, during the time we'd worked together.

"Sit down," I didn't mind suggesting, "and have a cup of something with me. I was just about to order."

This idea seemed to please her, for she sat, taking off her coat with those white, ethereal hands. Underneath, she wore a blue silk dress, sheer hose, and black pumps more suitable for later in the evening. In the warm glow of the lamps, she was paler than I remembered, with small hollows under her eyes. I thought privately that she looked ill, and wondered briefly if some sort of ailment had caused her to have to quit work.

The waitress sidled up and took my order of Irish coffee with extra whipped cream. Megan Watson simply shook her head.

"Have something," I said, feeling generous. "My treat. Really."

The blond hair brushed quietly across her shoulders. "No, but thank you. I'll just sit for a minute while you have yours. I really just wanted to talk for a minute or two. Just catch up a bit on things. You know."

Shrugging, the waitress went off.

There was a brief, somewhat uncomfortable silence. I said, "So what have you been doing since you left Life Mutual? We were all a little surprised when you quit."

"Were you?" She arched her eyebrows, pulling her small face into a frown. "I didn't really quit, you know. I suppose Mrs. White was angry that I just stopped coming to work."

"Mrs. White's words were unrepeatable." I grinned, remembering. Mrs. White was a strict old bitch, hard to work for and thoroughly unlikable. As far as I remembered, Megan had left work on Friday with her paycheck in hand and never came back. Job abandonment meant three days of no show, no call. Job abandonment was as good as not having the guts to quit without notice.

"She was pretty ticked." I admitted as my drink arrived, and I lifted a spoon to taste the creamy froth on top. "Why didn't you give notice? She'll blast every request for a recommendation she gets."

"Did she try to call me?" Megan asked, leaning slightly forward as if it mattered, and ignored my question.

I didn't know. I lifted my shoulders as a response. "Maybe not. She considers it a privilege to be allowed to work for her. The old bat." My drink was warm and comforting. My companion watched me delve into the cream and liquor with interested eyes.

"I've wondered a bit if anyone at the office had tried to get in touch with me. I know I only worked there for a short while, but I was making some friends." Her tone went soft and a bleak note crept into her voice. "Like you. I felt we had a lot in common. Remember when we had lunch downtown at Tony's?"

I barely remembered. Megan had been part of a group of us girls. All I knew we had in common was that we were both single, lived alone, and apparently hated cold, rainy nights. Somewhat embarrassed at her insistence on a friendship that was barely more than superficial. I lifted my cup and took a mouthful as I nodded, negating a need to answer. There was something about her whole demeanor that suggested a deep, needy loneliness that made me want to squirm in my seat.

She said with compelling earnestness, "Do you want to know why I never came back to Life Mutual?"

I didn't really. I just wanted to finish my drink and go back out into the rain. My own life was complicated enough without trying to solve someone else's problems and insecurities. Regrets about past mistakes were a dime a dozen.

"I met someone," she told me. "A man."

Not much of a surprise. A story as old as time. "Oh?" I murmured.

She sat there, so pale and fair, her thinness emphasized by the drape of her dark dress. A bland girl, nearly nondescript, nice enough but not memorable. She seemed to read my thoughts, for her eyelids flickered slightly. "His name was Rick. Rick Jones. I met him at a nightclub downtown. The Hill Street Pub. One of the girls at the office told me about it."

"And he promised to take you away from the hallowed halls of Life Mutual?" I made it sound like a joke, but neither of us smiled. By the time you're in your late twenties and unmarried, that phantom lover, the one with the sincere smile and good job, takes on the aura of legend. You just begin to doubt his existence.

Her smile was brittle. The fern hanging behind her shoulder loomed like a leering, bearded giant. "In fact, he did take me away."

"I guess he did." I agreed, "Did it not work out?" My coffee was nearly gone.

Megan said mournfully, "He wasn't the man I thought he was."

"They never are." My agreement was cynical. The cold rain still drizzled downward outside. I lifted my glass, drained the contents, and managed a decent social smile. "Well, it's been good to see you, Megan, but I've got to run. My car's still two blocks away and I'm dying to get these shoes off my feet."

She hesitated, then asked simply, "Could you maybe give me a lift home? It isn't too far."

I suppose I could have refused. But even as I stood and opened my mouth, I saw in Megan Watson's desperate gaze something that reminded me a little of myself. Of my empty dark apartment. Of my life going to and from work. I wasn't all that different in some ways. I might even believe the empty promises of an unreliable lover.

"Sure," I said with false brightness.

She stood as I fumbled with the money for the bill, donned her coat and silently followed me out of the restaurant like a small, insignificant shadow.

She directed me to follow Washington Street to the east, and I did so until the blurry outlines of rain-drenched houses and street lamps gave way to scattered farmhouses and dark, silent fields. Her definition of 'not far' certainly didn't jibe with my own, but for the same reason I hadn't refused her a ride, I said nothing.

Her profile was more darkness than light, and occasionally I caught the gleam of a white cheek or pale jaw as she sat next to me without speaking. Finally, about fifteen miles out of town, I had to ask, "How much farther?"

"Not far," she whispered. "Just ahead."

Her tone was so soft that I frowned at the slick expanse of road, her pallor and bleak expression still distressingly vivid in my mind. "Do you live alone?"

"No, I stay with another girl." I had the impression of a sidelong glance my direction.

"I've never been able to get along with a roommate for long." I said lamely, making conversation. Her stillness and silence were disturbing.

"We were kind of thrown together. Mere chance," Megan said slowly.

"Do you like her?" I asked curiously. The oblique line of our conversation was slightly irritating.

"I can't quite say. We're two of a kind, I guess." She might have shrugged. I wasn't sure.

She directed me to a turn off the main highway, and then to turn again. I drove now in complete silence, eager to be rid of my depressing friend.

The night was utterly dark except for the silver pellets of rain glinting in my headlights. The country road wound through dead fields of battered, rotting corn and empty rows of dirt. Here and there, we would pass dark, gathered bunches of trees at the edges of the fields. Farmhouses were far and between.

I kept to silence like a drowning man hangs onto a piece of driftwood. I actually jumped when she finally said, "Stop here."

"Here?" I asked, braking automatically, peering into the darkness. Trees lined either side of the road like an army of dark soldiers, quietly holding bare branches aloft like skeletal arms. I searched for the presence of a driveway even as I dubiously brought the car to a stop on the road. There was no light in sight.

"Where's the house?" I couldn't help but ask as my companion slid out of the car.

She didn't answer. The door shut with a dull thud. I watched incredulously as she walked away from me and faded into the slender ghosts of the trees.

I'm not sure why I got out of the car. Certainly it wasn't because I didn't mind my damp, aching feet. It wasn't because I was anxious to stay on that lonely road in full dark while it rained steadily outside and the temperature dropped degree by degree. It must have been because I couldn't reconcile driving away and leaving Megan Watson in the middle of nowhere in the middle of the night.

I was curious, too. Curious in a shivery, half-sick, disbelieving kind of way. The whole encounter had been strange and off-key.

It was very quiet. Water dripped in a chorus of liquid and darkness. The clump of trees thinned away on my right, but to the left, where she had gone, it was thick and black with hanging shadows. It was a desolate spot, and as I stood shivering on that road, I knew there was no house.

Megan Watson had disappeared.

Mrs. White had not tried to call Megan Watson to ask why she wasn't coming to work. When I asked, I was treated to a freezing stare and a lecture on the importance of work ethics among those my age. I don't know why I bothered.

Actually, I do. I bothered because Megan had seemed anxious over whether anyone had wanted to find out why she wasn't coming to work any longer. I bothered because my encounter with Megan bothered *me*.

I even got her address from the old employee address book and called her apartment complex. The man at the desk only vaguely remembered her, and would tell me next to nothing. However, I got the distinct impression she'd skipped out on her rent as well as her job. That, I told myself, explained the air of desperation. That explained the lingering persuasive aura of isolation and dejection. Burned bridges were difficult to repair. If Megan had given up on her job, abandoned her apartment, and all-around changed her life for some loser who turned out to be Mr. Wrong, no wonder she was glad to see a friendly face. Maybe, I convinced myself for most of the next day, there had been a house somewhere in the gloomy patch of woods where I'd dropped her off. Maybe I had just missed it. Maybe the roommate hadn't been home and no lights were on.

Maybe.

I left work early on the pretext of a headache. It didn't matter much to the company; I'd spent most of my morning trying to track down information on Megan Watson anyway.

The weather was better. Marginally. I drove the same route I'd followed the night before, viewing the banal landscape with a jaundiced eye. It was cold and dark gray with the threat of more rain we didn't need. White clouds puffed up into a leaden sky and a thin wind wailed softly past my car.

I had some difficulty finding the spot. In daylight, everything looks different, and instead of ominous shadows and afflicted countryside, I saw the plain downtrodden fields of Indiana under a dull November sky. It was flat, and it was dead, but it didn't scare me or fill me with foreboding.

What in the darkness had seemed a formidable patch of woods, proved to be nothing more than two hundred yards of trees lining the road, perhaps as thick as it was long. The area was farmed on both sides, and there was a house in sight, though it was far down the road. I parked in a small clear patch next to the road, and got out to breathe the persuasive aroma of decaying leaves and damp soil.

My footsteps made little noise on the sodden ground as I walked into the shelter of the trees. The ground was ankle-deep in wet leaves and dying fern, the fetid smell rising with every sinking footstep. I wandered in a few yards, my shoulders hunched against the chilly air, not knowing what I was looking for or why I had come. More puzzling was – why had Megan gotten out of the car at this particular spot? There was nothing to be seen, no place to go.

The wind sighed past. I felt cold, and vaguely angry, as if I'd been made a fool of, though I wasn't sure how. Walking back a little farther, I could see the fields past the trees, and more trees and fields in the distance. "Stupid," I called myself out loud, but my voice was lost in the silence.

Turning to leave, I took exactly two steps before I saw it. Then I stopped dead, feeling a cold much deeper than the November temperature seep into my bones and freeze my heart.

Almost at my feet was a delicate sculpture of arched ivory, the thin, bleached rib bones sticking out of the shifting autumn leaves. The skull was there too, but a bit to the side, as if coyly shy and turned away. The teeth gleamed dully in the obscure light. I had the impression of some tatters of dark material, maybe blue, amid the wet leaves cradling the skeleton.

I took several small stumbling steps backward, my breath rising in a great gusty cloud.

I'd found where Megan Watson was staying after all.

As weird as it was, I could not tell the police the truth. Mumbling something ridiculous about gathering fall leaves for my niece's school project was the best I could do. That didn't seem to raise too many eyebrows, though it was usually hunters that found bodies decaying in the woods, they told me.

Yes, bodies. As Megan had said, she was staying with another girl. That particular corpse, I learned later, had been there longer than Megan. *Just thrown together. Two of a kind.* She had told the perfect truth.

Two victims of the same man. Two tumbled remains rotting in harmony. Two of the forgotten, unmissed by the world.

I went to work the next day. What else was there to do? I didn't want Mrs. White to assume I'd left my position and replace me.

I didn't want to be forgotten. I didn't want to be passed over with a shrug. *We have a lot in common*, Megan had told me. If I disappeared tomorrow, would anyone look for me? Would effort be expended to find out where I had gone, or why?

I walked past the café after work, feeling loneliness like a stone weighing in my chest. Bleary streetlights winked through a misty gray twilight.

On impulse, I turned back and went inside.

Gone was the warm welcoming feeling of the other night. I edged my way into a booth and stared at my cold hands.

If I was waiting for a ghost girl to materialize, I was disappointed. Instead, the waitress stumped over and asked me what I wanted to drink.

I ordered Irish coffee again. Heavy on the liquor, I suggested with a shaky smile.

"Sure." Scribbling on her pad, she turned away.

"Hey," I called, "wait."

"Yeah?" Her disinterested glance flicked back to me.

"I was in here just the other night." I said hoarsely. "I sat here, in this booth. You waited on me."

"So?" Bored eyebrows went upward.

"A girl sat with me. She didn't order anything. A blond. Thin, kind of plain. Do you remember her?" I had to know. Had to ask. Had the illusion been mine alone?

The waitress laughed, pushing her hair off her forehead with a careless hand. "Honey," she said, "I don't even remember you."

November Girls first appeared in Potpourri Magazine, 2000 volume #12.

Can evil exist in an object we know to be alive, but to us is inanimate? I think it is a fascinating question, and it definitely led to the conception of The Tree. Is there true evil in the giant oak? Or are the characters just weak and seem to blame their flaws on some mysterious, primal power?

I invite you to read it for yourself and find out.

THE TREE
By Katherine Smith

"What a mess," said the woman standing next to him in the dusty driveway.

It was. He had to silently acknowledge her biting words. The house had slid insidiously toward total dilapidation: sagging gutters, crumbling shutters, flaking paint on walls dry with age and neglect. The inevitable advance of mildew and lichen crept across the old brick foundation like some progressive disease and the stench of last year's rotting leaves rose like a malevolent spirit.

How many years since he'd been there?

His boyhood seemed far past, farther than a barely recalled dream, like a dim shadow of a story he'd once heard and only half-remembered. He'd been young when he last visited the farm, barely a man, newly married, ignorant of what waited in his future.

A muffled laugh escaped his lips, torn from somewhere deep inside. It surprised him – that laugh – and it surprised his wife, who turned and stared with typical disapproval, her eyes narrowed and her lips slack and dry. He could see the tiny lines of age incised beside her mouth and nose, and the open holes of her pores glistening with mid-afternoon sweat. Her hair, once brown and thick, was now gray and lackluster, stuck like wire to her head.

"What's so funny?" she demanded. "This hovel you've inherited? I say laugh if you want, but it's all we've got."

Her head swung away and she started to walk off, shoes crunching the dry, unkempt grass as she headed for the front porch. He almost didn't catch the mutter as she moved slowly away, "Thanks to you."

It didn't flay him. Stinging words of contempt for his failures had long since lost their power to hurt him, as do all things of repetition. A human being can get used to almost anything of habit, even degradation. The old woman tramping angrily toward the wreck of his family home had no more power to wound him, no weapons of destruction. He wasn't sure what disgusted him more, her flabby, faded figure as she picked across the rabble of dead weeds and profaned grass, or the humiliating decay of the old house. His life, the life he'd once envisioned with hope and joy, had come to this. A crumbling old farmhouse, a bitter old wife he had never loved, and poverty to haunt his last years.

He was no longer capable of crying. A curious thickness grew in his throat but never reached his stinging eyes. The only thing alive, the only thing of beauty in the squalid surroundings, was the old oak tree in the corner by the far side of the house.

He'd forgotten it, or tried to forget. Standing there in the simmering heat of Indiana high summer, he was struck by memories, some good, some unwanted and terrifying. The past crowded close, impishly peering over his shoulder, laughing at his age and ill health.

His wife gained the porch and gingerly climbed the

creaking steps, turning to put her hand above her eyes and squint at him. "Are you going to stand there all day like a tired old fool?"

The smell of rot was acrid, strong, familiar. He obediently started across the grass, instinctively skirting the edge of shadow thrown by the huge old tree.

He remembered that much.

That night, he became a boy again. He lay in his narrow bed against the peeling wall of his old room, his breath soft and sweet out of his mouth, his eyes closed tightly against the dark.

Tap. Tap. Tap.

He heard the insistent call, a rapping at the tall undressed window, and all the old dread flooded back into his heart and limbs as if it were a half-century earlier. If he opened his eyes, he knew what he would see.

His lids were heavy, his childish heart pumping wildly.

Turning his head a fraction, he forced himself to look at the grimy glass. There was moonlight, but not enough, and his eyes were not what they used to be.

Tap. Tap. Tap.

Long thin branches from the old oak touched his window, as if begging him to answer the summons. Long, whippy branches with pointed ends, like evil nails on thin, emaciated fingers.

Drawing deep ragged breaths against the pain in his chest, he peered at the darkness beyond the glass. The tree remembered, he knew. It had waited these years, patient with the endurance of ancient life, and it had won. He was back. The cycle could begin again.

No, he agonized.

Tap. Tap. Tap.

If he just would open that window, as he should have done years ago, those wicked fingers would absolve his suffering. He could almost see them twining around his wife's scrawny neck and choking her life away. Sliding through his open window and sinking into her flesh like supple, deadly creatures.

He shivered in fear and anticipation.

Tap. Tap. Tap.

His eggs were lumpy and cold. He ate stolidly, chewing very slowly, his eyes focused on the chipped gray plastic top of the old kitchen table. His wife moved at the sink, fat feet thrust into soiled house slippers, her old robe carelessly worn over a faded nightgown.

The morning was hot and still, and the place stank of dirt and mold.

"I want to cut down the tree." He said the words quietly, lifting his coffee cup to his lips.

"What?" Turning around with a dripping plate in her hand, his wife looked astonished. "What are you talking about?"

"The oak tree. If we're going to have to live here, I want to cut it down"

"You're crazy." The plate drooled soapy water onto the floor, leaving a muddy puddle in the filth. "Your grandmother let this place fall to dust and we have no money to repair it. How could you want to destroy the only thing that gives this run-down ruin any value? That tree is hundreds of years old!"

Hundreds of years. It frightened him to think of how long

that tree had stood on the land he now owned. His hand trembled as he lowered his cup and gently set it on the marred surface of the table. "The house needs to be cleaned and painted, that's all. I don't want the tree."

Her quivering indignation slumped suddenly into contemptuous understanding. "Are you that superstitious, old man? Are you against the tree because of that old tragedy? That was years ago, before you were even born. I never knew you had so much imagination."

Tragedy, yes. It had been a tragedy when his grandfather had hung himself from the branches of the tree. The Great Depression had ruined him and driven him to seek solace in a rope and a high place. It was something his family had always spoken of in hushed tones of shame. He stared at his cup.

That wasn't the only story, of course. Just the only one she knew.

"Besides," a shrug lifted the shoulders under her old snagged robe, "it's hardly the fault of the tree that your grandfather was so weak and foolish. It runs in the family."

Foolish. He wondered.

"My sister tripped on one of the roots and broke her leg," he murmured, remembering, "and once a branch fell off and nearly killed my father while he was cutting the grass." His father had ended up dead anyway, not many months afterwards. One could hardly blame the tree for a German bullet.

But there was Albert, too. He never spoke of it.

His grandfather had died. His father had died. Albert had gone the same way. His grandmother was now dead, and the tree belonged to him. Troubled, he got to his feet abruptly and left the kitchen.

It was stiflingly hot outside. Weeds bent under his feet and slapped his legs as he walked over and stood perhaps fifty feet from the tree. It was a venerable specimen: tall, leafy, wide-branched, with a solid twisted trunk. A large knot about twenty feet up peered from the masses of greenery. That knot always reminded him of a human face in the throes of agony, with a gaping mouth and sightless eyes.

It was just a tree. God's gift to the earth, bringing shade and color and life.

But not one of the leafy branches, wide as they were, reached anywhere near his bedroom window. Not even with the passage of years, as far away as the tree sat, did the branches grow close enough to touch his window.

Yet night after night, since childhood, the tree had implored him to come. It whispered Albert's name to him in the dark.

Despite the summer heat, his shoulders hunched against a shiver.

They had been young – what – ten? He and Albert playing in the yard, tossing a ball back and forth like boys do, laughing and scuffing about in the grass.

It had been Albert – he was almost sure of it – who suggested they climb the tree. Albert, quick and clever and strong, had scrambled up to the lowest branches and extended a hand. "Come on."

He'd gone, of course. Albert always knew the best games. Albert, who had been his friend since they both could walk. Never mind that Albert was bigger and smarter. He'd never been jealous of Albert, no matter what people said.

So they'd climbed, laughing, up the tree until the limbs thinned and bent. He could still smell the sharp odor of bark and leaf, and hear Albert panting as he hurried to be first. To be best.

Not jealous. No. And he knew he had reached out to Albert to help steady him, not to push him.

The memory was vivid. Like yesterday. Cracking branches as the boy fell and bounced and screamed in pain. Killed outright of a broken neck by the time he reached the bottom. An accident.

An awful, tragic accident.

It was hot just standing in the sun. Like that day long ago.

Behind him, a voice said stiffly: "I can't believe you're really thinking of this, Jack. I can't. You aren't being practical, not that that should surprise me after all these years…"

He hated her voice, he thought. He hated it. Why had she followed him outside?

"Besides, you can't cut it down; it's too big, and God knows you have nothing to pay someone to do it for you."

Unmoving, he stood.

Evidently sensing her pleas were futile, his wife tried a different tack, coming forward so she stood beside him. "The tree doesn't represent bad memories to me, Jack." Her voice dropped to a cloying tone she hadn't bothered to use in many years. "Remember, you proposed to me under that tree. I couldn't stand for you to cut it down."

He remembered. It had been summer, and hot like this day, only nearer to dusk. At the same time every day, she would walk up the road, going slowly past the house. Her mother was just a cleaning lady at the Lutheran church and they said in town that she was *ambitious*, but he'd been young then. He had known she walked past on purpose, and as any young man, he was flattered, but his heart lay elsewhere. Yet every summer evening the cleaning lady's daughter walked past the farm and he had smiled at her.

She had taken to leaning on the gate and chatting with him, all above board and very polite, because it was well known that he had proposed to another girl and had been accepted.

How different his life could have been.

But somehow, one evening, he had invited her past the gate. Not to sit on the porch, as he normally did, but to sit in the shadows under the old tree. It was incredible to him now that he could have been so foolish, so easily led, but it had happened. He'd sat next to her as the dusk thickened toward night and somehow he had kissed her, put his hand under her skirts, and forgotten his future.

She had welcomed him with a sly joyous triumph, giving him her virginity under that tree, with his mother and grandmother just inside the house and the bats swirling slowly in the dark. Her smell had been wrong, and the texture of her skin, and the feel of her hair, but he'd done it anyway.

And then the reckoning. With poor Amy crying and him having to explain his folly with shame-faced honesty. That one act had cost him a lifetime.

His grandfather. Albert. His marriage. The tree had a lot to answer for.

His eyes moved involuntarily to the woman at his side. In the pitiless sunlight her scalp shone through her rusty hair, and the hard wrinkles under her eyes looked like soft leather. His manful decision to marry her had brought him no accolades from any side, and he had spent a slow lifetime with a hard scheming woman who neither loved him, nor gave him charity.

Something, some ghost of generosity or humanity, kept his tongue still. He wanted so much to right the hurt of a hundred wrongs by telling her the truth: that he had never wanted to marry her, or live with her, or spend his last years in her company. The tree was an abomination to him, and their unfortunate coupling those many years ago only added to his loathing of it.

Instead, he said calmly, "Yes, my dear. Perhaps you're right. The tree is a lovely thing, and I'm sure it adds value to this property."

Her relief was purely venal; he knew that. But the effect was the same. She turned in satisfaction and left him alone, stomping back toward the kitchen.

How sad they were, he mused wearily, trapped together by necessity and habit.

A slow breeze fluttered past his shoulder, touching the bright leaves of the oak tree. They whispered in response to the moving air, hushed voices carrying otherworldly tones into the hot, oppressive morning.

It was dark. It had to be dark, because otherwise she might stop him, or call someone to stop him. Her observation about cutting down the tree had made good sense; he saw that now, and he abandoned all thoughts of getting rid of it in such a fashion.

Instead, he had gone to town and spent several precious dollars on a can of gasoline.

He believed, in that torrid darkness, in the existence of evil. *I believe*, he chanted to himself, *that evil can inhabit a man, or a dog, or a scrap of earth. I believe it can sink bone-deep into the living core of a tree, and reside there.*

His actions affirmed his belief. He poured gasoline on the snake-like roots of the tree, and on the thick trunk, dashing it quickly and recklessly, as if in fear the tree would realize his plan and retaliate.

That finished, he stepped back and fished in his pocket for a packet of matches.

The pulse of shrilling insects filled the night air as he scraped the match. An odd triumph filled his body and he stood, flaring match in hand, his throat tight and hot with emotion.

The tree had stood for hundreds of years; how many lives had it taken in sacrifice? By fire, he could purge the sins and return peace to the only place on Earth left to him.

There wasn't a choice.

Giant branches quivered above his head. The leaves fluttered restively. *Do it*, he told himself woodenly, *just do it. Toss the match.*

The ghosts of his father and grandfather pressed him to do it. Albert called his name.

Oddly, he found himself turning to look at the house. Was it really the fault of the tree he was so miserable? Was it the tree, or his ugly sniping wife, the one who had deliberately trapped him into marriage and then became discontent with her trophy?

He hated her.

He hated *her*, not the tree. Hated with the same intensity he'd felt that day when Albert had reached the top first and jeered with typical triumph.

Incredibly, the match left his fingers in a perfect, thoughtless arc, not landing at the base of the tree, but on the dry dusty front porch of the old rotting house.

Fascinated, he watched as it smoldered and smoked, and then eventually came to life with bright licks of flame. Tinder-like, the porch was fodder for that hungry orange life.

What had he done? He knew better than to listen to the tree.

He sprang forward, tripping over the gasoline can and sprawling headlong in the dry grass. Was it the can? Had the tree tripped him? Heaving himself up, he stumbled toward the house, hearing the hiss and cry of fire, his mind's eye conjuring images of smoldering corpses and raging ghosts.

Hurry, hurry, hurry. The porch was ablaze, so he ran to the side door. As his hand touched the knob, the first pain came. Searing through his chest, knifing past his shoulder blades.

More pains, one after the other, until they became one. His body flailed at the wood of the door, clawing as darkness descended.

At that last moment, he felt the tree bending over him, triumphant, branches moving, leaves sighing, as if fascinated by yet another death.

"The Tree" first appeared in *Night Terrors*, June 2001 and is reprinted with the permission of the author, Abigail Brace.

About the Author

Katherine Smith is the award-winning author of seven novels and numerous short stories. Her short work has appeared in *Night Terrors*, *Crossroads*, *Potpourri*, *Hate: an Anthology of Mystery and Murder*, and the 2007 Eppies finalist for best horror, *Fear: an Anthology of Horror and Suspense*. Please visit her at http://www.katherinesmith.net

I was inspired by Clive Barker's ideas on Harlequins from his 'A-Z of Horror.' The harlequin (that is, clown) has the luck to be creepy, evil and darkly funny all at the same time. And they can get away with murder, too. How cool is that?

CLOWN SCHOOL
By J. Edward Tremlett

As far as Bill was concerned, there was no drive worse than the one that took his teenage daughter to or from her private academy.

It wasn't the long drive, up and down lonely, tree-shrouded roads to Michigan's Upper Peninsula, just over the Wisconsin border. It wasn't even that his ex-wife insisted he take the time to drive Sheila, or she wouldn't pay half the cost. And it wasn't the boredom, the sullen silence or the fights over what little radio they could get.

It was because his daughter made him hate her, his ex-wife and himself in near-equal measure.

"... stupid bitch thinks she's so smart," Sheila complained about her roommate, while pulling her long, brown hair through her brush. It was the first time she'd been able to have it down since school started.

"Maybe she is?" Bill offered. "How's *your* report card going to look?"

"She's only at Holbrook because her daddy's some ambassador," Sheila replied, avoiding an answer, "he doesn't want her 'mixing' with the kids where they live."

"Aren't they living in New York?"

"New York isn't all bad, Dad."

"New York is a pit, honey," Bill said, adjusting his glasses. "That's why we went to Chi-town."

"That turned out to be a pit, too."

Bill groused; he knew what was coming next, but was powerless to stop it.

"Not at all what it was like when you were a kid, huh?" she went on, no longer brushing her hair.

"Places change—"

"Besides, Mom's in New York."

"Your mom and I get along fine," Bill lied. "The job was what was important."

"Yeah, and then I try to make the best of it and—"

"Shut up," Bill said, exasperated already.

"I am so sick and tired of this shit," she hissed.

"That makes two of us, dear."

"You send me off to that stupid school so you don't have to be around me—"

"Now, we've talked about this—"

"You've *lied* about it! I don't need to go to some private academy! You just don't want me to hang out with my friends."

"They aren't your friends, Sheila. They're a bunch of losers. And if you hang out with losers, you're going to become one."

"*Fuck you!*" Sheila yelled.

Bill stomped on the brakes, pulled the car over into the ditch, and slapped Sheila across the face. She didn't even cry out. It was as though he hadn't done anything at all.

"Are you done?" he asked, red-faced and frustrated, not knowing what else to do or say.

"They're. My. Friends." Sheila repeated, still not crying from the slap. But she glared at him.

And when she did, the resemblance between her and her mother was uncanny – right down to the green eyes they somehow shared. Bill somehow fought back the desire to hit her again and again and kept talking.

"Half of your friends are on drugs. The other half just want to screw you."

"It's not like that—"

"Yes, it *is*. And if I have to send you all the way up to the U.P. to keep you away from them…"

"So it wasn't just for a good education, huh?" she shot back, catching him in his own words.

"That's not … it isn't—"

"Way to go, Dad. At least Mom tells me the truth."

Bill might have slapped her again, but if he started, he wouldn't stop. So he turned around, put his hands on the wheel, and started counting from twenty backwards, in his head.

"I want to talk to Mom," Sheila flatly stated when he got to ten.

"Not on my phone, you don't."

"Then as soon as we see a phone, I want to talk to Mom."

"I'm not paying for it."

"She gave me a phone card."

Bill looked at her and sighed. "Okay, fine. Next phone we see, I'll pull over."

"Yes," Sheila said, crossing her arms over her chest. "You do that, Dad."

He stomped on the gas as hard as he'd stomped on the brakes, and the car lurched out of the breakdown lane, spraying a thin cloud of gravel as it went.

Bill knew, deep down inside, that he must have done something wrong to deserve all this. Why else would his wife just decide to leave him after almost fifteen years of marriage? Why else would she have been having affairs for some time before she called a lawyer?

Bill had no idea. All he knew was that, in less than a week, almost everything he'd worked for was either gone or freefalling out of his control.

To round it all out, his usually keen lawyer completely bungled what should have been a favorable divorce. After all was said and done, Bill had lost all of his ex-wife's money, half of his own and both of their cars. His ex even got to keep the apartment she 'didn't want, anymore' just so she could sell it to someone who would.

She did leave him one thing, though – their daughter. Bill begged his ex to agree to joint custody, believing that Sheila needed both parents (which she did). But she refused, saying that she didn't want to be restrained in her quest to 'find herself.'

The years that followed had not been very kind. A transfer to Chi-town was not what had been promised, but he couldn't leave the company without breaking a strict non-competition clause. Their 'upscale' neighborhood turned sour, which was a large part of why Sheila was being sent off to school. And her grades had been so poor that her secluded pit of an 'exclusive' girl's school was the only good place that would take her.

Worse still, Sheila blamed Bill for what had happened to the marriage. His ex had set their daughter against him, using her increasingly infrequent phone calls to fill her ears with poison. And what could Bill really say in his defense?

So Bill went on, wiping the crap from his eyes with each new bad piece of news. His daughter resented him for what he'd had to do. His ex was happy to feed her lies and hate. The more Bill hated his daughter for becoming his ex-wife, the more he hated himself for feeling that way. And an empty, angry darkness behind his eyes screamed for release.

Something had to break, somewhere; he told himself that every morning as he counted the lines around his eyes, the gray in his thinning hair and the inches around his waist. He affirmed it every time he got another thankless assignment at the office or another harsh rejection at a bar. It had become his catechism as the bills mounted, the funds dwindled and his wife found yet another barely-legal way to weasel out of child support.

Something *had* to break. Bill just had to wait until the world was done making him shovel shit. Maybe there'd be a pony there, after all.

"I'm starving," Sheila said about five miles down the road. So far all they'd passed in their quest for a pay phone was a moldering shotgun shack and a closed-down gas station.

"So am I," Bill replied, grateful to talk about something pleasant. "What you hungry for?"

"What we got?"

"We passed a whole row of stuff in the last town."

"Which is, like, way back that way," Sheila cocked a thumb at the road behind. "What's up ahead?"

"I don't know."

The road turned to the left, the woods widened away from it, and there on the right was a field with a giant, white and yellow striped circus tent in the center. An uneven, gravel lot served for parking, and a few blocky, vintage cars were placed here and there.

'Clown School' read a big, wooden sign stretched above the tent's flap door. Gape-grinning clown heads smiled wildly on either side of the writing, and long, white and yellow pennants flapped slowly in the wind from either side of the heads.

"I don't think that's a restaurant," Bill said, taken aback. He'd remembered passing something, there, but *that*?

"I bet they have a phone," Sheila said.

"I don't—"

"They probably. Have. A phone," Sheila insisted.

"Okay, fine," Bill said. "But if they don't, you wait until you get home to call your mother. Deal?"

"That's not fair."

"Yeah, but I'm driving. Deal?"

She looked like she might spit on the dashboard, but nodded, grousing all the while. They had a deal.

The gravel crunched loudly underfoot as they walked up to the gaping flap door of the tent, and it was the only sound in the world. There were no other cars on the road, the woods beyond were strangely silent, and they could hear nothing from inside the tent – nothing at all.

"They probably don't have a phone," Bill said, hoping to be in and out before too long.

"Why not?"

"No wires."

"They might have a *cell*? You know, like the one you won't let me use?"

"Too far away from the towers," he replied, looking at his own. "No signal."

"You just need a better phone, Dad."

Bill was about to remind her that they couldn't *afford* a better phone – thanks, in no small part, to her poor grades – but then a clown came out of the darkness.

He was tall and gangly, wearing a silky clown suit that was the same white and yellow pattern as the tent. A small, conical hat was strapped to his head at an angle, a pair of outrageously big, black, empty eyeglasses was in front of his eyes, and a red rubber ball perched on the end of his nose.

"Well, hello!" the clown bellowed in a high-pitched, squeaky voice. "Welcome to Clown School!"

"Um ... hi," Bill said, taken aback. The clown made Bill remember the overly fawning eye doctor he used to go to when he was a kid. That guy always gave him the creeps.

"Are you here to enroll?" The clown chuckled, scampering up to the two of them with his big red clown shoes.

Bill chuckled, remembering their earlier conversation. Sheila just coughed.

"We're very sorry to disturb you, sir," she replied, using her best 'exclusive' school manners. "We just need to use your phone, if we could? I have a calling card, so it won't cost you anything—"

"Um, we realize you probably don't have a phone," Bill interrupted. "It's not really an emergency or anything—"

"Actually, it *is* an emergency, sir. He just doesn't want to admit there is one."

"Young lady, I am not—"

"Oh, we have a phone!" the clown said, kicking his feet up. "We do indeed have a telephone, right around the back."

"That's wonderful, sir," she said. "Thank you."

"But it's for clown use only!" the clown added, laughing.

"Ah ... " Bill said – figuring the clown was cutting him a break – and turned to head back to the car. "That's too bad. Thanks for your time, sir. Sheila, shall we ... "

"Sir, *please*," Sheila asked, putting her hands together as her eyes welled up with wetness. "I really need to talk to my mother. It's ... it's really urgent. Please?"

Bill didn't even bother to turn around; he knew she was pinching the web of her thumb to make herself tear up. She'd figured out how to do that when she was thirteen, and used it to get away with murder – at least until Bill caught on.

It worked like a charm, though; the clown went from laughing to fawning again. He leaned down, put a big, gloved hand on Sheila's shoulders and cocked his head at a loving angle.

"Oh, don't cry, little girl," he crooned. "You have such beautiful eyes, yes you do. I wouldn't want to see them full of tears."

"They're fake," Bill offered, but the die had been cast. The clown stood up, turned and gestured to the darkness inside the tent.

"Please come in!" the clown announced. "You can most certainly use our phone, and then you are both invited into the ring for this afternoon's big show!"

Then he honked his rubber nose a few times, then flip-flopped his feet forward, leading the way.

As they followed, Bill leaned down and whispered into Sheila's ear, "Just for that, you are not eating until we get home."

"Love you, Daddy," his daughter said, sweet as strawberry pie.

Every time Bill had been to a circus, it was inside a convention center, so he had no personal experience with what the inside of a circus tent should look like. But he'd been led to believe, by way of the movies, that the inside of the big tent should be ringed with wooden bleachers, with the center free for the show. That seemed the most logical thing to expect.

That wasn't what he saw. Inside the tent, just past the flap, was an open walkway between weighted, freestanding poles. Weathered and torn canvas barriers were lashed to each pole, stretching away into the darkness on either side. Past those poles were another pair, and then another, with yet more barriers lashed to them, creating a nestling series of corridors and hallways that stretched – and most likely curved – as far as the darkness would reveal.

Bill's eyes had trouble adjusting to that darkness, but his ears were now treated to what the outer tent had muffled. He could hear layers of laughter mixed with stomping, slapping, cracking, and moaning. He could also hear the barking of dogs and the neighing of horses, as well as what was either a dying elephant or a car with severe engine problems.

"We're all getting ready for the big, big show!" the clown announced, flip-flopping his shoes around in a big, sloppy circle. "It'll be so fun to have guests!"

"Well, we really just need to use the phone," Bill tried to protest, but there was something so sadly earnest about the clown's excitement that he didn't protest too forcibly. Saying 'no' and insisting on leaving as soon as possible would have been like hitting a child.

"I'm going to be a while on the phone, Dad," Sheila said, smiling right at him. That all but clinched the deal.

"All right, then," Bill said, looking at the clown. "If you could get me a front-row seat, I'd be happy to watch the show. I'm sorry, I didn't catch your name—"

"Well, I didn't throw it," the clown announced. "How about that?"

Then he laughed, reached into a heretofore-unseen pocket in his suit, and tossed a crumpled piece of paper right at Bill's forehead. Bill caught it on the way down to his feet and unfolded it, revealing a giant, staring eye. *"Dr. Peeky Boo"* was written above the eye, and below it was a grid of smiley-faces, all turned this way and that in a rough approximation of an eye chart.

"Well, Mr. Peeky-Boo—"

"Doctor Peeky-Boo!" the clown demanded, indignantly adjusting his big, empty eyeglasses. "I didn't get my P.I.E. so I could be called 'mister', thank you!"

"P.I.E.?" Sheila asked.

"Just like a PhD, only for clowns!" Dr. Peeky-Boo revealed. "You want to see mine?"

"Uh, sure—" she said, only to regret it; the clown produced a whipped-cream pie from seemingly nowhere, and deftly slopped it right into her face.

"Oh ... *fuck*!" Sheila pouted, wiping the gunk from her eyes, cheeks, and hair. And the moment she said it, the laughter and other noises in the tent completely ceased – all gone, as though someone had turned them off at the switch.

Bill knew he probably should have reprimanded Sheila for using that kind of language, just as he probably should have slugged the clown for doing that to her. But under the circumstances, all he could do was snort at the amusing spectacle; it was pretty damn funny, and she *had* walked right into it ...

"This isn't funny, Dad!" she howled, doing her best to get the slop off her face with her hands, and then off her hands onto her school uniform. "This dress is ruined!"

"Oh, I'm sorry," Dr. Peeky-Boo apologized, cocking his head this way and that. "Would you like me to help you get cleaned up?"

"*Yes!*" she demanded, and then received a face full of seltzer water, squirted from a bottle the clown had cocked just under his armpit. The bubbly water turned the gunk into white froth and it ran down the contours of her face, soaking the top of her dress.

Bill snorted some more, and then guffawed. This was getting funnier all the time.

"You ... " Sheila said, and it was all she could say to either of them. Her façade had cracked, and everything she might have used to respond – curses, threats or what Mom was going to say – was scrambled somewhere behind her eyes. Real tears fell out of her now, which made Bill feel a sting of parental shame.

"Okay, I think the joke's over," he told the clown, only to see that Peeky-Boo had already beaten him to that realization. The clown made the water bottle vanish, walked over to Sheila, and cupped her shoulders with his gloved hands.

"Oh, I'm so sorry," he said. "You have such pretty eyes. I'd hate to see them full of tears."

"You're ... *sick,*" she said, fishing around for words. "Sick and ... sick ... "

Then Peeky-Boo cocked his head, leaned into her, and whispered something in her ear. Bill couldn't hear a word of what was said, but whatever it was, it was highly effective. Sheila stopped crying, hitched a breath and just stood there, stunned.

Bill looked around, not sure of what he should say or do. As he did, he saw they'd been surrounded by an army of silent clowns all standing down the corridors, at the twilit boundary between what his eyes would let him see and what they wouldn't. Their white faces seemed phosphorescent in the near-darkness, and their eyes and mouths were like black pits.

How long had they been there, silently watching the spectacle? Bill had no idea, just as he had no idea how many clowns were there: dozens, or scores, or maybe even hundreds, there in the dark.

They came in all shapes and sizes, all kinds of costumes, no two exactly alike. Only their presence there, in the silent dark of this tent, made them part of a whole. And once they realized he'd seen them, they all took a quiet and respectful step back in eerie unison. They waved as they passed the barrier between what was seen and what was not, and then they were gone.

Only one clown remained – a large, hulking figure who came forward while the others slipped away. He wore a red and yellow silky costume, brandished a large cigar, and held three quick-moving German Shepherds on a leash. Each dog was skinny and wild-eyed and wore a white, conical hat strapped to its head.

"Oh, Bingo!" Dr. Peeky-Boo said, waving to the dog-handler as he came closer. "This young lady needs to clean up a little and use our phone. Could you give her a hand?"

The big clown smirked, put his cigar in his mouth, and used his now free hand to golf clap into the other. The three dogs reared back on their haunches when he did, as if he was asking them to perform some trick. Sheila gasped back what might have been a sob, and put her hands up to her eyes.

Again, Bill was dumbfounded. That was going more than a bit too far; he should have been angry, not amused.

But then, she *did* have it coming, didn't she? She'd insisted on stopping here and played the sympathy card in order to get in the door. Whose fault was it if these clowns – excellent students of human nature, one and all – decided to draw her into their world, just as she'd barged her way into theirs? Besides, maybe this was all just part of the fun – part of the wind-up. Maybe the seeming cruelty was just to separate out the rubes who 'didn't get it' from the people who could appreciate what this clown school had to offer. Maybe there was a really good show waiting for both of them: the kind that could make Bill remember what it'd been like to be a child and bring out the child in his all-too-grown-up daughter.

Maybe there was a pony waiting behind this massive pile of shit.

"I'll be in the ring with Dr. Peeky-Boo when you're done talking to your mother, dear," Bill said, smiling and putting his thumbs into his pants pockets. "Don't talk too long or you'll miss the show."

Sheila looked back at him – eyes glazed over with confusion, and possibly tears – and walked off, ever so meekly, with Bingo and his dogs. She might have tried to say something to him, but if so, she'd said it so low that he couldn't hear it. Then she was gone.

Dr. Peeky-Boo laughed, thrust an arm around the crook of Bill's elbow and flip-flopped them both towards the ring at the end of the walkway.

"I think this is the beginning of a beautiful friendship, Billy-Boy!" the clown announced, honking his nose as they went.

"I think so ... " Bill played along, idly wondering how Peeky-Boo had learned his name.

The pair walked into the very center of the tent, which was surrounded by canvas barriers and held up by a thick, central pole – one that took the roof of the tent up so high that Bill couldn't even see it. There were lights up there, he imagined, but only because something was adding a dim illumination to things as they went to their seats. It was as if the air was charged, somehow.

The ring was large (much larger than it should have been, Bill thought) and lined with the wooden bleachers he'd expected to see on the inside wall of the tent. There were four entrances through the canvas, each at a cardinal point and wide enough to take a rental truck through.

"Popcorn?" Dr. Peeky-Boo asked, producing a red and white striped box of it from nowhere. It smelled absolutely delicious.

"Thanks," Bill said, taking it as he was led to a seat on one of the bleachers, right in the front row. They were the sole audience today.

"How often do you have guests?" Bill asked, munching on a handful of popcorn. It was perfect: warm without being too hot, salty without being overpowering.

"Not as often as we'd like," Peeky-Boo said sadly, wiping a pretend tear from his eye. "It's a special day when we can show off what we've learned ... yes it is."

The clown doctor grinned, and there was something horribly wrong about the smile. But before Bill could react, Peeky-Boo turned, clapped his hands three times and demanded, "*Let there be clowns!*"

An unseen, wheezing pipe organ came to life, playing a jaunty tune that sounded like it might have been a circus standard. The music was just a little off, somehow, and Bill put that down to the poor sound of the instrument.

A trio of ball-juggling stilt-walkers trod in from the walkway to their right: three clowns in red and green motley, with impossibly tall, springy hats on their heads and five white balls apiece. Their stilts were tied together around the bottom with bright white lengths of ribbon, so they had to travel in perfect harmony to avoid falling down. In spite of their handicap – or because of it – they strode quickly and gracefully about the ring, making a perfect Figure-8 as they went.

Above the organ's groans, Bill could hear a car's engine. An old-style car – maybe a vintage Ford cab – puttered in from the left walkway. It was painted canary-yellow and held four clowns inside, all of whom were blindfolded. They weaved drunkenly around the ring, barely missing the stilt-walkers time and again, but coming just a little closer with each near-miss.

The result was inevitable; the car struck the stilt-walkers, right in the front. But the walkers remained standing – not even dropping their balls – while the car exploded like a toy. The sides, hood, roof and doors blew up and outward, as though they'd been jerked away by strings, leaving only the chassis, engine, rear and four blind, bewildered clowns in their seats, one still holding the wheel.

J. Edward Tremlett

The trunk popped open, and another clown leapt out. The stilt-walkers trod wide-legged around the car, eager to be on their way, and the stricken vehicle went forward again. As the car continued on its erratic, weaving path – now avoiding both its shed parts *and* the walkers – a new clown leaped out of the open, bobbing trunk, and then another, and another, until there were close to a hundred clowns in the ring.

The mismatched army of clowns formed a conga line – one that somehow kept clear of both the stilt-walkers and the car that had shat them out. The car lost its trunk, along with the last clown, and spun seemingly out of control as the driver increased his speed to an insane level. And all the while the walkers continued to juggle, not missing a single ball in spite of all that was going on around them.

Bill was not aware of how long the act went on until it came to a sudden halt. With no preamble, the car drove out of the right exit, the walkers strode out on the left, and the clowns all paraded out from where Bill and Peeky-Boo had entered. The car's lost parts were carried off by some of the more enterprising harlequins, and then there was nothing left but the shaky music of the pipe organ.

"Wow," Bill said, lost for exact words, "That was ... Jesus, that was amazing."

"That was just the warm-up act," Dr. Peeky-Boo said, giggling. "Just wait 'till you see what they do next ... "

Bill did, and was utterly enthralled by what he saw – at least, at first.

The clowns put on an amazing show. There was more juggling and acrobatics, with twists and turns in the acts that made them impossible to predict. There were complicated animal tricks with dogs and ponies, sometimes bending every notion of what Bill thought an animal could or couldn't do. There were slapstick routines, along with vignettes and skits that had him howling with laughter and unable to catch his breath.

The acts were superb performances of skill and trickery, and the show was a wondrous affair, one that would have delighted even the most jaded of audiences and put a smile on any child's face. Bill had only been able to call it 'amazing' earlier, but that was the word that fit it best – amazing, through and through.

And yet ... something was wrong here.

The worry started with the animal acts. The dogs and horses they'd trundled out were mangy and pathetic creatures – scarred, weak-legged and skinny as whips. The clowns were expert at keeping them on track through the acts, but the animals looked as though they might fall down dead or broken at any moment. The garish clown hats and coats they wore only added to the pity Bill felt for them as they performed.

Once Bill was feeling pity for the animals, he stopped laughing so much at the clowns' more abusive antics with one another, and started wincing. In each and every slapstick scenario, it seemed that one clown was on the receiving end of most of the abuse rather than everyone sharing equally. The one who took the first pratfall in each new act was doomed to take prank after prank, and fall after fall, without hope of revenge or deliverance – at least until the new act came on.

In one rather harrowing skit, a clown was grabbed by at least ten of his fellows and stuffed into a green and orange wooden barrel. They pounded the lid on and spent the rest of the act kicking it about, barrel walking atop it, and performing other complicated acrobatics with it as a centerpiece. All the while the poor clown was still inside, honking his nose loudly in fright and discomfort.

The skit ended as abruptly as it began. A clown produced a sledgehammer and struck the barrel, causing it to explode. The clown flopped out, 'dead', his hands over his chest and a limp, yellow flower stuck in one of them. The clowns laughed at the seeming cadaver and dragged him out by his nose, honking it as they went.

It was funny, yes, but Bill knew exactly how that clown must have felt. Wasn't that a perfect model for how his life had been for the last five years? He'd been ganged up on, tossed into a barrel, and used like a toy, too. His ex had even called him a clown, now and again, when he'd dared to ask for more support – or less venom – from her.

In Bill's mind, the unfortunate clown was wearing his own face. Or maybe he was now wearing the clown's? He was having a hard time visualizing where one left off and the other began.

And as he struggled to understand this problem, he felt a growing sickness within him: a nauseating divide between revulsion and self-pity that teetered between the two emotions like the tightrope walker from an earlier act.

But that was the last skit before the amazing finale of the show, and Bill was so overwhelmed by the showstopper that he forgot all about what had bothered him during the lead-up. Once again, he was lost to the insane, childish wonder he'd felt at the opening act, only multiplied by a thousand – one more taste of it and he was gone.

Then it was all over.

The clowns took a long bow and left, just as they'd entered – leaping into a moving clown car's trunk, one after the other. The car drove out of the opposite entrance to the ring, the unseen lights dimmed with a snap and a click, and that was the show.

"Wow," Bill repeated himself, too stunned to realize he'd dropped the popcorn box.

"Did you like that, Billy-Boy?" Dr. Peeky-Boo asked, replacing the empty, fallen box with a fresh one. "Did it make you a happy boy?"

"It sure did," he replied, not knowing what else to say, except: "Why wasn't Bingo out there? I was looking for him."

"He must still be with your daughter, Billy-Boy," the clown replied, pulling a big, toy stopwatch from nowhere and pretending to be amazed at the time. "I bet she's a talker!"

"That she is," Bill muttered, looking at his own watch. Amazingly enough, only a half-hour had gone by. He could have sworn the show was longer than that.

And why *wasn't* Sheila back yet? His ex-wife was normally only good for fifteen minutes on the phone at most, before ending the conversation with some tepid excuse. By all rights, she should have been back by now – even her mother couldn't pour that much poison into her ears in one sitting.

"Probably still talking," Bill answered his own question.

"Talking to yourself, Billy-Boy?" Peeky-Boo grinned. "That's the first sign of turning into a clown!"

"Naah," Bill said, getting up and stretching. "Not me, Doctor."

"Don't be too *surrrrrrrrrrrrrr-rrre*," the clown teased, poking a finger at him. Bill thought of himself in greasepaint and a clown suit, flip-flopping in front of an audience and taking pratfalls for laughs. It was a great thought for a moment, but the charm went out of it when he imagined his ex in the audience, scowling.

"So, what circuses do you guys work with?" Bill asked, trying to change the subject as quickly as possible. "It's been a while since I went to one, but I've never seen anything like that before."

"We don't work *with* people!" Peeky-Boo announced, leaping to his feet and stumbling into the ring. "What would be the point?"

"A clown's gotta eat, too."

"'Not by bread alone,'" the clown intoned, hands over his heart. "We work for the dream."

"Dream?" Bill asked, noting the faraway look crossing his host's white face when that word was spoken. He'd seen that look countless times before, mostly from door-to-door evangelists or crazed sidewalk preachers; it was the bliss and rapture of faith.

"Come with me, Billy-Boy," Peeky-Boo said, taking Bill by the hand and leading him out the way they'd come in. "There's something you need to see ... "

The 'something' was back down the walkway and to the left, heading along one of the barely lit, curving canvas corridors Bill had looked down when they'd first arrived. The only real light came from rips and holes in the outermost canvas, which added a strange, forbidding look to the way ahead. The small shafts of light seemed almost solid – skewed barriers meant to keep out intruders.

"You see ... a *real* clown has to understand pain," Dr. Peeky-Boo said, leading the way with a gloved hand. "It's not enough to make people laugh. You have to be able to make them cry, too."

"I didn't think clowns were supposed to make people cry," Bill said, feeling the worry from earlier swirl around him again like a cloud of dark, hot smoke.

"That's because the clown community has been poorly served by our role models," the clown replied, gazing wistfully ahead. "The last few years were really, really bad. Can you believe the clowns in fast food restaurants, enticing children to eat junk food?"

"Can't be any worse than shoveling elephant shit."

The clown made a face and shook his head. "That's not our way, Billy-Boy."

"Then what is the way?" Bill asked, then saw they were at the 'something'. A wooden arch was stretched across two poles, tied to both with something ropy and uneven. Beyond the arch, the canvas walls seemed to be heavily decorated with pictures and objects.

"Here is the way," Dr. Peeky-Boo said, clapping his hands three times, just as he had at the start of the show. There was a flicker, and then light as the ropy and uneven supports were revealed to be thick strings of carnival lights: red, yellow and blue. They cast harsh, unblinking glares on the arch – an incredibly old marquee reading 'Punch & Judy' – and the corridor beyond.

Bill's first thought was that this was some sort of clown museum. There were bits and pieces of costumes, odd and mostly unidentifiable artifacts, and old show posters and pictures in tacky, gilded frames. All the exhibits were festooned wildly upon the torn canvas walls, with no real sense of balance or order – almost as if they'd been tossed up at random by a blindfolded juggler.

Some of the pictures they passed were incredibly old; Bill saw daguerreotypes and tintypes, along with faded oil portraits and what might have been reproduced woodcuts. They were all of clowns in one social guise or another, with star circus performers and lowly harlequins all made equal by virtue of being here, in this museum.

But as Bill followed Peeky-Boo further in, he got the feeling this wasn't a museum. There were no plaques or notes by the exhibits to inform the uninitiated, and no sense of what, or who, the posters might have been of.

In fact, it felt more like a temple than a museum: a shrine to the history and artifice of clowns. And maybe something else.

"So, the way is?" Bill asked again, still wondering what this was all about, though becoming seriously worried about the possible answer.

"To get as far away from laughter as you can," Dr. Peeky-Boo said, almost reverently. "To bury yourself in pain and sadness and misery. To crawl on your hands and knees in the darkest places, until you can't remember the light anymore."

Bill grimaced, not sure he wanted to know what came next, but powerless not to ask the next logical question: "And then?"

"And then, one day, when you're as low as anyone could ever go ... you finally understand."

"Understand ... what?"

"What it means to be truly happy!" Dr. Peeky-Boo replied, honking his nose a few times. Maybe it was supposed to be some kind of Zen joke, but something about how the clown responded made Bill want to run.

Just then they came to a large, wooden puppet theatre sitting in the middle of the path and all but blocking the way. It was old and beaten down: wood splintered, yellow and purple paint flaking away like eczema. A name had been on the top plank once, but now it was all but unreadable.

"We find our students after they've been down the hard road, Billy-Boy," Peeky-Boo said, turning to face the theatre and clasping both hands over his heart. "After they've crawled down it, day after day, year after year. And if we're lucky, we get to them just before the world swallows them up like a goldfish ... "

The clown opened his mouth a little wider than it should have gone, then clamped his teeth together with an exaggerated *Chomp!* A fleck of blood might have flown from the tip of his tongue, but it might have been spittle – it was hard to tell in these lights.

"And then what do you do?" Bill asked, looking at the puppet theatre. Was it just another exhibit, or something else?

Dr. Peeky-Boo took his hands from his heart and clapped them together three more times. A harsh, bright light shone down from the darkness above, illuminating the puppet theatre. And from behind it, jerked up onto the 'stage' like a marionette, was the 'dead' clown from the show.

"Oh, my God ... " Bill whispered, looking at the 'dead' clown's face. His eyes were glassy – like those of a corpse – but he was still breathing.

He was also smiling widely.

"*This* is the way, Billy-Boy," Dr. Peeky-Boo said. "Our friend Slugger has come a long, long way since he first walked in our door. He used to be a mortgage broker with two houses and three girlfriends. And he made a million dollars each and every year! The world was sitting up and begging, just for him.

"But inside, he was crying," Peeky-Boo continued, wiping away a fake tear. "And he was crying because he wasn't really happy. Deep down, he knew something was wrong with everything. And that's why he came here, to Clown School."

"And now?" Bill asked, still not wanting to know, but powerless – utterly, totally powerless – to stop himself from asking. The words were all but forcing their way out of his mouth, just as his feet were gluing themselves to the ground.

"Now he's going to face his final exam!" Peeky-Boo announced, clapping his hands three more times. At the third clap, another puppet appeared, to the right of Slugger, and this time it was a proper one: a shiny 'Punch' clad in kingly purple and wielding a massive, black club.

Bill could tell from the angle of Slugger's left arm that he was the one controlling the puppet. But it was strange how Punch was highly animated – squirming, preening and all but leaping off Slugger's wrist – while the clown remained as motionless as a corpse.

"Hey there, Slugger," Punch said. And though Slugger's mouth moved, the sound seemed to be coming right from the puppet's frozen lips.

"Let the final exam ... *commence!*" Dr. Peeky-Boy said, laughing. As soon as he was done, the puppet reared back, readied his club, and swung it right into Slugger's red, rubber nose. There was a sound somewhere between a crack and a squish, and blood splattered past the club, out of the theatre and onto the ground.

"Ha ha ha!" Punch squealed – this time independent of Slugger's mouth. "That's the way to do it!"

Bill was rooted to the spot – helpless. He couldn't move or speak as the puppet laughed hysterically, pulled the club back from Slugger's bloody, mangled face, and swung it again and again. Each time the cracking/squishing got louder and wetter, more blood flew, and the club was pulled away and swung back a little bit faster and harder than the time before.

All Bill could do was stand there and eat popcorn, one perfect piece at a time.

"Yes, that's it, Slugger!" Dr. Peeky-Boo cheered as the puppet's motions became a frenzied blur of purple, black, and bloody red. *"That's it! That's the way to do it!"*

Just then, the puppet slowed in mid-swing and stopped inches from its target. The clown's face was completely bashed in: real nose gone, upper jaw smashed, eyes staring in different directions. Blood was pouring out of his mouth and nose – water-falling off his chin and onto the front of the theatre.

And as it spattered onto the wood, it ran over the edge, flowed down the front, then disappeared. It was as though the old, dry wood was drinking it down.

At that moment, Bill's paralysis dropped. He let go of the popcorn box and backed away from the theatre and Peeky-Boo. If the clown knew that his hold over Bill was gone, he made no sign; he simply stood and watched as Slugger collapsed behind the stage, puppet and all.

"Down he falls, Billy-Boy," the clown went on, looking at the now-bloodless theatre. "But when he gets back up again, he won't stop laughing..."

"You ... you all need help ... " Bill said.

"Nothing a hit of this won't cure!" Peeky-Boo announced, reproducing the seltzer bottle – again from seemingly nowhere – and squirting Bill right in the kisser.

The rush of wetness confused Bill for a moment; he stumbled around, trying to wipe his eyes clean of the smelly, bubbling froth. It felt wrong, somehow – stickier than it should have been.

The clown laughed – the raw, ripe belly laugh of a madman – and held the water bottle up for inspection. Three pairs of human eyes floated in the bubbly, pinkish murk, each one trailing ragged muscles behind and below.

"Here's looking at you, Billy-Boy," Dr. Peeky-Boo said, grinning all the more.

Bill screamed, stumbled back and fell down, a perfect pratfall that prompted another belly laugh out of Dr. Peeky-Boo. And as he scrambled back to his feet, he could hear the laughter echoing around them. Grinning, leering white faces filled every tear and hole in the canvas.

"What the fuck is wrong with you?" Bill screamed, but he knew it was useless for him to ask or expect an answer. He knew exactly what was wrong with them: they were madmen, one and all. He'd brought his daughter into a lair of madmen, and now they were going to die.

Bill screamed, running pell-mell back the way they'd come – or the way he thought, or *hoped* they'd come. The canvas dividers flapped and lurched as gloved hands reached out for him. Enterprising clowns started to push the dividers towards one another, clamping him like wood in a vise.

But he kept running and praying that he would somehow collide with Sheila, wherever she might have gone. He'd find her, get out of the tent, get into the car, and get as far away from here as fast as they could go.

After a few narrow scrapes and near misses, Bill realized the clowns weren't trying to catch him in the dividers after all. Instead, they were closing the gaps and rearranging them into a spiral, leading him back to the center of the tent. This meant his planned means of escape was completely cut off, but by the time he understood that, he was already in the ring – and trapped.

The lights of the ring were still dimmed, but Bill could see Sheila standing in its center, looking right at him. She was standing absolutely still – too terrified to move – and it only took Bill a moment to realize why.

Bingo was sitting nearby on a wooden bench. He had a covered, old-style metal garbage can next to him, with one hand on the lid. The other was holding a lit cigar. Between the smoke and dim lights, his face was almost hidden from view.

The clown's three German Shepherds were rolling on the ground by his feet, fighting tooth and claw over bones. Bill knew that at any moment Bingo could command those dogs to tear into Sheila with the same ferocity.

"You let those dogs loose, I'll kill you," Bill threatened, putting himself between the animals and his daughter. Bingo just grinned from behind the cloud of smoke, patting the lid of the trashcan with his big, thick hand. His dogs perked up their ears at the noise and started to whine and beg ...

"Honey, you just stand there," Bill said to his daughter, slowly backing up towards her. He shot a look back and was only half-surprised to see she'd done just what she was told, for once. She didn't move so much as an inch.

"Love you, Daddy," he heard her whisper.

"I love you too, honey," he said, backing up just a little

more. "Now, we're gonna get out of here, okay?"

"Love you, Daddy," she said again, her voice shaky and unsure.

"I love you, too. Now, you're gonna take my hand, and when I say so, we're gonna run for the door ... "

Bill knew this wasn't much of a plan; the door was blocked, and Bingo and his dogs were in the way. But it was the only thing he could think of just then, and he had to reassure his little girl—

"Love you, Daddy," Sheila repeated over and over again, getting faster as he came closer. "Love you, Daddy. Love you, Daddy ... "

Bill stopped as soon as he got close enough to take her hand. As he closed his fingers around hers, he was painfully aware of how frightened she was; her hands were cold and unyielding, just like a porcelain doll's.

"Love you, Daddy," Sheila repeated, as shaky as before but now twice as loud. "Love you, Daddy ... Love you, Daddy ... "

Bill turned around and looked at Sheila. Her face was hardly moving as she spoke, and her eyes were blank and unseeing – almost glassy in the half-light.

Then, with a click and a snap, the lights came back on full-force. It took Bill a moment to adjust to the harsh illumination, and when he did, he saw that Sheila's mouth wasn't moving at all. The sounds were coming from it, but she wasn't speaking – she wasn't even breathing.

And her eyes *were* made out of glass.

"Love you, Daddy," the thing before him repeated. "Love you, Daddy ... "

Bill gasped and took a step back. Then he heard the dogs snarling, and turned just in time to see them fighting over a fresh morsel from the trashcan. Blood and stringy muscle still hung from its joints, and droplets of clotted gore flew about the ring as the dogs tussled over the bone.

It was a human femur – raw and wet.

Bingo leaned back, smiling at his pets as they chewed on the bone. The front of his red and yellow suit was soaked clean through with drying blood. The trashcan was badly stained with it, and was covered with oddly quiet flies.

"Love you, Daddy," the doll wearing his daughter repeated over and over again. "Love you, Daddy ... Love you, Daddy ... Love you, Daddy ... "

"What are you really afraid of, Billy-Boy?" Dr. Peeky-Boo asked, suddenly standing in the entrance to the ring, blocking the only way out. "What is it that's holding *you* back? Why can't you just let go and have some fun?"

"Sheila ... " Bill whispered, not daring to turn around and look.

"Not anymore," Peeky-Boo said, extending his hands, the palms facing up. Each had a wet, bright green eye cupped in it.

(*Love you, Daddy*)

Bill screamed and kneeled on the floor, holding his head in his hands. He squeezed his temples in the vain hope he might explode his brains out of his skull and end this hell. But nothing happened, and nothing answered his screams, except the mad laughter of clowns.

Something inside him broke. Behind it was the darkness he'd always pulled back from. There was no escaping it now.

"Welcome to Clown School, Billy-Boy," Dr. Peeky-Boo said, grinning from ear to ear. The clown's mouth became part and parcel of the darkness, and Bill fell into it as he hit the floor in a heap.

He felt nothing. He *was* nothing. He was gone.

And when he finally came back up, he couldn't stop laughing.

About the Author

J. Edward Tremlett is a thirty-something writer who hails from ... well, all over. He's spent time in Ohio, South Korea, the United Arab Emirates and now Michigan, where he sells treasure to the unwary by night and writes by day, or at least twilight. His work has seen print in *The End is Nigh, Pyramid Magazine,* and *Nocturne*, amongst others. He is married with three cats and a car.

You can check out J. Edward Tremlett's live journal at:

http://jedwardtremlett.livejournal.com

The history of the Salem witch trials is sobering yet inspirational and still relevant. And the most moving event from that time centered on a man named Giles Corey. Part of his story is in the history books; the rest of his story is more disturbing…

CRUSHING GILES
By Stephen C. Hallin

The centuries-old building was purposefully dark. The gloom was artificial and slick in the tourist district. A cold drizzle wafted through the October mist.

Hollie seemed quiet and thoughtful.

"You can't park here. You're blocking traffic," she said

"We'll be fine. All of the parking spots are tight like this," James responded.

"It's too crowed here; we should come back some other time."

"Are you kidding? This is the week before Halloween in Salem Mass, the heartland of the witch-hunt. This will be fabulous."

Hollie sighed. "It's like every other dirty little town on the coast. Do we really need to stay for two days? I'm bored already."

"Listen, there's more to do than we have time for. But don't worry, I've planed our agenda. First stop: the Witch Museum for a history lesson."

"Uh-huh."

"Then we'll find the gravesite that I've been researching – where they buried Giles Corey."

"That's the real reason you dragged me here, isn't it?"

"And once it gets dark, we'll go through a haunted house I've heard about. The tickets are expensive, but it's supposed to be something special."

"I can't wait."

"And tomorrow, there's the House of Seven Gables, the old burial grounds, and maybe another haunted house or two."

"That all sounds good, but I'm visiting my mother while we're here."

"So that's why you've been so quiet. What's the harm in a quick stop?"

"Listen, ever since they moved here and my father disappeared, she's been more involved with that Wiccan garbage than ever."

"I know, but as long as we're here, maybe you could patch things up. She's still upset that you didn't go to your father's funeral."

"His *funeral*? That wasn't a funeral. It was a memorial service – they never found him, remember? For all I know, he's alive and doing God-knows-what."

A dark gray car stopped next to them. The driver apparently wanted the parking spot.

"We can't sit here arguing. Let's go in," James said.

The other driver honked his horn, as if trying to get James's attention.

"How far are we from the Witch Museum?"

"About twenty feet. It's right there." James hurried around the car to hold Hollie's door and helped her to the sidewalk.

The gray car sped away.

The museum was crowded and the air heavy with the mustiness of wet coats. There were younger groups, with patchworks of tattoos, piercings, and too-black hair on too-pale skin – the Goth gangs. There were older women layered in black lace and draped with odd crystals – the Wiccan nation. Two families in the far corner seemed out of place and nervous.

Despite the somber interests and gruesome past of the place, everyone laughed and joked as if waiting for a ride at an amusement park. Yet, something seemed different. James felt something more – something real and maybe significant, something more than just the sights and a few regurgitated blurbs of history. It dwarfed the approaching holiday ...

Something important lived here; something powerful. But what? Did this power come from some sort of primal Satanism or could it be something less profound? Maybe the Goths came here to be trendy; the Wiccans came to better know their heritage. James couldn't sort it all out, but he knew that something had pulled them all together.

As soon as he heard the announcement that the show was about to start, James squeezed his way toward the dimly-lit main room of the museum. The last of the lights switched off and there was a blinded moment before the presentation began. The only light glowed red above the door: EXIT.

"Welcome to Salem Massachusetts," began the guide. "We kill witches here."

She paused, obviously for effect.

"Or rather, we used to. So you guys don't have anything to worry about." The tour-herd tittered politely. "It started when the slave Tituba arrived from the Caribbean."

Lights clicked on behind James. He turned and was pleased to see that the visual aids were updated. Built on a small stage, everything in the life-sized diorama was more detailed. The skin on the figures looked real, almost alive. The coarse fabric and even the fit of the clothes was more authentic.

"The Salem girls loved Tituba. She was their nanny, their teacher, and their friend. They listened for hours to her stories about the occult. The girls knew it was wrong, but they couldn't stop. They mixed potions that never worked, they sacrificed a few stray cats, and, whenever the moon was full, they danced naked around bonfires in the deep woods. Soon their parents realized that something strange was happening and suspected a connection to witchcraft. Church leaders launched a formal investigation, and that's when the girls began having convulsions in public. That clinched it. The authorities needed no more proof; the hunt for the witches began. Neighbor turned in neighbor – everybody was a suspect."

"Sounds like the Department of Homeland Security. Everyone's a possible terrorist nowadays, right?" James whispered.

A heavy man wearing an American flag t-shirt glared indignantly at James.

"See? It's only a real witch-hunt when you can't call it a witch-hunt."

"Please be quiet," Hollie whispered.

The spotlights switched to the next scene, the arrest of a suspected witch.

The tour guide continued.

" ... and Giles Corey was accused in the early spring of 1692. There was a young neighbor girl who didn't like old Giles and this was her chance. When she announced that he visited her at night in various supernatural forms, he was immediately arrested and jailed. This was proof of his satanic activities – there was no defense. The punishment was death by hanging.

"Giles was stunned. He was a principled old guy and very religious. On Sundays, he was in the front pew singing all the hymns from memory. He read from the Bible every night and had paid for rebuilding the church when it burned to the ground in 1683.

"However, at that moment in Salem, *none* of that mattered. If you were accused of witchcraft, you were guilty and you were executed. Period.

"But this situation became even uglier; Giles didn't cooperate. He could have confessed and died quickly. However, Giles was too righteous and too stubborn; for months he refused to talk. By law, there was a harsh penalty for such silence. It was also death – but this was much worse. It was death by crushing.

"They finally realized that he would never admit guilt. So, in the fall of 1692, they laid a board on his chest and began placing heavy stones on top."

The tour guide slowed her speech and lowered her voice, as though feeling the drama in every word.

"With every stone, he was asked to confess. Bones bent and cracked; blood leaked. His breathing became more strained with every additional ounce. But he didn't say a word.

"This continued for two horrible days and nights. Even the executioners, hardened by the dozens of hangings, were deeply affected. They begged him to confess. They brought in his wife, his children, his friends, anybody that knew him ... tears in their eyes, they pleaded with him, they yelled at him in horrified frustration. It was excruciating. Then suddenly, the pile of rocks shifted and his torso collapsed to an unbelievable thinness. His bones were mostly dust, his internal organs all but squeezed dry. Once more, the lead executioner demanded a confession.

"And finally, Giles opened his mouth and strained for a gulp of air.

"This was it. It could all stop. At last, he was going to say what they wanted, he would hang and this madness would end.

" 'Confess *now*, ye wizard. Spare thyself, save thyself. What say ye? *What say ye?*'

"Giles grimaced, gathered his strength, and struggled to whisper his first words in six months.

" 'More weight.'

"The furious executioner threw everything he could find onto the pile. It's said that he climbed onto the rocks and wildly jumped on them. After a thirty-minute tirade, he was dragged away, gibbering and insane. And Giles Corey was nothing but a puddle of body parts and was – at last – dead. But this traumatic event shocked the community back to sanity; the witch trials ended, and the hangings stopped. The witch trials were horrible yet this was an incredible lesson for our country. From the McCarthy blacklists to the World War Two internment camps, sometimes Americans overreact. And whenever that happens, we need to look to our past and learn from our long-dead heroes, heroes like Giles Corey."

"That's the guy isn't it? Giles Corey?" Hollie whispered.

James nodded, trying to hide a half-tear. No matter how many times he heard this story, it always affected him. The tour ended and the main lights came back on. Silently, James and Hollie followed the witch-tourists back into the traffic and the dirty sidewalks, where the undercurrent of the real Salem was hidden and muffled.

"And you're the guy who will find his grave," Hollie said.

"Last time I made the same mistake that everyone makes – I tried to follow the roads from the old maps, but the village has changed too much. This time, I calculated the *exact position* from old maps, which we can find with this GPS receiver – see this? I've programmed it so an arrow will point to the position."

"And that's our next stop?"

"Yes."

He handed her the GPS receiver and carefully pulled into the busy traffic. Cars swerved in front of him and others tailgated him all the way to the western edge of town.

It was a relief to find a half-empty road.

The arrow pointed westward.

A huge hill – almost a mountain – was ahead and to the right. As they passed the hill, James noticed that Hollie wasn't watching the GPS.

"Isn't our hotel nearby? Let's get registered before we find the cemetery," Hollie said.

"He was buried at a crossroads, not a cemetery. Where is the arrow pointing?"

"Oh, crap, I think we passed it."

"I'll go back," James said as he made a u-turn. "Tell me what it does."

"Got it ... keep going. It's starting to turn ... it's turning, turning ... turning. Stop right here."

James eased the car onto the narrow shoulder. There was barely enough room for other cars to pass.

"Let me see," James said.

"Is it working?"

"Yes, but it's pointing at the hill. There wouldn't be a crossroads there. Something's wrong."

A gasoline truck washed by within inches. The car swayed.

"Yeah, fine, but let's not park here. Somebody is going to rear-end us."

During a brief opening in the traffic, James gunned the engine and they darted across the street. They passed a billboard-sized 'No Trespassing' sign and parked in a small pull-off. Looming behind the sign were two heavily-rusted trucks: a dump truck and a four-wheel-drive pickup with a plow-blade.

There was no one in sight; there was nobody to enforce the 'No Trespassing'.

The arrow on the GPS pointed steadfastly at the hill.

"Maybe the grave is on the other side. Are there any roads over there?" Hollie said.

"None. It's the largest undeveloped area in New England. It's owned by the Mathers ... as in Cotton Mather."

"The famous preacher?"

"Yes."

"Was he involved with the witch trials?"

"He may have played a behind-the-scenes role."

"Really." She seemed concerned.

James got out of the car, GPS in hand.

"Let's see where this takes us."

They started down a dirt road that led around the left side of the hill. When the road turned sharply up the slope, they left the road, and picked their way along the base of the hill.

"This isn't a real hill. This is a landfill. Look at all the half-buried junk. Those two trucks must be here to dump garbage," James said.

"Is that a trail up ahead? Let's get out of this."

"Let me check the GPS. I'm getting a little disoriented."

They were halfway around the hill – the arrow still pointed at the summit.

"This can't be ... "

"What? You're kidding," Hollie said.

"Why would there be a hill at a crossroads? Everyone was on horseback – no road would go straight up a hill."

"You said it yourself a minute ago. It probably started out as the crossroads, but they needed a dump."

"Well, let's take a look. It'll be easier to get to the top if we get back to the road."

"I don't have a choice, do I?"

They scrambled up some loose rocks and onto the deeply-rutted road. They passed a dozen switchbacks before the road steepened near the top. James stopped for a second and caught his breath.

As they crested the hill, the wind picked up. The top was flat and barren, almost smooth with dirt – loose fine dirt. Even up here, there were fresh tire tracks – this landfill was an ongoing operation. It was treeless, raw, and ugly.

According to the GPS, Corey's grave was at the precise center of the summit.

James unfolded a photocopy of an old map to double-check the position, but he couldn't hold it with one hand – the wind was too strong. He set the GPS receiver on a rock so that he could manage the flapping map. His feet slipped in the shifting dirt – there didn't seem to be anything solid to stand on ... it was almost like treading water.

The view was amazing. The entire town of Salem was below. Dusk was falling and the streetlights twinkled like neat rows of amber stars. Roads in old villages followed old cow paths or Indian trails or who knew what ... so being at street level made it confusing. From here, it made more sense. The lines of streetlights matched the lines on the old map. They meandered where they were supposed to meander, straightened where they should, and merged where they were supposed to merge.

Except when they approached the hill.

"I think they designed the entire town to stay away from this hill." James studied his map. "You're right. See that street over there?" he said, pointing, "it used to run right under us. It's a dead-end."

"James! There's a man down there – he's got a gun."

A burley man in a red plaid shirt waved a shotgun and yelled something. The wind was too loud and he was too far away; his words were unintelligible.

"He wants us to leave," James said.

The man aimed the shotgun at them.

"What's he doing? He can't shoot us," Hollie said.

The man lowered the gun and gestured angrily.

"Let's go," James answered.

The man pumped the shotgun and aimed again.

Hollie turned and ran. James followed. Luckily, the man was on the opposite side of the hill from their car, but he was also running toward their car.

Going downhill, they had the advantage. But what was the race about? Maybe he wanted to scare them off the hill. But if that was true and they were leaving, *why was he chasing them?*

Maybe he wanted to get them within range.

James decided that it didn't matter why that man chased them. The only thing that mattered was that he had a shotgun and they did not.

They scrambled down as many shortcuts as they could improvise. They were soon in the car. The engine started quickly. A folded piece of paper fluttered under a windshield wiper. There was no time to read it.

The gunman burst into sight as James careened onto the main road. The man ran after them, shouting.

"Okay, sir, I understand. I'll stay away," James murmured.

Accelerating through the speed limit, he left the deranged man far behind. Once they were safely down the road, he read the paper. Its message was in large black letters.

No trespassing!
$5,000 fine and one year in jail!

It was signed by Sgt Elias Mather, Salem PD. James turned on the windshield wipers and the paper flew away.

"Friendly folks around here, eh? Hollie, are you okay?"

Hollie nodded. "Perhaps we can go back and have a picnic there."

"One thing's for sure, I can't afford that fine. This pretty much ends the search for Giles."

"I agree. But maybe we should contact a historian about this. Who knows? Someone might excavate it and build another tourist attraction."

"It's worth a try. After all, Giles was the real hero here. He deserves a little recognition."

James checked his pockets for the GPS; they were empty. It wasn't on the seat, either. There was no easy or clever way to break the news.

"James, what's wrong?"

"I don't believe it. I have to go back," James said.

"What? You're kidding."

"I left the GPS receiver there. It cost over three hundred bucks."

"You want to go back *now*? What about the haunted house? What about the shotgun?"

"This won't take very long ... the haunted house is open till midnight. We'll go back when it's darker. I'll sneak in, get the GPS, and run like hell. I know exactly where it is."

"Why not go tomorrow?" Hollie said.

"The dump truck might bury it by then. I can't wait that long."

"I can't let you go alone."

James hid the car behind some trees. The shoulder of the now-empty highway was safe. The rising moon cast long ghostly shadows – it was light enough to see and it was dark enough to be invisible.

The dump truck struggled up the hill. In its lowest gear, it slowed to walking-speed.

"Let's get behind him. He'll never see us," James whispered.

They easily caught the truck and followed it at a careful distance.

The exhaust fumes were unpleasant and the engine's roar uncomfortable as it rasped and strained. Even so, following the taillights was much better than tripping up the hill in semi-darkness.

At every switchback, the truck lurched uncontrollably, almost stalling.

A hundred feet from the top, James and Hollie crouched behind a small ridge of rubble. The truck swung around and backed to the far edge of the hill. The driver sped away as the load slid out. He seemed determined to keep the tires moving.

With no more need for the switchbacks, the truck sped down a straighter, steeper road on the far side of the hill.

"He's gone. Let's get that thing and leave," Hollie said.

"Wait a second, I'm stuck." James's right foot slipped into some loose dirt, about half-way up his shin.

He braced his free foot on a large rock and pushed free with all his strength. He flexed his foot. Something inside, maybe a tendon, was torn and bruised. He'd have to limp, but he thought that he could run if necessary.

"The pickup is coming. It'll be here in a minute," Hollie said.

"He's too slow. We'll go down the other side, and he'll never see us," James replied.

James' injured foot bumped against unseen obstacles with every other step.

Was something inside cracked? He had a disturbing mental picture of a split leg-bone, its frazzled ends gnashing together with every step.

The growl of the pickup truck was closer. It was coming faster. There might only be a minute to find the GPS. This was crazy. In a year or two, he could buy one for ten dollars.

But this was the wrong time to try to explain *that* logic to Hollie.

Tiny thorns inside his foot sharpened – growing angry and loud. With this forced walking, there was more damage – maybe irreparable damage – occurring. Would he be able to run again? Would he need a cane? Was this a life-changing injury?

The bouquet of pain blossomed, twining upward.

"James, are you going to make it? We should stop – you look terrible."

"No, we're almost there."

He had to keep going.

Truth was, something coaxed him ... compelled him ... to return and find the GPS. It was the same reason he couldn't stop. And why he'd intentionally left the GPS behind. It was clearer now. From the beginning, he'd been driven ...

And it was too late to care that he didn't care.

Because this was why they all came to Salem. Something deep and powerful was here; it was humbling. Real history was here, an everyday-guy had stopped a massive witch-hunt, paying with his blood – saving thousands of lives. For three hundred years, Giles had gone un-mourned and almost forgotten. James and Hollie were his first proper visitors. It was an honor.

Finally reaching the top, James staggered over to the GPS receiver. Fully exposed to the moonlight, there was no problem finding it. He picked it up.

"Come on. Let's get the hell out of here," Hollie said.

Suddenly the ground split and James dropped into soft soil up to his knee. His bad foot was caught in a solid fist of mud. His leg changed, freezing into pain-overload, a pre-agony flavor of shock. James wanted to scream, but couldn't even breathe.

The pickup truck turned through another of the switchbacks. There were two more turns to go before its headlights would illuminate the top. The driver was bound to be Mr. Shotgun guy.

"James! Goddamn it, are you all right?"

He touched his leg – it flibbered like a wet washcloth. The jagged sensations were so intense and unreal that every thought was to stop them, every wish to lessen them. Crushed and leaking; his meat mixed with soil. Raw nerves jangled in dirt soup. It was unbearable.

As gently as he could, he tried to pull. And it worsened.

"I can't get out." He gasped.

The ground weakened again and he dropped in deeper. His other leg floundered in the softness.

Something squeezed his foot.

He screamed.

It squeezed again, gently this time. The earth here was strangely warm ... almost comfortable, almost relaxing ... the softness soaked through his foot. It melted into the wounds and there was something else ... unexpected relief.

It squeezed a third time, caressing his shattered ankle. The pain wasn't so bad. It was still there, but a shade spongier and more distant. It was now almost tolerable.

Again it squeezed, a gentle touch of penetrating heat and pressure at exactly the right spot. James closed his eyes; he moaned softly.

Hollie held out a long stick.

"James! Grab this. I'll pull you out."

The stick dropped from his limp hand; he was too weak to hold it. She came closer and tried to grab him. The dirt whirled between them; she backed away. It almost pulled her down.

The ground loosened and swallowed another inch of leg. There was no bottom to it. The pressure stopped and the pain exploded. It was torture.

Then, just as quickly, the pressure returned and the pain was gone – the change, excruciating. And it happened again. And then it happened once more ... and again, relief ... pain ... relief ... until the difference blurred between wanting the relief and needing the pain. It was almost the same. The shattered foot flipped around like a trout on a hook – that was what was causing all the pain. If only it weren't attached.

"Oh ... oh, my God," James whispered.

The earth squeezed rhythmically, harder and harder. But James wanted it to go faster. Pressure was the key. The harder it pressed, the higher it climbed, the faster it squeezed, the closer he got to something ... like ... ecstasy. His foot was attached by the smallest thread, his ankle barely there at all.

But it wanted more. It wanted him deeper. It wanted more *from* him. He stabbed his shattered limb downward. The limb swelled with blood – it thickened, it lengthened – the skin stretching and thinning, ripped and sore. The few inches of exposed thigh were layered with webs of crimson veins pumping more fluids downward, building even more pressure, tightening the skin, flooding the injuries. And the harder he pushed, the deeper he dug – the more intense the pain, the more exhilarating the relief. The foot! Somehow it had to be freed. James knew he couldn't do it by himself.

"Help me. Help," James said.

"The truck is almost here. They'll be able to dig you out."

"No ... not that. Not them ... not you."

The ground seemed to pulse furiously; fully synched with James – with what he wanted, with what he needed, with what he'd always needed. Tighter and tighter. Faster and faster. James could barely breath.

He stopped fighting the foot. He relaxed ever so slightly and suddenly the foot popped off with an incredible release.

The burst from the opened leg was hot and fierce. It was a welding torch, a gushing flamethrower, spurting his sticky bone marrow into the tight ground-throb. It was horrible. It was delicious. And when the last bead dribbled out, the compression crept higher on his leg, crushing more bone and milking out more. Glob by glob, it oozed out. Inch by incredible inch, it moved higher. A second was a year. A minute, an infinity. Would it ever finish? No. It mustn't ...

As it pulled him deeper, he heard a faint voice from far within the earth. At first, he didn't understand. Black curtains danced and grew across his vision, his ears buzzed. The voice became louder, deeper, and richer – a million orchestras resonating inside a monstrous earthquake.

In the moment before the blackness swallowed him, he understood. He knew what it needed and why it wanted him. It was an endless pursuit of perfection. And it spoke to him clearly.

"More weight."

It was Giles.

Hollie sat in the lobby of the emergency room holding an empty paper coffee cup. She was too tired to re-fill it; she was too dazed to throw it away. The night was almost over. The nightmare wasn't.

It was good to be out here – away from the babbling horror in the little white room, away from all of James' insane talk about the pile and why he needed to help add more. The hill had to be much heavier, Giles wanted it. The weight of living flesh was best.

Mother should be arriving soon, that would be a huge help. A car lurched into the parking lot and jerked to a stop. That might be her. Whoever it was, they were in a hurry. But wasn't that true for anyone going to the emergency room?

There she was, dressed in black, as always. But at last there was somebody that might help. Somebody that could think clearly, even if it was her mother.

The automatic doors whirred open and Hollie stood up. She realized that she wasn't prepared for this moment. She didn't know what to say. It had been at least ten years since they'd last spoken. Everything before that had been an argument. And not going to her father's memorial ... What could she possibly say after all that time and all that nastiness? What *should* she say?

They embraced.

Hollie wept.

"Oh, Mommy ... "

"It's okay, Hollie. I'm here," she said.

"Thank you for coming."

"How is James? Is he stable?"

"Yes. He has a surgery scheduled for nine this morning. They can't save his leg, but he'll be fitted for an artificial limb. Mom ... it was horrible ... the bone was sticking out and ... it was like ... like ... "

Hollie paused until she could form words again.

"It was like it had been in a pencil sharpener. His knee was shaved to a fine point."

"How the hell did *that* happen?"

"He slid into a hole. His leg was caught and it probably snapped when the pickup truck pulled him out. He was deep in some sort of cavity. When they finally got to him, I could only see the top of his head and he was still sinking."

"The bone was *shaved*? Where did this happen?"

"At that hill west of town."

"The hill on the Mather property?"

"Yes."

"Oh, no, not again. Is someone with him?"

"What do you mean? He's asleep – he's heavily sedated."

"We need to go now and watch him."

"He's in the back." Too tired to resist, Hollie led the way. "Follow me, but don't be alarmed. He's saying some crazy things."

"The only thing that matters is that *he'll go back*. Once they've been in the ground there. They *always* go back. That's how I lost your father."

"Now you're starting to sound like James. What the hell do you know?"

"Maybe nothing. Or maybe we need to get to his room. Right now."

Hurrying down the long hall, they passed the nurse's station, turned the corner and stopped.

"There's his room." Hollie pointed. On the white hospital tiles outside his door, there was a trail of bright red blood droplets, as though someone with a bleeding leg stump had hopped out of the room, heading away from the staffed section of the hospital. Halfway down the empty hall, there was a bloody smear. It looked as though the hopper had slipped and fallen when trying to turn toward a fire exit. In the middle of the smear, there was a small fragment of bone, sharp and shaved on one end like a toothpick, as though ...

Hollie opened the door to James' room. The bed was empty. She ran to the window; it had a view of the parking lot.

Their car was gone.

About the Author

Stephen C. Hallin is a retired military officer who has flown into hurricanes and typhoons. Currently, he teaches math and science at several colleges in Utah. He lives to ski bottomless powder and double diamonds. His website, the mighty http://www.HorrorMasters.com, is one of the most popular fiction sites on the Internet.

I'm told I have a questionable sense of humor. I guess I have a questionable way of thinking, too, because I often have macabre thoughts, frequently translating into very bad dreams. "Door Bitch" emerged from my pondering over what could happen if someone totally helpless but conscious was kidnapped by a maniac.

DOOR BITCH
By Dave Field

Chapter 1

"You know I'm always shitty when I've done a door bitch shift."

She rolled away slightly in the bed and he could tell Celine wasn't in the mood for fooling around. He sighed and stopped stroking down the side of her breast.

Maybe a change of subject.

"Why won't you come and live with me instead of us hopping back and forth between apartments? It would be a damned sight—"

"Oh, for Christ's sake, Bill!"

Celine flounced out of the bed and walked naked and luscious to the corner table he used as a bar. She grabbed a glass and bent to take ice from the tiny fridge underneath. Her hair, dark and something between curly and wavy, cascaded down each side of her face. Even in the semi-darkness, she made an arousing picture. Long legs and beautiful breasts. She poured a slug of whiskey over the cubes and sipped, gazing sightlessly up at the ceiling.

"Okay. Sorry. Can I have one, too?"

She turned and smiled, then began to fix him a drink.

"I'm the one who should be sorry," she said as she built it. "You'd think I'd be used to doing triage work in Emergency by now."

"I don't think anyone really gets happy with triaging work. Whatever you do, you're wrong by someone's standards – and it's often impossible to talk any sense into people when they're scared shitless. Whether they're the one who's hurt or someone who's dragged 'em into the hospital. They all think they should be at the top of the list."

She brought over his drink. He took it and caught her hand, easing her down to sit on the bed.

He could tell she was still bugged about things, and decided to keep talking.

"We both have the same sort of experience in that environment. We each started off rather like the injured – scared shitless – and then came to terms with the unpredictability and often the horror. It's the irrationality we encounter that causes the trouble. Always."

She'd turned to look at him as he spoke, and once again her beauty amazed him.

Eyes you could fall into.

He could see her features softening, the strain oozing away.

Is it me doing that – or is it the alcohol?

She sipped her drink, then put it down by the bed, slipped down onto her side and put her hand on his thigh.

"You're nice and warm. What are you doing tomorrow, anyway?"

"Around a million appendectomies, I suppose. No special surgery scheduled." He rolled onto his side, on one elbow. To be even closer.

"Funny. When I went into medicine, I figured it would be a bit more glamorous. It doesn't take long for it to be 'same old, same old', even when you're the bloody prima donna surgeon."

She pushed him down on the bed and clambered over him so that she had an arm and a leg on each side.

"I don't think you're a prima donna," she whispered. "I think you're a Don Juan."

She lowered her breasts gently onto his face.

She's relaxed.

Good.

Chapter 2

The late shift had been especially bad for door bitches, with the outcome of a pitched battle between two gangs to clean up. Knife wounds and small arms fire damage. Intensive care specialist nurse Celine Wilcox had been required to keep dozens of drugged-up screaming bums, all demanding assistance, in check. Emergency had been swarming with cops and security for hours as the members of the two gangs tried to bring their war into the hospital. The medical teams worked in an atmosphere akin to that of battlefield medics. It had been hell on wheels, the more so because there was also the usual litany of what passed for normal medical emergencies – kids poisoned with disinfectant, mothers damn near checking out on diet pills, an ectopic pregnancy, three cardiac arrests.

Celine was driving home through pouring rain and wanted nothing more than to be in bed. Alone. She was nervous, trembling with fatigue. Her mind filled with images of slashed bellies with intestines protruding, arterial bleeding, and the livid puckered wounds caused by gunfire.

She turned the car onto the freeway, slotting into a traffic stream stacked with vehicles at an intensity hard to believe at nearly three in the morning.

Where are they all going at this time of night?

The rainfall became heavier and she flipped the wipers into faster motion, then reached to switch channels on the radio, eyes staring steadily, warily ahead through the windshield. She saw a flare of brake lights and then, shockingly, the reason: a large truck had tipped and was blocking the three lanes on her side of the freeway.

Fleetingly, she registered that other vehicles, mainly cars, had slammed into the truck – that still *others* were doing so, right there where she could see it all happen, just like in the action films. Her foot pressed hard on the brake pedal and the car squealed to a stop, sliding only a little to one side on the wet pavement, and almost touching a nearly new Ford coupe.

Christ, that was close!

She sighed with relief.

Then heard tires squealing behind and stared into the rearview mirror. Something was bearing down on her, something big and out of control, and she watched in horror as its radiator grill became the only thing she could see. A rending crash, a sudden push in her back, and her head wrenched back agonizingly.

Blackness.

Chapter 3

Celine's eyes opened.

Something woke me. What?

She could see nothing other than a strange pattern of what looked like tiny ice cubes, very close to her face. She could smell a hot engine oil smell. Some of the cubes, she realized, were hurting her right cheek. Then it occurred to her she was lying on her right side with her cheek on the passenger seat. The ice cubes were pieces of broken windscreen.

Accident – had an accident. Get out.

She made to move. And nothing worked. She couldn't move. She instantly realized what had happened and a cold, nightmare sensation rushed through her.

Spinal trauma.

She worked through her limbs. Fingers, wrists, elbows, shoulders. Nothing. Toes, ankles, knees, pelvic joints. Nothing. Tried to turn her head. Nothing. To move her jaw – speak. Nothing.

Oh, shit!

Tears filled her eyes. She was helpless.

But I can breath ...

Noises outside. Sirens. Then red and blue lights painting the inside of her car. Livid colors. Someone yelling through a loudhailer. Someone else screaming, "Help me! Help me!"

Wait. Someone'll come. Someone. Just wait.

And then she realized she had no choice.

Chapter 4

She heard voices, quite close, and then a brilliant white light speared into the car.

A man spoke: "What have we here?"

She tried to answer. Nothing.

No more voices.

Suddenly, terrifyingly, the sound of a small engine and then the car began to tremble. She heard a wrenching, cracking sound. Moments later, the driver's side door was opened.

Outside noises much louder now.

Other motors running. People yelling. She felt a hand slide up her chest and rest against her neck, then slide back over her chest again.

He's checking my jugular pulse and respiration.

The man's voice again: "Well, lady, we'd better get you somewhere safe, hadn't we?"

Relief flooded through her and she tried to say just one word: *Thanks.*

But couldn't.

Another man's voice: "Need a hand with this one?"

"No. Triaged her out. Well, actually she didn't make it. She's dead."

Dead! I'm not dead!

She tried to speak again. No go.

"Shit." The owner of the second voice had obviously come for a look. He sounded very close. "And she's a looker, too. What a waste. Oh, well, plenty more to scoop up."

"Yeah."

Am I dreaming this? Red lights, blue lights, noise, can't move. It's a bad dream because of the madhouse in Emergency tonight. Just a bad dream.

Celine's bubble burst when a wind gust blew rain in through the opened driver's side door and wet her feet and ankles. She could feel the rain.

But she couldn't move her feet out of it.

Chapter 5

She heard someone by the door and recognized the sound of a hospital gurney being adjusted. Then the man who'd said she was dead spoke to her:

"Time for a ride, lady. We'll get this collar on first."

He unfastened her seatbelt and then grunted as he struggled to push the cervical support around her neck. Finally, he fixed it and slid his hands down over her chest again. Shock blossomed in her mind.

He's fondling my breasts! What's happening here?

The man slid a recovery board under her body and carefully maneuvered her until she was flat on her back. More grunting and he dragged her out of the car and onto the gurney.

She stared up into the black-gray night, rain falling onto her face, hurting her eyes. She realized she could close them.

That piece of me works. But what's happening?

A different voice, female: "Need a hand here?"

Help me!

"She's dead. Broken neck."

Celine's heart dropped like a stone as the man draped a sheet over her.

"That's four I've seen so far."

"Yeah. Still, look on the bright side – there's a great opportunity to harvest organs, huh?"

The female obviously didn't appreciate the comment.

"Was that supposed to be fucking funny?"

"Hey, it's a joke. Gotta laugh in this business. Or go crazy."

"Not my sorta humor." The female voice faded. And so did Celine's hope of rescue.

He was pushing the gurney through the wrecks. Celine heard snippets of sound – swearing, sobbing, wailing. A priest giving the Last Rites. The screech of tools, throbbing engines, red and blue light shone through the sheet. The fireworks display of sparks as metal was cut open. The deep beat-beat of a helicopter.

The gurney stopped. She heard vehicle doors opening and her little cart was pushed into what she guessed was an ambulance. The vehicle shook as someone climbed in and she heard the doors close.

Maybe I've got this wrong. Maybe I'm confused. Maybe …

The sheet was pulled down from her face and she was staring up at a middle-aged man possessed of brilliant blue eyes in a genial-looking, roundish face.

"Don't worry, pretty lady. You're in good hands."

She tried to speak. Nothing.

He reached over and pulled straps across her body, locking her into place.

Ran a hand over her cheek, brushing away glass fragments, then stood, slightly hunched over in the confines of the ambulance, and looked her up and down. She could see he was wearing ordinary rescue worker's coveralls with fluorescent reflective panels.

It must be me. It'll be okay. Soon they'll get Bill...

The man leaned down over her and licked her ear, her cheek. Took hold of her jaw and gently pulled it down. Pushed his tongue into her mouth.

Dave Field

Celine screamed in silent terror

Chapter 6

Bill knew there was something wrong. He knew because he'd been called in when the hospital learned of the multiple-car accident. He'd soon found that Celine had finished her shift. Gone home. She wasn't answering her phone at home, or her cell. And he knew she took the freeway route home. And the timing was right on.

Something's wrong.

He had to work, patch people up as they were dragged in. The interns could handle the simple stuff. He got the complications. He managed to get messages out, asking for help, to watch for a woman of Celine's description – pleas to the cops and firemen on the scene, the paramedics, the triage nurses.

The morgue people.

He worked into the dawn's light. Heard nothing.

Decided to do the worst part first. The morgue.

"I tell yer there ain't no stiff in here looks like that."

The attendant wasn't blessed with much diplomacy, but there was no denying he gave a direct answer to Bill's question.

He told me twice now she's not here.

Relieved, Bill looked around the trolleys, each with its miserable burden, then turned to leave – to try somewhere else.

"Exceptin' that one over there."

Bill stared at the man.

"Where?"

The attendant pointed towards a trolley at the far end of the morgue annex.

"Over there. The one near the extractor fan. Put it there 'cause 'er the stink. A burn-up, that one. No telling who or what without 'n autopsy."

Heart racing, Bill went over to the cart. Even ten paces away, he could smell it – despite the standard body bag. He lifted his hands to slide the zip. Paused. Then opened it to see the head. The sickening roast pork aroma of burned flesh spilled around him. He gagged. It was just possible to detect that he was looking at a face. Carbonized. No eyelids. No lips. Or ears.

He's right. Can't recognize her – it.

He slid the zipper open all the way, pulled back the bag. Stood away for a better view.

No fingers on the left hand. No right hand. No right foot. No skin. Anywhere. Except for a small area around and including the umbilicus.

He gagged again.

A voice, close behind: "You spew, you'll clean it up, buddy. You s'posed to be past that shit by now."

Bill turned to the mortuary attendant.

"It's not her. It's a man. You can tell by the pelvic bones. Thanks."

He walked off.

The attendant stared after him, then at the burned corpse. Grabbed the zipper. Muttered to himself:

"Prick coulda least closed the fuckin' bag. Fuckin' *medics*."

He snapped up the zipper expertly. Went back to his booth. Coffee, donuts, an adult film and a box of hospital tissues. All the comforts of home.

Chapter 8

Celine gazed at the ceiling. Her neck hurt. She had pins and needles in her left arm. There was a strong disinfectant smell. She scanned around as far as her eyes would move. She was in a semi-dark room painted a light off-white color. Her focus zoomed to a collection of obvious surgical tools hanging on a board as though it was in someone's garage. Knives, saws, retractors. Glittering metal.

What is this? What's going to happen to me?

She heard a door open. The genial-looking man came to stand by her.

"We'd better get you cleaned up."

He produced a pair of scissors and began cutting at her clothes.

No! No! Someone help me!

Tears rolled down her face.

He stopped a moment, looked at her. Looked along her body. Licked his lips.

"You'll feel much better."

In far too quick a time, he'd completely stripped her. The man stood back and eyed her. Celine sobbed, tried to beseech him – and realized he was watching her breasts shake as she gasped out her anguish.

He produced a bowl and added warm water to it. Picked up a large yellow sponge and a bottle of liquid soap.

"Hope you enjoy this as much as me."

He began sliding the soapy sponge over her.

Everywhere.

Echoes of Terror

The rain had eased, but the ominous gray clouds made a grim backdrop to the scene of the accident. The ambulances were long gone. A few fire trucks remained, their crews packing up equipment. Bill stood by his car and wondered where to start. The cop who'd let him get so close stood alongside, silent, obviously wondering the same thing.

"Any wrecks been shifted yet?" asked Bill.

The cop nodded. "Six or seven. Took 'em to the police compound like normal. We'll move 'em gradually as we log the details. Pictures 'n shit. All go to the compound with a big mess like this one."

"See a woman like this around?"

He showed the cop a picture of Celine. The cop shook his head dismissively. "Only been on shift an hour. You'd have to ask the others."

His transceiver squawked and he went off to deal with it.

Bill's heart sank as he turned back to the collection of wrecks. He could see camera strobes flashing as the details were documented. Here and there tow truck drivers were leaning against their vehicles, waiting for permission to move in and clean up. He decided to walk through the mess and ask about her car.

Glass crunched under his shoes, and he was continually stepping over and around bits of chrome trim, red and yellow lamp plastics, blood-soaked gauze swabs, oil pools. He approached a tow-truck driver.

"Seen a Toyota Highlander in this lot? Blue?"

The guy looked at him.

"Not blue. They're Indigo Pink Pearl."

Bill stared at him stupidly.

The man explained, "The color's Indigo Pink Pearl. I work in a body shop. I know. It's a prick to match."

"But have you seen one here? Or this woman?"

He offered the photograph.

"Good-lookin'. No. Haven't seen the car or her. Some cars 've been moved now. See the bright green tow-truck down there?"

He pointed and Bill looked.

"Yes."

"That's Archie Meacham's. He was the first of us here. He'd know. Archie don't miss nothin'."

"Thanks."

Bill walked on, past an astonishing array of wrecks. He paused and stared at a completely burned-out light truck. Thought back to the corpse in the morgue. Shuddered and then hurried away. More camera flashes. He heard chains rattling, a motor revving, and saw an old Chevy being lifted ponderously onto the back of a large flatbed.

His heart went into his mouth

As the Chevy moved, he saw a blue Toyota Highlander.

Bill broke into a run. The SUV was totaled, the rear end smashed in, the front bursting apart against another car. He tried to open the passenger side door. It was jammed. He saw the driver's side door was open and clambered over the SUV's buckled hood, to lean into the car.

No blood. No damage to the steering column.

No Celine. Where is she?

He saw her purse on the floor at the passenger's side, and picked it up. Inside he found her cell phone.

Christ! Where is she?

Chapter 9

"Now, that feels good, doesn't it?"

The man was carefully drying her with a large pink towel, very soft. She stared at him.

"We're going to be real good friends, you and I. Close, you might say. Now, you rest there a while and I'll go and get cleaned up. Then we'll get better acquainted."

He made to leave, then turned back and reached for her breast, kneading gently, rippling his fingers over the nipple.

"Real close," he said, and left her to her thoughts.

There were two men standing by the bright green tow-truck. Bill looked from one to the other. "Archie Meacham?"

"That's me. Wassup?"

He was short, dangerously fat and red-faced. Bill could tell instinctively he was poised for a heart attack or a stroke.

"I'm looking for this woman. She was driving the Toyota Highlander back there." He handed over the photograph and pointed. "The blue – the Indigo Pink Pearl one."

Archie examined the picture, passed it to the other man, who checked it, shook his head and returned it to Bill. Archie said, "Sorry. I'd remember her."

The other man lit a cigarette, began to cough violently.

A small car came to a halt close by and Bill wondered how the driver had gotten into the cordoned-off area. A middle-aged woman climbed out.

"Hey, Archie," she called out, "Gettin' it sorted out?"

"Hey, Sonya. Come back for another look as usual?"

Sonya grinned. "Had to. This was a big one."

Archie turned to Bill:

"Show Sonya. She's a paramedic. Been on this job for hours until we got 'em all out."

That's how she got in. She's part of the crowd.

He gave her the picture. She stared at it, then at Bill. The other guy wandered off, obviously not wanting to be involved.

Sonya seemed to be choosing words.

"What was she driving?"

He knew he was going to hear something bad.

"A blue Highlander."

"An SUV?"

He nodded. She slowly handed back the picture.

"Who are you?"

"I'm a surgeon at the hospital. Celine's an ER nurse. That's her car back there. We're—"

"I understand. Look, I can't see any way of making this easy. But you being what you are ... " She trailed off, stepped forward and took his arm.

"I briefly saw a girl who looked a bit like the one in the picture, on a gurney by the SUV. The paramedic – he told me she was ... gone."

She squeezed his arm. "Sorry."

Bill eyed the ground.

No!

"Sorry," she said again.

He shook himself, raised his head.

"Who – who said she was ... dead?"

"The paramedic. I don't know him. Doesn't work with us. Seen him a few times. Drives a weird lookin' ambulance. Private maybe."

Archie stared at her.

"Yer mean an old Ford? With 'Bernsten' on the sides?"

"Yeah, that's him."

The tow-truck driver knew him. "His name's Arthur Teale. Seen him at a few big prangs. Dunno who 'e works for."

It was enough for Bill. "How can I find him? Where would he take her? She's not in the morgue."

Neither of them could help.

Chapter 10

"Hello, darling."

The blue-eyed man wore a white toweling robe. His skin was pink, obviously from the shower, and Celine could smell a nauseating aftershave odor.

"Need to make you comfortable first," he advised.

She fainted when he catheterized her.

Bill pursued the chase.

"You sure she's not in any of the morgues?"

The voice from inside his cell phone assured him again everyone involved in the massive wreck had been identified – except for one burned corpse, now known to be male.

Cops – I need help from the cops.

He dialed emergency and explained who he was.

"I'm trying to locate an Arthur Teale. He's a paramedic who was working at the freeway accident last night. He's known to have removed a ... person from a wreck and taken her away. I need to locate him. And her – my ... Ms. Celine Wilcox."

A robotic-sounding voice at the other end told him his call was being forwarded. He could hear ringing, then a different voice – that of a woman – spoke: "Lieutenant Grears. Can I help you?"

Bill went through it all again.

"Hmm," she answered, "I guess you know all paramedics must be registered. Give me a minute and I'll check it out. I'll see if he's listed in the phone book first. How do you spell the surname?"

He didn't know for sure.

"Never mind. I'll try some variations. What's your number? Okay. I'll call you back soon."

She hung up.

He thought through what he knew.

'Benson' on the side of the ambulance. No – it was ... 'Bernsten'!

He made for his car. Bill needed a phone book, too.

Celine woke up. The man stood next to her. The robe was gone. What she could see of him was unclothed. She knew he was completely naked and she could smell his male odor even with the vile aftershave scent.

"Feel better now your bladder's empty, darling? Don't worry, the catheter's gone."

He held a violet-colored bottle up for her to see. She read 'Wildcat Erotic Massage Oil'. Closed her eyes – and found the images in her mind even worse.

God help me! Someone – anyone. Help me ...

The man whispered in her ear.

"I'm going to relax you now, my love."

She began to sob again as he poured oil onto her abdomen and breasts and began to massage her.

Bill burst through the diner door, startling the handful of customers. The woman behind the counter eyed him suspiciously.

"Emergency," he said, "Can I use your phone, take a look at your phone book?"

She handed up the book and the phone.

"Pay for each call after the first, no long-distance. Okay?"

"Sure." He threw a twenty-dollar bill down and grabbed the book.

"Coffee?"

He nodded distractedly, flipping pages.

Bernsten. Bernsten. Where is it?

No business name for Bernsten.

He checked the suburb name. *No.*

Desperate, he looked up surnames, finding eleven.

Do I call them? What can I ask?

He dialed the first number and a lady who sounded very old answered.

"Hello?"

"Hi. Is there someone there who's involved with Bernsten Paramedical Services?"

"What's that you say?"

"Bernsten Paramedical Services."

"Don't want any."

She hung up.

He tried the next number. Got nowhere. And the next. No go. And the next. The one after.

This is hopeless.

He kept going.

Number eight didn't answer. He rang number nine.

"Amelia Bernsten."

"Hi – I'm trying to locate someone associated with Bernsten. A paramedical service."

"You're too late."

"What?"

"We ran a contracting service for quite a while. Shut down five years ago – too much competition from the big companies."

"Is Mr. Teale there?"

"Who?"

"Arthur Teale."

"Never heard of an Arthur Teale."

"But he was driving a Bernsten ambulance last night. Working at an accident scene. He—"

"Don't know an Arthur Teale. And it wouldn't have been one of our ambulances. We sold three of the four when we closed down. Me 'n Vern – my husband – we kept one. He was gunna fix it up as a mobile home."

She sniffed. Bill guessed she was a little emotional.

She went on, "But he died a year-and-a-half back. I sold it."

Bill's mind raced.

"Mrs Bernsten, this is real important. Who did you sell it to?"

"I advertised it. Didn't want to get ripped off by those dealers. Sold it private. Hang on, I'll see if I can find ... "

She put the phone down.

Bill waited.

Come on!

Chapter 11

"Good, isn't it," purred the man as he slid his hands over her breasts again. She could hear the soft crack of the oil as he worked his fingers, could feel the stickiness under her breasts, where her thighs touched. Around her sex. The oil had an offensive cheap scent.

"Now," he said. He stepped away a little and bent slightly. She heard a faint whirring sound. Celine realized that whatever she lay on was sinking down. She closed her eyes. Seconds later the whirring stopped.

"Look at me," the voice whispered.

No! No! He's going to rape me! Over and over. Surely someone can help me – Bill – help me!

"Look at me."

Fearfully she opened her eyes. He stood very close, aroused.

She closed her eyes. Heard him moving.

He slithered on top of her.

This can't be happening. It's not real. It's in my head. What can I do? Why can't I wake up?

"Hmmmm ... " He sighed. And wriggled on her.

Mrs Bernsten finally picked up the phone.

"It was a man called Morris Adderson."

"Morris Adderson. Do you know where he lives?"

"No. He came and picked up the ambulance. Gave a good price for it, too. Better than the other offers. Do you want their names as well? They're all here on my list. No? Okay. Vern used to say I hoarded everything. I suppose he was right. I mean, what's the point of keeping this list when the ambulance is sold? I won't be ringing them again, will I?"

Bill was thunderstruck.

"Are you saying you have the phone numbers on your list? You have a number for Morris Adderson?

"Sure. I've got 'em all. I—"

"What's the number for Morris Adderson?"

She told him, and as he wrote down the number his cell phone rang.

"Have to go. Thanks."

The cell phone call was from Grears.

"Sorry I took so long. Didn't have much to tell you anyway. We couldn't find an Arthur Teale and there's no paramedic registered with that name. I talked about it with a few of the guys and someone remembered a weirdo from a few years back. He was arrested for necrophilia. Worked in a morgue. They lost the body of a young woman. Found he'd stashed it away in a locker. They put him away for two years under some deal to keep things quiet. But it doesn't really fit, does it? Celine's still alive. Right?"

Bill didn't answer the question. Instead, he asked his own:

"This weirdo – was his name Morris Adderson?"

Celine was revolted. She wanted to throw up, didn't want to choke on her vomit. The man was slobbering all over her, pawing at her. She knew it wouldn't be long before he parted her legs and—

A tremendous splintering crash made the body on top of her freeze in surprise. A thumping sound.

Running feet. Help me!

Another crash and suddenly the room seemed filled with figures in black. The man was wrenched off her.

Someone said, "You scum." Very quietly.

She heard the blue-eyed man's voice:

"I can explain—"

"Aargh," said Celine. Suddenly the room went very quiet. A hand touched her neck. She turned her eyes to look up. A pair of astonished eyes stared back. They belonged to a policeman.

"She's still alive! Get an ambulance. Cover her up. And get this piece of shit out of here."

Celine looked at him through a torrent of tears.

"Aargh," she said.

I found another piece of me that works.

"So, it wasn't so bad moving in with me after all, was it?"

Bill was putting stuff in the dishwasher after lunch. Celine spun around and around in the wheelchair, laughing.

He stopped what he was doing.

"Careful. If you fall out of that thing, we'll probably end up spending another four hours digging clots and shit out of your spinal cord. Just because you didn't break your neck last time, doesn't mean it can't happen next time."

"I'm already wearing the cervical collar. I'll be safe enough."

Celine stepped out of the chair and came over to him. Awkwardly reached to kiss his lips.

"And when I get the damned thing off permanently, " she looked at the calendar, "in three week's time, I'll show you just what I can do with a mixture of lips and neck."

He laughed. "I can't wait – but I will. Anyway, I know *you*. When you take the chair back tomorrow, you'll volunteer for light duties instead of tooling around here all day. And you'll start getting those shitty moods on again. Won't you?"

"That's for me to know and you to wonder about, Don Juan."

Bill shrugged into his jacket and grabbed his medical bag. Gave her a kiss.

"See you tonight, hon."

She smiled at him, as he walked away from her backwards, grinning madly.

"Maybe," she said.

"Only one word to describe you," he retorted, stopping by the door, "Bitch."

About the Author

Dave Field is an Australian author and editor. Much of his story "Door Bitch" is based on his experiences while working in a British general hospital many years ago. If you like his story, chances are you'll like more of his writing. He has two novels out with the publisher Whiskey Creek Press – *Profile Three* and *Hurtling to Oblivion*. Check out his website at http://www.authorsden.com/daveffield for novel excerpts, more short stories and articles. Dave lives in Darwin in the Northern Territory with partner Margi and dogs Max and Bonni.

After my car broke down one dark and stormy night, I found myself walking through an old graveyard pondering one of the horror genre's greatest themes: being trapped in a seemingly inescapable situation. Just then a twig snapped! Yellow eyes glinted in the murk! Suddenly I ... Okay, I give up! I got the idea for Tempest while lying on the living room floor and staring at the ceiling. Go figure.

TEMPEST
By Matt Hults

They'd traveled halfway around the lake when the storm started to get bad. The wind picked up fast, coming out of the north, and it whipped through the trees like an angry specter, carrying a hailstorm of dead leaves across the trail.

Logan's skin prickled. The weekend had been unseasonably warm for early November, but the temperature continued to plummet with the increasing wind. Despite the chill, he peeled off his flannel shirt and handed it to Kelly, leaving himself with just a tee-shirt.

"Thanks," she said, adding a smile of admiration that helped to dispel the cold.

Beside them, Rob and Tina watched the exchange. None of them had thought to bring jackets, and when Tina turned to Rob with the pleading expression of a shivering baby kitten, he merely hugged his own shirt tighter and quickened his pace.

"Real chivalrous, asshole!"

They all laughed for a moment, and then continued their trek in silence.

Ironically, Logan had seen this coming before they even left the cabin. The sky appeared dark and featureless now, but he'd noticed the latent ferocity in the thunderheads at sunset, and when the girls first suggested one last hike up to Liberty Beach for a final bonfire before returning to the city, he'd almost advised against it ...

Almost.

Instead, he came along for Kelly. They'd been dating for two weeks and things had been progressing at a slow but friendly pace. That didn't bother Logan too much. He liked her, and she liked him, and he knew caution had its merit in a new relationship. Rob and Tina, on the other hand, had been going together for maybe half as long, yet over the last two nights, Logan had lain awake in his bed listening to the two of them rattle their headboard to near-destruction in the adjacent bedroom while Kelly slept down the hall. Earlier, when he'd seen the eagerness in her eyes at the idea of the bonfire, Logan hoped it was finally his turn for some action.

So much for nobility, he thought.

Now it was clear they weren't going to make it to the beach.

Lightning flashed and the forest became a chaotic bramble of shadows. Thunder shook the air around them.

"We're never going to make it back to the cabin before this breaks," Rob said as he led the way down the trail.

"Tell me something I don't know."

His friend's teeth chattered together. "Maybe we should check some of the other cabins," he suggested, "see if we can find somebody who'll let us wait this out? You've got to be as cold as I am. Once the rain hits, we'll be headed for hypothermia city."

"It's the end of the season," Logan reminded him. "Not all of these places stay open year-round. I'd bet that half the cabins are already closed up for the winter."

"We should still try," Rob pressed.

Logan nodded. He didn't like the idea of knocking on some stranger's door in the middle of the north woods, but he already detected the first hint of moisture in the air and combined with the wind, it felt like icy needles pricking his skin.

"Okay," he agreed. "We'll try the next access."

The DNR had prohibited waterfront construction on this side of the lake as part of a land-management program focused on the preservation of the lake's natural borders. No cabins, no docks, no private beaches. Instead, dirt paths or portage trails tethered the properties to the shoreline, minimizing the evidence of any human presence.

After thirty yards or so, they came to one of the paths, a plain dirt trail marked by a carved wood sign that identified the property owners as 'The Miller's'. They told the girls the plan and started up the path with the harrowing sound of creaking tree branches issuing overhead.

They'd gone twenty yards when the rain began to fall.

Logan heard it patter through the treetops higher up – in those that still had leaves – then on the ground around them. The sound of it stopped him in his tracks.

Each drop seemed to … hiss.

"Do you hear that?" he asked.

The others came to a halt beside him, looking around, listening, but before anyone could answer, Rob snapped his hand to his chest as if pulling it out of a fire.

"Ouch! Crap! That hurt!"

"What—" Logan started. Then he felt it too, a searing pain on the back of his neck, like hot oil scalding his flesh. "Damn!"

The rain hurt.

"Argh!" Rob yelped again, his cry followed by shrieks of pain from Kelly and Tina.

"What the hell! This shit burns!"

Logan wiped the sizzling drips from his arms and pulled his shirt collar over his head. "Come on," he said. "Run!"

He led the group forward, sprinting up the trail, trusting its course ran in a straight line. They heard the fiery drops hissing all around them now, cutting through the forest, and each new impact sounded like flipping a hamburger on a hot grill.

But the scary part came with the realization that it was still just sprinkling – and the trees were blocking most of it.

What will happen when the storm really lets go? Logan wondered. *How long would we survive in a cloudburst of this stuff?*

He didn't want to find out.

After another thirty yards, the trees thinned out and a clearing opened up ahead of them, revealing a large two-story log building with a covered wrap-around deck. At first glance, Logan only saw dark windows and an empty yard with no vehicles in sight, but right now, he only cared about the presence of the overhang above the deck.

Howling and cursing, they raced across the open ground and bound up the front steps, making it to shelter. They all gasped for air as if the short run had been a thirty-mile marathon.

"Damn!" Rob said once out of the weather. "What the hell do you call that? I've heard of acid rain but this is crazy!"

"You got me there." Logan puffed.

Kelly took off his flannel shirt and stuck a finger through one of the dozens of holes that had been eaten through the material. "I'd say acid rain pretty much describes it," she replied. "Is everyone okay?"

They made a brief assessment of their injuries and found that their exposed skin had turned bright red, looking like a bad case of sunburn. It stung like it, too. Rob and Kelly had been somewhat protected thanks to the long-sleeved shirts, but both Tina and Logan had scatterings of small blisters on their arms.

"It's a good thing we got out of it when we did," Tina commented, glaring at Rob.

"What do you think could've caused it?" Kelly asked. "We're miles from anything!"

As if to answer, an elongated pulse of lightning flickered overhead. It flashed on and off throughout the storm like a kilowatt strobe light, revealing the clouds hidden within the darkness above.

The group fell silent, stunned by the sight.

The sky had become an enormous spiral of twisting black vapor, a vortex covering the entire region, all of it swirling like a miniature hurricane.

"Jesus Christ," Rob whispered.

And then the view vanished as the darkness returned.

Now the rain came down at full force. It poured out of the sky, hissing through the trees with that bacon-sizzle sound. Logan watched leaves disintegrate almost instantly in the tempest, and within less than a minute, it had stripped every branch in sight bare.

"My God." Tina gasped. Everyone else remained speechless.

The wind gusted and a sheet of the acidic rainwater blew under the deck's overhang, dappling the floorboards near the group's feet with a scattering of burn marks. They all lunged backward, flattening to the cabin's outer wall.

"We can't stay out here," Kelly said. "If the wind changes direction, it just might reach us next time."

Logan nodded his agreement and hammered on the cabin's door, shouting for help. He tried the knob.

"Locked."

"Hold up the shirt," Rob said, pointing. The door had nine panels of beveled glass, and Logan positioned his tattered flannel over the pane closest to the doorknob, holding it in place as Rob used his elbow to shatter the glass. Neither of the girls objected.

Rob reached in, undid the deadbolt.

They all filed through the door.

"Hello," Logan called, already knowing there'd be no answer.

The cabin looked more like a new house on the inside. The decor appeared to be Scandinavian in style, judging from what little he could see of it, utilizing lots of pine woodwork to perpetuate the rustic theme – an image that was somewhat broken by the presence of a digital readout thermostat and an intercom system. When lightning flashed outside, the rooms appeared as any other family household during a nighttime storm. If not for their unusual predicament, the normality of it might have been soothing.

Kelly tried the light switch beside the door while Rob went left, into an appliance-crammed kitchen.

"No power," Kelly informed him.

"Phone's dead, too," Rob called from the shadows.

"That means we're trapped here," Tina said.

Thunder exploded overhead, rattling the windowpanes like invisible hands clawing at the glass.

"Look," Logan said once the commotion had passed, "this place is obviously someone's second home. It's well stocked and probably maintained on a regular basis. Let's look around and see if we can find a cell phone or a radio."

They all nodded.

Overhead, the rain on the rooftop sounded vaguely like percolating coffee.

"See if you can find a flashlight while you're in there," he said to Rob and Tina. "We'll check the other rooms."

Across from the entry, a carpeted staircase led to the second floor, its right-hand railing open to the large main living room. Over that area, the vaulted ceiling reached at least twenty feet high, and the windows along its tallest outer wall let in plenty of ambient light to see by. The upper hallway at the top of the steps was also exposed to the lower room, and Logan counted three doors on that level.

"Upstairs or down?" Kelly asked.

"Let's stick down here for now," Logan replied, listening to the tapping on the rooftop.

A huge stone fireplace dominated the far back wall of the cabin, whereas the space to their left, just beneath the stairs, housed a massive entertainment center with a wide screen HD television, satellite receiver, surround sound speakers, TiVo, and DVD player. A leather couch and a matching pair of chairs made up a central seating area between the electronics and the huge windows on the right, but to Logan, they looked like a group of monolithic tombstones in the dim light of the room.

"This is someone's idea of roughing it?" Kelly asked.

Logan smiled. "Camping must mean no central air."

She laughed, but her amusement carried a forced undertone to it.

As Kelly went to search the far end of the room, Logan paused to check a cordless phone that sat on an end table between two of the chairs – just in case. The moment his fingertips touched the handset, something hissed from behind him.

He jumped and spun around—

But saw nothing.

After three seconds of silence, the sound repeated itself, and this time he saw what created it. Rainwater dripped on one of the chairs, causing the leather to bubble at the point of contact, raising small wisps of steam.

He looked up in time to see a third droplet nose-dive out of the darkness overhead.

"It's eating through the roof," he called out to the rest of the group. "I think we only bought ourselves a limited amount of time."

"Logan, quick, in here!" Kelly called, having disappeared through an open doorway to the left of the fireplace. He perceived an encouraging note of excitement in the tone of her voice and hurried to rejoin her.

The door opened into a short hallway, and he found her in the first of two rooms, a small office, standing next to an olive-green metal box.

"A radio!" she said.

"I found a flashlight!" Rob called from the front of the house. "It works, too!"

"Bring it here," Logan told him.

"Do you know how to work it?" Kelly asked.

"I'll figure it out." He took her hand and squeezed it. "You might've just saved us."

Rob and Tina appeared, and they all hunkered in front of the machine while Logan examined the controls. He located a power switch on the front panel, but when he tried it, nothing happened.

He pulled the unit away from the wall and cursed at what he saw.

"Damn, it's electric."

"Well, what else did you expect?" Tina asked.

Logan met her eyes, but saw only trepidation in her features.

"I was hoping it might have a battery back-up. If it does, it's dead."

Rob smacked the desk. "So we're back to where we started."

"Not quite," Logan replied. He took the flashlight. "All we have to do is get the power back on. The breaker box is probably in the basement, or a utility closet."

"There's a door with steps leading down as you enter the kitchen," Tina stated. "It's right next to the refrigerator."

Logan snapped his fingers to emphasize the ease of the task. "If that's all the problem is, then we'll be in business in no time."

"What if it's the storm, though?" Kelly asked. "What if that acid stuff melted the lines?"

Logan saw everyone's optimism falter at the thought. "Most of the power cables around here are buried underground," he said. "It helps protect against forest fires started by downed wires." He didn't know if that was true, but it sounded good and seemed to restore their faith. He went for the door, then stopped short as more corrosive liquid began dripping from the ceiling.

"We don't have long," he thought aloud. Turning to the others, he added, "You three, go check the upstairs and see if there's any heavy clothing we could use as protection against this shit. We might need it." He faced the hallway again. "There might be more leaks, though, so watch yourself—"

He halted in his tracks, snapped up the flashlight.

"What's wrong?" Rob asked from behind him.

Logan opened his mouth but didn't answer. He'd been about to step through the doorway of the room across the hall from the den – a small bedroom by the look of it – when he thought he saw something move. The sight only lasted for a split second, but in that instant, he glimpsed a stout shape silhouetted against the far window, on the opposite side of a bed. Then it was gone.

As if it ducked behind the mattress, he thought.

But when he angled the flashlight's beam in that direction, it revealed nothing but clean tan-colored carpet.

"Dude, what is it?" Rob prodded.

Logan shook his head. "Nothing, I guess. I thought I saw someone by the bed."

"What?" Tina demanded with a detectable trace of fear in her tone.

"It was just a mistake," he replied. "There's nothing here." He did a cursory sweep of the room with the light, but other than the bed, it looked empty.

Lightning flickered again, coming in through the window, and the flash reaffirmed what the handheld light had already proven. But now Logan's mind had turned toward thoughts of horror movies – four people trapped in a cabin with a spooky storm raging outside. Where had he seen that one before? – and he quickly shone the light at the base of the bed, expecting it to reflect back in a hateful set of yellow eyes peering out from underneath. On the contrary, the bed sat barely three inches off the floor; not a prime hiding spot for a killer.

"Come on," he said, eager to leave the tight hallway. "Check the rest of the rooms and be quick about it. I'll get the breakers on."

"I want to stay with you," Kelly said.

"Okay," he agreed. "But let's hurry."

They moved toward the kitchen as Rob and Tina headed upstairs. The rain continued to pour out of the night in great torrents, and the patter-peck sound of it on the glass made him glance out the massive living room windows.

Kelly had been right earlier. The wind had changed direction. It had picked up speed, as well, and now the downpour outside whisked wildly in every direction, spraying clear across the deck, against the outer walls of the building.

But the sight didn't compare to the view of the woods.

Despite the blustery wind, a haze of white fog had arisen within the encompassing forest, an obscuring white vapor of steam or smoke that wafted off the trees. Even as they watched, several of the taller pines in the distance tipped and fell to the ground.

"Oh, God." Kelly gasped. "There's no way we'll make it out of here in time."

"Yes, we will," Logan corrected, but his words lacked the level of confidence he'd meant to convey. "Come on." He took hold of her hand and continued forward.

They found three new leaks in the kitchen. Two just dripped, but one streamed from the ceiling to the floor at a steady pace, buckling the linoleum tiles.

Focusing on the task at hand, they went straight to the narrow door Tina had described and opened it, finding it led into an imposingly dark stairwell.

Logan scanned the steps with the flashlight then started down.

At the bottom of the steps, the cinder block stairwell gave way to ancient rock walls of fitted stone and a bare dirt floor that gave off the odor of a cave. Moisture floated in the air like restless spirits, felt but unseen, making the space musty and dank. Runoff from the leaks upstairs trickled between the ceiling joists somewhere deeper in the darkness, sounding like mocking impish laughter.

Kelly uttered a soft sound of disgust but said nothing, and Logan trod off the last runner of the staircase like stepping onto the moon.

He guessed that the basement had to be a full century older than the structure above it, suggesting that the original cabin had been torn down and rebuilt. Whereas the rooms upstairs looked modern and aesthetic, the basement was a pit.

He panned the flashlight across the earthy chamber, straining his eyes to pick out detail in the murk. The light's beam seemed weaker here, less revealing. Large old appliances littered the room, casting jagged shadows on the walls – a wood stove, a wringer and washbasin, a rusted water tank, a well hand-pump, a tangle of copper piping – items probably from the cabin's first incarnation that the owners weren't ready to throw away yet.

"There," he finally said, halting the light on a gray metallic box mounted to the far wall. They hurried across the room, and Logan flipped open the panel's cover to divulge twin rows of grime-coated circuit breakers.

Kelly screamed.

It came out as a piercing sound of mixed terror and surprise, a cry so loud and unexpected in the silent black junkyard of a basement that it startled Logan into dropping the flashlight.

Kelly ran. She crashed past a stack of empty paint cans and clambered up the steps before Logan even had a chance to bend down and retrieve the light.

Part of him wanted to follow her, find out what had frightened her before coming back, but he knew they needed power to call for help, and he resisted the compelling urge to chase after her.

He scooped up the light. Aimed it at the far wall.

And saw what had made Kelly scream.

A blob.

An oblong yellow-green blob of slime.

It sat in the nearest corner of the room, tucked behind the heaped appliances, backed against the stone. It couldn't have been more than three feet tall and slightly narrower in width.

At first glance, his mind's elementary perception classified it as a mold of some kind, or a giant accumulation of naturally occurring mucus. But it had eyes! They blinked and squinted the second he turned the flashlight on it – at least two-dozen of them, gold with irregular black pupils – each varying in size and moving independently from the others.

The creature had sucked itself into a tighter ball when the light exposed its hiding place, and a number of stubby tentacles flipped up as if to shield it from an attack.

"What the … " he began, but found himself unable to finish the thought.

The thing's numerous pupils quickly adjusted to the light, and after a moment, the stunted appendages lowered, relaxed. Even as Logan watched it, he realized that the blob was now studying him in the same manner he was inspecting it.

"What are you?" he finally managed.

Six of the thing's eyes lifted from their sockets, supported on thin green stalks that escalated two feet above its gelatinous emerald bulk, dribbling yellow ooze as they rose.

Logan flinched but didn't flee. He stared at it in awe, perplexed, not really seeing the blob as a threat until a wide mouth split across its viscous body and opened to disgorge a thick pink tongue over countless rows of white triangular teeth.

Then it was as if he were six years old again, running from a nightmare, screaming like he'd glimpsed a moonlit hand reach out of the closet. It wasn't so much the sight of the being's tooth-filled maw that inspired such panic, but what he'd heard come out of it – a noise that not only implied intelligence but malevolence.

The thing had laughed at him.

Logan shot toward the steps. He jumped the first three risers and took the others two at a time. Rob and Tina appeared in the kitchen at the same moment he crossed the doorframe, followed by Kelly, who stopped at the entryway.

"Stay back!" Logan shouted.

"What the hell's going on?" Rob asked. He and Tina both wore padded winter coats with hoods and held several other articles of clothing in their arms.

Logan slammed the door. "There's something down there!" he yelled.

"That's what she said," Rob replied, nodding toward Kelly.

Kelly remained at a distance, hugging herself and shaking. "They don't believe it," she said.

Rob looked to him. "She said there's a monster down there. How the hell would you react?"

"She's telling the truth." He gasped. "I don't know what it is, but it isn't human."

Rob tossed the extra coats on the counter. "Yeah, but a monster? Are you sure you didn't see—"

"I'm sure," Logan and Kelly both replied.

Everyone paused in silence for a moment, watching the door, uncertain what to do. The sound of the rain drumming on the roof filled the room, and from farther away came the sound of another falling tree. Logan also thought he detected the acrid smell of rotted wood.

"What about the power?" Rob asked. "Did you find the—"

"Yes," Logan answered. "But that thing surprised me before I could flip the switch." He looked around, ashamedly adding, "I lost the flashlight, too."

"So what do we do?" Tina asked. "I'm not staying in here if there's a—"

"We can't go anywhere else," Rob cut in, gesturing toward the window. "And if that storm keeps up, this whole damn place will come down on our heads!"

Logan glanced around and saw that the number of leaks coming through the kitchen ceiling had tripled, forcing Rob to maneuver around them as he crossed the floor to Logan's side.

"We have to get that power on," his friend said. "Do you think one of us could run down there, hit the switch, and get back up without ... whatever it is you saw doing anything to us?"

Logan shrugged. "I don't know," he admitted. "It didn't look like it could move very fast, but it sure as hell has teeth. Lots of them."

A crash boomed from somewhere upstairs, instantly followed by the sound of rushing water and hissing steam, causing everyone to jump.

"The bedroom," Tina said, looking up. "When we were up there, the ceiling in one of the rooms looked ready to cave in."

Rob faced Logan in the gloom, looking all the more determined. "We need to try it," he said. "Or at least go to the bottom of the steps and check it out."

Logan hesitated, but then agreed. "Okay."

Rob picked up a broom that leaned against the refrigerator to their left, gave a nod of readiness, and Logan opened the door at the exact same moment a bolt of lightning flashed outside, filling the black stairwell with its light.

The blob was coming up the steps.

Half its eyes hovered above its gooey body now, suspended like antennas, and multiple tentacles plastered the stairwell walls, pulling it upward. Its horrid mouth still hung agape, and Logan saw fat globules of slime drip heavily from its rolling tongue.

"Holy crap!" Rob blurted.

The lightning blinked out, and the creature vanished in the prevailing dark.

Logan threw the door closed again. "See what I mean!" he roared.

Rob's face appeared livid. "W – what the fuck?"

"What was it?" Tina pleaded. "What did you see?"

Suddenly the door bucked, rammed from the other side, and everyone screamed. Rob and Logan threw themselves against the wood, holding it in the frame, but the driving force rivaled even their combined muscle.

"Lock it!" Rob cried, pushing with all his might.

Logan looked to the knob in his hands. "There is no lock!"

"Shit!"

Tina shook her head with denial. Kelly sobbed into her hands.

Logan turned to shout at them for help when he felt something bump into his foot. Looking down, he saw that one of the creature's eyestalks had oozed through the thin gap between the door and the floor and now stared up at him.

He cried out and stomped on the quarter-size orb, feeling it pop through the sole of his shoe, like stepping on a fat grape. At that same instant, a fierce and haunting wail of pain arose from the opposite side of the door, an alien sound that vibrated through Logan's bones.

"We need weapons!" Rob screamed at the girls.

Kelly dashed away from where she stood and retreated toward the living room, leaving Tina alone. The other girl remained bolted in place, looking like one of the many victim statues in a wax museum of horrors.

A tentacle extended under the door and slapped up against the wood.

Then another. And another.

Logan kicked at each, but they resisted his assault. He heard a brief chatter of splintering wood, then a loud firecracker pop as the door split up the middle.

"Jesus!" Rob barked.

Kelly abruptly reappeared at the entry of the kitchen, carrying a fireplace stoker, scissor tongs, and two logs of wood. "Here," she said. "It's all I could find."

Logan took the poker, Rob the tongs. Together, the three of them began beating at the trio of ghastly tentacles, hammering them as hard as they could. Unlike its eyes, however, the creature's limbs appeared to feel no pain, and each of their blows landed with no visible sign of damage.

"Damn!" Rob huffed.

There was another hollow-bone snap and the crack in the door lengthened, reaching all the way to the top. Logan could feel the wood bowing inward now, about to break in half.

"This can't be happening," Tina cried.

Logan searched right and left with frantic twists of his head, finally spotting an empty water dish and food tray at the base of the refrigerator, the kind designed for pets.

Without a word, he grabbed the dish and pushed away from the door, holding the plastic container under the fastest running ceiling leak. Rob shouted at him, screaming that he couldn't hold the door by himself, but Logan knew it wouldn't matter in a few more seconds; the thing was coming through. He just wanted to buy them enough time to get clear of it.

With about a cup of rainwater in the bowl, he turned and splashed the acidic liquid on the blob's exposed tentacles. Black smoke billowed from the monster's flesh on contact, hissing and popping like water on hot grease, and the three limbs jerked back under the door, recoiling to the sound of the blob's freakish howl.

Logan jumped back, reclaiming the poker.

Rob ran to the far counter, started yanking open drawers.

"Open the front door!" Logan shouted to Tina. "We'll force it outside when it comes through and burn it to ashes!"

The idea seemed to appeal to her, and for the first time since the melee started, Tina reacted. She undid the locks and opened the door. Its cratered outer paneling trailed a million thin streamers of smoke as it swung inward.

Rob pulled a butcher knife from one of the drawers.

Kelly readied more water.

The shattered door to the basement jolted. Sagged back. Jolted again.

"Get ready!" Logan warned.

With a loud bang, the wood burst into pieces, half of it clattering to the floor in a hail of destruction, the rest dangling at awkward angles from its tortured hinges. The blob appeared immediately. It slid into the center of the kitchen as if gliding on ice, its multitude of eyeballs raking the scene.

Tina shrieked. Until then, she'd been the only one who hadn't seen it.

Logan fidgeted about eight feet away, poker in hand, ready to swing, but he hesitated to move closer. The creature barely came up to his waist, but after what he'd seen it do to the door, he knew he couldn't underrate its abilities based on its size.

"Hook it!" Rob yelled. "I'll get it with the tongs!"

Logan nodded and took a step forward, then it swiveled in his direction, aligning him with its mouth, and he instantly backed off.

"Kill it!" Tina screamed.

But Kelly acted first. Without warning, she lunged at the monster and flicked the contents of the dog dish at its globular body. Corrosive rainwater drenched it from top to bottom and more black smoke erupted from a hundred rupturing blisters.

"Yeah!" Rob shouted. The blob undulated wildly, wailing in pain, and he took advantage of its torment, slicing with the knife.

The blade lopped off one of the eyestalks.

It dropped to the tile, twitching like a spasmodic serpent.

Rob drew back for a second attack, but the creature turned on him before he could strike. Its tongue shot out of its yawning mouth like a fleshy-pink cannonball and smacked him square in the face, rocking his head back as if he'd been punched by a professional boxer.

He staggered backward but didn't fall over. When his head tipped forward again, Logan saw five or six slender black spines protruding from his face. They stuck out at downcast angles due to the trajectory in which they'd gone in, all clustered around his nose and right cheek. One had entered through his upper lip, pinning it up in a gum-flashing snarl.

"Rob!" Tina screamed.

Their friend looked dazed, not sure of what had just happened, and he dreamily raised his free hand to the offending objects that now jutted from his flesh, touching them lightly. The ends of each had sagged slightly at first, Logan noticed, as if soft and pliable, but then quickly straightened out as they hardened before his eyes.

Rob grasped one and pulled.

He had a good three inches to hold onto – and another six came out of his head. Logan gagged at the sight. The sound it made coming out proved just as bad, like fingernails on a chalkboard, and Logan felt a scream building in his throat at the contemplation of *why* it sounded that way.

With the bony needle extracted, Rob's eyes rolled over and he collapsed to the floor. The blob lunged at his legs.

"No!" Logan roared. He'd been stunned immobile by the raw hideousness of what had transpired, by the mind-boggling reality of their entire ordeal, but now he leapt forward, hammering the fireplace poker down on the top of the slime-coated monster.

Tina screamed throughout the whole episode, her cries steadily escalating, passing from mere fear into the realm of hysteria.

Logan struck the creature's blubbery torso twice, swinging with rage, swinging with vengeance, but to little affect. On the upward arc of his third try, a *second* mouth ripped open on his side of the blob, expelling a savage growl. Although smaller than the first, it seemed to include the same quantity of teeth.

Its tongue exploded out and seized the poker, wrapping itself tight around the shaft. This close, Logan could see the prickly tips of a dozen more spines and quickly relinquished his grip, abandoning the tool.

Kelly splashed it with more water and it recoiled in agony.

"No!" Tina continued to shriek, feverishly shaking her head, backing away from the beast. "No, this isn't real! This isn't happening! None of this is happening! It can't be! This just can't be real!"

She ran out the door.

"Tina, don't!" Kelly shouted. But the other girl had already leapt from the deck, swallowed by the deadly downpour. Kelly tried to chase after her, and Logan grabbed her by the arm, pulling her back.

Tina made it ten feet from the cabin before she fell, gaining another two yards as her momentum carried her to the ground. She crashed to the mud screaming, enveloped in a cloud of steam coming off her skin and clothing, flopping through the noxious rainwater.

"She's melting!" Kelly cried as Logan held her back.

He reached out with one hand and threw the door closed, knowing there was nothing they could do. Right now they had their own crisis to deal with.

The blob was moving toward them.

"Let's get in the living room," he said. "There's more space in there. Maybe we can lead it away from Rob."

He looked past the beast, to where Rob had collapsed against the far cupboards. In a quick flicker of lightning, he saw that the skin of his friend's head had swollen grotesquely, almost doubling in size.

"Now! Let's go!"

They both turned and charged into the airy chamber, entering the room in time to see a *second* blob emerge from the far hallway, out of the doorway by the fireplace.

And this one stood at least five feet high.

"Oh, God, no!" Kelly shouted, stopping hard in her tracks.

Logan thought of the bedroom across from the den, the shape he'd seen in the window. There *had* been something under the bed! Three inches of clearance might not accommodate a human prowler, but it obviously posed no problem for these jelly-bodied monsters.

"Upstairs," he said, and they twisted around, raced up the staircase.

The leaks spilled down everywhere here. They dripped, streamed, trickled, and gushed from dozens of locations, peeling the wall paint and smoldering in the carpet. Logan got hit twice as they hurried up the risers, and he gritted his teeth in pain as the liquid ate into his skin.

Over the right-hand railing of the open hallway, he could see the heavier blob oozing across the floor below, eyes fixed on them, heading for the stairs. It passed under several of the ceiling leaks that showered into the living room, but despite taking damage, it kept moving forward.

At the base of the steps, the smaller blob had already started up.

"We need to find a place we can barricade ourselves in," he stammered.

As he recalled, he saw three doors on this level, and they tried each in succession. The first one opened into a bedroom. A large section of sheetrock had fallen across the bed, leaving a gaping hole in the ceiling, and Logan guessed that this was the room Tina had commented on earlier, the source of the crash. Wet pink insulation hung from the opening like disemboweled intestines.

They went to the next door: a kid's room. He spotted a set of bunk beds and combination desk/bookcase that could've made good reinforcements for the door, but the ceiling here looked in immediate danger of mimicking the damage they'd seen in the first room, so they quickly moved on.

The last door opened into a medium-size bathroom. Unlike the rest of the cabin, no leaks rained from the ceiling in here and the overhead sheetrock appeared smooth and intact. On the other hand, the flimsy construction of its hollow-core door didn't inspire great levels of confidence.

"Logan," Kelly mewed, grabbing his arm. He swung around to see her facing the way they'd come and witnessed the first blob slip off the steps. The second one trailed right behind it – followed by a *third*!

"This'll have to do," he said. "Quick! Get in!"

No sooner had he closed the door and engaged the push-button lock when he heard the first hard thuds from the opposite side. A single window broke the room's near-perfect darkness, but, other than during a lightning flash, only let in enough light to scarcely define its basic dimensions. Though he couldn't see them in the dark, Logan sensed the movement of the blobs' green tentacles as they began squeezing beneath the door.

"Get back!" he yelled.

A blaze of lightning lit the air, and Logan saw four slippery appendages squirming into the room.

"We need something to stop them," Kelly said.

Feeling blindly in the gloom, Logan tore open the medicine cabinet over the sink and began searching through its contents, needing to handle each of the items in order to tell what they were. He felt for razorblades, rubbing alcohol, hairspray, anything. But the owners obviously restocked the cabinet's supplies with each visit, and right now the only items he could find were tubes of antibiotic ointment, band-aids, and skin lotion.

"Damnit!"

Two of the tentacles abandoned their sightless search and curled upward, audibly suctioning to the door. The wood groaned.

Logan ran a shaky hand across his face, frantically searching for something to fight with, when his eyes settled on the toilet.

"Yes!"

Moving swiftly, he lifted the lid off the toilet's water tank and placed it on the floor, wrapping it in a shaggy rubber-backed rug that lay next to the tub.

"Look out," he told Kelly. "Get in the tub and close your eyes."

"What for—"

"Just do it!"

As soon as she moved out of the way, he raised the bundle above his head and smashed it down on the floor as hard as he could. The impact shook the whole room, and Kelly let out a sharp cry of surprise in the dark. When he unwrapped the rug, the ceramic lid had fractured into a score of thick, wicked-edged shards.

He seized up one of the pieces. "Let the amputations begin."

Logan whirled around even as the wood splintered and began hacking, slicing, cutting at the rubbery limbs that strove to break down the door. He attacked with blind slashes, but he felt the succumbing contact of the creatures' flesh and heard the satisfying howls of pain.

He laughed in triumph as he chopped, a sound that came out a little too unrestrained, like the first suspicious sound made by a car engine running full tilt with no oil.

"Who's laughing now, slimeball?"

Another flash of lightning illuminated the bathroom and he saw that the tentacles had retreated, leaving behind a mess of withering severed segments.

"Logan!" Kelly suddenly gasped. "Logan, there's a car outside!"

He stood, peering into the storm, and when the next flash came, he saw the garage – a large aluminum structure about sixty feet away, nestled in the tree line. Two roll-up doors and one person-size entry gave access to the front of the building, and he immediately noticed that the first of the big twin doors rested partway open. There, in the shadowy interior, Logan made out the front grill of a vehicle parked inside.

"Do you think we could reach it?" Kelly asked.

"Are you kidding? I doubt we'd even make it to the ground!"

"Logan, we could get away from here!"

"You saw what happened to Tina!"

"Yeah, but she didn't have this!" she said, and yanked on the shower curtain.

Logan opened his mouth to protest, then didn't. Instead, he reached out and felt the smooth vinyl material, letting the idea sink in. He recalled how the dog dish hadn't melted.

From deeper in the building, there came an augural bellow of stressed timbers, low and foreboding, a noise closely pursued by a distressing shift in the cabin's overall balance. The entire room suddenly felt slanted.

"Looks like we might not have a choice," he said. "Let's try it."

Kelly pulled down the curtain while Logan carefully opened the window and knocked out the screen, snapping his hand back when he felt the sting of the rain.

"Give me the curtain," he said.

Draping it over his arm, he slowly reached out into the storm. The rain pattered noisily off its surface but didn't seem to harm it.

"This may just work!" he cheered. "Damn good think—"

Something metallic banged against the sink, making them both flinch and cry out. Logan yanked his arm back inside and pivoted to face the noise, as did Kelly, and what they saw arrested their breaths in mid-draw. All had been oddly quiet on the other side of the door, and now Logan understood why; he spotted the room's overhead vent cover lying on the floor, and when he looked to the ceiling, he witnessed one of the blobs ooze into view, emerging from the ductwork!

Kelly shrieked as five plum-sized eyeballs dangled into the room.

"Out! Now! Let's go!"

Logan shrouded himself and slipped outside, using the toilet like a step, then held out the shower curtain to shield Kelly as she made her egress onto the roof.

The blob in the vent spilled free and plopped to the floor.

They found themselves on the furthest side of the building from the point where they'd entered, and it became apparent that the covered deck didn't fully encompass the cabin as Logan had originally presumed. The overhang here proved minimal, maybe a foot and a half of standing room between the outer wall and the drop-off. On the good side, the owners had chosen slate roofing tiles to augment the building's lodgelike façade, and the stone shingles appeared to have withstood the caustic properties of the rain.

Nevertheless, as they adjusted their position, shuffling out of reach of the window, Logan felt the tiles displace beneath their feet, slipping precariously, like they floated in mud. Evidently, the water had affected everything else beneath them.

They traveled to the left, edging along until they located a section of ground that didn't have standing pools of rainwater. The route took them away from their intended target, but upon exiting the window, Logan had noticed the section of roof to the right – the direction of the cabin's chimney – didn't look safe. The massive tower of stonework had separated from the rest of the building, tilting a scary three feet outward, and he didn't want to be near it if it fell.

When he glanced at it again, he caught fleeting glimpses of green shapes moving within the bathroom's window frame but nothing had followed them outside.

They eased to the edge of the overhang and looked down.

"This is going to hurt," Logan said. "If we move fast, get up quick enough, maybe it won't be so bad ... " He took her hand. "Are you ready?"

Kelly's face looked ashen and frail, but determination shone in her eyes. "I'm ready."

"Hold on tight."

They counted to three – and jumped.

Logan remembered launching himself off the ledge of his tree-fort at age eight, a stunt he preformed on a regular basis back then, but a nine-foot drop for a skin-and-bones boy became a whole different experience for a 174 pound man twenty years later.

The landing equated to voluntarily leaping feet-first into the path of a runaway truck. His heel bones felt like they exploded on impact, and thank God he'd remembered to roll or his chin would've imbedded in the mud directly between them.

The rain hit instantly, biting into his skin with toxic brutality. Then he was standing, ignoring the pain, yanking the shower curtain back over his head. He'd separated from Kelly in the fall, but she sprung up just as fast and appeared by his side before he needed to look for her.

Her face pinched with agony, sizzling sounds issuing within her shirt.

Logan felt it, too, searing down his back, across his

arms.

"Go!" he shouted through the pain. "Run as fast as you can!"

They moved in tandem, blazing through the night, the shower curtain fanning out in their wake like a cape. The garage door stood only halfway up and they ducked to get inside without slowing their pace, shoes slapping across the concrete slab floor. The moment they encountered dry ground again, they flung the curtain aside and started tearing off their shirts, pants, shoes, and socks, casting them away. They exhaled haggard breaths, panting out of pain and exhaustion, but faint smiles crept onto their faces in the wake of their maneuver.

"Still alive?" Logan asked.

"Still alive."

Logan didn't let the small victory overpower his better judgment, though. He searched the darkness as he stripped down to his boxers, sweeping the shadows of the garage. He systematically evaluated the security of their new surroundings, inventorying what items he could see, planning their next move.

But, overall, he was looking for blobs.

Someone had to open the door, an inner voice cautioned.

He kicked away his last sock and started to turn his attention toward the vehicle – a shiny black vintage Camero – when a thunderous crash boomed from outside.

He spun around and pushed the roll-up door higher, revealing a spectacle that left his jaw hanging. The chimney side of the cabin had totally collapsed to the ground, the roof of the living room having caved-in over the gap. The rest of the building disintegrated in slow motion as he watched, its shape contorting oddly, sagging and bending lower and lower, warping to the ruthless affects of the rain.

"Jesus," he whispered. "We barely made it."

He glanced to Kelly. She too had stripped to her underwear, wearing only her bra and panties now, and though she had the toned body of an athlete, he saw nothing erotic about her condition. Wet and shivering, her skin a patchwork of cold pale flesh and contrasting red burns, she hugged herself across her chest, looking out the open door, standing barefoot on the hard concrete like the apparition of a dead girl. Logan ached with compassion for her at that moment, realizing how much he cared for her. He wanted to hold her tight, shield her from this dreadful night, to somehow make her safe.

He had no time for romantics, though.

He turned to pull the door down so the rain wouldn't blow in, when his gaze landed on the rectangular casing of a switchbox mounted to the wall. To his astonishment, three overhead fluorescent lights flickered on when he tried it.

"Holy shit!" he laughed. "We've got power!"

The two of them resurveyed the interior of the garage, now able to view its entirety. They stood beside the car in the middle of the open space, directly across from a long workbench and a number of gas-powered lawn care appliances. In the stall on the other side of the car sat a trailer with two fiberglass canoes.

Logan's gaze drifted to the area beside the workbench and he gasped at what he saw: Slime. It coated the floor and a good portion of the wall, all of it concentrated around a tall electrical box similar to the one he'd seen in the basement of the cabin. PVC conduit rose from the floor beneath it, connecting at its base.

The panel hung open and when Logan approached it, he saw what he'd feared.

He pointed at the piping. "That's how the blobs got into the house," he said shakily. "That's why the garage door is open: they broke in here first, then they slipped through the underground conduit to the basement the same way they oozed through that air vent."

Kelly remained silent, but by the worry expressed on her face he guessed that she already knew the danger.

"They could use it to get back here."

She shook her head at the idea, her eyes begging for him to take it back. "But the house is gone. It caved in, for God's sake! They couldn't have survived. Not after that!"

"We can't take the chance," he said. "We're getting out of here!"

He located a large stand-up toolbox at one side of the work area and opened the first few drawers, selecting a thin flat-head screwdriver and a hammer from the items inside.

"Do you think it'll be safe to drive in that stuff?" Kelly asked as Logan approached the muscle car. "I mean, what if the tires melt, or the roof leaks?"

"The rain only seems to affect organic material," he answered. "Or maybe it just works *faster* on biological things. Either way, we should be okay long enough to reach town."

He'd been prepared to smash out one of the back windows to gain entry to the vehicle, knowing he could duct-tape a section of the shower curtain over the empty frame, but the doors proved to be unlocked.

He slid in across the passenger seat and fit the screwdriver's blade into the ignition keyhole, using the hammer to forcibly drive it through the tumblers.

"Look!" Kelly suddenly cried. "They're coming!"

Logan glanced to where she pointed and heard a burbling noise coming from the circuit breaker box. A cluster of slime bubbles seeped from the piping.

He twisted the handle of the screwdriver, but nothing happened. He struck it twice more with the hammer. "Get in the car," he said. "In the back!"

"But we'll be trapped!" she replied. "They'll ooze through the vents!"

He trained his gaze on the electrical box, saw eyeballs sprouting from inside the panel. "Oh, crap, you're right!"

He leapt out of the vehicle and bolted to the far end of the workbench – watching the eyes track his movements – and raced to where various garden tools hung neatly on wall hooks. Beside them sat a riding lawn mower, a hedge trimmer, a chainsaw, a leaf blower; all devices that required...

Gasoline!

He found a plastic five-gallon container of it in one of the lower metal cabinets, as well as a small propane tank fitted with a pistol-grip starter. Perfect.

The first blob had already partially extracted itself from the box by the time he returned to the car and uncapped the jug. It clung to the wall like a massive glob of snot, and he quickly doused it with the flammable liquid, sloshing it from a distance. The monster didn't even seem to notice.

Logan backed up to the open door of the car and got in, tossing the empty can at the blob. He opened the shut-off valve of the propane tank and clicked the trigger, instantly igniting a bluish-orange flame.

The first blob moved off the wall, onto the fuel-splashed floor.

A second one secreted from the electrical panel.

"Get down," he told Kelly. Then, using the door like a

shield, he reached out and lobbed the propane tank through the air.

Whoosh!

The blast only lasted for a split second, but during that moment the whole room transformed into a nebulous orange fireball; suddenly, flames consumed everything: the floor, the walls, even the air. It was the fumes, Logan knew. Trapped within the confines of the aluminum building, they'd become concentrated and filled the space with explosive vapors. He recoiled from the heat as it pulsed through the paneling of the car.

Thankfully the explosion burned itself out almost instantly, leaving only the area drenched in gas leaping with flames.

Logan peered out through the window and saw the blobs completely encased in fire, his satisfaction further enhanced by the fact that both of them lay still. A second explosion of sparks erupted in all directions from the circuit breaker panel, and the overhead lights went dark, leaving the blaze as their only source to see by.

He felt a smile of success creep across his face as he watched the burning heap, heard Kelly sobbing with joy from behind him. But the smile quickly faded and the cheers ceased as the blob on the floor began to *grow*.

Logan stared in disbelief as the thing inexplicably expanded!

"No way!"

Covered in fire, it bloated to almost twice its original size, swelling like a threatened puffer fish; then suddenly it popped!

Numerous flaming globules splattered against the door and windows, each hit sounding like the impact of a slushy snowball. In the aftermath, Logan counted twenty or so slimy cantaloupe-size fragments spread across the room.

And each was alive!

Suddenly they weren't just facing one creature; they were surrounded!

The fire, Logan's mind raged. *It doesn't kill them ... it makes them multiply!*

The smaller blobs on the car began to slide around the hood and windshield, some moving blindly, others with eyes, and Logan knew they had just minutes – or perhaps only seconds – before the creatures located the ventilation openings and got inside.

Logan picked up the hammer and went back to work on the screwdriver, pounding the blade harder as the miniature monsters explored the exterior of the car.

Beyond the open garage door, a burst of lightning lit the region, accompanied by a deafening grumble of thunder, and before the flash extinguished, Kelly gasped in shock and grabbed Logan's arm.

"Oh, my God, Logan, look!"

He thought for certain that her cry of surprise pertained to the blobs on the hood, having witnessed some horrific new ability of their unearthly opponents, but before he could ask for clarification, she pointed out the windshield and said, "I think I saw Rob!"

"What?"

"In the flash of lightning," she explained. "I saw someone come out of the wreckage near the front of the cabin, under the remains of the deck overhang!"

Logan looked again, trying not to notice the creatures in the foreground of his vision. He strained his eyes to cut through the dark, desperately trying to pick out detail in the near-impenetrable haze of the storm.

A fresh blast of airborne electricity lit the grounds around the cabin, spotlighting a slumped and staggering figure that limped along the outer remnants of the building.

"I see him!" Logan exclaimed. "You're right! He's alive!"

"He's dazed, though," Kelly observed. "Oh, Jesus, if he steps out from under there he'll be dissolved in the rain!"

"Not if I can help it!"

He bashed the screwdriver one last time with the hammer, striking it as hard as he could, and the tool stabbed deeper into the mechanism with a cruel snap of metal.

Kelly drew in a sharp breath, about to say something, when the entire car jolted. It rocked up on the passenger side, thumped down hard, and the next thing they knew yellow-green ooze covered the windshield.

Kelly shrieked with a new degree of terror at the throng of eyeballs now glaring at them through the glass, and Logan gaped at the vast tooth-filled mouth that opened less than eighteen inches away. The creature's pink tongue thumped obscenely back and forth against the glass, the blunt sound of its fleshy collisions emphasized by the scratching noise created by the countless sharp spikes concealed within its tip.

Kelly screamed. Logan screamed. The windshield cracked. And that entire racket abruptly reduced to mere background noise when Logan gave the screwdriver one last twist and the Camero's powerful engine roared to life.

Still shouting, he put the vehicle in gear and stomped on the gas. The high-pitched squeal of spinning tires filled the room, then the rubber caught, and they rocketed forward, scraping off more than half the blob on the windshield as the muscle car bullied its way out the partially open garage door, ripping it off its tracks. They plunged into the full fury of the storm, the blob shrieking in pain. It bubbled and thrashed like a leech dropped in saltwater, and before long, its gelatinous green mass vanished within heavy clouds of sooty-black smoke.

The rain cleansed the car in seconds.

With his field of view cleared, Logan realized he was racing pell-mell toward the forest, having kept his foot pressed on the accelerator in the terror of the moment.

He let off the gas, snapped on the headlights.

They were on the side of the cabin where they'd first arrived, ten feet from barreling down the footpath that had brought them here to begin with. Logan spun the wheel, simultaneously applying the brakes.

The car swung around, headlights sweeping the cabin wreckage.

"There he is!" Kelly pointed. "There's Rob!"

Logan saw him, too, and both his heart and his stomach clenched at the sight. Revealed in the vehicle's high beams, Logan discovered that his friend had become a puffy, swollen hulk. He recalled the inflammation he'd seen around the spines in Rob's face, but the effect had spread, and now he looked less like a human being and more like … like one of the blobs.

Logan gagged at the thought of it.

The overstuffed figure lurched and stumbled under an outcropping of fallen roof, turning to face the car. Despite his current physical deformities, Rob's mind obviously still existed in there, even now searching for a way to escape. But he was hurt, confused, and in his traumatized condition, he must not have realized what he was doing when he saw the car.

He shambled toward the lights.

"Oh, God!" Kelly cried. "Not again, Logan! I can't watch it again! Stop him!"

Logan floored the gas pedal but the tires whirled uselessly in the mud for precious seconds before catching traction. By the time they'd crossed the distance and pulled the car alongside him, wispy sheets of steam veiled Rob's distended form as he staggered toward them.

Kelly leaned up between the seats and opened the passenger door.

"Get in!" she called, reaching out to help him.

The blob exploded from Rob's torso. It lunged between Kelly's outstretched arms and slammed into the center of her chest, tackling her into the backseat.

Logan saw it coming a second too late. Their friend was already dead; he'd been dead from the beginning. The moment the balloon-version of Rob's body leaned against the waiting seat, Logan glimpsed the bloody slit up the middle of the man's belly, viewed the churning green mass filling the hollowed-out space within. One of those things had crawled *inside* him! The bastard had used his skin like a raincoat!

He'd tried to alert Kelly, but it leapt on her before the warning left his mouth.

Now lightning streaked overhead, and what happened next seemed to be captured in the swiftness of a camera flash.

Logan struck out, trying to shove the thing back out the door even as the husk of Rob's melting corpse dropped to the ground. The monster poured forth in a thick wave, flowing over the passenger seat to completely smother Kelly, cutting off her cry of surprise. At the same time, he pressed on the gas, trying to get away.

The monster encased Kelly's body in seconds, her last choking shouts muffled to near-inaudibility behind the ooze.

"No!" Logan roared. He twisted around to fight the beast

off her, not thinking in the grip of panic, and both his feet mashed down on the accelerator.

He saw Kelly lying on her back, submersed in green goop, saw the liquid demon pouring into her mouth and nostrils, gold eyeballs and all. He fought wildly, seizing fistfuls of slime, tearing off eyestalks.

The monster's mouth sprang open and its pallid tongue blasted at his head. He ducked fast, dodged it by inches, and spun around in his seat to see the car plunge head-on into the woods.

Even in its current gear the vehicle acted like a bulldozer. It plowed into the undergrowth, leveling everything from bushes to saplings. Logan grasped the steering wheel and spun it hard to the right, cutting a path toward the road that accessed the property.

The car burst from the tree line and hit the driveway embankment going nearly at the same speed it had entered the woods. A terrifying jolt shook the car's frame like a shockwave and the front end jumped skyward. It blasted through an explosion of mud and landed with another heavy crash as the tires met the pavement.

Logan bounced around in his seat like an unsecured crash test dummy, hanging onto the steering wheel for support, and the car careened across the road before he saved it from reentering the trees on the opposite side.

He got the machine under control, kept it stable in the furious wind.

A tentacle lashed around his neck from behind.

Another slapped across his forehead.

He yelled out as they tugged him back, forcing him to arch over the seat. He gripped the slick appendage wrapped around his neck with one hand and held onto the steering wheel with the other, fighting to pull free.

He chanced a glance behind him.

Kelly was gone. At least that's what it looked like. In reality her corpse probably still lay there, covered by the monster, but his overstressed brain imagined that she'd already been consumed by the thing, her mass absorbed, added to its bulk.

"You pile of green shit ... " he croaked. "I'll kill you ... I'll kill you!"

He cranked the steering wheel to the right, then back to the left, swerving the Camero back and forth across the rain-polished asphalt, zigzagging like a suicidal drunk. And the stunt worked! The sudden gyrations proved too much for the blob, forcing it to let go as its amorphous body got sloshed from side to side like a water balloon.

Logan saw his one chance at defeating the beast.

He stepped on the gas, making the engine bellow with power.

He swung the car right, jerked it hard to the left. The road ahead appeared as a phantom line made solid in the headlights, but its distant course remained continuously elusive in the violent weather. He knew that one unexpected turn at this point could mean disaster, but right now, his desire for revenge outweighed the threat of a collision.

He crisscrossed the route left and right, half-laughing, half-crying at the sludgy noises coming from the thing behind him, watching it slip to and fro across the seat in the rearview mirror.

"Must suck not to have arms, huh, jizzwad?"

Still veering dangerously, he leaned across the passenger seat and unlatched the door, throwing out the seat's lap belt the moment it flew open. He swung the car back across the road, not giving the blob a chance to recover, and when the door slammed closed with the movement, the buckle of the dangling safety belt prevented it from latching shut.

"Your turn at some hurt," Logan growled. "This is for my friends!"

He angled the Camero to the right, giving the engine another burst of fuel, and at the last second before going off the road, he cut sharp to the left. The passenger door leapt open with the momentum, swinging wild, and there came a harsh squawk of ruined metal as its hinges bent past their limit.

Logan held on tight but dared to crane his head around to watch the blob go flying out into the rain, wanting to relish the spectacle of its gelatinous ass getting cooked.

But the blob was already gone. Kelly's body, too. The backseat was empty.

He faced the road again, leveling the wheel before going off the road, and—

Felt it on his feet!

He looked down to see countless stubby tentacles hugging his legs, clasping around him even as the creature oozed out from under the seat! Tiny mouths burst open on the tips of some of the reaching limbs and began to snap at his bare skin.

"Ah!" he cried, feeling the first set of teeth.

He kicked and stomped and flailed, but the mouths didn't let up. Each one he crushed divided, creating another, and soon it felt as though he'd waded knee-deep into a school of piranhas. He pulled his bloody feet up onto the seat in a futile effort to escape the tortuous jaws below and looked forward again in time to see the tree in his path.

A huge pine. Lying across the road. Only a car-length away.

His eyes widened.

The Camero hit it full force—

And blasted straight through it like a bullet. The car barely slowed down!

The rain, he thought. *It must've turned the wood to pulp!*

The car may have made it through the obstacle undamaged, but now it careened out of control, sliding sideways down the wet road. Logan battled the wheel, trying to direct the tires into the skid, but the blob's weight continued to press down on the gas pedal at the same time, making the Camero go crazy.

The engine raged, pushing them faster and faster.

Logan looked down at the monster, at its horde of snapping mouths, and clenched his teeth in dire preparation of plunging his feet into its mass with the hope of hitting the brakes.

That's when the lightning struck.

It blasted across the center of the road, simultaneously blinding him with its glare and deafening him with an unbearable bawl of thunder. The next thing he knew, he was flying through the air, out the open passenger door, tumbling end-over-end across the asphalt. He didn't see what caused the crash, but his last heart-racing memory before the lightning was of a huge gray shape towering before him in the storm, materializing out of the sea of rain like a cresting leviathan.

He came to a rest on his back, splayed out on hard concrete, in agony but coherent. Everything hurt – *everything* – and he struggled with an even mixture of profound dread and relief when he discovered that the pain came from inside him, not on him.

He hadn't landed in the rain.

He could still hear the downpour bucketing on the road nearby, could feel the high wind pucker his skin with goosebumps. But where the hell was he?

Lying on his back, he saw a series of dark steel beams overhead, long metal struts supporting a flat concrete structure.

A bridge!

He'd been thrown under a bridge. That's what he'd seen coming through the rain – or, more accurately, seen himself speeding toward. The car must've hit the outer embankment on the way in, and he'd been tossed clear, landing under the overpass. Hissing with the pain it caused, he turned his head to the right and saw the ruined Camero mated with one of the bridge's inner concrete walls, its hood and engine compartment now a peaked and smoky mountain range of bent metal.

The blob lay between them.

Logan gasped – then winced at the paralyzing stab of pain the inhalation triggered. The creature was still alive! But, then again, why wouldn't it be? Its globular body was ideal for absorbing the force of the crash. Logan, on the other hand, felt as broken up on the inside as the car looked on the outside. The blob knew it, too. It crossed the distance to him at a leisurely rate, its froglike eyes gleaming with a hungry anticipation of things to come.

It stood less than four feet from his legs when something tittered not far away. Logan's overstrained mind failed to decipher the meaning of the chirpy noise, and he almost thought he'd imagined it until the blob's eyes whirled in their sockets to face the source.

Logan heard a brief electronic whine, followed by a shimmering globe of yellow light that shot out of the darkness and exploded against the blob's backside.

It disintegrated before Logan's eyes.

No sound, no stroboscopic flare. The monster just turned to ash and crumbled, reduced to an infinitesimal number of microscopic particles that blew apart in the wind, as if the beast had never existed.

With the blob gone, Logan saw three figures approaching through the storm, even now stepping past the ravaged Camero, walking out of the rain. They all wore glossy black armor and helmets, their faces shielded behind reflective visors.

And they all carried guns.

Big guns.

Really big guns. Cannons!

Logan had never seen anything like them outside of sci-fi movies and comic book pages. Each weapon had to be over six feet long with a barrel wide enough to accommodate a basketball.

Two of the men – soldiers? – stopped to search the Camero while the one in the lead marched straight over and leveled the enormous bore of his weapon two feet from Logan's face. He heard the electronic whine issue once again and watched a red-orange flower of light blossom within the deeper reaches of the barrel.

"No," he whimpered, feebly raising a broken arm as if it could somehow shield him from the coming blast.

Then he heard the tittering again, like the singsong call of an exotic bird.

The glow died away and the weapon lowered as one of the other armor-clad strangers came forward. The musical bird noise jingled in the air a third time, now from Logan's would-be killer, and he suddenly realized he was listening to voices.

The newcomer produced a pistol-shaped device and pointed it at Logan's body, once again causing him to tense, but when he pulled the trigger, it discharged a fine white mist rather than an energy-ball of electrical death.

Logan watched the faintly luminescent vapor settle on his skin, not certain what to expect, and before he knew how to react, he saw a gold, cherry-size eyeball emerge from one of the bite wounds on his left leg. It struggled from the gash on three diminutive green tentacles, pulling itself out of his flesh and dropping to the ground.

The moment the mist touched his skin all his aches and pains had departed like an exorcised devil, but the sight alone conjured a scream just as loud as any cry of agony.

The gunner kicked the tiny orb away and fired at it.

Noise. Light. Ash. Gone.

Logan quivered. He looked to the stranger at his side, the one with the mist gun, and when the armored figure squatted down to Logan's level, he met his mirror image in the visor. Then the stranger spoke.

"You're lucky," he said. His words sounded like individual sound bytes plucked from separate audio recordings and seamlessly patched together. "That was the last one."

With that, the stranger stood and began walking back the way he'd come. His companions were already several yards down the road, well clear of the bridge, and Logan jerked with shock as, one-by-one, bolts of white-hot lightning struck each of them on the head, and they vanished in the flash.

Logan stared after them, paralyzed in the grip of awe.

The rain had stopped, the clouds were dispersing.

Overhead, the stars became visible through the evaporating thunderheads, distant groupings of faraway fires that appeared nothing like the constellations he'd become so familiar with over a lifetime of camping trips. These stars were in the wrong places, too bright, too evenly spaced and concentrically positioned.

No. Not stars. Lights.

Lights on the underside of a vast machine, a craft miles in diameter.

He knew it even before the vessel rose higher, moving noiselessly, ascending toward the upper atmosphere, finally revealing the true nighttime sky behind it.

When it was gone, Logan fainted.

He came to sometime the next morning.

When he awoke, noise blared from all around – the hard, concussive sound of a large engine – and once his eyes flickered open, he found himself looking up at a cloudless blue sky and the silhouetted underbelly of a helicopter hovering far overhead.

He lay on his back, strapped down in some kind of stretcher or basket, covered with blankets. His arms and legs had been secured tight against his body, his head locked in a neck brace.

Everything still hurt, some areas worse than he remembered, and in his semi-conscious state of awakening, he caught the sound of voices yelling over the thump of the rotors. He couldn't make out all of it, just snippets of conversations, but he heard mention of broken limbs, dislocated joints, a shattered pelvis, and a punctured lung.

A saber of sunlight stabbed at his pupils, and he closed his eyes to shield them against it. When he opened them again, he found himself floating in the air, closer to the helicopter, though he couldn't remember lifting off the ground.

The neck brace limited his ability to look about but didn't immobilize him entirely, and when he angled his head and eyes to one side, he could see over the lip of the basket. Now that he was airborne, he got his first real glimpse of the surrounding area and saw firsthand the true enormity of destruction caused by the storm.

The forest was gone, thousands of acres leveled. In its place lay a wide expanse of blackened field, flat charred terrain broken by winding paths that were once roads and dotted sporadically with the skeletal remains of those few trees that hadn't succumbed to the downpour. It was a sight more suited to the aftermath of a wildfire or a volcanic eruption, but certainly not a rainstorm.

As Logan lifted higher, he saw the lake in the distance, dry now, and even spotted an irregular patch of barren land among the wreckage of the woods that might've been where the cabin had stood. Not his family's cabin, but the one where—

He closed his eyes again, not wanting to recall it.

The basket reached the side of the helicopter and came to a halt parallel an open door where two medics waited. The hoist's steel arm retracted and seconds later Logan was inside the craft.

"Can you tell me your name?" one of the men yelled over the noise of the rotors.

"Logan," he replied, and the word came out surprisingly clear. "Logan Mitchell."

"That's good," the man said cheerily. "That's excellent. Now, Logan, you've had an accident, and you're being air lifted to a hospital. Do you understand me?"

He grunted a yes.

"Are you allergic to anything? On medication?"

He grunted a no.

"Okay, then," the man smiled, still shouting over the roar of the chopper. "You just try and relax and we'll take care of you from here. We'll have you right as rain in no time!"

"No rain," Logan groaned.

"Huh?"

"Blobs," he added.

The medic's face sobered and he nodded his understanding. "You're the tenth person we've come across who's said that," he replied.

Then the man spoke into his headset mike as Logan once again let his exhausted body slip toward unconsciousness, hearing him say: "Tell the General we have another witness to question," before he drifted into sleep.

About the Author

Matt Hults lives with his wife and two children in Minneapolis, Minnesota.

His fiction appears in the anthologies *Undead: Skin and Bones*, *Fried; Fast Food, Slow Deaths*, and *Horrors Library, Volume 2*. His first e-book, *Skinwalker*, will soon be available from Wild Child Publishing.

You can contact the author through his web site at http://www.NewHorrorFiction.com

I was researching odd things about the number thirteen and came across an article on bakers in Egypt, a baker's dozen being thirteen. It told of how their ears were cut off and hung on the wall of their shop if caught shortchanging their customers, to let people know he was a thief.

A BAKER'S DOZEN
By Nancy Jackson

He walked down the cobblestone road, straightened his pants and checked that his shirt was tucked in neatly. At the corner of Parker and Thirteenth Avenue, his bakery sat lodged between a used bookshop and an old-fashioned ice cream parlor. The morning was still overcast and brought a slight chill to the often-damp area of downtown Braxston in the dodgy section of Illinois. Rolland Patterson unlocked the paint-scratched ivory door and pulled the shades up. In the backroom, he threw on his starched white uniform and donned a hat that did more to make him appear tall than hide the onset of gray hairs. His reflection was one to be proud of – in his father's eyes, though he tried to fit the role that was placed upon him at infancy. Each generation of Patterson's resulted in baking, in one aspect. While other three-year-olds had received coloring books, yo-yos, and bouncy balls for Christmas, his home sewn stocking was full of rolling pins, cookie cutters, and fresh dough to practice on. Rolland was the thirteenth Patterson to become an official baker with his very own shop, a prestigious honor, though somewhat uneventful. He was undecided if he liked the business or not, but it was a trade to fall back on when everything else fell apart. His reputation and name would pave the way for a lifetime of flour and powdered sugar. It had been his decision to close the shop while he tried his hand as a banker.

Money had been his enemy since he could remember. One way or another he lost it to ungrateful siblings, or had it stolen by schoolyard bullies, or gambled it away. His father had also mismanaged money, which in turn meant none of his seven siblings would ever set foot in a university to further their education. Rolland believed his father paid off many unsightly people to keep food on the table when his business was doing poorly. One recurring image kept playing in his mind; it was of a man in a long wool coat, with the collar pulled up over his ears and face. His talk was somewhat garbled and colorful, especially for young ears. Rolland had been caught listening when he was ten-years-old, and was whipped that night, until he begged for mercy. His father made him promise to never ask about what he'd witnessed, and to this day, he'd kept his word.

With a wife and a daughter to feed and clothe, he didn't want to be considered cheap and unable to be a provider. Rolland figured as a bank teller he would redeem his relationship with money, and work decent hours to satisfy his family's needs. No other job in town allowed one to take the weekends off and still profit. In a tourist town, money was made on the weekends; so closing down was a death sentence for mom-and-pop owned stores. Unfortunately, Rolland was a creature of bad habits, and the forty-five-year-old man did what came naturally. He stole money. Most of it was just small change, nothing extravagant, but he had his moments of greed. Those moments had almost caught up with him. When eyebrows were raised, he blamed his then-friend and co-worker, Wallace Price. On the thirteenth of

September, Wallace was given the pink slip and traded it in for a ride underneath the local train. His severed body was found the next morning by the railway tracks, the look of disillusion painfully etched on his decapitated head.

Rolland felt horrible, and was racked with guilt, but couldn't let on for fear of disappointing his family. His wife would have left him and it would have tarnished the Patterson name for years to come. He'd called around in hopes to find the whereabouts of the strange man in the wool coat his father had done business with, but came up empty-handed. After four months, he left the bank business and reopened his bakery. The new location brought in more customers than the last one, so all in all it had been a profitable move and somewhat of a life-lesson.

Rolland re-checked his image in the mirror, licked his fingers and smoothed the straggly ends of his eyebrows down to frame his worn hazel eyes. He walked out of the backroom and smiled. Several of his loyal customers stood patiently outside the door, waiting for him to switch the sign to read 'open'.

"Morning," two elderly women said in unison.

They were his favorite customers. "Mrs. Davis, Mrs. Samson, as always it's lovely to see the two most beautiful women in all of Illinois. Will it be the usual?"

They nodded their heads and watched him load up two bags of sweet rolls.

"We're very much appreciative for the extra sugar you give us," Mrs. Davis gushed. "Just more sweets for two sweet ladies," he replied and counted back their change.

The women giggled like two young schoolgirls and waved as they walked out the door. Rolland had been getting away with overcharging his customers since the beginning, and found it a difficult habit to break. He found no correlation between stealing from the bank – a severe offense – to that of a little extra pocket change from his bakery. Besides, he owned the place, it was his right to tip himself, as he deemed appropriate. He saved money by doing all the work, and not hiring an assistant. It only made sense to bend the rules. By placing several tubs of sugar and folded up napkins at the bottom of the bags, he could charge the people full price by the weight, and they wouldn't know any different. He found he not only saved money, but also made the customers feel extra special. Rolland smiled to himself as he calculated the added change he would have in his pocket by the end of the week.

It wasn't long before the door opened, bringing in tiny pellets of rain. A man entered wearing a mahogany trench coat with the collar pulled up high, concealing most of his face. Rolland held his breath for a moment, and watched the stranger close the door behind him. Except for the obvious difference in overcoats, the man bore an uncanny appearance to the one he'd seen as a boy.

"We sure don't need anymore rain around here." Rolland sighed, hoping to start a conversation.

"Nope," replied the man. "Hate the stuff myself."

"Anything in particular I can help you with? I don't believe I've seen you in my shop before."

"Nope, first time in. I'm fairly easy to please, though, and I know exactly what I want."

"Great, what can I get you?"

"Your money, life, and family," the stranger answered in a gruff voice.

Rolland wondered if some flour had gotten in his ears. "Pardon me?"

The man's eyes narrowed. "I'll start with your family if you want."

"Is this some sort of a charade?" Rolland asked. "I don't appreciate threats made against my family."

With a sneer, the stranger chuckled. "Oh, is that so? I'll try and pretend that I care. Sometimes, we do things to people that cause them a lot of pain and hurt. Why should it be different between us? We're such good pals."

Rolland shifted his weight from one leg to the other. "I don't believe I know you." The baker feared it was indeed the man he'd seen in the trench coat, and that he'd come to collect on his father's old debts.

"Oh, trust me, we know one another. Different body, same agenda. Now look here, we're going to come to an understanding and you'll give me what I ask for."

"We'll see about that," Rolland countered.

"I'm two seconds away from causing a brilliant accident at your wife's workplace. She is on the thirteenth floor, correct?"

Rolland felt the blood rush out of him. The thought of harm coming to his wife angered him. She'd always been a loving woman, and gave his life a glimmer of meaning. "Who the hell are you?"

"I'm just a guy with a whole new outlook on things, thanks to you."

The stranger pulled out his hand from a pocket. A sharp blade reflected against the fluorescent shop lights. He stepped behind the counter and effortlessly put Rolland in a headlock. With all his strength, he wrestled him to the black and white checkered floor.

"It wasn't long ago I was just like you, Patterson. A hard worker, always on time, needed to make some extra cash from the bank to support my growing family."

Rolland's eyes widened. He strained to hear the familiarity in the voice.

"Things were going smooth for quite some time, until one day a man walks in out of nowhere and decides he's the big cheese, and starts hoarding money for his own betterment," the man continued. "To make matters worse, I befriend the guy only to be accused of stealing the money myself. I was only thirteen days away from a bonus and a nameplate in my own private office."

Rolland was speechless; the guy was trying to play mind games with him or something. "Do you expect me to believe you are Wallace Price? Aside from the obvious fact that Price committed suicide, you look nothing like the man. I'll give you credit on his voice, but you can't con a con man."

"Come on, buddy, your ears don't deceive you, but if you aren't careful, they will be the first things to go off of your head," the stranger said.

The baker's throat filled with cotton as his imagination worked into overtime. Imposter or not, the man knew too much. He decided to stop struggling and figure out how he was going to handle things. Rolland put his hands out, in an effort to show surrender.

"Good. I think we understand one another," Wallace said, and helped the baker up. "Now let's talk business. I lost my reputation, job, family, and my life because of your selfish greed. What shall be your punishment in return?"

"Look, I'm sorry for what happened to Wallace Price. I've lost a lot of sleep over it and I still grieve the man to this day. I don't know if you're a member of his family, but I'm not in the mood for games. I'm not responsible for his death, the guy committed suicide. Who are you really, his brother or something?" Rolland kept his gaze on the sharp blade in the stranger's hand.

"Those ears of yours won't be missed, it's obvious you don't listen much. I *am* Wallace Price," he said. "You ended my life and I aim to make you pay, one way or another."

Rolland shook his head. Sweat beaded atop his forehead and slid down his nose.

"Look, even if what you say is true, which is impossible, I can't take back what happened. For now, I'll humor you and pretend you are who you say you are. In all honesty, I had no idea you were up for a bonus or anything of that magnitude. When I heard rumors that someone had been stealing and the manager was going to have the man locked up for life, I panicked. Before I knew it, your name spilled from my lips. You were always so quiet and well respected; I didn't think they'd believe me. Everything happened so damn fast, it was too late to change my answer."

"Well, it seems they took your word for gold, because the manager went straight to me, told me to pack up my stuff, and that I should expect a lengthy and expensive procedure until I was behind bars," Price growled.

"You didn't help matters by committing suicide," Rolland added. "You only sealed the guilt with them."

The man paused and turned the blade in his hands several times.

"Yes, well, that is all in the past, now isn't it? But let's look to the future ... your future to be specific. I'm not about to walk out of your life until we've pulled you apart piece by piece."

"You'll never get away with killing me," said the baker. "The police will find you and lock you up. I have a good reputation around here."

"Yes, as a thief. But if you squeal, think how foolish you will sound. A dead man is stalking you, and threatening your life? How would you like to explain that one?"

The door to the shop opened and a young couple strolled in. Rolland straightened his uniform and plastered a smile across his face.

"Hello, what can I do for you today?" he asked.

"Good day," the young blonde woman greeted. "We're looking for some pastries for a casual dinner party tonight. The host is somewhat of a chocoholic, but likes things fancy. Any recommendations?"

"I've got just the thing you're looking for. Éclairs. Delicious, fancy, and drowned in chocolate. You can't go wrong there."

"That sounds perfect," the young woman smiled and hugged her partner. "Could we get a couple boxes full, please?"

Rolland worked hard to steady his hands while he piled the éclairs inside the cardboard box. As was his habit, he carefully filled in the extra space at the bottom of the box with napkins and tissue, to charge more money.

"Two boxes worth will be fifteen dollars," he said.

Without hesitation the woman paid him and the couple left, animatedly talking about the dinner party.

"Look there, you cheated more innocent people," Wallace said, shaking his head in pity.

"What I do in my business is just that, my business," Rolland replied, rubbing his hand against the back of his neck.

"Not anymore. You and I are going to be partners for a little while. Remember it's just a quick call to the wife's work, or your daughter's school and *boom*," he said with a dramatic gesture of his hands.

"There's no reason to involve my family, is there?" Rolland asked.

"I don't see why I should care about them. Let's not forget that you left my wife and three sons practically penniless with another baby on the way. Forget that my insurance policy was worth about two months' rent and they had to move out of the only home they'd ever known. Their lives took a severe turn, just as mine did, and I'd say they certainly didn't deserve it. You didn't seem to give a damn about anyone but yourself at the time, why should I be any different?"

Wallace strode over to the door, locked it, and closed the shades for added privacy. He pulled the baker into the backroom and steadied the knife. In a swift move he nicked Rolland's left ear. Blood dripped onto the starched white uniform like splatter marks from a paintbrush.

Rolland hollered something fierce.

"Tell you what, Mister Baker Man, I'll give you a chance to redeem yourself and keep your family alive," he said, and cleaned the knife on a nearby cloth. "Did you ever hear about the story of how the term 'a baker's dozen' began?"

"N-no," stammered Rolland, holding back tears.

"Well, it was said that in Egypt they cut off the ears of a baker and nailed them to the doorpost of his own bakery if he was caught shortchanging customers. It seems the act of thievery is as old as time, especially in the workplace. Can you imagine the horror, to have your ear cut off and hanging in front of your nose for the whole world to see? I don't know about you, but I'd be ashamed and embarrassed. Sort of like the whole 'scarlet letter' theory. Think about it, everyone would know you're a thief and you'd lose your pride and their trust. Your reputation would be at stake and the future of the Patterson's would come to a standstill. I hear your wife is pregnant with a son on the way; he may not be too keen to be born into such a dishonest name. It hurts my own ears to think about it," Price said. "I've spent the last thirteen days watching you and have seen you take from your loyal customers, and all the while you've let them think they were getting more. You haven't changed a bit since the days of the bank. You're stealing. It's deceitful, and I'm not about to wait around and do nothing this time."

"I'm through talking with a dead man," Rolland shouted. "You're a crazy son of a bitch, and I want you to get the hell out of here!"

He reached for the wooden rolling pin, but the stranger was too quick. His arms flailed around, making it seem he was everywhere at once.

"No, I'm not dead yet, not in the way you think death means. I sold my soul and bought myself more time," Wallace said. "I have all the time in the world to bring you down."

Price stepped closer to the baker, until they were nose to nose. He reached under his neck and pulled up the flap of loose skin that lay jagged and torn. Rolland fought the nausea as he saw blood, bone, and decay from a badly mutilated face. The baker tried to run but Wallace wouldn't let him. He held the knife to his throat, and jabbed it into his skin several times.

"Okay, what do you want me to do?" asked Rolland.

"That's better. You, my friend, are going to start making a baker's dozen for everything you sell," he said. "I want to see thirteen brownies, thirteen pastries, and thirteen loaves of bread go out to each customer. There won't be anymore stealing. You're going to give more and take less."

"Fine, that's easy enough," Rolland said and shrugged.

"There's more," Wallace interrupted. "There is much more."

From his coat, he handed Rolland a large bag filled with a white substance.

"What is this, flour?" asked the baker. "I have plenty in my shop."

"You're a naïve one, aren't you? No, you fool. Poison."

"There's no way in hell I'm going to poison my customers!" Rolland cried.

"Then Hell is where you'll go," Price sneered. "Listen carefully to the plan, partner. Every thirteenth customer will receive a free loaf of bread or pastry made with this powder. For every unexplained death, a small trace of this poison will be found and soon it will lead back to you. If you don't comply, I'll expose you for the fraud you are."

"I will not be responsible for the death of innocent people," the baker challenged.

"Actually my friend, you already are," added Wallace.

Rolland swayed in the doorway. His head started to spin. This couldn't be real. For the most part he was a good man, though he had his faults. It was never his intention to hurt others.

"You decide right here and now. Your family or your customers," Wallace said. "Because in the end you'll be hurting one of them."

"Yes, yes, I'll do as you say. Just leave my wife and daughter out of this." Rolland sighed dejectedly.

"Good man. Now I suggest you get to work and bake those potent pastries right now."

Rolland opened the bag and dumped a pile of the poison on the table as he set to work to bake fresh bread and muffins. An hour later, he reopened the store and mentally took inventory of his customers. In a special bag, he placed muffins laced with the poison, and handed them out with the order of every thirteenth customer.

Wallace followed the next chosen customer to his house and watched the poison work its magic. From outside a tiny oval window, he observed the elderly man walk across his living room and fall to the carpet in a full-blown seizure. Wallace broke in through the back door and stood over the man with a wide smile across his face. When he was sure the old man was dead, he took out his knife and sliced off the right ear. He put it in a bag with the others he'd collected and made his way back to the bakery. While Rolland was busy with customers, he went into the backroom and set to work on his ultimate masterpiece. He covered it up so the baker wouldn't notice until it was the right time.

At the end of the day, Rolland was closing up shop when Wallace came calling.

"How's that bakers dozen?" he asked.

"Fine, I seem to have more customers today than I've had all week. Everyone was commenting on the extra treat. I only remembered to give out six free muffins, though," he said.

"It's your first day, so I'll cut you a little slack, partner. You'll just have to hand out seven tomorrow."

Rolland stared at the floor. "I don't think I can do this again, it's just not right."

"I'll tell you what. I'll be more than happy to pay your family a visit," Wallace challenged. "Kids love to get a big bag of muffins for free. Pregnant women are quite easy to please when it comes to sweets. See you tomorrow morning, bright and early. I'll be watching you, don't worry. It's not like I need to sleep."

The next morning, Rolland arrived early and substituted his own bag of flour for the poison. He didn't care what Wallace threatened, he'd be sure his family was safe, but he wouldn't harm anymore of his customers. The fine line between reality and a nightmare had been crossed. He didn't know whether to believe the man was Wallace or a man paid to play the part.

Once again his mind drifted back to the time when he was a boy, and he'd seen the man in the big wool coat. His father had been handing him a lot of money, and the mysterious man had held something shiny in his other hand. Then they shook hands. The words had been muffled and set to whispers, but it was the first time he'd heard his father's voice shake, like he was scared. When his father turned around to see him, he couldn't run fast enough up the stairs. The man in the overcoat had smiled at him, but not one that was friendly. Shivers still went up his back when he visualized that awful grimace.

Rolland decided to take back some of the control. He believed the man who claimed to be Price, was one in the same as the man in wool. Same vengeance, different psycho. They represented heartless criminals with nothing but revenge and money on their minds. Fear, threats, scare tactics, those were the things that made them loom like monsters and live in the lap of luxury. One person's death was another man's profit. He couldn't sit back in good faith and allow that to happen. Rolland set to work rolling the fresh dough, *sans* the poison, and appearing busy.

A short while later, Wallace walked through the door whistling a tune.

"I think today's going to be one of the better ones," he announced. "We've a busy schedule ahead of us."

Rolland watched the impersonator walk around the shop, eyeing all the décor and product.

"I can see why you'd like to be in this line of work," he said to the baker. "It has many perks. Not only are you the boss and pick your own hours, but you get to make people happy every single day. I almost had that at the bank, until you squashed all my dreams."

Rolland's eye twitched. "How many times must I apologize? If I had it to do over again, I would. I never thought they'd treat you the way they did. I expected a full investigation where all evidence would point to me."

"Yes, well, if I could change things, it would've been your body on the railroad tracks with a severed head and broken body. Now let us not forget the special treats for those lucky customers of yours. I'll be in and out most of the day, but trust me when I say that I'm always keeping an eye on you."

By noon, Rolland had given away four more free pastries with what Wallace thought was the poison. With the increased feelings of empowerment over the situation, he almost neglected to see that he was free of his own addiction. The extra money he often pocketed didn't seem important to him anymore. It was the smiles on the faces of those who came in, with a twinkle in their eyes and a craving for something rich and sugary. The satisfaction came with being proud of where he was at in his life, and he wouldn't let that sense of pride get away from him again. Fear had enabled him to put things in a new perspective. He turned on the radio and put it to a station playing an upbeat forties' tune. Rolland snapped his fingers and danced around the shop until the door opened in his face.

Wallace stormed in, scowling, with a bloodied white bag over his shoulder. Rolland followed him into the backroom, his heart beating right out of his chest.

"What the hell do you have there?" he asked.

"You'll find out soon enough."

He watched in horror as Wallace nailed several human ears up on a wooden panel, each one presented like a trophy of some sort. Rolland fought to keep the three sugar doughnuts down that he'd had for breakfast.

"What is all this?"

"Remember the story I told you about where the baker's dozen punishment originated? Well, I decided to give it a twist. All good stories need a twist somewhere to keep things interesting," Wallace mused.

Rolland was afraid to ask. "I don't understand. Whose ears are those?"

"Why, they belong to thirteen of your lucky customers." Price's words dripped with pride.

The baker put his hand on the wall to keep from falling over. He was living in a nightmare. "Pardon me?"

"These are the souvenirs of your thirteen special customers that you gave the poison-laced muffins to," Wallace said.

"But I didn't give out thirteen treats," Rolland whispered, his throat dry and scratchy. How had Wallace known? All his strength and confidence slipped to the floor and disappeared into the cracks. What had he done?

"I'm sorry, would you repeat what you just said?"

"I said, I didn't give out all thirteen treats," he repeated.

"You're quite right, you only gave out six, but I had to improvise. I kept count myself and finished off another five customers who should have received the tasty treats. Then, to keep things interesting, I got these two as a bonus."

The baker's mouth dropped open, his lips quivered.

"Look familiar, don't they? I made damn sure to get this one here with the pretty sapphire encased by diamonds. I guess it's true that diamonds are a girl's best friends. Now, about the smaller one, would you say it belonged to a twelve, or thirteen-year-old girl?"

Rolland sank to his knees. The image of his wife and daughter, petrified as a stranger cut off their ear, was almost too much.

"Tell me they're still alive!" he begged, his hands plastered together in prayer.

"Well, the bread basket I gave them looked completely empty last time I checked," said Wallace. "Don't worry, I gave them an extra dose so they didn't feel any pain. They looked quite peaceful."

The room spun, a bevy of colors flashed before Rolland's eyes. He tried to stand but his legs buckled.

"Just kill me, why don't you just kill me?" he pleaded.

Wallace's eyes narrowed. "Hell no! I want you to live with what you have done to me, our families, and your customers. I want you to feel remorse for stealing, cheating, and betraying those close to you. I've destroyed your family and life like I said I would," Wallace mused. "The only thing missing on this trophy board is one of your ears. Tomorrow the paper will run a story about your arrest and that should take care of your job and reputation. I'll have done all I set out to do. Destroy you."

"Will you be happy then?" asked Rolland.

"Perhaps."

Rolland screamed as Wallace raised the knife and cut away at his ear. Pain tore through his head and made his fingers and toes tingle. Warmth rushed down the side of his neck and pooled along his shoulder. He watched in stunned silence as Wallace attached the ear to the wooden panel.

"Now I must bid you farewell, I have a devil with my soul to contend with."

Rolland gripped his ear, and tried to stop the blood from spilling between his fingers. He looked around, but there was no sign of Wallace anywhere. A stampede of footsteps came up behind him. He turned in time to see several police officers with their guns pointed at him.

"Hold up your hands, sir, you are under arrest for the deaths of many people in the area. I understand you cut off their ears as a reward?" an officer said. "We'll be taking a look around your bakery, sir."

Thirteen days later, Rolland sat in his cell, his new home for life. Horrible nightmares had plagued him each night, and he was racked with exhaustion. He kept thinking that the man in the wool coat was coming for him still. Wallace Pride wanted him to think he'd returned from the afterlife, but he knew it was all a ploy. His father had somehow found out about his stealing from the bank, and had paid some grisly man to make him suffer. It was all out in the open now, complete with a life sentence. He had no one to blame but himself.

"You have a visitor," one of the guards said. "It's a lady, so be on your best behavior."

Rolland stood and rested the weight of his body against the bars. A beautiful brunette walked into the room, a woman he didn't recognize. He noticed the swell of her belly, and guessed she was about eight months pregnant, just like his own wife had been. Tears welled up in the corners of his eyes, and he brushed them away in one swift motion.

"Hello, Mr. Patterson," she greeted, her voice full of confidence. "You may not remember me, but I used to be a regular customer of yours, back when you had your shop on the other side of town."

"Oh, yes, that one was a much smaller shop. What brings you here?" he asked.

"You were always our favorite baker, well of my kids and I. After I heard the report on the news about the recent events, I just had to come see you and let you know that I don't believe everything I hear."

Rolland turned the side of his face with the missing ear away from her at the mention of the word *hear*. It made him feel inferior. Everyone had been convinced he cut off his own ear to make himself look innocent. When he'd mentioned

Wallace Price, his attorney suggested an asylum would be a better fit for him.

He smiled at the woman and cleared his throat. "Thank you for your belief in me," he said.

"The officer said I could leave these with you." She moved to the right of the bars and placed a card, a photo, and a loaf of fresh baked bread through the small opening. "I made this myself, though I'm sure it won't compare to the things you've made. I must go now, but please, enjoy." The woman smiled as she walked away, her shoes clacking loudly on the floor.

Rolland waited until he was alone before he looked at what she'd left. His stomach growled and he immediately started to chomp away at the bread. In the photo, he saw the faces of three handsome boys, all redheads with freckles. There was a familiar look in their eyes, but he couldn't put his finger on it. He wondered if his wife had known them at one time. Rolland opened the card and read it carefully. The last bit of the bread fell to the urine stained floor. On the inside were the words 'a baker's dozen' written over and over. The poison seared through his veins, and burned his insides. He swore he could hear Wallace's laughter echo inside the dank walls.

"Isn't my wife a beauty? And in case you are wondering, yes, now I am happy. I'll get my life back just in time to watch yours end."

About the Author

Nancy Jackson's work can be found in *Cthulhu Sex Magazine*, *FEAR Anthology*, *Project Contagion*, *Horror Carousel*, *Nocturne*, and *Embark to Madness*, as well as the upcoming publications *Sha Daa: Tales of the Apocalypse Book One*, *Harvest Moon Hotel*, *Black Ink Horror Magazine*, *Parasitic Sands*, and *Dark Sins and Desires Unveiled*. She is also the Pacific Northwest Regional Representative for the International Order of Horror Professionals.

While her website is under construction, she invites you to visit her blog at: http://www.myspace.com/nancy_jackson

I wrote "Interludes" partially as a sub-plot of a NaNoWriMo novel following being released from a 6-year position I loved, as well as not getting the final result of my divorce when I expected it. The anger and bitterness exploded, spraying a torrent of blood and gore in 60,000 busy words ... "Interludes" shone as an examination of how someone could become free of emotional and physical pain.

INTERLUDES
By Jodi Lee

How often does it happen? How often would a woman totally lose her mind without anyone around her noticing? Particularly when she lives with two other people and interacts with at least a dozen others every day. And to top it off, she *tells* them, *almost daily*, that something just isn't right, that it's *wrong*. But she hadn't seen anyone but him for so long ... maybe they weren't even real? Oh yes, they were real.

Had they listened, things would have been so much easier on everyone. But was she real? Was *he*?

Kaine read the file the nurse had put in front of him.

The patient was Claire Davis, a fairly successful freelance writer. She had begun to be 'noticed' by the print publishers, through her freelance work online. And it hadn't taken long either; not six weeks after her first article was published on her very immature website, the publisher of a small newsletter had requested permission to reprint it on page two of his next issue. Shortly after her second article was posted, the owner of a large syndicate in the United Kingdom requested reprint rights. If she worked and posted her material on her website, she was fine. Then she was hired by a big-name content provider.

In her file, Claire stated she hadn't expected to stay as long as she did, nor get as involved as she did. After plugging away at two other content providers, she knew they didn't last long; one of the places that had published her material had folded within six months of the grand opening. Not this one, though. This one had stuck it out, through a couple of changes in ownership and management. She wrote that she'd worked hard for them even when they stopped paying the fee, and began paying in 'shares'.

And then they fired everyone. No notice, no payment; they'd simply fired everyone. Claire had an emotional breakdown.

Something wasn't right about this case, but Kaine couldn't put his finger on it. He sighed as he pushed the file away, sliding it across the immaculate desk.

In the Internet Age, everyone and anyone could publish, and Claire firmly believed that it was this mentality bringing down the entire journalism world. Over half of the other content providers she'd worked with shouldn't have been allowed to live on their own without 'special help', let alone publish the oddities that flowed from their fingertips.

Memories, tinged with nostalgia; it had been a long time. Claire's fingers brushed the keyboard gently, softly outlining where she had once tap-tap-tapped away the afternoons. Looking closer, she saw the scaly, brown marks over the more frequently used keys. E was almost obliterated by the stain.

She licked her finger, wiped E clean, then put the flakes of ... whatever ... into her mouth. Savored the taste of long-dead blood. Smiling, she relished the memories the dead moments brought her. And that's when it had happened, that's when she realized she wasn't alone.

Kaine watched from the two-way mirror installed between his office and the reception area.

The woman seemed to be drifting, her mouth open and her eyes glazed. Suddenly, she snapped out of her reverie, smiled politely to the nurse sitting beside her, and turned back to the task at hand; filling out the insurance forms was almost as tedious as writing the introductory story he always asked for.

Kaine. He shivered as she looked up, directly into his eyes. He could have sworn she'd whispered his name, right into his ear. For a moment, he was positive she could actually see him.

The nurse stood and took the clipboard from Claire. Kaine watched as the old bulldog went over the paperwork, shaking her head. She turned away and disappeared from his view – he knew she was going to bring him the forms to go with the rest of the file on his desk.

Claire, meantime, sat with a tiny smile creating lines on either side of her mouth and the shadow of a dimple on one cheek. For a moment, she seemed to try and stifle the giggles, which shook her shoulders, but as Kaine heard the door close to his office, and the nurse began to talk to him,

Claire began to shake; he heard the laughter and a chill worked its way down his spine.

"The faster she's out of my waiting room the better," the nurse spoke. "There's something about that one out there, and if she thinks she's pulling one over on me, she's mistaken. I've been working reception nearly thirty years, and I know a lie when I see one. She's from out of state."

"Your point, Nurse Kelly?" Kaine responded, still distracted by his observance of the woman waiting beyond the glass.

"You won't be paid for this one. You aren't licensed for out-of-staters. I am tired of trying to—"

"Kelly, let me worry about that, okay? Just ... go tell her I'm ready to see her."

A cold wave crashed over him like water, as he continued to watch Claire. He could actually see the transformation. Her hand rose, trembling, to her mouth. Kelly was out there now, telling her that Kaine would see her, and Claire actually turned to her in shock. *See who? Why? Where am I?* Kaine thought he could actually hear the questions formed by Claire's lips.

He watched as the woman's expression changed to one of absolute fear – and then her head whipped back and to the side, and the expression was the same as before the laughter; cold and cruel. It was as though someone had slapped her.

Kaine's blood ran cold, but he kept his face immobile, his eyes aloof, watching as Claire sat watching *him*.

Oh, he'd asked all the right questions, sure. He just could not have been prepared for what she would say in response. He had never expected a woman like her to be sitting across from him, in his office. Bound by his oath, he could not repeat a single word she'd said as she rambled on for forty-five minutes. They existed, those poor souls that had to share a physical existence. *Multiple Personality Disorder.* He'd known, of course he'd known – the textbooks and journals were full of the case studies. But to have one sitting so prettily in the chair reserved for patients was beyond luck.

"Why did you come here, Claire?" He spoke in tones barely above a whisper, and yet because of his training there was a forcefulness that compelled most patients to speak. "There are hundreds of psychiatrists in the city, and you chose to come to me. Why?" Shifting in his chair, he pulled his notebook closer, ready to add her comments.

"I think you know why, Dr. Kaine. Can you not even suspect? Why don't you tell me why I'm here. Why I chose to open up to you, and only you." Claire smirked, and even though he wasn't looking at her, he could hear it in her voice. She *mocked* him. The tables turned; now it was he who was uncomfortable. Put on the spot, nonetheless.

"Claire, I really don't know." Kaine didn't want to look into her eyes. Didn't want to see his truth reflected there. "I suppose you chose me from the phone book just as so many others do."

"No, Kaine. I chose you because you and I know each other. We've known each other almost all my life, so to speak. You were there at the beginning of all of this, and now, here we are again. Together, at the end. You will finish this off with me, and then perhaps, we'll let you go."

"Claire?" he asked, watching her face as an almost physical change betrayed the change in personality. Kaine observed how she moved from cold, heartless and cruel to scared, abandoned and weak, and back again. He noted the smirk that returned to twist the woman's features.

Claire stood, and stalked to the water-cooler for a cup of the liquid she so rarely partook of. "You really don't remember me do you? You, of the wondrous seductive, deductive abilities. Think back, Kaine. Go back to med school. Anything interesting and out of the norm happen while you were there?" Pulling the chair closer to Kaine's, Claire arranged herself in a semi-lotus position, allowing her skirt to reveal a little more of her body. She noticed him noticing her thighs, despite his sudden fear. "Would you like some help remembering, Kaine?" She laughed.

This wasn't her, Kaine thought. *She'd been blonde, and blue eyed. She was older than this woman. Could Claire be her daughter? No. They were careful.*

"Listen, Claire, I don't know what you're on about, nor do I think this is truly appropriate. I'm afraid I'll have to ask you to leave. Our time is up anyway." He rose, brushed past her bare knees, and strode briskly to the door. Before he could open it though, she'd grabbed his shoulder, and flung him around. Shoving him back into the chair, she braced herself on the arms.

"You will remember, Kaine. You and you alone are responsible for what I've become." The hate in her voice startled him, causing him to attempt crying out to the receptionist or nurse.

Grasping his face in her hands, Claire leaned in and pressed her lips to his, maintaining eye contact but cutting off his scream. As he struggled, he inhaled in shock, and she exhaled. Abruptly he stopped struggling and even began to give in, in some way. Her breath was sweet, almost like ether. She watched, making him more terrified and he closed his eyes to get away from her; it was then she sank her teeth into her own tongue, and forced the gushing blood into his mouth.

Swallowing convulsively, Kaine's eyes flew open. Claire pulled away then, knowing he saw her now as she was then.

"Jesus Christ!"

"Oh no, love. He has no business here, nor can he help you now. You know that."

And Claire began to laugh as Kaine sheltered his face in his hands and sobbed.

Kaine and Claire drove out of the city until there was nothing but darkness on the horizon behind them. Neither of them spoke a word, and yet Kaine seemed to know exactly where Claire wanted him to go.

Three hours later, they arrived at a little house on the outskirts of a small town. Claire stepped out of the car the moment Kaine had put it in park, and when she walked in front of it, the headlights cast an eerie glow to her face; it shimmered and shifted, almost as though she were wearing a mask. She motioned for Kaine to follow her. He did so, feeling as though he were walking wraith-like through someone else's dream. *Nightmare, more like*, he thought as he stumbled up the steps.

Claire had left the door open as she went inside. The smell coming from the house was thick with something he couldn't quite place, but it left him gagging. The familiarity of this whole situation was starting to give him pause. Claire herself was beginning to seem a little transparent. She'd become a great deal whiter since they'd entered the house. A trick of the light, nothing more.

Nevermore.

Kaine felt as though his grip on reality was slipping away as he watched her hair swing back and forth and shiver in different colors. His sanity was drifting right through his grasping fingers and sifting to the floor like so much dust. Still, he followed Claire through the ruins of the house, the smell getting thicker and heavier until even his very eyes stung with the obscenity of it.

She turned at the top of a flight of stairs. Beckoning once more, she descended.

Where are you going Claire? Where are you taking me? Kaine thought as he followed her down the stairwell. His hand tried to grasp the railing, but it was slick with some viscous fluid. Startled, he jerked his hand away and looked at it. Nothing there. Wiping his palm against his slacks anyway, he quickened his pace. He didn't want to lose sight of her and get lost in this ... God-awful mess. And that smell! Why couldn't he just turn around and leave?

Kaine finally dragged his handkerchief from his pocket to cover his nose and mouth. *Where, Claire? What is this place?*

She only looked back at him and nodded towards the bottom of the steps.

"We're almost there, Dr. Kaine. Don't worry." After another twist in the stairs leading down, they were on a solid floor again, one which looked to be concrete.

Claire stepped towards the middle of this room, and pulled the string hanging from a light fixture in the ceiling. When the light splashed over the horrors in front of him, Kaine doubled over and vomited.

"Welcome to Hell, Dr. Kaine. I do hope you enjoy your stay." Claire spoke calmly, spreading her arms in a welcoming gesture before brushing her skirt down in a nervous movement. Kaine thought he saw horror and confusion on her face then, but in a flash, it was gone again and the woman was composed once more.

Kaine couldn't believe what he was seeing. What he had at first thought to be paint, was actually blood. His mind had blocked the color and scent; the oxidized brown of dried blood and the rusty, musty odor. God help him, it was like a charnel house! Horrified, he staggered around the room, eyes bulging out of their sockets as though they wanted to dance on his cheeks.

"*Why,* Claire? Why bring me here? Why show me this?" he screamed. He didn't know her; didn't really care to know her, truth be told. Fuck the doctor-patient confidentiality blather; if he got out of here alive, he was going straight to the cops. For that matter, fuck the Hippocratic Oath; if he could, he'd kill her. "Who are you, Claire?"

"If you honestly don't know, Kaine, that's not my problem. I don't know, either. Not for sure. Not for real. For the time being, let's say you once helped a pseudo-family member of mine. And when you did, you caused some sort of short circuit in the mental wiring. I ... used to ... " She shook her head, then spread her arms wide, urging him to take in the entire room. "This is what the short circuit did. This is why you are here." Claire stepped toward him and attempted to take his hand. He jerked back reflexively, stumbling over the mess on the floor and scrabbling to get away from her. Her twisted laughter followed him around the room as he searched for the stairway.

"There's no point in looking, Kaine. I sealed the door. The stairway to Heaven is no longer available. Why don't you take a seat? Perhaps, if you cooperate, you will see your Heaven. Sooner, rather than later, I'm afraid."

When Kaine turned to look at her once more, she was gone, and he'd been left alone to suffer the room on his own. Almost at the moment he realized he was now alone, the light snapped off, causing him to scream in panic. Crawling over to the farthest corner of where he *thought* the stairway had been, he pushed himself against the wall as tightly as he could. Drawing his knees up to his chin, he encircled his legs with his arms and ducked his head. In-between prayers, he cried. In between the sobs, he screamed.

Somewhere in the darkness, Kaine heard a scratching sound.

Not long after, something touched his leg and he pulled back as far as he could. When the reaching, snatching thing pushed against him again, he stood and stumbled across the room. The scratching followed him, sounding like the scurrying feet of half a dozen rats.

The sounds came from all around him. Sinking to his knees, Kaine gave himself up to whatever it was that wanted him. It ripped and tore at his clothes until he was left naked and shivering. The hands brushed against his skin as though he were a favorite family pet. Petting him, stroking him, kissing him.

In his terror, the shrieks issuing from his mouth nearly deafened him. And when he could scream no more, he fell silent and became still.

It had been hours in the dark; waiting for Claire's return. Kaine hadn't quite slipped into the safety of insanity, but he was dancing precariously on the edge. The creatures that had pawed at him at first seemed to have drifted back into the darkness. He had heard a few mutters after he'd stopped screaming, and assumed the hands that had touched him were human, and alive. *God above, they had to be alive!*

His worst fear had not yet proven itself to be a reality. Nightmares had plagued him for years after his stint in the morgue at the hospital ... nightmares where the dead returned to life and stalked him in the corridors. They had only intensified when he interned with the doctor in charge of research at the psychiatric facility. The said doctor had given lethal doses of various drugs to the catatonic patients who had no family to notice the loss. When there was a loss. Often, he would revive them after various periods of time.

They came back different. So much so in some cases that Kaine had thought it would be best to kill them a second time, and leave it at that.

He had himself excused from that place as soon as he could. Occasionally, he'd read papers from the Research Department there, and shuddered to think how they got their material. Oddly enough, he'd never spoken of the horrors that went on there. The deaths were secondary to some of it. But there were gaps in his memories, and he thought perhaps there was something *there*, that would be an explanation of *here, now*.

He tried to place Claire's face to any of those memories, and couldn't. In fact, he tried to place Claire's face to anything he'd been involved in that was in any way untoward. Still, he came up blank. He was sure he'd never met the woman until she strode into his inner office.

Kaine's senses were twitching, so when he heard the footsteps on the floor above and then descending the stairs, he was ready. Maneuvering himself into a crouching position, he was ready to spring at her the moment she turned on the light. But, instead of coming into the room where he waited, she passed the door. He listened to her steps as long as he could hear them, then strained to hear more.

Another voice ... male ... was barely distinguishable on the other side of the wall. Claire's voice in reply, and then anger from the man. He could catch snatches of their conversation as it became more heated, but none of it made sense in any way. The man was obviously reprimanding Claire for something, and Kaine felt perhaps it had to do with him. She cried out once, then quieted as the man laughed.

Cautiously, lest he disturb the creatures in the dark, or Heaven forbid, touch something that was rotting on the floor, he slowly made his way across the room, and finally felt the wall on the other side. Exhaling sharply, he realized he had been holding his breath.

Pressing his ear to the wall, he listened.

"You must let him go. I don't think he had any idea what was going on. I did what I could, but he doesn't believe it is his fault. Honestly, when I did the exchange, I could feel that what happened to you wasn't directly his fault. He was ... "

"ENOUGH! I tell you he was responsible, and he will be punished. Just as the other was, and just as the rest of them have been. He is the last. When I am done with him, you and I can finally be together."

"I'm sorry. I just thought," mumbling then, "I just thought that we could end it all now, and still be together. I could find a better specimen; a younger one. One more like you were before."

"Stop your sniveling, girl. Just leave me for now. He will do fine, and in the end, you will see that I was right."

The laughter that came from the next room sounded quite familiar to Kaine. *Too familiar.*

His tenuous grip on reality slipped and he found himself sitting in the research lab at the facility.

The boy that had been strapped to the table was barely alive. There was blood seeping from his nose, ears, and eyes now; it was his eyes that shocked Kaine the most.

They were moving. Patient 1164 had never moved his eyes in the six months Kaine had been here. Not once. They had to be closed for him at night, and opened for him during the day. A nurse went around once in a while to make sure he was blinking, and when necessary, give him a dose of lubricant.

If they sat him in a chair, he stayed there. If the nurses put his arms over his head, they stayed there. Typical catatonia. Kaine hadn't been here when the kid arrived; he was a long term resident according to his chart. Admitted by social services at age eleven, he was now thirteen. Just past his birthday actually. Since he was the youngest resident here, the nurses had given him a birthday party.

Kaine thought it was morbid to give an obvious vegetable a party he couldn't understand. He had only read the current parts of the kid's file, nothing from his previous life outside the walls of the psychiatric facility. If he had, he would have known this kid had been catatonic only two years. It had been his eleventh birthday when he slipped into the darkness.

Nor did Kaine read the notes about the brainwave activity. The kid's brain was wild with activity – he was most certainly aware of everything that went on around him. He was *not* a typical case. Which was why Shrink had ordered him brought down here, to the lab. Again, Kaine had no idea why.

The kid had been strapped to the table, had the rubber ball stuck in his mouth – and been zapped numerous times with electro-shock. He'd actually broken into a mad sort of giggle then. The attending doctor had practically jumped at this; immediately his nurse was sent out for the tray of other devices from his office. Kaine had a sudden urge to leave the room. If he did though, he'd be questioned later and he could not lose this residency.

It was all very wrong. Very, *very* wrong. He knew what was coming, and thought a child was too much.

When the nurse returned, the attending went to work. The man had been a doctor at this facility for fifteen years, and every two months of that fifteen years, they'd given him a patient to do research on. It was the kid's turn. Simple as that, in his mind.

Kaine was ordered to attach the EEG wires to the kid's head, while the nurse pulled off the rags that passed as pajama bottoms. When the preps were finished, the doctor started his research.

Eventually, the kid's bladder let go, and not long after that, he began to scream.

Testing on the kid went on for months, not just the standard two. Kaine began to realize, albeit slowly, that there was something different about this one, something that the staff had been waiting for. As he was just the 'Rez' and the 'Shrink' didn't think he needed to be informed about every detail of their work, he was left in the dark as to what it was they'd been looking for, and why.

And every week, the kid improved. The catatonia was slipping away, and although there hadn't been massive improvement, there was some. Kaine had helped prep the kid a couple of times, and wrote in his own notes that if they put him in a chair, he settled himself into it; if they put his hand up, he did leave it for a moment, then he put it in his lap.

There was still no intelligence in the eyes, though. Nothing there to indicate sentient life.

"*REZ*! Get that kid over here and strapped to the table. We have to proceed to the next level of testing," Shrink hollered when Kaine didn't immediately answer to 'Rez'. He responded with a curt: "Yes, sir, Shrink." And wheeled the kid over to the table.

Obviously, there was *something* in there; the kid started to cry silently. Just one drop, rolling down his cheek and plopping onto the hospital issue gown he was wearing. "Sorry, kid, it's my job," Kaine whispered into the kid's ear as he lifted him up onto the table.

There was to be no electro-shock today, which was okay. Kaine had often wondered if a good old-fashioned lobotomy wouldn't have been more humane than killing the brain with electricity. As he strapped the kid down and removed the gown, he noted the trembling in the legs. When the gown was off entirely, Kaine could see the dozen or so scars all over the kid's body; cigarette burns on his chest, and what looked like a fresh burn down lower, into the sparse hair that had begun growing on the kid's groin in the last year.

What in God's name is that guy doing to you? Kaine thought, not daring to risk Shrink's anger by saying it aloud. If he did, next thing he knew, he'd be the one strapped to the table.

Shuddering at the thought, Kaine pulled the last strap tight over the kid's forehead, and left the room to stand behind the observation glass. He knew what today was, he had a gut feeling. Today, the kid would die.

Shrink entered the room carrying his own tray. When he pulled back the cover, numerous needles and an IV bag were revealed. Kaine noted that the kid's stare was following Shrink as much as it could. Kaine opened his mouth to tell Shrink, but thought better of it. *Not worth losing your residency over, man. Get a grip.*

He did make note in his notebook, though. Entered time and date, and all the details he could before the nurse entered the observation area. She didn't even see the notebook as he tucked it back into his pocket.

Kaine flinched as the first needle was inserted into the kid's skinny arm. The kid began to shake violently, Kaine thought perhaps in a grand mal seizure. As quickly as it had started, though, it was done. Foaming drool dribbled down the side of the kid's face and pooled on the table.

The kid's eyes had rolled back, but the lids hadn't lowered, giving him a ghostly, zombie-like look. He was out; whether by the drugs used, or fainting, Kaine wasn't sure. Shrink motioned for the nurse, who immediately dashed to his side. She catheterized the kid, then closed his eyes, taping them down.

Before she left the room, she had a moment of compassion and gave the boy's hand a squeeze. When he squeezed back, snapping one of the bones in her hand, she screamed. She continued to scream as the monitors around her showed no life signs in the body that wouldn't release her hand.

Kaine heard echoes of the woman's scream for years afterwards, always at the edges of dreams he could never recall.

When the doc brought the kid around, after extricating the nurse from the cold hand, he was once again catatonic. Kaine didn't believe it – there was something in his eyes now, that wasn't there before. That had *never* been there, as far as Kaine could tell from the records. When the kid had eye contact with someone, cold sweats broke out on their backs and they *knew* they'd looked into the abyss a little too long.

Nietzsche would have loved this kid.

The kid seemed to be able to play the doctor in just the right way. Shrink was getting the results he wanted clinically, but psychologically, the kid was dead. Or so he thought. Kaine new better; he and a couple of the ward nurses swore they'd seen a gleeful snarl on the kid's face on more than one occasion. Shrink didn't give a shit; he was getting his results.

Kaine stayed late one night, several months after what had become known as the 'zombie incident'. From the window in a little used, upper floor office, he watched as Shrink and his latest nurse-toy left in a flashy sports car.

Kaine knew Shrink kept the office locked, and had therefore taken the liberty of relieving one of the nurses of her keys during coffee-break in the afternoon. Since she rarely moved her ass from her chair at the desk in the evenings, Kaine knew he was safe in taking hers.

Waiting a good half-hour before leaving his hidey-hole, Kaine finally emerged when he heard a group of nurses shout one floor below. Making his way down the stairs, he listened as the shouts grew louder, and more aggravated. When he entered the hallway through the door at the stairwell, the nurses didn't have time to question, and he could see the reason for the excitement.

The kid was standing in the middle of the TV room, gracing his audience with a lowered head, chilling grin; he was staring up through his bangs at the circle surrounding him.

The laugh ... that laugh was one Kaine thought he'd remember for the rest of his life. Time heals all horrors, though, and it turns out he didn't. That night it froze the blood in his veins and nearly enticed him to piss in his own pants. And the kid stood there, laughing through the psychotic haze he'd been put in. Kaine ordered a sedative, and when it was brought to him, he advanced on the kid, apologizing as he went.

The head nurse later told him it was bad form to apologize to the patients when trying to administer meds. Kaine told her to take her idiotic advice and cram it up her ass, along with her attitude, and where the *fuck* had she been during the little drama anyway? Sitting on her chair at the desk, watching in relative safety, that's where.

The kid dodged back and forth, and was strangely quick for a kid who could barely move not all that long ago. Kaine finally lunged when the kid ducked, and the needle connected with the fleshy part of his thigh.

Kaine couldn't help but scream when the kid bit him, though ... his upper thigh not all that far from his sac, actually. For a moment, while the nurse was sewing him up later, he thought perhaps the kid *had* been going for the sac. Nevertheless, the deed was done, and the kid eventually tucked back into his bed with 'security wraps' around ankles, wrists and chest, rather than a security blanket. He wouldn't be going anywhere anytime soon.

When Kaine was patched up, he excused himself and made like he was going to the Rez office to collect himself. One quick turn to the left after the Rez office door, and he was in the hallway leading to Shrink's office. After shaking the shit out of the keys as he tried to find the right one, he finally got one into the lock, and it turned.

He opened the door and slipped inside; he didn't bother with the light, he'd come prepared with a pen light he'd been given as a gag gift. He was slightly shocked to see that Shrink's file cabinets were not locked, but was thankful for that small mercy. When he found the cabinet that should have had the kid's file, he pulled open the middle drawer, and quickly scanned the names there. As with so many things that night, later he would stop to wonder why the files weren't alpha-numerically filed, rather than simply by name. All the institute's files were done alpha-numerically.

When he found the kid's file, what he read there was simply horrifying. Beyond horrifying. For one thing, according to the records, the kid didn't exist outside these walls. The county simply considered him a 'lost child'; Shrink himself had reported him missing from the institute.

Shrink could do what he wanted with this kid, and no one would be the wiser.

Kaine read notations here and there, nothing spectacular and nothing interesting. In the final few pages of the file is where he found what he'd been looking for. Shrink's plan for further testing on the kid, and then something he referred to as 're-induction'. Kaine's eyes grew wide, beads of sweat formed on his forehead and he had to clamp his hand over his mouth to keep the moans from escaping. He couldn't let this happen.

Kaine didn't want to stop and think, he just wanted to stuff the kid's file under his lab coat and get the fuck out of Dodge. He didn't think the nurses would let him leave with the kid, but he could take the file, and come back for the kid later, with the authorities.

If they'd believe him. There was always that possibility, that one in a million chance that after having read the file, they'd think he'd lost his own mind working here.

What the hell was he going to do? He supposed he'd have to stop and think, and just as he was leaving the office, he realized one thing he *could* do. He could photocopy the kid's file, and stick the original back into the cabinet. Shrink would likely be back tomorrow, but there wouldn't be any testing going on until next week ... he was sure of it. Not one hundred percent, but sure enough.

He'd have time to think of something to do. Time to get something concrete planned out. As he snuck down the hallways and inner offices until he got to the photocopy room, he let his mind go blank. Step by step. Nothing could go wrong now or he'd lose his residency and the kid, too. One or the other, but not both, and preferably not the kid.

Kaine managed to get all of the file copied and sorted and ready; it was on the return trip to Shrink's office that he kept looking over his shoulder, swearing someone was behind him. He *knew* he'd heard footsteps. Probably that young nurse, the one that made puppy eyes at him all the time. She never failed to be on his shifts, following not too far behind him during rounds, and hovering in general. Kaine stopped as he was about to open Shrink's door.

The nurse!

She could help him get the kid out of here, and she'd likely be more than willing. He wouldn't even have to explain that she could lose her job over this – he'd let her read the file before they'd spring the kid. She'd never been down to the lab, and he didn't think she'd been on the job long enough to have become jaded. Nodding to himself, he continued on into Shrink's office.

After he'd made sure the room looked exactly as he'd originally found it, Kaine moved to leave, backing out of the door. That was his big mistake. He ran right into the head nurse.

She'd gotten up off her chair and wandered all the way down here, just looking for something to bitch about.

"Resident Kaine! What do you think you're doing in Shrink's office?" Without waiting for Kaine to reply, she continued, "I think the patient we sedated this evening may have managed to get my keys. I can't find them. I didn't want to sound an alarm amongst the staff until I'd talked to you." Busily checking over her shoulders so no one else heard tell of her incompetence, the woman didn't even notice as Kaine slid her keys carefully into his pocket. "I want you to go in to his room and look for them, if you would. Please, Rez ... I just, I can't ... " She drew herself up to her full height and stuck out her chest a little, like a man would, when drawing up his courage. "I am a bit afraid of that kid, Doctor Kaine. There's something about his eyes. He's in there all right, and I think he's faking." She wouldn't meet Kaine's eyes and looked as though it wasn't just her keys that were making her ashamed. She was actually ashamed to be afraid of one of the patients, and maybe ashamed that she'd resorted to buttering up the resident, calling him *Doctor* Kaine for once.

"Nurse, you have every right to be afraid of that patient. A lot of us are, including me. He is in there all right. He's in there, and he's waiting." Sure, why not feed the fear? Kaine did believe the kid was in there, but waiting? Waiting for what, exactly? It certainly wasn't a moment to spring on someone and kill them.

Shivering, Kaine realized it could well be that very thing. Maybe the kid was beyond redemption. Maybe this wasn't worth losing his residency over.

NO! You have to help him, some usually quiet and unassuming voice inside him said. Taking her by the elbow, he led her away.

"Let's go, madam, and see if we can find those wayward keys of yours. And, I'll keep quiet about it, if you don't tell anyone I was in Shrink's office. You see, the couch in there is a sight more comfortable than the one in the Resident's Lounge. I just had a little catnap is all." He smiled, knowing that little lie slipped past her radar.

The pair searched for the missing keys in the kid's room, all the while the kid watched Kaine's every move. Sedated or not, he was definitely awake, and definitely aware. Kaine was beginning to feel as though the kid was begging silently to be released from the bonds he'd put on the scrawny arms and legs.

"Let's hurry up, shall we? I don't think they're in here." He said quietly to the nurse: "Let's look around the nurse's station once more. Perhaps we'll find them there. Two sets of eyes and all that ... " Again, he took her by the elbow and this time, he didn't need to nudge her along, she went of her own accord.

"Rez, he's awake. He was watching you," she spoke as they walked down the hall. He simply nodded, wanting to get this done and over with so he could go back to being horrified. And perhaps, he could track down that little nurse while he was at it.

Meanwhile, the little nurse stepped out of the private bathroom that was part of the kid's room. She'd been waiting in there, behind the shower curtain, until Nurse Bitch and Doctor Gorgeous left the room. She'd been in, sitting with the kid, and heard them coming. She'd dashed for cover – she was supposed to be checking on all the patients. If Nurse Bitch caught her lollygagging around, particularly around the kid, she'd be on reprimand.

She leaned over and touched the kid's cheek. He opened his eyes, and smiled at her. Shocked a little, but only a little, she sat on the edge of the bed and began talking to him. In a little while, he began answering her.

Kaine searched high and low for the blonde nurse who wouldn't ever leave him alone. He'd finally managed to get rid of the head nurse long enough to duck into the bathroom in the staff room, and as he relieved himself, he dropped her keys under the sink, nudging them over closer to the garbage can with his toe.

After he washed his hands, he opened the door. She was standing there, as he figured she would be. He made like he was about to turn out the light, when … oh! What have we here? Are these your keys?

Jim Carrey couldn't have done it better, he was sure. He excused himself, and left the head nurse standing there, apparently wondering how her keys managed to get in there, since she never used that bathroom. Shrugging her dumb shoulders, she went back to her chair, and her charts.

Kaine finally gave up searching for the blonde, thinking perhaps the nurse wasn't on duty tonight after all, and be fucked if he was going to ask the head nurse. Then there'd be all sorts of commentary from her – their brief conspiratorial friendship was now over. Back to normal, left foot, right foot, and so on. In fact, he was beginning to feel as though she'd likely tell Shrink he'd been in the office, despite the threat of his telling that she lost her keys. *That* was in fact, a larger offense, really. In the grand scheme of things, that was. Any nurse caught without her keys could be fired instantly.

But, on the other hand, any resident being caught out of bounds was also grounds for immediate dismissal, plus the said resident would lose residency. No residency, no qualifications, no glorious job in the future.

In short – Kaine had the distinct feeling he was fucked. From many directions at once.

He had plenty of time to think about all of this as he searched for that damn woman. He thought again about giving up, but then the thought flitted through his head: perhaps he hadn't been the only one wandering out of bounds. Taking his own set of keys, he unlocked the door that led to the lab. Descending the stairs rapidly, two at a time, he was momentarily freaked out by the red glow given off from the emergency exit signs. The only illumination in this stairwell during the night hours, actually. He hadn't realized that, and he still had an irrational fear of the near-dark. Total dark was okay; near-dark, and he was panicky.

He pushed open the door to the lab at the bottom of the stairs, and checked the observation room. Nothing and no one there, and no one in the theatre, either. What he did notice – and that had changed since early afternoon when he'd arrived – was that there was a new machine there. It looked like a defibrillator, but not quite. It hummed and whined in the pale flush cast by the theatre off-hour lights. In his panicky state, Kaine thought he saw a body on the table, and it had been flayed open. Shutting his eyes tightly, and squeezing the heels of his palms into his eyes, he told himself that was impossible.

When he opened his eyes, the vision had dissipated, and he turned to leave. Kaine ran up the stairs, taking them three at a time, and exhausting himself. After he locked the door in the main hallway, he hung his head down and braced his arms against his knees, catching his breath. He stumbled, shaking, along the edge of the hall, holding the wall as best he could, until he got to the Staff Room.

Once there, he pulled open the fridge, and grabbed a bottle of water. Sitting in one of the many armchairs, he propped his feet up, while resting his head on the back of the chair and closing his eyes.

He dreamt he was still in this position when the nurse came in. She was so petite, and so very blonde. He watched as she approached him, and then pulled his feet off the table in front of him. He didn't move, only looked at her. She smiled, and unbuttoned her uniform, sliding it off her shoulders and giving him a damn good view of the bra, and the cleavage the uniform had hidden. He knew he was dreaming. But he didn't want this to stop. He admitted to himself how much he did want her.

She slid in between his legs, unbuckled his belt and lowered his fly. As she knelt, her fine, slender hands found his cock tucked away and rubbed against it. He closed his eyes as she pulled it out, lifting his hips and groaning as she brought her tongue to the tip. Licking all around the top, and then sliding it into her mouth, she sucked him hard. When she sank her teeth into the base of his dick, he squirmed, but she'd put her hand over his eyes ... he couldn't see, couldn't move. She released him.

She stood, turning her back to him. He reached up and lifted the edge of her skirt, not shocked at all to find her bare assed underneath. He pulled her down onto his lap and ground her against himself.

He awoke just as his dream-self was about to come. He looked down at his crotch, verifying he didn't even have an erection, yet he still felt as though he was about to shoot all over in his pants. He wiped his hands over his eyes, and had another swallow of water.

By the time he started out of the room, and down the hall to look for the nurse again, he'd forgotten all about the dream.

As he walked past the kid's room, he heard voices. Before stepping into the room, he pushed the door open only a crack, and listened. Someone was in there, talking to the kid, and by God, *he was answering*! A cold chill ran down Kaine's spine as he heard the voice for the first time. It was higher than most thirteen year olds; the kid hadn't used his vocal cords often enough to get them warmed up, but the wisdom in those words was ... far beyond his thirteen years. Far beyond.

Clearing his throat as he stepped into the room, Kaine was stunned to find the nurse he sought, sitting there, holding the kid's hand. She didn't bounce up when he came in, she stayed put. *Score one for her nerves*, he thought. The kid turned to look at Kaine, and he grinned. The grin made Kaine want to piss in his pants, turning his insides to liquid fire. Why was he reacting like this? He was just a kid, and he was a kid in danger. A kid Kaine *wanted* to help. What the fuck?

"No, Kaine, I'm not in danger. Come in, why don't you?" The eyes that regarded him glittered with something Kaine wasn't sure he wanted any part of.

The kid laughed; it was infectious. When Kaine began to laugh with him, he knew he was lost.

Kaine came around in the hovel Claire had brought him to. The coppery-salt smell of the blood that had been splashed around the room seemed to be getting stronger. Perhaps it was just his imagination playing tricks with him, but he didn't think so.

It was still dark, but he could now see bits of light shining onto the floor in front of him; shining from between ill-placed floorboards above, from a blacked-out window to his right. The scuffling sounds were still around him; but as with the last time he came around, there were no pawing, clawed hands grabbing at his feet. He heard absolutely no sounds coming from above, nor from the room next to him. Rising, he turned to look at the window more closely.

He began to scratch at it carefully so as not to make too much noise. Whatever was down here with him seemed to be sleeping now, and he also didn't want to have the person in the next room catching him. It didn't take long, really, to scrape off enough of the paint (he assumed it was spray paint) to get a fairly large patch of light on the floor. It had, in fact, illuminated the little room rather well, not only that lonely piece of floor, but also allowing his eyes to see into the murky grey that was his cell.

As the patch of light grew larger, there were sighs and grunts, and sounds of sliding across the floor. There were definitely other people down here with him, but he wasn't sure what state they were in. He didn't want to know, really. Kaine might be a doctor, he may have survived med school – but he'd put all of that behind him when he chose to specialize in psychiatry. Whatever their condition, they moaned as they scuttled further into the shadows.

In the next room, he heard a chair slide across the floor, a few steps to the door, and it opened just as he slid back to his own little crouching spot in the corner. Feigning sleep, he watched through lowered lashes as the person he assumed was his true captor strode across his cell to stand over him. A toe nudged his thigh, and still Kaine pretended to sleep.

"Shall we not play this game, Dr. Kaine? I know full well you are not asleep, so just give up the act. I want to speak with you, and I want to do it in relative civility. Get up, put this on, and follow me." Again, the voice's familiarity annoyed Kaine into puzzling over who he may be. Thoughts were cut short as a robe of some sort had been tossed over his lap.

He stood, shrugged the robe on, and followed with relative docility.

The light in the next room hurt his eyes, even after adjusting them slightly as he peered at the window while he worked on it. He blinked several times then put his hand on his forehead, shading his eyes. He still couldn't quite make out the figure on the other side of the table, but he thought he would in no time now. He knew it had to do with the Facility, and he was suddenly sure that perhaps this grown man before him was ...

"Yes, Dr. Kaine. I was the child that Shrink spent so much time and diligence in first killing, then resurrecting so many times. I was that child in the bed; the one you thought you freed from a prison of unmentionable terror. Sit down."

Kaine sat, his mouth flopping open and closed like a guppy out of water.

"Oh, do stop that. Just keep it closed for now." The man turned and carried a small tray to the table. Setting it in front of Kaine – still out of the circle of light cast by the overhead bulb – he motioned for Kaine to fix himself some coffee. "I so enjoy coffee first thing in the morning. It's that first cup ... always special."

Kaine fixed his mug with the motions of an automaton, adding his sugar and cream from habit rather than deliberate action.

"The woman who introduced herself as Claire Davis, is not in fact, Claire Davis. Claire is ... Claire is somewhere else right now. I asked Joanie to fill in for her. I am rather surprised you didn't recognize her right off the bat, Kaine. You used to find her as annoying as a bug. She used to follow you around the Facility, remember? Her hair has darkened over the years and she dyes it darker still; I suppose you would have recognized her, if you'd been presented with someone whose age would match their appearance." The kid sat down across from Kaine and leaned in, under the lights. Kaine saw that his face had really not aged that much; he didn't look fourteen any longer, but he also didn't look like he'd be in his thirties.

"What happened to you? Why have you got me here?" Kaine whispered hoarsely.

"I've done some rather, *troubling* things in the past few years, and I felt the need to discuss them with the cause." He stopped long enough to take a sip of his coffee, and continued, "You see, Kaine, you took me from the Facility before Shrink had finished his work. I was ... for lack of a better word ... unfinished. Therefore, I have some fundamental mistakes in my wiring. Joanie loves to call it that. That's how I know when she's slipped out and Claire's personality has gone somewhere else. Mostly, it's Joanie, acting as Claire. Claire, when she's out ... " He fell silent for several moments, hands searching pockets for a pack of cigarettes. Finding none, he rose and searched the cupboard above the counter on the far side of the room.

Finding his pack, an ashtray, and bringing the coffee pot with him, he returned to his seat.

"You see, Kaine, I was not the only one being created in that dark basement. I was learning rapidly, and I found the weakest link amongst the women. Joanie was so infatuated with you, she was ripe for manipulation. It didn't take long for her to see past you to me."

Kaine sputtered coffee over himself. She had to have been at least twelve years older than the kid when they escaped the Facility. Kaine had slept with her, for Christ's sake, while they'd been on the road. And yet, *hadn't he known then?*

"I see you are coming to the realization. Good. Means we can move on. After you left us, Joanie and I went north. Spent some time moving around with a group of people, pretending I was her son. Obviously, after I started fucking her, that story wasn't going to fly."

"You have been with her since the Facility then?" Kaine asked, almost dumbfounded, but not quite.

The kid nodded. He lit a cigarette, and offered Kaine one, who shook his head. "Yes. About three years after you left, I began seriously playing with her mind, here and there. Putting her under hypnosis, making suggestions, bringing her back." The man waved his hand as if it were nothing more than a game. "For a while, she was just a close friend, a caretaker, while I went to school. I met someone there, and although Joanie was raging jealous, she accepted it. That person was Claire."

He snuffed out the cigarette, and pushing the ashtray away to the side, he leaned across the table again. "I even took a new name, Kaine. Billy Davis. It's nice to meet you."

The twinkle was back in the man's eyes and Kaine felt hot urine splash over his feet as the realizations hit and his bladder let go; he'd read the papers. He knew who Billy Davis was, or had been. All those people, and the woman he'd been married to. Shot. He'd been shot, and it had been her lover that killed him, he'd been …

"But you're dead. You were shot and killed."

"No, Rez. I *was* shot. I *was* declared DOA by the attending emergency responders. My body was taken to the Facility, at Joanie's request. Did you know, Shrink was still there … He performed a marginal autopsy on me, as much as he knew he could get away with. Once he'd done some repairs to my skull and put me into physiotherapy for a while, I was almost as good as new. Almost."

Kaine just stared at the man seated in front of him. What in God's name had Shrink been doing down there in that lab?

The kid, the man – Billy – sat across the table, smirking as Kaine took it all in, as he tried to understand what his part in all of this was.

"Why, Billy? Why have you got me here? I didn't start this."

"No, Kaine, you didn't. But you'll finish it."

With movements lithe and fast as a wildcat, Billy was up and over the table, grabbing Kaine by his throat. Nails dug into Kaine's windpipe, the skin ripping with the pressure applied by Billy's hand. "You won't die easy, and it won't be fast. You'll die as I did, on that table, so long ago. Do you remember, Kaine? Do you remember getting caught?"

Kaine blacked out before Billy even finished his question.

Light was blinding him, even though his eyelids were drawn shut over his eyes. When he tried to raise a hand to shade them, he found his arms useless. He couldn't even open his eyes – they'd been taped shut. His throat was raw, and Kaine realized with a start that he was ventalized. Joanie must have put him on the ventilator, Billy couldn't have had the experience to do it without damaging his already partially crushed and swollen airway.

Kaine cried, silent and still, tears leaking out from under the surgical tape. He couldn't feel his feet, and didn't know he was lying in a mess of his own fluids. The high-epidural would wear off soon, and that was when Billy would make his work complete.

They waited, silently, in the observation lounge. Billy's hand caressed slow and lazy circles on Joanie's back as she serviced him with her mouth. He showed no signs of pleasure, nor of pain when she bit down on his straining penis.

His face never twitched, his hands never stopped their motion, even when he ejaculated.

When it was done, he pushed her away and rose, zipping his pants before leaving the room. Kaine was awake, and it was time to begin.

Billy didn't speak, simply ran the blade from Kaine's collarbone to his navel. The effects of the spinal anesthesia had only just worn off, and Kaine screamed; the sound was muffled and choked by the ventilator, but it was obvious by the straining. Kaine *screamed*, until his nerves overloaded, and he shut down.

Billy waited.

Kaine became aware of more than the pain. The sounds were familiar, but not ... It was the sound of a defibrillator charging, and going off, then charging again. With each sharp conclusion, Kaine's body jerked from the table. He was alive.

He could feel his heart racing; Billy was shocking him and throwing his heart out of sync. The electric charge, the delicate balance ...

Kaine thought he was gasping for air, that he had no oxygen. He felt as though the walls were caving in, as though his lungs were no longer in his chest. He was suffocating.

Another jolt across his body, causing his mind to scream when his body just could not.

Why, why keep his mind awake? Why keep him alive and cut him open?

Why?

Flames of pain trickled along the finer nerve endings across his torso; he felt the machine take over for his heart, for his lungs. Fire ran through his veins and his mind would not close off, would not let him escape. Tears slipped unnoticed from his eyes, now free and open so he could watch the removal of his organs in the mirror above.

Billy took the heart and one lung to the table beyond Kaine's range of sight. When he returned, Kaine could not be sure if the organs he carried were his, or someone – *something* – else's.

Laughing manically, Kaine thought to himself: *from this*

vantage point, they would look different … He realized he felt no more pain as Billy sewed him together again. No pain, until the defibrillator charged and Billy applied the paddles once more.

Three times, and he was out. Billy laughed under the mask when Kaine's eyes rolled into his skull.

"Kaine. Kaine, *Kaine* … in a moment I'm going to remove the pads. There will be no more pain. You will feel nothing, ever again. Be glad I allowed you a sedative. Be glad you are ventilated. Be glad I've been merciful."

Kaine awoke to several more jolts from the machine. He remembered. He remembered everything now.

Shrink had been sure that people, on their deathbeds, could leave their bodies and survive in the ether until a new vessel was found. Claire was in Joanie, and Kaine … well, Kaine had the same problem as Billy. He was unfinished; body dead but functional and a mind corroded by the pain from the procedures. A mind corrupted by hate and anger, a mind stuck between the physical and the final interlude.

Dead, but fueled by a fire no other would understand. No other, but Billy.

After his recovery, Kaine not only forgave, but thanked Billy for the opportunity. Together, they sought new vessels. Those that survived the procedure would join them, and together, they'd help the entire world to see what a joyous, *free* world could rise from nothing more than exquisite pain.

About the Author

Jodi Lee is a 30-something year old writer from Manitoba, Canada. She has spent almost her entire life on the Canadian Prairies, which she credits for her over-active imagination. Nothing breaks the monotony like the occasional zombie chasing her two daughters, or a flesh-devouring mutant alien mosquito. When not working on selling other authors' works to publishers world-wide, she reads slush for Apex Digest and attempts to meet her own word count goals. Visit her website at http://www.jodilee.ca

The premise of this story came to me when a dear, sweet telemarketer decided to call me one day and wreaked havoc on my good mood and my sanity. Unlike the persistent telemarketer in this story, my telemarketer did not get a sale that day, nor did he on the second, third, or fourth day he called me back. But he did get a short story dedicated to his pertinacious nature.

ONE HELL OF A DEAL
By Giovanna Lagana

"Damn, that blasted phone!" Jack cursed as he sucked his throbbing, red finger. He accidentally burnt it touching the scorching-hot frying pan when the first shrilling ring came.

He twisted around quickly to the sink and turned on the cold-water tap, shoving his middle finger under the flowing water.

The phone kept ringing and ringing in persistence, making his eardrums vibrate, and sent surging pain through his head. "Why isn't the damn answering machine kicking in? Yeah, yeah. I'm coming."

He shut off the running water, shuffled over to his frying eggs, and turned off the burner, then walked up to the phone on the wall.

He checked the answering machine. It was on. *Weird.* Maybe it was broken. Then he looked at the Caller ID name and saw 'Mélanie Clavier' on the screen. A smile spread across his face. He hadn't heard from her in over a year. Boy, did he miss her. Yeah, he missed her long sexy legs, her full, delicious breasts, and that curvy behind of hers.

Every inch of her spelled sex in the first degree. Too bad her mouth never shut up. But he hadn't had a dose of Mélanie Clavier in over a year and his manhood was in dire need of a romping with the famous Mademoiselle Clavier. Oh, yes, indeed that would be a nice way to start the day and get rid of the hangover from Hell. Maybe she could suck on his burnt finger and make it all better. Maybe she could suck on something else and make that all better, too. *Oh, yeah!*

As the phone rang a tenth time, Jack grabbed it forcibly. Rubbing one side of his temple, which felt like every vein in it would burst, he answered: "Hey, baby. I haven't heard from you in over a year. How have you been?"

The name on the screen switched to 'Unknown' as a jovial voice on the other end replied: "Good morning. May I please speak to Mr. Truman?"

"Yeah, it's Jack Truman. This isn't Mélanie. Who is this?"

"Ah, Mr. Truman. Hello. Allow me to introduce myself. My name is Adam Temper and I'm calling on behalf of Serpent Publishing."

"If this is about a publishing deal, talk to my agent."

"No, no, Mr. Truman. I am calling because of this special we have this month on our books."

Jack wanted to force his fist through the phone and punch the genial telemarketer. "Look, Mac ... "

"Ah, it's Adam Temper."

"I don't give a shit if it's the Queen of England. I'm not interested!"

"My, my, that is awfully rude of you, Mr. Truman. I mean, you haven't even let me tell you what we are offering."

"I don't care if you are offering me a king's ransom. I'm not interested. And where the hell did you get my number?"

Hesitation radiated through the voice's words. "Ah ... I have it in the company's phone listing."

"Bull! My number is unlisted!"

"Are you calling me a liar, sir?"

"Damn right. Look, I don't know who gave you my number or what you paid to get it. The point is I'm not interested."

"Please, just let me tell you about our offer."

Jack banged his head against the wall in frustration. *Big mistake*. Stars fluttered in his vision and a surge of nausea churned its way up his esophagus. It took only a second for it to subside and he could talk again. "What part of 'no' don't you understand, Mac? I'm not interested. Final!"

The convivial tone over the line morphed into a wicked, deep, and vile one, growling, "I'LL TELL YOU WHEN IT'S FINAL, JACK!!!!"

A sensation of dread pulsated through him. The voice ... the voice sounded inhuman. Beast-like. In reflex, Jack hung up the phone and walked away, almost afraid the phone would detach itself from the wall and a huge, horrible demon would crawl out of it and attack him.

"What the hell was that?" he uttered to no one but himself.

Of course, when he got no answer, he shrugged off the panic and walked back to the stove. His eggs looked all gooey and disgusting. More acid ascended to his mouth at the view. "Ah, the hell with it. I ain't gonna eat. Where are the damn Aspirin?"

He walked over to the corner cupboard and started to rummage through the box of medication he had tossed in it. Half of the bottles were expired. After a minute, he found the container at the bottom of the box and took out two. He shoved them in his mouth and chewed them as he walked over to the cooler to get a glass of water. A gagging reflex made his gaze turn to the ceiling. Aspirin tasted horrible, especially when he crushed them in his mouth, but that was the only way Jack could take them. He had problems swallowing pills ever since his cousin from New York came to Montreal for a visit when they were kids and put him in a choke hold he had seen on a wrestling match on TV. His throat seemed to shrink then and he could never swallow pills without chewing them first.

Years ago, he had gone to see a ton of O.R.L specialists for his problem. The doctors had all said there was nothing wrong with his thorax and that it was only stress. *Yeah, right.* When they couldn't figure out what was wrong, they always blamed stress. How convenient for them and not so convenient for Jack. There was nothing he could do but just cope with it.

As he rinsed away the sour, revolting tang from his mouth, the phone rang again and he jumped. A part of him shook in his slippers. Another part of him wanted to go to the phone and scream like a maniac to tell the telemarketer to go to Hell.

Before he made up his mind what part of him would take over, the phone rang again. He took a deep breath and walked over to it. He picked it up and stated assertively: "Look, Mac, I'm not interested. Don't call me again."

He was about to hang up when he heard the low sound of a familiar voice say: "Wait, Jack!"

He looked at the Caller ID and realized who it was. He put the receiver to his ear and responded: "Roy? Is that you?"

With a slight giggle, the caller said: "Yeah. It's me. Who is 'Mac' and what are you not interested in?"

Jack leaned against the wall, sighing in relief. "Oh, a telemarketer from Hell. That's all."

"Ah, aren't they all. How come they called you? Your number is unlisted?"

"I'm asking myself the same question. Do you think they got it through the publisher?"

"Nah, no way. They keep your address and number highly confidential. They could get into big problems if they ever let it slip out."

"So where did he get it?"

"Maybe through a friend of yours. You know those chicks you pick up could easily have passed it on. You really ought to be careful who you give your number to, you know. I mean you are Jack Truman."

"Yeah, yeah. I get the point. Anyway, I doubt he'll call back again. I made it perfectly clear I wasn't interested."

"Hmmm, I hope so. But once you are on their list, you'll be called up again. I suggest you call the phone company and change your number. By the way, don't you have Caller ID? Maybe you can trace the call?"

"Yeah, at first it read a girl's name I know, then it turned to Unknown. Freakin' weird, man."

"Maybe it's some kind of blocking device these telemarketers have to conceal their private lines. A lot of them are calling from their own homes, you know?"

"Yeah, I know. This whole telemarketing scene was invented to rid us of our sanity, man. There's no doubt in my mind."

"Ain't it the truth." There was a brief pause and then Roy said: "Jack, can you come to the office this morning?"

Jack looked at his underwear and slippers. He was in no mood to shower and get dressed, let alone drive into the city and into downtown. Not with the walloping headache.

"Roy, can't I come tomorrow? Or this afternoon?"

A sigh. "Look, Jack, I have an important meeting this afternoon and this news can't wait."

Panic took over his senses. "What? What is it, Roy?"

"I'm sorry, man. I can't tell you over the phone. Be here in two hours, will you?"

Before Jack could protest, Roy hung up.

Jack rubbed his eyes in reflex. Something deep down in his gut sounded an alarm. He had a bad feeling that the telemarketer from Hell was only the start to a very awful day.

"Yeah, Jack, I knew you'd be happy with the news," Roy Steinman enunciated with a priggish grin.

Jack bowed his head, smiling. "I sure am, Roy. You don't know how long I have been waiting for this. It's been a long time coming."

He slouched onto the couch in Roy's office and combed his hands through his sandy blond hair. His emotions were running high. A surge of relief flowed through him. He had been on pins and needles ever since Roy called him earlier asking him to come to his office.

From his past experiences with Roy, his literary agent, he figured Roy had bad news to deliver and Roy always delivered his bad news in person, in his office. As if it would dull the shock or the disappointment. *Right.* That was a farce. Bad news was bad news, no matter how or where it was delivered.

But today, his pessimistic thoughts were uncalled for. Today, the news was good. Damn good. The type of news Jack had been waiting for for over a decade – before his wife left him for his best friend, before he lost custody of his daughter, before he drowned his sorrows in alcohol and women. Definitely before writer's block set in and turned his creative mind to spoils, making his writing career plummet into practical failure, and he was branded a has been by the media.

To make sure he wasn't dreaming, Jack asked: "You sure about that, Roy?"

Roy pushed his burgundy, leather chair back and twirled it around like a child on a merry go round. "Yeah, Jack, there's no doubt about it. You've been nominated for the Nobel Prize in Literature. I couldn't believe it myself until I got the call. Now tell me my idea a year ago was stupid."

"No, Roy, I got to admit you were right and I was wrong. The day you suggested hiring a ghostwriter, I thought you were nuts. I thought there was no way this writer could pull it off. It's not like I write like anybody out there. I mean, you know my style, how I add my random and philosophical thoughts into the narration. And weave my metaphors into a graphic image for the reader. I honestly thought Belial couldn't pull it off."

"No doubt about it, Jack, your style is unique. And when Belial called me back then and offered to be our ghostwriter, I practically laughed in his face. I mean he had no credentials, no past experience. But lucky for us I like a guy with balls. And Belial has balls. He kept calling and calling until I finally asked him to send me his manuscript."

"Yeah, I remember when you brought it over to my house. I practically had a heart attack after I read it. It was like ... like ... "

"Like you were reading your own stuff."

"Yeah, but more than that. It's like a déjà vu thing, you know. Like I could have sworn I wrote it or thought of writing it some time or other. I don't know how to put it."

"Well, that déjà vu thing isn't important. The fact that he could write like you ... or rather how you used to is what is important." Roy bent down and opened his left drawer, shuffling papers. Then he sat up and spread articles and clippings from literary magazines, *The New York Times*, and *The Chicago Tribune* on his desk, all praising the rebirth of Jack Truman's writing career. "See, Jack. Everyone believes it. Everyone believes Belial's novel is yours."

"Yeah, they do. But what happens now, Roy?"

Roy's forehead crinkled in perplexity. "What do you mean?"

Jack pushed himself to the edge of the couch and brought his hands together in complete seriousness. "What happens with Belial and me? Will he want more money? Is he willing to write another novel for me? What?"

Roy smiled, beaming with reassurance. "Don't worry, Jack. The contract I made the lawyer write up, which you and Belial signed, is totally legal and binding. No, he won't ask for more money. Yes, he will keep his mouth shut, and yes, he is writing the sequel to the novel as we speak. He will deliver it to you at the end of the month. Don't worry, Jack. We hired the best lawyer for this. I took no chances. This is the publishing business, for Christ's sake. If this didn't happen all the time, ghostwriters wouldn't exist and be making business, would they?"

Jack shook his head in affirmation. "Yeah, I guess you're right. If someone would have asked me ten years ago if I would ever hire a ghostwriter, I would have kicked him out on his ass and told him never to insult me like that again.

"Who would have thought I would be hiring one a decade later and rising back to fame and be nominated for a Nobel Prize."

"Don't wreck your brain thinking about it."

"Yeah, but I feel like I'm cheating some way."

Roy shook his head negatively. "Cheating! Are you serious! Look, if Belial had gone on his own and tried to sell that story, he would have gotten nowhere. He had no experience, no name, nothing. Through you, he's $100, 000. richer and will be getting more royalties from the second book. And your fans are happy they get to read a book that took ten years to write. Who loses out, Jack? Tell me, huh? Who?"

"Yeah, if you put it that way ... "

"Damn right I'm right." Roy looked at his watch. "Holy shit! It's almost noon. Sorry, Jack, but I got a meeting with another client at one sharp, which I need to get ready for. So I hope you don't mind if I kick you out now."

Jack got up and straightened out his tight jeans. Even at forty-five, he still had a firm butt and the body of a twenty-five-year-old. The over indulgence in booze hadn't put a damper on him physically, only his mental self. "Okay, Roy. I got to go and do some things myself. Take care."

As Roy picked up the phone on his desk, he motioned with his index finger. "Don't forget you've got a book signing at The Book Depot tomorrow afternoon."

"Yeah, I remember. Will you be there?"

"When have I ever missed a book signing, kiddo? Yeah, I'll be there."

"That's what I love about you, Roy."

With a wide smile, Roy responded: "That and the fact that we've known each other for over twenty years."

"Yeah. It's been a long time and a great friendship. Okay, I'll see you tomorrow."

Jack closed the door and headed for the staircase as his cell phone rang. He had downloaded a Sci-fi sound, which sounded like a cross between the soundtrack from Star Trek and Star Wars. It sounded pretty cool a few weeks ago, but its novelty was wearing thin, to the point it became annoying. He'd have to search the Net later on for a new, invigorating tune.

Isn't Modern Technology wonderful!

As he flipped the metallic silver cover of his cell, he saw the name 'Mélanie Clavier' flashing in the tiny box on the phone.

Oh, oh! Dread came rushing in on its high horse, levying his complete attention.

As Jack stared at the display, it turned to 'Unknown'.

Shocker?

Not!

That feeling in the back of his conscience he had at his home a few hours ago had never completely gone away even when Roy told him the amazing news. It just temporarily rolled over to dormancy, but now it came to its full awareness once again.

He whispered: "No way, man," and turned off his cell.

For a brief moment, he felt in control once again. Was poor Jack fooling himself? Hell, poor Jack hadn't been in control of anything ever since Sylvie, his wife, left him for another man ten years ago.

And sure enough when he thought he had gotten rid of the pestilent telemarketing call, his phone began to ring again. Only this time it wasn't the Sci-Fi music. It was gothic. Scary gothic music full of bass and a macabre feel. Freaking out, he pulled out the battery from the back of the phone.

It went dead. No ringing. Just silence. "Finally," he whispered, putting his phone back in the pouch on his belt, and then started to descend the stairs, heading for his car, which he parked in a space at the end of the street.

Before he got to the end of the long stairway, his phone started vibrating. He jumped. At first, it was weak, almost tickling.

"Bloody hell!" He screamed and then looked around instinctively. Luckily, no one was around to see him freak out.

He tried to open the pouch and remove the phone, but the pouch transformed before his eyes and blood red roots began to grow and spread around his waist. The vibration evolved into painful, vigorous shakes.

Panic struck him at full force again. His lungs shrunk, depriving him of oxygen, as the bloody roots spread and tightened around his abdomen and chest. His vision began to blur and the veins in his face protruded and pulsated with each agonizing vibration from the god-forsaken phone.

In desperateness, as his face turned blue and unconsciousness seeped into the deep crevices of his mind, he thought of answering the beast within the phone and thus stopping this living nightmare.

As if the phone, or the creature lurking on the other side, could sense his thoughts, the monstrous phone morphed back to his old, tame cell phone. No blood, no throbbing veins, and no deadly shaking. He took a deep, long-needed breath and waited a second for the blood in his head to flow back down. Then he removed the cursed phone from the pouch and answered with hesitation and a stutter: "Hell-lo?"

"Jacky-boy!" the demon voice responded. "Or should I say *Jackass*!"

"What do you want?"

"I told you before. I want to tell you about this special Serpent Publishing is having."

"Who are you? And what do you want with me?"

"Jackass, has all the booze numbed your brain cells or have the women you've been fucking fried them completely? I told you I want to tell you about this special Serpent Publishing is having."

"Okay, okay, what is it?"

"Well, for five hundred thousand you can have all the books in the Serpent Publishing library."

"Five hundred thousand!" he shrieked. "I don't have five hundred thousand!"

"Oh, come now, Jackass. How stupid do you think I am? You made a fortune with that book Belial wrote for you. Five hundred thousand is peanuts. You can afford it all right.

A pause. "How do you know about that?"

"I know many things, my friend. It's my job to know these things. So is the answer yes, or do you dare to say no? I'm warning you, Jackass, you'd better not say no. I'll get angry." He chuckled. "If you think I am bad now, just wait and see how I get when I don't get my way. I'm a real Hell raiser then."

Jack took a big breath, and knowing he had no choice, he responded: "Okay, but it will take me a while before I can get the money."

"I'll give you a day."

"Okay, I'll try."

"No, Jackass, don't try. DO IT! The bank you need to transfer the money to is the Bank of the Underworld, the account is 666. The name is Adam Temper," said the demon and hung up.

Jack threw the phone against the wall, making it shatter into a hundred pieces. "FUCK YOU!"

As he left the building and walked toward his car, his hands were shaking and he perspired like crazy. Passersby looked at him dumbfoundedly as if they feared he was tripping on some type of potent street drug. Jack was also wondering the same thing. Damn, it had to be one hell of a drug to make him trip a demon that had targeted him through the phone.

As he passed a phone booth, walking towards his car, the phone in it rang. Jack trembled even more and looked around him. He asked a tall man passing him if he could answer it.

The guy ripped his hand out of Jack's grip, and frowning said: "Answer it yourself, wacko. It ain't ringing."

Jack stood there and wrapped his arms around his torso. Even though it was the middle of summer, and with the humidex, the temperature was 35 Celsius, he was cold. Ice cold.

He stared at the phone that kept ringing relentlessly, which apparently no one else heard or was bothered by. Finally he answered: "Yeah."

"No, Jackass, FUCK *YOU*! You have one day. I'll call you before dinner time to make sure you went to the bank to make the transfer."

"But the bank you said doesn't exist."

A roaring, haunting laugh echoed through the phone. "After all that's happened to you today, can you honestly say it doesn't exist? It exists, all right, Jackass. Only not many people know about it."

"Fine, I'll go to the bank now and make the transfer."

"Good." And the phone went dead.

But the ringing in Jack's ear still remained – the ringing of utter fear and despair.

Jack got home at five o'clock. He had spent two hours at the bank. They made him sign a million papers and called a hundred places for authorizations and verifications. Sure enough the Bank of the Underworld existed, with an account 666 for an Adam Temper.

The bank manager had told him the money would be transferred electronically by nine o'clock the next morning.

Again, isn't Modern Technology wonderful!

Jack felt like he'd been run over by a truck. His body ached, and the headache from Hell still had a vise grip on his brain. He rummaged through the freezer looking for something good to eat. Maybe if he ate something, he'd feel better.

The freezer was full of frozen gourmet meals. A famous downtown fine cuisine restaurant's chef had precooked and frozen many of Jack's favorite meals. Jack paid a hefty price for the prepared meals, but every cent of it was worth it, because he was a terrible, lazy cook.

As he slipped a tray of Veal Parmigiana into the microwave and set the timer on High for five minutes, the phone rang. Not surprisingly, the ring tone was the same eerie gothic music from earlier. The beige phone turned into a blood red color and twisted into a shape of a beating heart. Talk about one hell of a Caller ID. No refuting who that was.

Jack freaked, he couldn't bring himself to pick it up. Who would? Within a minute, his phone turned back to the way it was, and then Jack finally answered it. "Hello."

"Hey, Jackass. What took you so long? I see you completed the transfer. Good. The books will be delivered tomorrow morning at ten o'clock once I see the money deposited into my account. Be home to accept the delivery, will you?"

Before Jack could reply, the demon hung up.

For the first time in the entire day, he felt a wave of relief pour over him. Even though he was broke, he still was alive. His next royalty check was just a few weeks away. And from what Roy had mentioned, it would be double the last amount.

He walked over to the bar and served himself a big glass of cognac.

He needed it badly, really badly.

By eight o'clock that evening, Jack had drunk himself into a stupor and toppled onto his bed fully clothed and drooling, feeling as if the worst was over. The weatherman had reported on the evening news blue skies were in the forecast tomorrow. For once Jack thought he got the forecast right.

Jack woke up the next morning to a buzzing sound. He turned around trying to ascertain where he was. After a minute, he realized he was in his room on the floor. The carpet reeked of urine.

His urine.

Gross.

He sat up and the whole room spun around him. He closed his eyes and waited a few seconds before he opened them again. The twirling room finally came to a stop and he was able to stand. He looked at his alarm clock on the mahogany nightstand. It was ten o'clock.

The buzzing sound came again, only this time he realized it was the doorbell. "Holy crap!" he uttered as he shuffled to the front door.

He peeked through the peephole and saw a deliveryman on the other side. *Good. No demon.*

He opened the door and the smiling deliveryman looked at him in apparent surprise. The pungent odor of urine must have attacked his nose because a look of disgust spread over his face. He asked: "Mr. Truman? Mr. Jack Truman?"

Jack smiled in embarrassment. He could only imagine what he looked like. He already knew what he smelled like. It was all Jack could do to keep his stomach acid from erupting with every acrid inhale he took. But the man was there to deliver the books and then he'd never have to see him again.

"Yes, I'm Mr. Truman."

"All right, Mr. Truman, may I come in? I have a delivery for you."

"Yes, yes, of course." Jack opened the door fully and stepped aside.

The deliveryman stooped down and picked up a heavy, huge box as if it weighed as much as a box full of feathers and walked in with it. He placed it on the floor in Jack's living room and took out an electronic pad and stylus pen. "Please sign here."

"Sure," said Jack as he picked it up and signed. Then handed it over to the deliveryman.

The deliveryman looked at the signature and began to laugh.

Perplexed, Jack looked at him and asked: "What's so funny?"

The deliveryman said nothing only turned to him and laughed louder and more sinisterly. Then he instantly transformed into a blood red demon with horns and a ghastly face so frightening, Medusa herself would surely turn to stone gazing upon his face of horror.

With the same eerie, vile voice Jack had heard on the phone, the demon said, "GOT YOU!"

Jack walked backwards in fear. "I don't understand."

The demon followed him slowly. "What's there not to understand, Jackass. I GOT YOU!"

"If you mean you got my five hundred thousand. Then yes."

The demon laughed even louder. "Yes, I got the money, but I also got *you*."

Jack shrieked, "No, No!"

The demon brought up the electronic pad to Jack's eyes. "Read, Jackass. Read the fine print. You just signed over your soul to me."

Tears began to well up in his eyes. "No! No! I didn't know what I was signing."

Again the demon laughed. "Jack, Jack. After over twenty years in the business, haven't you learnt that isn't an excuse? No, the contract is signed and I own your money and your soul." The demon looked at the screen and said: "Oh, and you owe me a phone number."

"No, this can't be happening!"

"Yes, Jacko, it is, and you owe me a number, look at the fine print. It says you owe me a number."

Through filmy eyes, Jack stared at the pad. Sure enough it was all there, like the demon said. Jack searched his memory trying to come up with a number of one of the tramps he bedded. Of course none came to mind. 'Love them and leave them' was his motto. So why would he memorize their numbers?

The demon tapped his claw-like foot on the floor. "Come on, Jackass, tell me a name or I'll take the first number on your phone over there."

Panic surged through his mind. Sylvie's name was on there. The demon would go after his ex-wife, then his daughter. *Never.* Jack would never let that happen. He blurted out the only damn number he had memorized in his puny brain. "All right! The number is 555-3575!"

The demon smiled and worms and maggots from inside his mouth fell to the floor. "And the name?"

"Roy Steinman."

Jack could swear the demon knew Roy's name from the expression on his face.

"Good." The demon took a few more steps towards him.

Jack trembled and whispered: "What are you going to do to me?"

"Eat you, Jackass, and take your soul."

Jack screamed: "NOOOOOO!!!!" as the demon plunged his razor sharp fangs into his neck.

The demon finished eating his meal in minutes, absorbing Jack's soul into his grotesque body. Jack made a scrumptious dish. After he was satisfied, he sat on Jack's couch and laughed to himself. He looked at Jack's bony remains and said, "Poor Jackass, you never saw me coming, did you? If you would've done your research, you would have realized Mélanie Clavier gave me your name and number over a year ago when she signed my contract and sold me her soul.

"You would have also realized Belial was me and that the story I sold you was actually your stupid story you had buried in your warped, damaged brain. I just stole it from you with my voodoo demon magic. Yeah, I had a blast playing you and Roy Steinman like puppets. That arrogant asshole got on my nerves almost as much as you did, Jackass. But of course, I couldn't go after him unless his name was given to me through the contract clause. And now that it has," he giggled wickedly and rubbed his claw-like hands in anticipation of the havoc he'd wreak on pathetic Roy Steinman's soul, "it'll be so much fun."

He sighed and then continued: "Ah, Jackass ... you and Roy weren't smart at all, were you? You should have realized what the name Belial meant."

"I love that name, don't you? I also love Temper, too. Classy, huh? Those are the only names used in the Bible that I adore. That stupid name Beelzebub makes me sound like a Neanderthal and Satan is so tame."

"Yeah, man, I've been around for centuries. Millennia, actually, and to this day, I still get goose pimples thinking of how Man has evolved."

Belial got up and looked at his disgusting flesh and laughed again. "Okay, maybe not goose pimples. How about warts?" He spun his long distorted finger in the air and a vortex suddenly appeared in the center of poor old Jack's living room.

Before he stepped through the wormhole stairway to Hell, so he could devise his next trap for Roy Steinman, Belial turned back to Jack's bones and finished his speech. "Yeah, Jackass, decades ago, it took me years to get poor, stupid humans to sign over their souls to me, but now, with today's innovations, it takes me mere seconds."

He stepped into the maelstrom with his final statement and smirked. "*Isn't modern technology wonderful!*"

About the Author

Giovanna Lagana has been writing for several years. Many of her poems and short stories have appeared in magazines, e-zines, and anthologies. She's also the Senior Editor of Lachesis Publishing. When she isn't busy playing with her kids, writing, or editing, she spends her time reading.

She has written a horror/romantic suspense novel *With Black & White Comes The Grey–The Battle Of Armageddon–Book 1,* which was rated a top-ten Best Horror Novel in the Preditors & Editors 2005 Reader's Poll. She is also a contributor, and co-editor, of *Love, Hate, Fear and Hope* anthologies.

For more information on her and her writing, please visit her at: http://www.giovannalagana.com

People always ask... "Where did the inspiration for your story come from" and usually, the writer can't give a good answer. In the case of "Ice Cold Shakes", I do have an answer though: a dream. I generally don't remember my dreams, but one night, I had a particularly vivid dream, and the next morning when I woke up, I immediately scribbled down what I could remember of it, from fragments of images that included a snakelike woman and a band of co-eds hiking in the Appalachians. That week, I wrote "Ice Cold Shakes", trying to recapture the intense surreal weirdness of the dream. I don't think fiction can approach the power of dream ... but here's what I came up with:

ICE COLD SHAKES
By John Everson

The glowing eyes should have sent me running. At least they should have given me a clue. But at the time, I just thought they were sexy. I mean, what would you do if you were shivering in a musty sleeping bag in the middle of godforsaken nowhere and this incredible woman suddenly slithered in beside you – wearing a stitch of nothing? I'm sure you'd throw her out because she had overly bright green eyes. Right?

But I suppose I should start at the beginning. While I hate to blame the poor guy, it *was* all Bob's idea. "Let's get together this summer and road trip," he begged us a week before finals. The 'us' included three-fourths of an inseparable collegiate quartet – Ann, a bafflingly pretty Poly-Sci major;

Bill, a dedicated 'liberal arts-undecided' jock, and myself, a bookworm English major. We were all brain-dead from putting in all-nighters in our various curricula and Bob (a computer geek) tantalized us with dreams of the open road. We agreed immediately. It was the best way to shut him up so we could get some cramming done.

Bob – being Bob – didn't forget. A week later, as we were packing to leave the dorms for the summer, he corralled us to his room. "So when do we go?" he asked, eyes bugging out in single-minded anticipation – as if we'd automatically know what the hell he was talking about! Bill looked at his watch.

"Fifteen minutes?"

It wasn't that easy. Ann had a summer job lined up – just a couple months of office work for a state congressman, but she needed the money. Bill's summer calendar would have inspired awe among the contestants of *The Dating Game* and I, well, actually I had nothing to do at all but dig into some Milton – or maybe attempt *The Divine Comedy* again – but I couldn't admit to that, could I?

So we all went home to sort out our lives. After two months of phone tag and crossing bad weeks off the calendar, we ended up in the backseat of Bob's dilapidated dirt brown Pontiac Bonneville. We had two weeks to kill before heading back to school, and we needed a destination. I favored something in the way of a big white sand beach, bronzed, bikini-clad women trouncing everywhere – sort of a delayed Spring Break thing. Bob wanted to head east.

"The Appalachians," he pronounced.

The three of us looked at him blankly. Ann stretched out her tiny legs, hoisting a bare knee over Bill's lap, and yawned. She didn't care where we went as long as she didn't have to make coffee and answer the phone.

"I've always wanted to drive up into the hills and camp out in the Old Country," he explained.

I wanted to ask when the East Coast had officially been designated as the Old Country, but I kept my mouth shut. Bob had babbled on before about how he was descended from Mayflower pilgrims and I didn't want to hear the story again. So Massachusetts, not Middleton, was his old country. Whatever.

Bill, to my surprise, offered monosyllabic agreement:

"Cool."

I'd gathered that his summer gigolo schedule had backfired in some embittering way because when I countered Appalachia with the idea of beach babes, his only reply was: "No women".

Ann gave her eye-popping orange and green tube-top an exaggerated examination.

"Should I leave?" she whined.

"You're not a woman, you're Ann," Bill replied in that playful frat boy demeanor that allows him somehow to tell a woman he'd rather sleep with a snake than her, and leave her feeling complimented – I've seen it happen. I shook my head in wonder as Ann leaned against his beefy shoulder.

"I'd only get sun burnt on a beach, anyway," she said, holding out her arms to show an utter lack of a tan base.

I was obviously not going to see a beach.

Three days later, we were careening through West Virginia. Bill had obviously outgrown his heartbreak; he and Ann seemed to be getting too friendly for friends in the backseat while I suffered through another interminable lecture on the ever-exhausting life of Bob in the front. Some road trip.

I have to admit, the scenery *was* getting impressive. We'd switched to secondary roads that morning to see some of the surrounding country. Thick forests of trees, green everywhere, the occasional wisp of fog hanging over the lush vegetation at the bottom of a valley – if I was a painter or a photographer, I wouldn't have been happier. As it happens, I'm not, so a couple hours of the view were pretty much enough for me. We stopped at a bed and breakfast that night, at the foothills. Bob and Bill and I had switched off driving for the past forty hours and it was time for some stretching out. We should have gotten back on the highway and just kept going.

But the Blue Mountain Inn was a cozy little place – bearskins and deer heads grafted to the walls, oaken beams supporting the roof. We checked in, and the old man at the desk had a mouth as uncorkable as Bob's.

"So, where are ya'll from? What are ya'll doing way out here? Where are ya headed?" he badgered.

It was twenty questions from Hume Cronin. I let Bob deal with him (it seemed fitting, somehow) while I wandered the room. It was homey. Floor to ceiling fireplace of rough, irregular boulders. Plank floors covered with hand-crafted throw rugs. A rocking chair. I happened to glance out the front window at Ann and Bill who were perched on the hood of the car. Their faces were fused at the lips. My stomach shriveled. I had a sudden premonition that after this trip our little group was going to be immeasurably altered.

"Okay, it's all set."

Bob looked very pleased with himself. I couldn't imagine

what he could be so proud of 'setting'. All he had to do was book us a room.

So I asked him.

"I got us two connecting rooms. I figured Ann and Bill were going to want one and you and I would take the other. Then tomorrow, Jack – that's the owner – is going to get his son Jack junior to take us upriver. He'll drop us off at Wichitaw Lake, and then we hike from there."

"Hike? Nobody said nothing about hiking!"

I was picturing us all lost in the middle of a mosquito-infested bog screaming for help. I'm not by nature the adventurous athletic type.

"Yeah, it'll be great. This way we can get up into the hills where no one ever goes – really get back to nature."

"Did you ever think that maybe there's a reason nobody ever goes there?" I asked dryly.

"Yeah, cuz there are no paved roads. Come on, let's go tell Bill and Ann."

The couple nodded impatiently as Bob outlined our itinerary.

"Sounds great," Bill agreed, nodding and wrinkling up his mouth like my dad always does when Mom over-pushes a point and he wants to make sure she sees he agrees with her totally (even though most of the time he doesn't, he's just waiting for her to leave the room so he can get back to the NBA game).

"Can we have our room key? I want to lie down and catch a nap for a while before dinner."

Bob dropped the keys into Bill's extended hand.

Ann followed him, pausing only to catch my eye and wink. Sleep was not what Bill was about to catch. I stared at Bob's angular back and sighed. It was him and me. I loved

Bob and all, but he was not my idea of the ideal backwoods date. I hoped this Lake Whichever had a beach.

An hour later, the four of us were the sole occupants of the inn's kitchen. Jack's wife, a plump graying woman with a limp, served us fried chicken, biscuits, and gravy. We ate like pigs. I was halfway through my second helping when my appetite bowed out. Ann was licking the chicken grease off Bill's fingers. Don't ask why this bothered me, but it did. A month before, Ann would have made fun of anybody doing that to 'Lughead Bill'.

"I'm turning in," I said.

Bob looked at me like I was nuts. "Don't do that. It's early. I figured we could all shoot some pool in the sitting room. Jack said it's a great table."

"Sorry. I'm beat and if we're getting up early, I'm getting some sleep. 'Night."

Of course I didn't go to sleep. I lay in the musty, afghan-covered bed staring at the antique floral wallpaper, listening to the laughter of my friends downstairs amid the clinking of billiards. I had, if truth be told, looked forward to this trip. The four of us had been friends now for two years, and, while Bob occasionally got on my nerves, I would gladly do anything for any of them. But now love had entered the picture – or lust – and spoiled the whole equation. Before, when one of us had problems with the opposite sex, we turned to each other for comfort – a fortress of four. Now the walls had been undermined from inside. Instead of four equal friends, we were becoming two couples. And I wasn't happy with the breakdown.

Jack Jr. turned out to be a pretty cool guy, kind of a Ron

Howard type – carrot hair, freckle face. By nine o'clock the next morning he had us rowing up river, backpacks stowed beneath our seats. His attempts to dissuade us from venturing out on our own were futile.

"There's a main road that goes right up to the top of this mountain here, you know," he told us before we climbed into the boat. He pointed at the white-capped peak miles away. "There's a great little lodge right up at the top there. Unbelievable view."

He waited for someone to burst out with something like "yeah, let's go get the car and drive up."

No one did.

"We don't want to go where everyone else has been," Bob jumped in. "We want to see the unspoiled country. The Old Country."

There he went again with the Old business. I flipped the baseball cap off his head.

"They didn't wear Sox hats in the Old Country, pal. And where's your bearskin coat and your beef jerky?"

"Shouldn't he have a peace pipe or something?" Ann ribbed.

Jack just shook his head at us and pushed the boat into the water.

We were at the lake by nightfall, and there was no beach. In fact, I didn't think it was much of a lake. More like an extended marshy pond, with cattails ringing the border and thick puke green scum covering most of the surface. Lilly pads fought with the cattails for squatters rights to the edge and giant glittering violet and blue dragonflies darted back and forth, apparently quite disturbed that something foreign had broached the calm of the place. The bank (what I could see of it) was steep, slick with smelly mud. No, I wouldn't be doing any swimming here, I decided.

We pitched our tent a little ways from the shore between some incredibly tall evergreens. I looked back at the way we had come. It was as if the forest, the lake, the green scum – had all dismissed our presence. There was no trace to show we had come through, and no path ahead for us to follow. Bob had truly succeeded in getting us to the middle of nowhere.

Jack laid out the country with a pointed finger:

"To the west, you've got the river and the inn, and to the north is open forest and foothills for longer than I can say. If you stay east, you'll be climbing the mountain itself. It gets pretty steep about a half day's hike from here. Probably two days will get you high enough that you can scope out the whole range. You should also be able to see the lake pretty well after a day or so, because you'll be above it. South of here, there's a little town called Nocturne. I'd stay away from it if I were you. Folks there are weird. Creepy as a black widow spider, Pa would say. We get one of 'em comes in to town by us once a month or so in a pickup, loads up on gasoline, rock salt, some other dry stuff, and then disappears. And they always seem to come by at night. They mostly keep to themselves and we steer clear of them. So I'd stick due east, climb the mountain for four days or so and then head back. I'll meet you here on the night of the eighth day. If you've gotten lost n' aren't here, I'll light a fire and keep it lit for a couple days – you can follow the smoke back.

He grinned, half closed his eyes and looked furtively right and left. "Unless the Nocturne's get ya."

Bill lobbed a clod of dirt at him. Ann just looked into the

fire. Jack knew he had an audience, and pressed on.

"Folks tell around here that the Nocturners like the taste of human flesh. They say if you're in Nocturne after dark, you won't be coming out. And people in these parts do have a habit of disappearing, I'll tell ya that. Don't know how many times I've caught the lights of state cops along the highway flashing their spots into the bushes, looking for tourists that left their cars along the road and never came back. And sometimes I'll wake up in the middle of the night and hear a scream – cops say it's just an owl lighting on a coon or a cat some such, but I tell you, they don't sound like cat screams to me."

The darkness descending upon the mountain seemed to light the fire of credibility under Jack's ghost story. Ann now clutched Bill's arm tightly. The skin outlining her hand was white. Bob, for once, didn't have anything to say.

Nobody did, until something flitted through the trees above us and gave out a sharp screech. I was on my feet in an instant, Ann was hugging Bill.

Jack laughed.

"Just an owl folks. What, did I scare ya with that story? You gotta be tougher than that if you're gonna play king o the hill up here. Come on, let's turn in."

We nearly ran for the tent. Jack zipped it up behind us, shining a flashlight all along the floor edges.

"Don't want any water moccasins slithering in here. They'll follow the warmth and cuddle right up next to you if they can. Worst thing in the world is waking up next to a water moccasin, cuz generally you jump, scare the snake, and it bites you. You get bit by a moccasin, you better have a good friend who'll suck on your blood pretty quick or yer history. I heard of one guy, name of Art, who got bit when he sat down on a stump. The guy he was with couldn't bring himself to kiss Art's ass. Art cried and pleaded, with his pants there around his knees, and that other man just walked away shaking his head. But he was so ashamed when he come back to find Art dead that later he shot himself – right through the forehead."

"Do you know any stories with happy endings?" I asked.

He chuckled and turned over in his sleeping bag. Bill reached over and clicked off our electric lantern. The night crept in, a heavy, fearsome blanket. I lay in my bag, listening to the chirps of crickets and locusts and all the other little sounds of night in the forest. Rustles in the brush. Frog croaks sporadically rising above the dull background insect chittering. Something splashing in the lake – a frog? a fish? a snake? I drifted off to troubled dreams.

Jack left us the next morning to head back to the inn. He cautioned us again about zipping the tents, and then pointed south. "Now don't go heading into Nocturne!" He laughed at us and waved as the boat moved into the water. "See you in eight days, adventurers!"

We broke camp and got underway. I was miserable within the hour, scratched and cut by burrs and brambles, pushing spiny branches out of my way, sweat running from my forehead into my eyes. I have to admit, Ann surprised me – she was a better hiker than I, never once complaining. Bob was our leader, followed by Bill. I took up the rear.

Watching Ann's backside swaying in front of me all day left me: A) knowing what Bill saw in her, and B) hating myself for thinking that way. I was really wishing we were back in the dorm, with things the way they were; Ann needling Bill about his overly active social life and picking apart whatever bimbo he happened to be seeing this week, Bob fretting over some test he'd undoubtedly aced but making like he probably failed, and me sitting there in the middle, just soaking in the conversation, the vibes, the ...

My homesickness was cut short when I got slashed in the head by a particularly thorny branch and blood welled down my cheek. At that point, we decided to pitch camp for our first night alone. Ann got a bottle of whiskey from Bill's pack and rubbed it into the gash across my forehead.

"Don't want that head infected, babe. It's big enough already." She smiled. Bill was helping Bob build a fire. It was just the two of us – for the first time since the trip had begun. So I let go.

"What are you doing?"

"I'm putting booze on your forehead instead of your mouth. Some people'd say you have a drinking problem. Others would just say you smell bad."

"You *know* what I mean."

Her voice got softer. She glanced across our clearing at Bill, currently showing us his butt as he bent over the pile of twigs.

"Don't be mad, babe. I just realized this summer, while I was working in that office ... the guys I met there, I kept comparing to him. I mean, you and Bob, you're great and we'll always be close. I like you guys a lot. But I realized when I missed Bill so bad that I liked him as a lot more than a friend. And I know it's probably hard for you guys to watch us but ... " She suddenly threw her arms around me and whispered in my ear. "I can't tell you. It feels better than it has with anyone. I love him."

"Hey, take your arms off my woman, stranger," Bill yelled over at us. We all laughed. But not, I thought, as loudly as we once would have. Ann and I went over and helped cook dinner – more beans and franks – and then got around to using the whiskey for its rightful purpose. By midnight, we were all pretty gone. The moon was full, high in the sky, lighting up the campsite better than the fire. We were singing Grateful Dead songs. I think we closed on "Friend Of The Devil", in retrospect, maybe not such a good choice. Bob fell on his face when we finally decided to go to bed, and Bill lent an unsteady shoulder. I scooped Ann up and the odd couples stumbled into bed.

The next thing I remember clearly is feeling a cool tongue tickling the wound on my head. My first thought was that I'd better be still, it was a water moccasin, and that we'd been so drunk no one had closed the flap. But when I gathered the courage to slowly open my eyes, I could tell by the lack of light that the tent *was* sealed. That's when I saw her eyes.

"SSSSHHHH," she hissed, her lips moving slowly down my face to caress my own.

"Who?" I began to ask, only to have my oxygen cut off by a probing kiss. Her eyes met mine, cool, mutating green like the tuner light on my grandpa's antique radio dial – they hypnotized me. The mystery, the lure of her animal eyes cut through my fear, warmed my heart, and sped my pulse. With a deft movement, she kicked her feet inside the bag and moved her body in next to mine. She was cool, smooth, outlined in gentle woman curves that hid nothing and offered everything. I lay still next to her, my mind racing with possibilities. Was she here to tease me, and then cut my throat? A fingernail grazed my neck at that moment, and I shivered. Her lips slid from my forehead to my chin. Then she rolled on top. Her eyes were glowing orbs of emerald fire, flickering in a dance of lust that sucked me in like an ant to honey. My veins pounded with a mixture of fear and desire. Her tongue slid slowly from between pale lips, swam in the cleft of my chin, and traced the outline of my mouth. She taunted me with her thighs, squeezing and shifting, then going still. With fingernails long and pointed, she drew intricate designs on my chest; my breath came in faster and faster gasps as this strange, frighteningly erotic woman moved me closer to the edge. Sliding her feet around my ankles, she took me inside her just as I was sure I would die from desire. The scent of her was like the earthy tang of crushed leaves, the power in her gaze drove me to reckless surrender. In the heat of our wordless dance, she grew wilder, pounding me into the ground with her body. She bent to taste my mouth once more and her teeth raked my tongue. I tasted iron and then she sucked hungrily on my mouth, while her nails gouged long and painfully orgasmic currents from my shoulder to my groin. I thought maybe she would take her pleasure and then kill me with her bare hands at the moment of our release. I found I didn't care and thrust my body into hers.

When I woke up, she was gone. Bob saw me looking around the tent in dismay.

"Lose something?"

"Somebody."

Ann and Bill sat up in tandem. She playfully nipped his ear and a tremor ran through me. That innocent sensuality no longer seemed guiltless after my dark entwining. Bill stretching out his arms and yawned.

"What's up?"

Bob laughed. "He can't remember where his dream date

went."

I stared at him. How could he know? Had he watched? Did he see her leave? Bob took my silence as anger.

"I was just kidding," he offered, looking quizzically at me. "Come on, let's start breakfast." He leaned over to the entrance and unzipped the flap. I saw it was all the way down, sealed from the inside. There was no way anyone could have gotten in and then resealed it that tightly without *being* on the inside. I wondered if I was losing it. But there were scratch marks on my neck and chest that weren't there the night before, and the memory of her eyes didn't lie. She'd been here.

As I rolled up my sleeping bag, something fluttered to the floor of the tent. An empty snake skin. Proof double. I had lain with the snake and lived. Worse yet, I had enjoyed it. I craved it. I wanted her back, whatever she was.

I shook my head and stumbled out into the morning.

By lunchtime, I regretted that I'd ever met Bob. I hated hiking. I hated the mountain. My legs and back were killing me, my arms were covered with scrapes and mosquito bites, and my clothes were rank with sweat. The sun blazed overhead, and I don't think any of us were prepared for the exertion. Even our great leader was starting to look frayed. Around three o'clock, we came to a plateau that made at least some of the pain worth it. The valley we'd left unfolded below. Lake Wichitaw was a sapphire in a jade setting. The river leading to it quickly changed from a discernable blue to a murky green that melded into the growth of the forest. We called it an early day and pitched camp. Bill scouted the perimeter and found a nearby stream, which we all took much-needed turns bathing in. Then we collapsed in the tent for a pre-dinner nap. Dusk slipped into night when we woke up, stiff muscles evoked more than a few groans. Bill and I were trying to get a fire going when she walked into camp. I almost ran and threw myself at her feet.

Her hair was black as ink against a face of cotton white. She wore a bright yellow sundress that revealed seductively sculpted leg. She was sleek, sexy, and seemed every inch an average – if darkly attractive – human woman. I stared speechless and confused. I'd halfway managed to convince myself that she had been nothing more than a dream, or a hallucination caused by the fang scratch of the serpent who left her skin behind in my bedroll. The painfully familiar intruder nodded, but gave no other indication that we'd met in unholy union the night before.

"Hi ya, strangers. Whatcha cookin'?"

She had a backwoods accent, but mingled its homey twang with the whisper of something cool, something foreign.

Bob took the lead.

"Looks like SpaghettiOs tonight – if we ever get this fire going. You from around here?"

"My name's Lisha," she said, flashing him a pearly smile. She seemed to drag out the 'sh' of her name. Like a lisp – or a snake. But I was ensnared. I had lived inside her last night, and if she was the Devil come to open my chest and swallow my heart, I would have followed her command then. I looked for the unearthly fire in her eyes. They didn't seem at all unnatural now.

"And yes, I live around here. Just a little walk down that trail," she continued, pointing at some invisible walkway behind her. "If you'd like to come with me, I'm sure I could find you something a lot tastier to eat. I know Melville's makes some excellent vanilla and strawberry shakes."

Too easy. The promise of her, real food, shakes – or

anything cool – was the answer to my daylong prayer. I could see Ann nudging Bill and nodding. They were as tired of this ill-begotten journey as I. Bob was the only dissenter.

"Thanks a lot, but we didn't come all this way to eat in a restaurant. We're out here to commune with nature, to get in touch with ourselves, to … "

"*Ice cold* shakes," Lisha prodded.

"We'd love to," I interrupted. I had ulterior motives that didn't involve nutritional sustenance, but Ann innocently seconded it.

"It wouldn't be right to pass up the local hospitality," she pushed gently.

Bob pouted.

"Fine. You all just go on, abandon the hike. Maybe they'll put you up in a nice hotel and you can watch HBO."

He turned away and stomped towards the tent.

But Lisha didn't let him get away. In three steps, she had blocked him from sanctuary.

"You don't have to come, but I'd really like to show you our little town. We don't get many visitors up here."

She put her hands on his shoulders and looked deep into his eyes. Her voice dropped a notch.

"Please come. For me?"

I could see Bob was caving. I didn't think many men could stand up to that stare.

"I'll have you back to the camp before midnight," she drawled appeasingly.

Bob polled our faces and looked again at Lisha. A smile crept across his lips. "Ice cold shakes, huh?"

After introductions were made, we followed our guide across

the glen, down an incline through a dense cover of brush, and out onto a gravel road. After feeling a million miles from anywhere, to walk five minutes to our right and discover we'd been barely skirting the cusp of civilization was a letdown. Bob monopolized the conversation, telling Lisha all about our journey and finally, after about 15 minutes of walking through the dark, he got around to asking where we were going.

"Nocturne, population 27," she said with a laugh.

We came to a simultaneous, abrupt halt. She couldn't help but notice.

"Oh no, have you heard *those* stories?"

Nobody answered.

"Look, we live up on a mountain, we're pretty isolated, and so we probably seem kinda weird to outsiders. But we don't *eat* people or any of that other silly stuff they say about us. Do I look like a cannibal?"

She smiled that melting smile, and everyone seemed to relax. I thought her eyes gleamed overly hard and bright in the hot dark air. And maybe her teeth *did* look like they enjoyed the ripping of bloody flesh. But I followed her anyway and nobody else noticed the irony in her smile. Pretty soon we walked out of the black tunnel of trees and into a clearing.

Our gravel trail abruptly merged with cobblestones and we stood at the entrance to a quaint little town. Like a turn of the century postcard, the main street was lined by stately Victorian homes etched proud by arches and pillars, and lit by gas lanterns bordering the red-stoned street. Music played somewhere nearby – something rootsy and primal. And if Nocturne only had a population of 27, then the whole town walked towards us. They came out of the houses, out of the general store down the block, out of the bushes. When we set foot on the cobblestones, a signal must have gone off.

"Howdy, strangers," came the voice of one old man, followed by a chorus of: "Hello there's." We were soon surrounded by smiling faces; hands extended in welcome. There were polyester-clad, grey-haired, bouffant-topped housewives, long-haired, bearded men wearing garish purple-orange paisley. They were, without a doubt, the most colorful group I'd ever seen gathered in one spot. We rode the human wave down the street to a blue frame storefront with white-rimmed windows. A large placard above the door read *Melville's* in ornate script.

A small hand attached itself to my own.

"C'mon, mister. Let's git a shake."

She was a wan little urchin, barely taller than my knees, with coppery braided hair and dirt smeared on her chin. I reached down and pulled her up to sit in my arms. She squirmed and slithered to escape my grasp.

"So you like ice cream, do ya?" I asked. She stopped struggling and squinted at my face, nodded vigorously. I thought I saw her eyes light up like green crystals, but when I looked closer, they were a cozy brown.

The doors opened ahead of us, and a silver-haired man in an apron beckoned us inside. At first glance, his face looked straight out of a Norman Rockwell painting. But when I stared harder at him, I could see a feral glitter to his gaze, and could imagine that wrinkled hand now offering the ice cream scoop instead wielding a razor.

"C'mon in, everyone," his voice boomed. "I've just finished churning a fresh batch of ice cream. So to celebrate, tonight Melville's specialty is on the house. Shakes for everyone!"

A cheer went up all around us, and we were swept through a dining room of white Formica tables to a brightly lit ice cream counter. A line formed rapidly, and a young woman appeared in front of me to claim my passenger.

"She does love her ice cream shakes," the woman murmured shyly as the little girl bridged the gap between us. They disappeared into the mob. Another hand gripped mine. This one was stronger, but still coolly feminine. It belonged to Lisha.

"Hi, stranger. Did you miss me this morning?"

She winked at me.

"How did you ... "

She shut off my question with a kiss.

"Not now. I like strawberry. Do you like strawberry?"

We were almost at the front of the line.

"Yeah, sure," I answered, looking around for the rest of my group. Bill and Ann stood a few paces behind me, Bob was over in a corner, already trying to score with a fair-skinned blonde wearing a ripped purple tie-die shirt and cut-offs.

"We'll both have a strawberry," Lisha ordered for us. The old man scooped and blended, tossing juicy red berries into the mix. I caught his eye as he reached for another scoop of strawberries. He didn't look away. But his hand gripped the berries, harder, tighter. A trickle of pulpy berry blood dripped from between his fingers into the steel cup. Then his grasp loosened, and the mutilated strawberry remains tumbled into the cup as well. The right corner of his mouth twisted up and he punched the blender button. I looked away finally. His eyes had never blinked or left my own. If it was a warning, it had its desired effect. I shivered and I hadn't even tasted the frozen drink.

They *were* great shakes – but for all her boasting about them, I ended up finishing most of Lisha's as well as mine.

"I'm so full I could burst," I said, spooning out the last icy berry chunk from the bottom of the glass.

"Come with me," she whispered. Her eyes flashed that eerie emerald color as she said it, and she smiled provocatively. Remembering last night, I rose so fast I nearly upset the table.

She led me by the hand out into the night. We crossed the street to a grand three-story frame house, the path to the door rimmed in perfumed flowers. She pushed the door open without knocking and led me straight up a flight of polished stairs to the bedroom. Hardwood floors recorded the echoes of our steps as we crossed the threshold. An antique chest of drawers hugged one wall; another opened out to a balcony above the town's main street. But the center attraction was the four-poster bed, which took up much of the room. A canopy draped over the top obscured the mattress from the outside world.

"Take off your clothes," she commanded. Her voice seemed to lisp with excitement. Again I wondered if she would open my throat when she finished with me, but I couldn't stop myself. I craved the cut of her claws on my skin. I yearned for the bite of her jaws on my neck.

As I unbuttoned my shirt, she stood frozen two feet away, staring. When the garment dropped to the floor, her breathing audibly increased. Her eyes gleamed like evil spotlights. Her chest heaved. As I loosened my belt, I asked, "Aren't you going to undress, too?"

"If you like," she murmured, hypnotic eyes sparkling with anticipation. As I kicked off my pants, unveiling my flushed and hungry skin, she pulled the sundress over her head and let it drop. She wore nothing underneath. She stood, a porcelain statue, a perfectly white vision of lust incarnate. Small, sinfully pointed breasts jutted above the outline of her ribs. Their nipples protruded, blue with cold excitement though the night oozed slick, humid heat. A faint line of dark hair pointed the way to her femininity, which lacking any modest cover of down, showed itself eagerly awaiting the intrusion of my own red, burning flesh. Ice and fire longed to annihilate themselves in each other. I was inflamed by her litheness, her lean but muscular smoothness. By her hairlessness. By the delicate flowerings of blue that raced across her skin, marbling the chalky perfection with the tracings of mortality, the maplike runnels of the currents of her heart.

"Lie down on the bed," she hissed. Her eyes flashed once more, and I did as she commanded. In a second, she was on top of me, her tongue licking the sweat from my arms and face. I tried to hold her mouth with mine, but couldn't keep her. Her tongue and teeth trailed across my body, tracing every curve, every knot. And then, as I fought to contain my anxious desire, she straddled my waist, wrapped herself around me, and began to grind. I was in ecstasy. She leaned down to lick my face, her breasts slid across my chest. Her palms flattened mine to the bed. I was only an instrument, I knew and accepted. She held me down, she used me, and I conceded. Her gaze settled to my face, a deadly gleam overtook the hypnotism of her corneas. They burrowed into my face, into my neck. I knew for sure she was going to kill me. She was going to rip through my chest and, oblivious to the gore spattering her body, eat my bloody, still-pumping heart.

Her arms were steel bands, holding me in thrall. Saliva

dripped from her mouth onto my face. She moved with sensual carnivorous grace still atop me, grinding me into grateful submission. Whatever she was, I knew that she was deadly. And still, I gave myself to her in that instant. Her lips pulled back to reveal all her teeth, white and polished as fossilized ivory. Her gums accented them in cool blue-purple. She giggled then as my cries approached orgasm, and opening that sickly chasm still wider, I watched all her teeth suddenly retract, leaving only the hungry gleaming of twin canine fangs. Her spit covered my face now, frothy with the hurricane of changes her mouth underwent. Her lower jaw was thinning, receding into her cranium, her nose flattened. Now with the glare of angry green hunger glowing poisonous in her unblinking, unlidded eyes, her huge snake's head descended to touch noses with me. A wet ribbon slicked the foam from my eyes and dug through my lips into my throat. Its length passed my tonsils, the tickle causing an involuntary spasm in my stomach. And then she took back her too-long tongue, and in slow motion lowered, her horrible shifting face to my neck. Teeth pierced my skin.

It was a needle prick that crescendoed to a knife's slash. As the pain exploded through my veins, I thrashed to escape, only ripping her bite further into my neck. Her hands, which had seemed to playfully pin my wrists in sexual bondage moments before, closed in earnest. This was no longer a pleasure game. I was prey, and she the predator. She locked my hips with her own, my manhood trapped in an agonizingly crushing vise. Her legs scissored to restrain mine. She was half my size and twice my strength and her teeth were milking blood from my neck in a deadly siphon. I could feel my heated pulse showering away, spent, into the sweaty night. I moaned. I cried. At last the fear came upon me. This was no longer an excitingly dangerous rendezvous of strangers. This was my death, and I suddenly wanted very much to live. I pleaded with her.

"Let me go. Please. I'll do whatever you like. However you want. You can scratch me, bite me, but please. Let me live. Please."

My words were gargled with the pressure of her fangs, but she disengaged from her feast. Swirling emerald marbles locked with my eyes. Dots of gold swam like electric current within those swirls of luring green. Her mouth was now lipless. The crimsoned tips of her teeth jutted out over scaly ridges of bloodless flesh. Her head had elongated into that of a fishbelly white snake. She rocked gently from side to side, a hypnotic dance designed to lull the victim, I knew. Her eyes never left me.

"Sssssshh, my love. I won't drain you dry. I only want to tasssste a little. But mmmm, the ssstrawberry ssshakes in you are ssssoooo gooood."

With the speed of a rubberband released, she buried her mouth in me once more. Her long, raven-black hair covered my eyes, but I could hear her slurping with undisguised hunger on my life. I was twisting between the lines of pleasure and pain, dancing on the blades of death. I could feel an icy burn racing from my neck to my chest, to my heart, to my arms. I shivered uncontrollably. Was she fully a snake? Was it frigid poison she pumped into my captured body, so that whether she drank all my blood now or not, I was dead anyway? Would she turn me into a damned creature like herself?

"Please, no more." I gasped as the room began to spin wildly and nausea threatened to heave whatever remained of the shakes in my stomach onto the bed.

She didn't answer, but after another minute, she pulled away, and collapsed next to me on the bed. Her mouth hung slack, a thread of crimson dangled between her lip and the exposed ivory needle that had drawn it. Her nose seemed to jut back to its former delicate triangle, and her teeth poked back through her gums, now crimson-tainted with the wine of her dinner. Her eyes were closed; her hands hugged her chest and belly. She licked her lips and consumed the bloody traces they held with erotic, savoring slowness.

"Mmmmm," she moaned. "Stay with me. I'll keep you alive ... forever."

It seemed a command rather than an invitation. And while I admired – indeed, still lusted for – her creamy body stretched out before me, I knew that I might have only one chance to escape. Even now I felt ready to renounce life to be her blood slave for eternity. My resolve slid back and forth. But when a light snore escaped her sated mouth, I knew that this was it. If I waited another hour, I knew I would never leave. It had to be now. The room had steadied, and though I felt as weak as a baby, I rolled out of the bed and tiptoed to the window.

The mob of Nocturnals were just now coming out of the ice cream parlor and streaming into the street. There were three distinct groups, each centered around one of my friends. Bill hung limply between the shoulders of an old man and a hippie. Bob was shirtless and held by a half dozen women. He didn't seem to struggle; he looked dazed. Ann thrashed between the hands of the ice cream merchant and two heavyset men. The streetlights caught her face just enough for me to see the naked terror as she leaned back suddenly and let out a piercing scream. One of the fat men took the opportunity to sink his head into her shoulder. He came up a moment later, eyes blazing green, teeth dripping blood. Ann had quieted at his bite.

"Vanilla," he yelled.

Some of the people around Bob moved to Ann's circle when Bob's keeper announced: "Strawberry."

The little girl I had held earlier was the first to sample Bill.

"Vanilla," her pixie voice proclaimed. She no longer sounded innocent and cute to me, but evil, obscenely sluttish.

One by one the townspeople moved in to sample the blood of my friends – apparently by shake flavor preference. I was certain they wouldn't stop until every drop of life had been consumed. I wanted to run. I wanted to abandon them all and just get out of there alive. But I couldn't leave them. I had to try to do something to distract the monsters from the kill – and I probably had only minutes to work with. Grabbing my pants, I stole down the stairs and found a back door out of the kitchen.

I ran through weedy, overgrown back yards until I stood at the gravel road. I could see the mob only a couple blocks away, but their attention seemed firmly centered on dinner. Or dessert. I crossed the roadway and worked my way through the backyards on the other side of the street to the general store. I entered through a back door and crept through its half dozen aisles looking for something I could use. I pulled a hand-axe off the wall, and found a five-gallon barrel of kerosene. I almost laughed out loud at my luck. Leaving a trail of colorless liquid behind me, I dashed from the store to the wood-framed house next door. I splashed its doors, its windows, its porch. Then I ran a trail to the next house, which I anointed the same way. I worked my way down the block and then decided I could spare no more time.

As I dug in my pocket for a book of matches, the grass behind me whispered. I turned, squinted into the black shadows of the waving weeds. In the distance, I could hear the whoops and laughter of the Nocturnals. They had turned the slow murder of my friends into a festival. The stench of kerosene was stifling in the heavy air, and just as I gave up my wary vigil, I saw something move at me from the corner of my eye.

Then I was lying on the ground, my head lanced with white pain. A giant of a monster sat on my chest, with putrid eyes and yellowed teeth. He bent to drink from my neck, but as his fangs reopened Lisha's wounds, I brought my arm up from the ground and connected with the back of his skull. The kerosene can thudded hollowly against his head, splashing us both with the noxious liquid. As he lost his balance and bellowed in surprise, I rolled away and aimed a kick at his head. A fang punctured my heel, but I heard the snap of vertebrae moving in the wrong direction. His scream was deafening, the kind a man might make while viewing his own castration. He rolled spasmodically on the ground, and he was shrinking. His head retracted – farther than Lisha's had – so that he truly resembled a giant milky snake. Between the pain in my skull and the overpowering smell of kerosene, I almost passed out. But his screams served as my lifeline. They wouldn't let me slip away.

Striking a match, I tossed it at the metamorphosing snake-man, whose yells had devolved to angry hisses. The flames leapt up his dwindling body. Wherever they touched, the skin instantly blackened, bubbled, and shriveling. The smell was hideous – like hamburger left to rot in the sun. His head seemed frozen at a right angle with his body, which flopped about on the ground like drops of water in a hot frying pan. At last he flipped so that his eyes were facing me, their accusation complete and deadly. Then the flame seemed to explode over his head, burning brighter and whiter until with a sizzling pop, his body seemed to just ... implode. The flames however continued, having met the line of kerosene leading to the house. My stomach did give way then, and as it emptied onto the unkept lawn, I watched as the flames sped around the windows, across the porch, and flared down a path to start the next house – and the next and the next.

Now I could hear the sounds of celebration in the street turning to dismay and anger, but I couldn't stop to see what they did about it. I limped across the street and one by one put each house ablaze, slowing only when I came to Lisha's back door. I looked up at the windows on the second floor and envisioned her lying there, naked and asleep on the bed. I pictured her sleek white body covered with suppurating sores as the fire toasted and tortured her skin. No, I said to myself. She had not killed me, and I couldn't light the match to incinerate her. I dropped the nearly empty canister in the yard and dragged myself around the front to see what had become of the street feast.

The cobblestones were nearly bare. Ann, Bill, and Bob lay abandoned in the center of the street, crumpled in odd, lifeless positions. Was I too late? Had their souls already escaped with their blood? I heard yells and saw the blur of shapes running through the night between the fiercely burning homes, and with a fervent hope that they cared more for their lairs than revenge, I ran out to try to rouse my friends.

Their clothes were torn and shredded around their shoulders, where blood still seeped from a myriad of gashes, but with relief, I saw they all breathed. I shook and prodded and got Bill and Ann to open their eyes, but Bob remained unconscious. His face seemed ghastly white; his chest barely moved. I listened for his heartbeat, and only heard the faintest *lub-lub*. Bill staggered to his feet as I worked frantically to revive Bob. It was no use. I dragged Bob to a sitting position and pulled an arm across my shoulder. The wound in my neck throbbed with pain at the pressure, but I managed to lob him over my back keeping a grip on his legs. Ann tried to rise, but fell weakly to her knees. Bill helped her up and, without saying a word, the four of us began lurching away from the shrieks and the flames.

We got to the edge of town. There, lolling across the roadway was a six-foot coil of white death. It hissed at our approach. I could see the electric anger of its eyes from yards away. Lowering Bob to the ground, I motioned for Bill and Ann to stay put. Pulling the hatchet I'd purloined out of my belt, I advanced on the hissing, spitting creature with slow deliberate steps.

"Get out of our way or I'll kill you," I said from between clenched teeth. I held the short axe ready. The snake gave no ground.

"I torched your little town, you bastard," I taunted. It came out sounding tough, but my knees felt ready to collapse. "Shouldn't you be finding another hole to hide in?"

It struck then, or tried to. As it shot across the stones, I brought the axe down, cutting the viper cleanly in half. A spray of hot blood covered me as its two halves twitched and wriggled spewing insides into the air as it whipped back and forth on the dark-stained street, fangs still bared for the kill. I brought the axe down again and cleaved the head from one of the halves, and after a moment, its flailing subsided. Leaving the bloody mess as a warning, I hefted Bob onto my back again and we weaved our way down the gravel road. Somehow, we reached the camp and started a fire. Bob still didn't wake. His face looked ashen, even in the orange flicker of firelight. We primed his lips first with water and then with whiskey, but nothing brought him around. His breathing had slowed to a couple of wheezing gasps a minute.

The three of us sat around him through the night, the twisting undulations of the flames surrounding us in an unnatural aura. The Nocturnals could have knocked us out without a fight then. I don't know why they didn't.

We didn't speak; we didn't touch.

All we could share was a common sight: the slow but unstoppable leaching of Bob's life. He seemed to melt into the ground, diminishing, growing closer to death with every hour. When the first rays of the sun filtered through the cool air of morning, he was gone.

We buried him then, scratching out a shallow grave between the trees a short way down the hill from our camp using my hatchet and some flat rocks. We covered it with a cairn of stones, broke camp, and made our way as far back down the mountain as we could stagger. We had to wait at the lake for over a day before Jack picked us up. In that time, we did nothing but agree on a common story. The rest of the hours, we simply stared silently out at the lake.

Bob's parents flew in, and the police went with us back to the campsite. We told them that Bob had slipped away from the camp in the night and hadn't come back, which was, in a metaphysical sense, true. The sheriff knew better. His glance kept resting on the scabs covering each of our necks. Once, when he patted my back and said: "We'll find him," without any promise in his voice, his hand lingered on my shoulder and gave a firm, knowing squeeze. "You kids go on home now," he said softly. "Don't think about this no more." I saw a secret anguish in the lines of his face, perhaps the memory of a similar loss of his own.

They never did find Bob, of course. I don't think they really looked that hard. They knew he wasn't lost.

Since returning to school, I've been reading up on various facets of the occult, trying to understand what we stumbled upon. I have found no answers; but now I wonder if that grave still holds Bob's decaying carcass. Did the worms and ants and excavating grubs get their due? Or did his body collapse in upon itself, transforming with the power of injected toxins to allow a shiny white serpent to emerge under the soft rays of the moon from its cocoon of empty, bloodied clothes?

I wonder too about Ann and Bill. A silence stood between us on our return that repelled as powerfully as Bob's endless chatter had once glued us together. Their romance slipped away as quickly as the summer. Bill never even returned to school after Christmas Break. I haven't seen Ann in months. And now, as the hot perfume of summer washes over me once more, I keep seeing Lisha's evil eyes. I hear her promise 'forever' and I wonder.

I wonder when I see the tender white flesh of a woman's neck, how it would taste to push a kiss beyond the skin.

I wonder if I returned to the mountain, would I find Nocturne? Would they have stayed and rebuilt their timeless town?

I wonder would Lisha keep me as her own, or kill me for the destruction I brought?

I wonder if I would find that Ann and Bill were already there on the mountain ahead of me, waiting patiently arm in arm with ice-cold shakes and a newly fanged, green-eyed Bob. Waiting for the four of us to be together again. Forever.

And I wonder how much longer I can live without finding out.

Ice Cold Shakes was originally published in the small press magazine anthology *Shapeshifter*, 1995

About the Author

John Everson is the Bram Stoker Award-winning author of the novels *Sacrifice* (Delirium Books, 2007) and *Covenant* (Delirium Books, 2004) as well as the novelette *Failure* (Delirium Books, 2006). Much of his short fiction has been collected in three short story collections – *Needles & Sins* (Necro Publications, 2007), *Vigilantes of Love* (Twilight Tales, 2003) and *Cage of Bones & Other Deadly Obsessions* (Delirium Books, 2000). He is also the co-editor of the *Spooks!* ghost story anthology (Twilight Tales, 2004), and the founder of Dark Arts Books (www.darkartsbooks.com). For information on his fiction, art and music, visit John Everson: Dark Arts at http://www.johneverson.com

New releases this coming spring

Out of Darkness (written by Vanessa deHart)
Romantic suspense

On a darkened street in the Old Quebec City quarter, a car swerves, cutting Genny Lynn down. The driver momentarily stops to enjoy his handiwork then drives off leaving her for dead.

Lost in the darkness of her mind, Genny Lynn wakes, her disoriented gaze capturing that of a handsome stranger staring ominously at her from the foot of a hospital bed.

For three years, Luc Savard has fought his wife's terror tactics – wrestling for control of his family's fortune. He has longed for freedom from her evil presence. Until now.

Could a cease-fire be possible, when she looks at him with such vulnerable and seemingly innocent eyes and asks: "Who am I?"

Would he dare risk his fortune, and his heart, on the off-chance that this lighter and whimsical version of his wife would stay? Could love shed light on the truth and drive out the darkness that has shadowed their marriage for so long?

The Jaguar Legacy (written by Maureen Fisher)
Romantic suspense

Journalist Charley Underhill barges in on a remote archaeological site headed by Dr. Alistair Kincaid to get the scoop of the decade. But the hunky archaeologist, renowned for his aversion to the press, protects his latest discovery with zeal. A battle of wills and wits ensues. Meanwhile, danger stalks on velvet paws when strands from a past life intertwine with the present. Torn between redeeming her soul and betraying the man she loves, will Charley find the answers that will heal her heart?

I WILL RISE (written by Michael Louis Calvillo)
Horror

THE HUMAN VIRUS MUST BE DESTROYED!

I WILL RISE is an apocalyptic love story about faithlessness in humanity, personal insecurity and destructive choice in a world where symmetry rules and contentment within one's own skin is nearly impossible. Funky, grotesque and ferocious, I Will Rise is a rollercoaster ride of literary horror that will infiltrate your senses and alter your perceptions forever.

IN TWENTY-FOUR HOURS ...

Upon death, a bitter, societal outcast named Charles is given the ability to annihilate the human race. Risen and relishing the opportunity to make the world suffer, he embraces his bloody destiny, but, as his killing touch spreads death and destruction, his new status affords unexpected human interaction. Second thoughts surmount as he falls for Annabelle, a fiery redhead tasked with guiding Charles and orchestrating mayhem. As feelings deepen, Charles wonders: Has he been excluded by society or is his lonely existence a product of his own narrow ignorance? As realization flowers and regrets begin to surface a choice must be made between the legion of the dead and the pleas of the living.

... EVERYONE YOU KNOW WILL BE DEAD.

Does all of humanity really deserve to perish at his hands? Is it too late for Charles to defy death, escape meat cleaver wielding pro-human maniacs, prevent zombie hordes from rising and stop the cataclysmic forces raging inside his body? Is it too late to discover purpose and rejoin the ranks of the living? Unfortunately, Charles is already dead. Unfortunately, even if Charles could find a way to throw his deathly state in to reverse, Annabelle isn't having it. Driven by anti-human rhetoric, red herrings and forces unbeknownst to Charles, she wants to see the world suffer and die so badly her insides jitterbug madly when she envisions the infinite end.

Printed in the United States
74214LV00004B/3